INDECENT

DARCY BURKE

ZEALOUS QUILL PRESS

For the Hot Sexy Six, my daily dose of sanity, hilarity, and damn good friendship. You are so smart and amazing, and I'm so glad we're a gang!

INDECENT

Society's most exclusive invitation...

Welcome to the Phoenix Club, where London's most audacious, disreputable, and intriguing ladies and gentlemen find scandal, redemption, and second chances.

If Bennet St. James, the Viscount Glastonbury, doesn't find a bride with a sizeable dowry, he'll be in the poorhouse along with his interminable number of female relatives—all of whom he loves but are a drain on the negative fortune his father left when he died of a broken pocketbook. Desperate, he hatches a scheme to snare an heiress only to be foiled by a most vexing and alluring—and unfortunately equally destitute—paid companion.

Lady's companion Prudence Lancaster is single-minded about finding her mother and filling in the missing pieces of her life. But a villainous viscount interrupts her plans, and his surprising charm and understanding tempts her in the most indecent ways. Soon, she's dreaming of the future instead of wallowing in the past.

But when Bennet shares a dark secret, her hopes are dashed. For he won't break the promise he made to his family, even if it means losing the greatest love he's ever known.

Don't miss the rest of *The Phoenix Club*!

Do you want to hear all the latest about me and my books? Sign up at Reader Club newsletter for members-only bonus content, advance notice of pre-orders, insider scoop, as well as contests and giveaways!

Care to share your love for my books with like-minded readers? Want to hang with me and see pictures of my cats (who doesn't!)? Then don't miss my exclusive Facebook groups!

Darcy's Duchesses for historical readers
Burke's Book Lovers for contemporary readers

Want more historical romance? Do you like your historical romance filled with passion and red hot chemistry? Join me and my author friends in the Facebook group, Historical Harlots, for exclusive giveaways, chat with amazing HistRom authors, and more!

CHAPTER 1

England 1815

Jolted awake as her head banged the side of the coach, Prudence Lancaster mumbled something extremely unladylike. If there wasn't a sack over her head, she could see where she was going or if it was still night. She assumed it had to be. While she'd managed to doze, the rough road didn't allow her to rest for long.

She had no idea where she was going or who had kidnapped her, let alone why. That anyone would go to the trouble of snatching her—an unimportant paid companion—was perplexing to say the least. Hopefully, she would have some answers when they got to wherever they were going. She prayed that would be soon.

With her hands and feet bound and a cloth tied around her mouth, she was quite uncomfortable. She'd long ago tumbled from the seat and hadn't been able to get herself back onto it. Her captors were not the least considerate.

The sound of rain against the roof soothed her, at least.

She rolled to her back and was grateful that her hands were bound in front instead of behind. She'd prefer they weren't bound at all, of course. Every attempt she'd made to loosen the rope had been utterly futile. She'd given up some time ago.

How long ago was that exactly? She wasn't even sure what time they'd abducted her because they'd roused her from a dead sleep.

All she recalled was that she'd fallen into a dreamless slumber upon returning to the inn in Croydon after the boxing match. She'd rushed there from London with Cassandra, the duke's daughter to whom she was companion, so Cassandra could find the man she loved. Lord Wexford had been one of the fighters. He and Cassandra had been happily reunited, then they'd gone to spend the night wherever he was staying.

Since Prudence was not a chaperone, as she'd reminded Cassandra repeatedly, she'd done nothing to stop them. On the contrary, she was thrilled that Cassandra was so happy.

Decidedly less thrilling was the manner in which Prudence had been rudely awakened at some point in the night. She hadn't seen the face of whoever had grabbed her before a cloth was tied tightly around her mouth and a bag pulled over her head. Shock and terror had quite stolen her senses.

They'd then bound her hands and feet, and the pair had carried her downstairs and out of the King's Arms. She assumed they were a pair since she'd heard only two voices by that point. They'd joined a third man outside before setting her into the coach saying she'd "be with him soon" and there was "nothing to fear."

With whom? And how in the bloody hell could she remain unafraid given their careless handling of her? Many parts of her ached from bouncing about the floor of the coach, and there was a thoroughly disgusting taste in her mouth from the cloth they'd used to gag her.

But Prudence refused to break. She'd eventually get free.

And then what?

She supposed that depended on whom she'd be with soon. Since they'd said she had nothing to fear, Prudence clung to that. Perhaps there was a good explanation for her abduction.

The dread that had lived in her spine these many hours said otherwise.

The rain increased to a heavy staccato, and she hoped it wouldn't slow their passage. She wanted to get wherever they were going. The thought of stretching her body and taking a deep, unhindered breath was incredibly appealing.

Eventually, she closed her eyes and was again lulled into a half sleep where she remained aware of the bump and rustle of the coach. Then the coach stopped. That catapulted her into full wakefulness.

She sat up just before the door opened—behind her, she realized.

"Oi! She's on the floor!" one of them called out.

"Just pull 'er out!" another responded.

Large hands hauled Prudence from the coach into the rain. *At least my head's completely covered*, she thought wryly. She was also glad for the cloak they'd thrown over her night rail before dragging her from her room.

The man tossed her over his shoulder and carried her some distance. She was cold and wet by the time they walked into a building. Warmth suffused her, and she closed her eyes in a mixture of relief and gladness.

The emotions didn't linger, however, as she realized she was surely about to meet the "him" she wasn't supposed to be afraid of. Tension knifed through her, and unease swirled in her gut. Bouncing against the brigand's shoulder as they climbed stairs didn't help matters.

A door opened, creaking softly, before they moved inside. She heard it close behind them. Then they set her on the floor, but the one who'd carried her kept his arm around her. As much as she would have preferred that he erupt into flames instead of touch her, she needed the support.

"What the devil have you done?" a fourth gentleman, who sounded vaguely familiar to Prudence, not that she could place him, asked with a mixture of shock and anger, his voice low.

"We brought 'er 'ere just like ye said. Where's the money?"

"You were supposed to *bring* her, not truss her up like a pheasant after the hunt!"

A pheasant after the hunt? This was a gentleman, but she would have guessed that based on his refined speech alone.

"We don't take chances when there's this much blunt involved," the same brigand responded. "Now give us what you promised, or we'll take the chit and go."

She heard a thump and wondered what that noise could be. How she wished she could speak!

"I hope you didn't wake the innkeepers."

"We came in quiet, just like you said to. Now give us our blunt."

"Fine," the gentleman said caustically. There were footsteps and some shuffling. "Here."

"Count it," the brigand growled.

"It's all 'ere," another of the kidnappers said. "Let's go."

"Pleasure doing business with you, m'lord." There was no mistaking that the brigand was smiling as he said this.

Then the arm around her was gone, and Prudence wobbled. Another set of arms came around her, along with the scent of pine and bergamot. *This* was the gentleman.

The sound of the door closing filtered through the sack covering her head just before it was whisked away.

"My apologies, Lady Cass—"

Prudence blinked into a face she knew. Bright blond hair and stunning blue-green eyes, chiseled features with sculpted lips. Lord Glastonbury?

He recoiled in horror. "You aren't Lady Cassandra!"

Prudence's response was muffled by the gag. He'd planned to kidnap her employer? Not that Cassandra was her employer, but Prudence *was* her paid companion.

"Oh my God." He reached behind her head and untied the infernal piece of fabric.

As soon as it was loose, she spit it from her mouth. "A drink, please."

"Yes, of course."

"Perhaps after you untie me," she rasped, her body suddenly screaming of thirst, but not as loudly as it was for freedom.

Glastonbury hastened to pluck the rope from her wrists, then bent and did the same at her ankles. When she was free, she contemplated sending her foot into his chest and knocking him back on his arse. Instead, she rubbed her wrists and glowered at him as he stood to fetch her a glass of whatever was in the bottle on the table.

He handed her the glass, his brow deeply furrowed. "I don't understand what happened."

Prudence drank half the glass—it was ale—before pausing. "You had me kidnapped, it seems."

"Not you. Lady Cassandra."

That he'd planned to steal Cassandra, the daughter of a duke, from her very bed was beyond astonishing. "As you can see, they nabbed the wrong person." And Prudence could guess why.

"I don't know how. I told them where she would be and

what she was wearing—a purple cloak." His gaze dropped to the purple cloak draped around Prudence.

"We switched cloaks." Prudence glared at him. "They woke me, gagged me, put a bag over my head, tied my hands and feet, and dragged me who knows where in the middle of the night. But you intended for that to happen to *Lady Cassandra?*"

His face flushed red. "I didn't intend for them to do any of that. I paid them to bring you to me without being seen." He frowned, his gaze dropping to her reddened wrists. "It seems they took things too far."

"You think so?" she asked with razor-sharp sarcasm. She finished the ale and thrust the glass back at him. "Do you have anything stronger?"

"I do not. Would you care for more ale?"

"If that's all you have. Though, port or madeira would be preferable," she muttered darkly.

He flinched, then refilled her glass. "Miss Lancaster, I am terribly sorry for all this."

She was shocked he recalled her name. Most gentlemen wouldn't.

Though Prudence might have preferred a fortified wine to ease her pains, she was grateful for any flavor, even ale, to wash away the taste of the last hours. She took several more sips before lowering the glass. Then she walked to the hearth, where a low fire burned, and held one hand out to the warmth. "Your apology is inconsequential. I am glad they took me instead of Lady Cassandra. To think of her suffering what I have..." She shuddered.

Turning, she pinned him with a furious glare. "Why would you do this?"

He hesitated, frowning more deeply than before. His gaze flicked to the floor. "We were going to elope."

"I'm fairly certain elopement involves both parties' agreement and consent."

His head snapped up. "How do you know she didn't give them?"

Prudence scoffed. "I'm her companion. I know precisely what we were doing in Croydon, and it had nothing to do with *you*."

He exhaled. "Not an elopement exactly, but I feel confident she would have been amenable once she arrived here and saw me."

"Amenable after being dragged through the night trussed, as you say, like a pheasant after the hunt? Tell me, Lord Glastonbury, how many pheasants have you trussed?"

"None. Others take care of that."

"Of course they do," she whispered through a sneer. "Your kind don't do anything for yourselves. Mustn't soil your hands when you can have someone else do it for you."

"*My kind?*"

"Entitled gentlemen."

Wincing, he extended his hand toward her, but promptly dropped it to his side again. "You clearly think quite poorly of me, and you've every right, but let me explain."

"Explain what? How you would have ruined Lady Cassandra with your actions? You're despicable. And that isn't just *my* opinion. Anyone would objectively think that after what I've been through and upon learning you orchestrated the entire ordeal."

He had the grace to look pained. Remorseful, almost. Actually, he did look as if he regretted his actions, but Prudence wasn't going to forgive him. "I was desperate. I thought this would work—Lady Cassandra and I like one another. I was certain she would accept my proposal. But then her father meddled. I just needed to explain to her—"

Gripping her glass, Prudence took a step toward him.

"What would you have explained?"

He said nothing, his features a mixture of obstinance and regret, the latter of which was beginning to annoy her.

"You would have stolen her choices—her entire future. She's in love with Wexford. I expect they will be married." Which meant Prudence would need to find a new position, and her sudden disappearance could greatly endanger her prospects. Her outrage increased.

The viscount's face didn't register surprise. There was resignation. And anger.

Prudence went on. "You would have stolen her from the man she loves, and for what? To refill your empty coffers?"

He opened his mouth, then snapped it closed, his lips whitening.

"There is nothing for you to explain and certainly nothing to excuse. And I think you know it." She took another long drink, her gaze glued to his.

His jaw worked, and he finally looked away from her. "I regret my actions. As I said, I was desperate. You can't possibly understand. I'll return you to London in the morning."

"Where are we?"

"Hersham. About twenty miles southwest of Mayfair."

"I can't begin to imagine the extent of your nefarious plot —where you were going, what you planned—but I hope the shame remains with you the rest of your days. Now, if you'll excuse me, I would like to sleep."

"Your bag is there." He pointed to her case, which must have been the thump she'd heard when the sack was still over her head.

"I'm surprised they brought that," she said before tossing back the rest of the ale.

"I asked them to." He blinked at her. "I'm not completely horrid," he added softly.

She set the glass on the table and curled her lip toward him. "You can tell yourself that as much as you like. Just know it isn't true."

Lifting her arms, she stretched, and it felt glorious. What would feel even better would be to wash up. She glanced toward a dresser with a ewer and basin on top. "Is that water clean?"

"It is."

"Good. I don't know where you're sleeping, but it's not in that bed."

"I wouldn't dream of it." There wasn't an ounce of sarcasm in his tone, but she gave him no credit.

When he didn't move, she narrowed her eyes at him.

He straightened. "I'll just leave you alone." Turning, he left the room, closing the door softly behind him.

What an absolute disaster. But it could have been so much worse. Hopefully, Prudence wouldn't be missed by anyone other than Cassandra. In all likelihood, her reputation would be fine and her chances for future employment unhindered. That didn't mean there wasn't some amount of risk—if the truth of her situation ever got out.

The viscount's behavior was shocking. She knew he was in need of funds, that this was the entire reason he'd courted Cassandra, but to be so incredibly desperate as to become a villain?

You can't possibly understand.

His words echoed in her brain. He'd been shocked to see her—not just because she wasn't Cassandra, but because of the way the brigands had handled her. He'd also apologized and seemed genuinely remorseful. What couldn't she understand? Curiosity pushed her outrage aside, at least a little.

If he'd managed to kidnap Cassandra instead, this truly would have been a catastrophe. She would have been ruined, her reputation shredded. In truth, Cassandra had already risked it by rushing to Croydon to find Wexford. However, they would wed, and all would be well.

And where would that leave Prudence? Without a job and with a potentially reputation-killing disappearance hanging over her. The thought of losing her hard-won security shortened her breath. Not too long ago, she'd been completely alone in the world, an orphan with no prospects after having to leave her position at a school for young ladies when the father of one of those young ladies had propositioned her most grotesquely. She'd had no choice but to depart unless she wanted to accept his disgusting advances.

Driven to desperation, she'd embarked on a foolish errand to find employment, only to find luck when she'd met Lord Lucien Westbrook, Cassandra's brother. He'd rescued her from certain doom when he'd offered to help her find a position as a governess or a companion.

She would not allow Glastonbury to ruin her good fortune. She had to get back to London as soon as possible.

~

*B*ennet St. James, Viscount Glastonbury, jerked awake in a cold sweat despite the fact that he was sprawled in a chair near the warm hearth. Blinking, he saw that the first gray of dawn was just slipping over the chamber.

Glancing toward the bed, he detected the lump of Miss Lancaster and for the thousandth time berated himself for his stupidity. Not only had this turned into a horrible ordeal for the poor companion, he'd lost a pile of money for what amounted to total failure.

Rubbing his hand over his face, he forced himself to breathe. This was not the end of things. It was, however, one large step closer to defeat.

Unless he came up with a new stratagem. It could not, however, include marrying an heiress, since the Duke of Evesham would tell everyone that Bennet was a breath away from the poor house. Could viscounts even be admitted to workhouses?

Bennet shook his head. That wouldn't happen. He would always have a place to live. Aberforth Place was entailed, and Bennet was stuck with it. Just as he was stuck with an abundance of female relatives to care for, some at Aberforth Place and others...elsewhere.

He could hope that Evesham—Cassandra's father—wouldn't tell anyone, but Bennet knew better than to expect that. Especially once everyone heard what Bennet had done, that he'd kidnapped Lady Cassandra's companion and that he'd intended to abduct Lady Cassandra herself. His stomach folded over itself. If she went to Bow Street, there would be no stratagems and his family would be lost. What in the bloody hell had he been thinking?

He groaned softly, then sucked in a breath when he heard rustling in the bed. Leaning from the chair, he tried to discern if the companion had awakened. When she didn't move again or make noise, he exhaled with relief. He wasn't quite ready to face her furious disdain again. Though, he deserved nothing less.

What *had* he been thinking?

He hadn't, and that was a terrible concern. People in his family sometimes acted impulsively, without concern for others, and, as with his behavior the previous night when *he'd* acted impulsively, bad things happened.

He'd been incredibly distraught upon receiving the note from Evesham in which the duke had informed Bennet that he was aware of his dire financial woes and would not allow him to wed his daughter. Frustration had turned to rage, and Bennet had lost sight of, well, everything. He'd been so close

—the proposal was imminent, and Cassandra had given him every indication she was amenable to his offer.

Except she'd apparently been in love with Wexford instead. Not that Bennet had thought she loved him, nor did he love her. That might have come, however, since they liked each other at least.

All of it was moot now. And his chances of finding another heiress were slim. Once the ton learned of his destitution, he'd be labeled a fortune hunter, and no one would want to marry him. Save a wealthy merchant's daughter in search of a title. He ought to consider that direction.

This was such a calamity! If only his father hadn't lost every bit of money at the gaming tables, Bennet and the rest of his family wouldn't be in this mess.

He glanced again toward the bed. He'd been livid after losing the chance to wed Lady Cassandra. He'd allowed his emotions to get the better of him, completely ruining the fight he was supposed to win and losing to Cassandra's future husband of all people. That fight was supposed to change his fortune, just as marrying Cassandra would have done. If all had gone as planned, Bennet's problems would have been solved.

Anger began to rise in him again. The boxing match had been his idea. He'd offered himself as a lure—a viscount fighting in a bout—to the owner of his boxing club. Frederick Dodd had immediately warmed to the idea and had even agreed to give Bennet a healthy portion of the ticket sales. If he won.

Instead, Bennet had lost—not only his pride, but a major source of income he'd been expecting. How in the hell was he going to meet his obligations? It wasn't as if he could continue to let them lapse, especially where his relatives were concerned.

He began to shake as a familiar sensation of panic and

desperation crept over him. His skin felt cold and clammy, and the room began to fade. This couldn't be happening. He'd staved it off for so long, but he worried his collapse was inevitable. Last night's criminal actions had proved that Bennet was no better than the most afflicted in his family... those who fought to keep themselves in check, to battle the darkness that threatened to overwhelm and drive them into inescapable despair and delusion.

Sitting up, he dropped his head between his legs and braced his palms on his thighs. He took deep, staggering breaths, willing himself to settle before his mind was completely out of his grasp. That had never happened—not yet. But it would. Someday.

Gradually, he began to calm, his pulse slowing and his breathing becoming more even. He could manage this. He *would* find an heiress. There was nothing wrong with marrying into the merchant class.

And what of Miss Lancaster? He looked toward her again, feeling weary. Was there a chance she wouldn't tell what had happened? Surely, she'd want to protect her reputation.

He closed his eyes and silently cursed himself. Not only was he destitute and a scheming criminal, he was also an absolute scoundrel. The worst sort of gentleman.

But when he thought of those who would suffer because of his father's actions, Bennet felt a renewed purpose. They were his responsibility, and he would ensure they were taken care of for the rest of their days.

Pushing himself up from the chair, Bennet caught the thin blanket before it slid to the floor. He set it on the cushion and stoked the fire, building it back into a low flame. Satisfied, he meandered toward the bed.

Miss Lancaster lay on her back, one hand resting beside her cheek against the pillow. Her features were barely visible with only the light from the kindled fire and the gray dawn to illuminate her. She was very beautiful, far more attractive than he'd ever noticed, truth be told. But then she'd always been a part of the background. Now she was in the center, her outrage demanding attention.

Her blonde hair was braided, but wispy curls had escaped, some brushing her temple and jaw. Long lashes curled against her cheek. Beneath them glittered moss-green eyes that had appeared almost jewellike in her well-justified fury. Pink bow lips had berated him with great effect, and her pert nose had wrinkled with her distaste of him.

He felt truly awful about what had happened to her. Hiring a trio of questionable fellows at the fight had been an abominable idea, one borne of abject desperation. But a part of him must have known Cassandra wouldn't want to come. Why else would he have hired men like that or arranged to have them deliver her to him here, twenty miles from Croydon? He was a villain, deserving of Miss Lancaster's outrage and much more.

"I'm so sorry," he whispered. "I'll get you back to London first thing."

And then what would happen? Would she tell everyone what he'd done?

Her employer was the Duke of Evesham, who was already inclined to at least dislike Bennet, if not loathe him. Perhaps the duke would prosecute him for kidnapping.

A ball of tension formed in Bennet's gut, and he expected it to remain for quite some time.

Turning, Bennet fetched his boots and threw on his coat. He left the room, careful to close the door quietly behind him. He crept downstairs and was glad to find the innkeeper, Mr. Logan, already about. The man was old enough to be Bennet's father, though he was far more helpful and caring than Bennet's own had ever been.

"Morning, my lord," Logan said with a smile. "I trust your

betrothed arrived last night as planned?"

Bennet had informed Logan and his wife that his future viscountess would be joining him. It wasn't as if he could have hidden her, and he wasn't going to have her stay in another room, not by herself.

"She did, thank you," Bennet lied. Logan didn't need to know that Miss Lancaster wasn't the woman he'd expected.

"Splendid. I'm sorry you won't be able to leave today, but it's just as well since the rain is so heavy."

On his way to the table situated next to the hearth, Bennet snapped to attention. "What's that? Why can't we leave?"

Logan's brow creased. "Begging your pardon, my lord, I thought you knew about the coach. The journey with her ladyship seems to have been rough, and the brake block is in dire need of replacement."

"Can your stable master fix it?" Bennet asked. Riverview wasn't a typical inn with a steady stream of travelers where problems like this could more easily be repaired. It was unfortunate that his own coachman, Tom, wasn't with him on this trip. He'd been ill, so Bennet had hired someone to drive his coach to Croydon. Then he'd hired a horse to ride here on his own while the men he'd paid to take Lady Cassandra had driven his coach to the inn.

"Indeed, my lord. However, the stable master will need to send his lad into town to purchase a block when the rain settles down a bit. It's unlikely he'll be able to finish the repair and get you on the road before late afternoon or evening."

Bennet had known they couldn't leave until afternoon, at least, since the horses would need to rest, and he couldn't afford to switch them. He'd already been struggling to afford to hire someone to drive to Aberforth Place, which wasn't necessary now. Still, he needed someone to drive them to

London, unless he wanted to add to his notoriety by playing coachman. Christ, this had been an incredibly short-sighted plan.

"What will that cost?" Bennet asked cautiously. "I don't carry much blunt on me—don't like to travel the road with a great deal of coin, you understand."

Logan smiled. "Of course not, my lord. Never mind the cost. I know you'll cover it on your next visit."

Bennet had always done that. He did his best to pay his debts, and so far always had. Settling his father's debts, however, was another matter entirely.

"Thank you, Logan, I appreciate you very much." The innkeeper and his wife were unfailingly kind. Bennet had stayed at Riverview several times on his way to London from Aberforth Place. Their small inn, which was as much a farm, was outside Hersham and thus cheaper, which was why he'd chosen it the first time—everything Bennet did was based on economy. It was why he'd had ale last night and not the fortified wine Miss Lancaster would have preferred. And frankly should have had.

"I'll let Mrs. Logan know you're down. She'll want to bring your coffee personally." Logan gave Bennet a warm grin before bustling off. He was a small man, but bursting with energy and surprising strength. Bennet used to wonder how he and his wife managed everything, but after coming to know them, he understood completely. They worked hard and found joy in their toil. The innkeeper liked to tell Bennet that if one wasn't bone-tired at the end of the day, he ought to redouble his efforts the next.

Bennet had taken that advice to heart when it came to finding a way out of his financial mess. He winced inwardly as he realized that had led him to make some very poor decisions. Such as kidnapping an heiress on a whim.

Sitting at the table in front of the cozy fire, Bennet vowed to indeed redouble his efforts. He had to. Too many people depended on him. His retainers, the tenants at Aberforth Place, and most of all, his family. He thought of his many aunts and cousin, especially Aunt Agatha, who relied on him the most. If he didn't settle the payments owed for her care, he didn't know what he would do. She'd have to come home, he supposed. And who would care for her there?

Hell, it was all so bloody complicated.

Frowning, he silently cursed his father. Though, Bennet supposed it wasn't even really his fault. The man had tried to fulfill his duties and had even occasionally been successful. He hadn't chosen to be afflicted in the way he was, nor had any of Bennet's other relatives. Still, his father hadn't made the best choices. A lack of self-awareness had been one of his greatest flaws. Along with his inability to manage his emotions, especially his terrifying rage and heartrending anguish. At least Bennet was aware that he carried the family curse and could very well end up like his father…

"Here you are, my lord." Mrs. Logan brought him a steaming mug of coffee. "Just the way you like it." She'd added a dollop of cream on his first visit, and he'd quite fancied the taste.

He smiled at her as she set the mug on the table. "You are too kind."

"Mr. Logan says your bride arrived. I'm so looking forward to meeting her." Mrs. Logan's blue eyes moved to the corner where the stairs were located. "Good morning, my lady!"

Bennet leapt to his feet and turned to see the companion at the base of the staircase. Her blonde braid was coiled and pinned atop her head, and she was dressed in a plain blue traveling costume.

He hated to have to be the one to tell her that they wouldn't be going anywhere.

CHAPTER 2

*P*rudence surveyed the common room, a cozy space with two small tables and a comfortable seating area, but her gaze was drawn to the tall, blond scoundrel staring in her direction. Yes, he was a scoundrel, even if he was devilishly attractive. Devilish, she decided, was the perfect word to describe him.

As was attractive. He looked handsome despite his somewhat rumpled state. She'd noticed the blanket on the chair in their chamber and deduced that was where he'd slept. While he wore a waistcoat, he hadn't donned a cravat, leaving a bare triangle of skin from his upper chest to the hollow of his throat. She'd never imagined that view could be alluring, especially on a man she considered a villain. And yet it was. Disturbingly. Prudence averted her gaze.

A middle-aged woman with light hair and a welcoming smile stood near him. "Good morning, my lady," she said.

"This is Mrs. Logan," Glastonbury blurted as he took a step forward. "Allow me to present my betrothed, Lady Prudence."

He knew her Christian name too? And apparently

expected her to masquerade as his future wife. Well, she supposed she could do that for the short time they were here. She was anxious to leave.

Mrs. Logan dipped into a brief curtsey. "Can I fetch you some coffee, my lady? Breakfast will be ready soon."

"I'd prefer tea, if you have it? With a bit of cream and sugar, please."

"Certainly!" Mrs. Logan took herself off, and Prudence eyed the small round table that Glastonbury stood next to.

He gestured to a chair. "Care to join me?"

"I suppose I must if I'm your betrothed." She slid into the chair.

He sat opposite her with a weak smile. "I hope you don't mind pretending. It seemed easiest."

"For you," Prudence noted. "I'm eager to be on our way. Cassandra is going to be worried sick about me."

"Ah, perhaps not," he said, wincing in discomfort, his cheeks flushing.

Prudence pursed her lips in irritation, wondering what else he hadn't told her. "Why wouldn't she be?"

"Because you wrote her a note." He glanced toward the fire. "Rather, Cassandra left a note explaining that she was eloping. That way, no one would come after her."

She blinked at him. "Except Cassandra isn't gone."

"She was supposed to be, and the note was from her so others wouldn't worry. I didn't sign it since I have no idea how she writes her name."

"How scheming of you," she murmured. "I might think you planned this well, if not for the way your hirelings handled me."

"It was a ridiculous plan from the start." He sounded bitter. And even disgusted.

She had better descriptions for his stratagem. "Nefarious and ill-conceived." She appreciated that he didn't look affronted. In fact, he seemed to silently agree with her. "You were foolish to think no one would come after Cassandra. Of course they would—Wexford, her brothers, her father. You really didn't think this through."

He exhaled. "I told you I was desperate."

Mrs. Logan returned with the tea, but didn't linger, for which Prudence was grateful. They couldn't discuss what was actually happening or had happened in front of her.

Glastonbury drank his coffee, his brow set into contemplative lines.

"I don't know how you can drink that," Prudence commented. "So bitter."

"Perhaps I'm a bitter person," he said.

She'd thought he seemed so, but was surprised to hear him describe himself that way. "Are you?"

He only shrugged in response. "I hope the tea is to your liking."

She took a sip and found it quite delicious for such an isolated place. "It is, thank you. I can't believe you authored a fake note. You really are a blackguard."

"Yes. I'm afraid your opinion of me and this situation is about to get even worse. There is a problem with the coach requiring repair. It won't be ready to leave until tomorrow, which is probably for the best since the rain has likely made the roads quite slow. It would take us twice as long to reach London."

They were trapped here for another night? "I didn't think my opinion of you could sink any lower. I was wrong." She took another drink of tea as anger swirled inside her. The problem with the coach might not be his fault, but the fact that she was even here was. If not for him, she'd be on her way back to London with Cassandra right now.

"I am deeply sorry for everything."

"So now I must keep up the charade of being your

betrothed for an entire day." She glowered at him. "I want a separate room."

"The inn only has two rooms, and when I arrived, Logan noted that the smaller one has a leaky window. He indicated that he wouldn't be taking any other lodgers because the room isn't fit for habitation at the moment. I am confident he wouldn't allow us to sleep there. He takes our comfort very seriously."

That was certainly convenient, she mused—for Glastonbury. Except he hadn't planned to be closeted with her. He'd expected Cassandra, who would have been even more upset by this situation. She had a family and a man she loved, and Glastonbury would have ripped her away from that. What had he taken Prudence from? A job that was likely coming to an end soon. Friends, but no family.

Did that mean her life was somehow less? That she wouldn't be missed?

She shook the silly, emotional thoughts away, as she'd done for years. Ever since her father's death when she was fifteen and her mother had admonished her to "tuck away" her grief. She'd said, "No one wants to see your emotions, Pru. They're messy and ultimately useless."

"Even love?" Prudence had asked. Her mother had said that love was something to be held close to the heart and that those worthy of the sentiment knew they were loved, as she knew Prudence loved her and she loved Prudence. It had felt like a secret, a bond that only they shared. In the wake of her father's death, she'd found comfort in that. Then, after her mother's death, she'd buried everything away. Emotions *were* useless when life and everything in it was so incredibly fleeting.

Bringing herself back to the present, Prudence asked, "How did you even find this place? It barely seems like an inn."

"Years ago, on my first trip to London, I wasn't able to make the final leg of the journey due to rain."

"Sounds familiar," she said quietly.

"I ended up here. It's a farm, but they also operate as an inn, albeit a small one."

"So you routinely stay here? I assumed you chose this place because it's isolated. Less chance of being caught with a kidnapped heiress."

"That's rather cynical."

She narrowed an eye at him. "But accurate, yes?"

"Yes," he admitted with a sigh. "However, I would have chosen Riverview anyway. Because, as you said, I routinely visit on my way to London from Somerset."

Prudence sipped her tea, then frowned. "I wish you hadn't used my Christian name. In fact, I am surprised you even knew it."

"I pay attention. No one will know who you truly are, if that's troubling you."

He was right. No one here would ever think she was Miss Prudence Lancaster, paid companion. Here, she was Lady Prudence. "Is my father a duke?" she asked sarcastically.

"Do you want him to be?"

"My father was a teacher," she said quietly, looking down at her tea as she recalled the man who'd raised her until he'd died. Her real father wasn't a duke, but he wasn't far off. She began to panic that Bennet would somehow read her thoughts—that she'd been adopted and that her entire life was a fabrication that could fall apart with the wrong utterance. Fleeting, indeed. She jerked her head back up and rushed to divert the subject of their conversation. "I'm still struggling with how you could be so desperate to do something this despicable. I understand you're in need of money, but this is beyond the pale."

His features, which had softened, now stiffened, his jaw clenching. "You wouldn't understand."

"You said that last night. Because I'm not from your class?" Prudence kept herself from snorting in derision.

His eyes widened briefly. "Not at all. My father wasn't nearly so lovely as yours. He left me a mess that I've been trying to tidy for the past year."

"Why would you say that about my father?" she asked. "How could you know?"

"I can see you remember him fondly. I do not hold my father in the same regard."

"Oh." She regretted allowing Bennet to glimpse even the faintest of her thoughts or emotions—it soured her mood. Eager to turn the conversation away from herself, she asked, "You didn't have a good relationship with your father?"

His jaw tightened. "It was difficult. *He* was difficult. His legacy includes insurmountable debt, an estate in disarray, and other…things."

"I'm sorry to hear that. It doesn't seem you're having much success with your efforts at fixing whatever he did."

"Yes, thank you for that," he said with as much sarcasm as she'd done earlier.

They glowered at each other over the table, each sipping their drink. Prudence hadn't meant to prick his ire. She was too caught up in her own irritation. This was why emotions were to be avoided.

"My goodness, but the love between you is evident to any observer," Mrs. Logan, who'd somehow arrived at the table noiselessly, remarked. She beamed at them as she set down a basket of rolls as well as plates before each of them. "How lovely. I'll be back with some ham."

As she hurried off, Prudence arched a brow. "*Evident*," she remarked softly.

"Evidently." He smirked. "You are correct about everything. I am despicable, and it was a horrible plan."

"Your dastardly kidnapping scheme aside, you should have been honest with Cassandra about your financial state."

"That too," he admitted. "In my defense, I assumed it would preclude me from courting her—and I was right. As soon as the duke learned of my shallow pockets, he ended our association."

"Do you think he approved of Wexford?" Prudence shook her head with a humorous smile. "His Grace will be horrified when he learns his daughter wishes to wed an Irishman. Given the duke's reaction to him, you'd think Wexford was one of hell's minions."

Glastonbury flinched. "I don't envy him. He's a nice fellow. I hope they'll be very happy." His gaze fixed behind her. "Mrs. Logan is returning," he murmured.

Mrs. Logan set a crock of butter on the table along with a plate of ham. "I'll check on you shortly. Enjoy!"

Prudence plucked a roll from the basket and slathered it in butter. "Do you really hope that? That they'll be happy, I mean."

"Of course I do. I'm not *that* despicable."

She was glad to hear it. Not that it mattered. Once he returned her to London, she'd likely never see him again. And if she did, it would be in a busy London ballroom or someplace similar, and they wouldn't acknowledge each other. Why should they?

They ate quietly for a few minutes. Prudence hadn't realized how ravenous she was. Apparently, being tossed around a coach half the night made one rather hungry. And sore. Her back and backside were somewhat tender.

After finishing two slices of ham and a roll, Glastonbury leaned back and perused her a moment, making her feel slightly self-conscious.

"What?" she asked dubiously.

"What do you plan to tell Lady Cassandra?"

Prudence shrugged. "The truth. What else should I tell her? That I eloped? I'm afraid that would be a difficult lie to uphold. Not that I would want to."

"Perhaps your husband died tragically just after the wedding. Imagine the freedom you could enjoy as a widow."

"I am already a lady's companion, a spinster. You'll have to come up with a better reason than that for me to keep the truth from Cassandra. Perhaps you ought to bribe me."

His brow furrowed for the briefest moment. Then he laughed. It was a rather jolly sound. "You possess a keen wit, Miss Lancaster."

"Careful. If you're committed to this ruse you concocted, you'd best call me Prudence. Or Pru, if you'd like to seem familiar." She finished the last bite of her roll.

"Shall you call me Bennet, then? Pru." He said her name slowly, even though he used the shortened version, as if he were trying it out.

"If you're to call me Pru, I shall call you Ben. Does anyone call you that?"

"My Aunt Agatha used to." His gaze drifted to the fire and remained fixed upon it.

Prudence was tempted to ask if his aunt was still with him, but it sounded as if she was not. He'd been kind enough not to prod after she'd foolishly mentioned her father. She would show him the same courtesy. It wasn't as if they needed to get to know one another, even if they were trapped together for a longer period of time.

She studied his profile, acknowledging that he was a very handsome gentleman. He also seemed most remorseful, not that his contrition alleviated the trouble he'd caused. Was it a trouble? She'd been frightened and uncomfortable, but she was unharmed and safe. Presumably, her reputation would remain intact. Would it if she was revealed to have been alone with Glastonbury for several days? Elopement would ensure she wasn't ruined.

Except she didn't want to marry him, nor was he asking. But if she hadn't eloped, what could she say she'd been doing? And why had she written the note? She'd have to reveal him and the truth of his actions.

It would be bad enough for him with everyone learning he had no money. Did she want to pile on his troubles by telling everyone he'd kidnapped her?

No, she refused to take any responsibility for the mess he'd created—not just for himself, but for her too. She shook the thoughts from her mind. Since they were stranded here, she had plenty of time to compose a plan.

"What shall we do all day?" she asked.

He looked back to her, his blue eyes brilliant in the light from the fire. "I thought I might take a nap. The chair wasn't terribly comfortable."

"You still aren't sleeping in the bed," she said. "Not even for a nap."

"I wouldn't think so. I'd planned to ask for extra blankets so that I may make a pallet on the floor."

"How enterprising of you." She stood abruptly, and he jumped to his feet. Glancing at the window, she said, "I'd take a walk, but it's still pouring buckets."

"A nap it is, then. Perhaps cards? Backgammon?"

Prudence found his charm disconcerting. He was contemptible. "I'd rather you didn't try to be nice to me."

"Makes it hard to stay angry, doesn't it?" He flashed her a brilliant smile, and her traitorous stomach had the nerve to do a small but noticeable flip.

"Do not flirt with me, Ben," she said sternly, immediately regretting using his name. It sounded far too intimate—and tasted that way on her tongue. She gave him her haughtiest glare.

Then she spun on her heel and marched back upstairs. Once there, she wondered what in the devil she'd do next.

∾

*F*ollowing dinner that evening, Mrs. Logan approached their table with a bottle and two wineglasses. "I've brought our best port. May I pour for you?" she offered with a smile.

Bennet tried not to think of the cost. Surely the best bottle of port here was at least moderately affordable? Not that he had even a shilling to spare.

"Thank you, Mrs. Logan," Pru said primly. She was very proper, but then he supposed she had to be as a lady's companion. Especially working for the Duke of Evesham.

Had he ruined that for her? Revealing the truth about where she'd been, that Bennet had kidnapped her by mistake would damage her as much as him. Had she considered that? He wanted to discuss it with her, but he also didn't want her to think his motives were selfish. He was finished—and he knew that. That didn't mean she had to be too. He'd been half-serious about his elopement-with-a-dead-husband suggestion.

Mrs. Logan departed, and Bennet lifted his glass over the table. "Shall we drink to an improvement in the weather?"

"Has it improved?" Pru asked, glancing toward the window where it was now dark outside. "It seemed to rain all day without interruption."

"It's more of a prayer," he said with a benign smile before taking a drink.

She gave a slight shrug, then also sipped her port. "This is delicious." She eyed him a moment, seeming hesitant.

"Is there something else you want to say?" he asked. "I think you more than deserve to ask me anything."

"Can you afford this?" She inclined her head toward the port.

"I didn't ask for it." That would have to suffice as an answer. He preferred to avoid admitting the true depths of his insolvency. "But I want you to enjoy it. You deserve that too."

She took another sip. "What will you do after you return me to London? Do you plan to stay for the rest of the Season?"

"If you're wondering whether I'll slink back to Somerset with my tail between my legs, the answer is no. I do need to go home to check on things, but hopefully, I'll find an heiress first." He lifted a shoulder. "Someone will want to marry a viscount. At least I have a title to sell."

She frowned gently, her lush lips pulling down. Lush? He ought not characterize her in such a way. She was not for him to lust after. Still, it was difficult to ignore her beauty.

"You can't marry for love, then," she said matter-of-factly.

He gave a humorless laugh. "I haven't the luxury of that, I'm afraid. I will hope to marry someone I like and admire—as I did Cassandra."

"I can understand. Love *is* a luxury, isn't it?"

"Why do you say that?" He found her to be rather enigmatic. She was very stiff, save her bouts of pique, which he'd thoroughly earned. Except for the brief mention of her father—in that moment, Bennet had seen love in her eyes.

"Love brings obligations and...messiness," she said offhandedly. "I'm alone now, and it's far more convenient—financially, emotionally, in all ways, really."

He couldn't argue that love was untidy. He had only to think of his family. They loved one another dearly, even his father, but there were plenty of other messy, complicated emotions and situations. "You've no desire to fall in love? To marry?"

"No." Her response came fast and strong. "Then I'd have to worry about someone other than myself, including children." Her shoulder twitched.

She didn't want children? How extraordinary.

Bennet took a drink of wine, thinking it was far better than he'd expected. It was, quite possibly, expensive after all. Blast. Ah well, he'd find a way to settle his account with Logan. There had to be another painting he could sell.

He changed the subject because he wasn't sure where they could go from there without venturing into rather personal, private territory. She'd already demonstrated she preferred to avoid that.

"What are you going to do now that Lady Cassandra is marrying Wexford?"

Prudence tensed, her shoulders stiffening along with her jawline. "I expect things will work out. They did after my previous charge eloped."

"An actual elopement?" he asked in surprise. "Who was that?"

"Lady Overton. When she and Lord Overton eloped, I went to Lady Cassandra. The two are close friends, so it was a convenient—and fortunate—move."

"I should say so. Does Lady Cassandra have another friend?"

"I can't say, but I believe she'll do her best to ensure I find a position. It may be that I shall work for someone older."

"Would you prefer that?"

She arched a brow. "I suspect there would be far less intrigue."

He laughed softly before taking another drink of port. "I suppose accompanying your charge to a boxing match and being abducted for your trouble is not likely to happen if you are companion to a dowager."

She smiled, and he wished she would do it more often. "I should hope not."

"It seems you haven't worked for an older woman as yet. Does that mean you haven't been a companion long? You seem rather young for the position, even if you are a spinster." He wrinkled his nose. "I dislike that word."

"It doesn't bother me. Anyway, I'm not as young as you probably think I am."

He noticed she didn't answer his question about how long she'd been in her line of work. He wouldn't press. "I'd say you were two and twenty. So perhaps you're actually thirty. That would make you older than me." He waggled his brows before recalling that she'd instructed him not to flirt with her. Was he really flirting? Probably. He couldn't seem to help himself. He liked her.

Her cheeks flushed light pink. "I am not thirty. Nor am I two and twenty."

"Something in between, then." He finished the port in his glass and refilled it. Lifting his brows in silent query, he held the bottle toward her wineglass, which wasn't quite empty.

She gave him a slight nod, and he replenished hers too.

"I really do feel very badly about last night," he said. "Are you recovered?"

She seemed to be, but she struck him as a stalwart young woman. He doubted she'd tell him if she wasn't.

"I am," she said, predictably. "Your hirelings were blackguards, however."

"I can't say I disagree, and if I see them again, I'll beat them to a pulp."

"All three of them?" she asked in surprise.

"I'd certainly try. You did not see me at my best in the bout last night." He tried to quash the feeling of self-loathing that rose in his throat. Not because he'd fought poorly but because he'd lost control. "I'm typically a better fighter."

"I see. Still, I should think it unadvisable for you to challenge three men at once and those men in particular. They seemed rather ruthless."

He couldn't disagree. "Which is why I shall never forgive myself for what I did and for involving you in it."

She opened her mouth, but pressed her lips together before speaking, her gaze moving to the side.

Bennet turned his head to see Logan had come into the common area. "Evening, Logan. This is a very fine port."

Relief flashed across the innkeeper's features. "I'm glad. I asked Mrs. Logan to bring it as an apology since you won't be able to leave on the morrow."

"What?" The word came from Bennet and Prudence in unison as they both turned more fully in their chairs toward Logan.

Logan's dark eyes sparked with distress. "You didn't know? My goodness, I thought Mrs. Logan had told you. Young Davy couldn't get to town today. The road is washed out from the rain, and the wind was just brutal. We're hoping things die down overnight, but it will be rough going. Hopefully he can get the box tomorrow and complete the repair, but I daresay you'll be here another night. I'm so sorry to have to tell you that news. I know how anxious you must be to get to your wedding."

Prudence coughed, and Bennet shifted his attention to her.

"All right, darling?" he asked.

She arched a fair brow and murmured, "Fine."

"I am sorry," Logan said again.

"It's not your fault," Prudence said brightly, surprising Bennet. "We appreciate your hospitality. I wonder if you might bring some extra blankets to our chamber. As you can imagine, his lordship and I are not sharing a bed until we are wed. However, my dear Ben insists we sleep in the same room for safety's sake. He slept in the chair, but now that we are here for more than one night, I daresay he would be more comfortable on a makeshift bed, if you can manage it."

If Logan found the request odd, he didn't show it. But then the entire situation was inappropriate. He trusted that Bennet was an honorable man who was simply impatient to wed the woman with whom he was madly in love.

"That's no problem at all, my lady. We'll set it up right away."

"Would you also prepare a bath for her ladyship?" Bennet asked. He should have thought of it sooner. But now that they were here for two more nights, he wanted her to be able to bathe.

"Yes, of course," Logan said with a nod. "If you'd also like a bath, my lord, we've a room off the kitchen you're welcome to use."

"That would be heavenly. Thank you." Bennet lifted his wineglass. "To your unparalleled hospitality."

"Hear, hear," Prudence agreed, raising her glass as well.

Logan blushed before hurrying off.

Prudence closed her eyes. "A bath. How lovely that will be." She opened her eyes and scrutinized him closely. "Promise you won't come back to the room for an hour."

"I will make sure you are finished and the bath has been removed." He gave her a sheepish look. "I am very sorry we can't leave tomorrow. This is turning into quite a disaster."

"Well, it's not as if anyone is worrying about me," she said.

There was an edge to her voice, and he couldn't discern why. "It's not because they don't care. I'm sure Lady Cassandra would be quite concerned if not for that stupid note."

Prudence said nothing as she sipped her wine.

"Since we're stranded here another day, what can I do to entertain you? You didn't seem interested in cards or backgammon. Chess? Some other game?"

"I don't play games."

"Why not?"

"I never had the time. Or the inclination," she added hastily.

He wondered about her life before she'd become a companion. Her father had been a teacher. *Had been*—was he dead? What of her mother? Did she have siblings? He thought about what she'd said, *it's not as if anyone is worrying about me.* Did she mean she had no one? The notion made him feel as though someone had carved a large hole in his chest.

"What do you like to do with your free time?" he asked.

"I suppose I read. Usually. I also like to take walks, though that seems unlikely given the rain and sodden nature of the ground."

He cracked a small smile. "It does indeed. I could read to you. I often read to my great-aunts. They like me to make silly and dramatic voices."

She stared at him. "I can hardly imagine. They live with you?"

He nodded. "Great-Aunt Flora has always taken her name quite seriously. She likes to press flowers. Indeed, she's never seen one she hasn't wanted to pick and press between one of her beloved newspapers. She's also an avid reader of the news, gossip in particular, I'm afraid. Her sister, Great-Aunt Minerva, is a painter, though she only paints a small number of subjects. She also rescues animals. Or more aptly, they probably rescue her." He left out the other things—how they might stay up all night with their obsessions and even become frantic over them. Their quirks were different from his father's and yet similar. They were all birds of a feather. Well, most of them.

"They sound fascinating."

He chuckled softly. "That is one word to describe them, yes. I've other relatives as well, but I shan't bore you with them. I've already blathered enough. Now, as to reading?"

She took a drink of port and lowered her gaze. "That might be amenable. If we've time."

"I daresay we'll have plenty tomorrow." He'd seen a flash of curiosity in her eyes before she'd looked away. If she wanted to ask him something, she was preventing herself from doing so. It was likely she didn't want to form any kind of attachment with him, even if it was only temporary. "I'm not a bad person," he said quietly. "I've treated you badly— not on purpose, but it is still my fault. If there is a way I can make it up to you, I will."

She studied him a moment, a light crease running just above her brows. "I believe that. Which is why I am torn as to how to characterize my disappearance when I return. If I tell them the truth, you'll be utterly ruined. I doubt you'd be able to find an heiress at all, even with your title. Or if you do, she may be someone you'll regret marrying."

"Because any intelligent young lady would stay completely clear of me," he said.

Her brows and shoulders briefly darted up in response.

He shook his head. "You mustn't let any of that determine your actions. You must do as you think necessary."

"That's terribly gallant of you, especially considering the utter scandal you stirred."

"I deserve the consequences of that." He finished his port once more, gripping the stem perhaps a trifle too tightly.

She emptied her glass as well, setting it on the table before her. "While that is true, I find myself wondering if it's necessary."

Every fiber of his being froze for a moment. Had he heard her right? "What does that mean?"

"It means I'm still pondering, and it seems I have an extra day to continue doing so. I'm not sure I can go through with pretending to have eloped with someone, but I won't rule it out. However, that would require a story as to who he was, how I knew him, and why I kept it from Cassandra. I'm just not sure it will be possible." She rose, and he did the same. "Do let me know if you think of something else. Good night."

A quick but beguiling smile passed over her lips, and Bennet found himself staring at her mouth until she turned from him. "Good night," he said as she started up the stairs.

The companion was proving to be a remarkable woman. He sat back down and poured himself another glass of port. And tried very hard not to think of her lips. Or the fact that she was shortly to be bathing in their chamber.

Instead, he endeavored to dream up a reason for Prudence's absence and for why she'd leave a note saying she'd eloped. Honestly, if he wasn't so bloody hard up, he'd just marry her himself.

CHAPTER 3

*P*rudence awoke in the dark—far past midnight, but not yet morning—as wind and rain battered the inn. If the weather didn't improve soon, she feared how long they'd be stranded here. Together in this room.

Opening her eyes, she looked toward the other end of the small room, where Bennet was asleep on his pallet near the hearth. His bed might be less comfortable than hers, but he had the warmth of the fire nearby at least.

This was a nice bed actually. As comfortable as the one she slept in at Evesham House in Grosvenor Square. That she inhabited such a prestigious address was still strange to her, but then so was acting as companion to the daughter of a duke. For someone who'd grown up in much less elegant surroundings, who knew how to cook and clean, and had always dressed herself, this world she'd entered a few months ago was foreign. It was becoming less so, and she was adept at acclimating—or so her friend Ada told her. Ada had also had to acclimate to a new position when she'd become the bookkeeper at the Phoenix Club, so she understood.

The Phoenix Club, London's newest exclusive social gathering place, brought Lord Lucien Westbrook to mind. Not only was he Cassandra's older brother, he'd been the one to help Prudence become a paid companion. But that was what he did—help people. He'd done it repeatedly for people of all social classes with a variety of problems. Lucien was a singular gentleman, and Prudence would be lying if she didn't admit he'd rather enthralled her with his charm and kindness. He was also breathtakingly handsome and perhaps the most likeable person she'd ever met. *Everyone* adored Lucien.

As owner of the Phoenix Club, he'd created a place that, while exclusive in its membership, invited people who were perhaps not widely welcome or at least not terribly popular. In fact, those sorts of people were often ignored with regard to membership. Prudence didn't know Lucien well, but she suspected he'd started the club because in some way he felt excluded. But that was just her supposition and one she would never present to him.

Especially not when he'd been so helpful to her, stepping in to change her life at a moment when everything had seemed particularly bleak. It was because of this that she wondered if he could help her with her current predicament, as in where she could say she'd been if not eloping. Furthermore, why would she have said eloping if she wasn't? Bennet had set up a real mess.

To ask for Lucien's help, she'd have to be very creative in how she explained the situation. She couldn't tell him about Bennet at all, not without revealing his plan to kidnap Lucien's sister. Prudence wasn't going to expose Bennet to Lucien's wrath—for while Lucien was the epitome of a kind and considerate gentleman, he would never permit such villainous behavior, particularly when it came to his beloved sister. Lucien issuing a challenge to a duel would not surprise

Prudence. For that reason alone, she would keep Bennet's role in this secret.

She looked toward where he slept again and wondered why she didn't despise him. She had. She should! But he'd demonstrated exceptional remorse and a surprising kindness. Furthermore, there seemed to be good reason for his motivations—it sounded as though his father had left him in a very bad situation—even if his decisions had been quite poor.

He made a noise. It sounded like a word, but Prudence couldn't make it out. Was he awake?

Slipping from the bed before she thought better of it, Prudence crept toward the fire. His eyes were closed, one bare arm thrown over his head against the pillow.

Bare.

He wasn't wearing a shirt. And the covers were low enough that she could see the breadth of his upper chest. He was muscular, which was to be expected given his boxing habit.

A sudden and rather forbidden thought flashed across her mind. She imagined how they might spend their time while trapped here. Her eyes darted toward the bed, and she silently chastised herself for such scandalous thoughts. Would she have found them scandalous before becoming a companion, before she'd been expected to demonstrate exemplary behavior? Not that she didn't have a reputation to uphold, even as an employee at a school. Indeed, it was in protection of her name—and even more of her person—that she'd left and found herself in dire straits to begin with. If not for the unwanted attention of that student's father, Prudence would still be at that school.

She ought not think of Bennet as anything other than a nuisance. She oughtn't think of him as Bennet either, but they were past that now. They weren't friends; however, they'd formed some sort of…connection through this experience and in the dark hours of this moment she allowed herself a flight of fancy.

She took in the masculine sweep of his nose and jaw, the supple line of his lips, the golden fan of his lashes. In her mind, she saw the vibrant hue of his blue-green eyes. They seemed able to see things about her that she didn't wish to share—or at least they tried to. He didn't look at her and discount her presence as someone of unimportance. He'd actually known her name, which had been astonishing enough.

This was madness. She had no right to stand there and ogle him, even if he had—accidentally—abducted her. He was trying to make amends. It wasn't his fault the weather was making a hash of everything.

Spinning on her heel, she retreated to the bed and burrowed beneath the covers. Flights of fancy were fine, but she daren't hope for more.

Even if she should be entitled to it.

~

*U*pon waking, Bennet was surprised to find Prudence had already gone. But then, he'd slept later than normal. Which was to be expected since he'd had trouble falling asleep. He worried over getting her back to London and ensuring she didn't suffer for his behavior.

He went downstairs to see her situated in a chair reading a book. "Good morning," he said. "You've had breakfast?"

She looked up, her features serene and lovely in the gray morning light. The rain had stopped for the last while, and it wasn't quite as dark as it had been. "I have. Mrs. Logan's rolls are delicious. If we stay too long, I may double in size."

He laughed, for he felt the same about Mrs. Logan's cooking. "Wait until she makes a trifle. You'll want to devour the entire thing. It will make you quite rudely gluttonous, I'm afraid."

"We wouldn't want that," Prudence said, her gaze returning to her book.

Bennet sat at the table just as Mrs. Logan came in with a tray. She bade him good morning as she set his breakfast and coffee on the table.

"I was just telling Pru about your trifle," he said, grasping his mug.

"Oh!" Mrs. Logan blushed, then waved her hand at him. "You're spoiling my surprise for later. How did you know?"

"I didn't. I merely hoped."

"You are too kind, my lord, too kind." Smiling, she shook her head as she left.

Bennet tucked into his meal, glancing occasionally toward his pretend bride. When he was finished, he leaned back in his chair and sipped his coffee, holding the mug between his hands. "Did you sleep well?"

She looked up, blinking. "Well enough. The wind was rather loud."

"I'm afraid I slept like the dead." The pallet had made a much better bed than the chair. "What are you reading?"

"*The Chronicles of Christabelle de Mowbray.*"

"I've read that to my aunts. My offer to read to you is still available."

She hesitated, then held out the book.

Bennet set his coffee on the table and stood. Stepping toward her, he took the book. "Where are you?" She pointed to a place midway down the page. Nodding, he glanced over the lines before that and tried to recall the story. Then he launched into the dialogue with robust enthusiasm.

By the time he turned the page, she was smiling. As he

moved to the following page, she laughed softly, her humor increasing as he increased his volume—and absurdity.

When he turned the page again, she held up her hand. "Please stop. I can't take anymore."

"Are you certain? I could try to be more sedate."

One of her pale brows arched. "Can you?"

"Yes. Though it's not nearly as amusing." He returned the book to her, and their fingers touched briefly. Too briefly. He wanted to clasp her hand, to look into her eyes, and... what? He shook the thought away.

"I never would have thought you possessed such a sense of humor. Or do you save it for your aunts primarily?"

"My aunts require a sense of humor," he said with dark sarcasm. He loved them dearly, but eccentric didn't begin to fully describe them. Add in fussy, obstinate, and mercurial and the characterization got closer.

"How did you come to read for them?" she asked, holding the book open in her lap as she sat forward.

Bennet pulled his chair from the table and sat back down. "I grew up with them, and they used to read to me. They taught me to read before the governess could—by making me read to them. Over the years, I became more animated, I suppose."

"How nice to have an extended family living with you. But I imagine your house is quite large enough to support that."

"Yes, Aberforth Place is almost too large." Thinking of the cavernous rooms, many of which were now empty, he revised his statement. "It *is* too large. Especially for me and my two great-aunts." He really ought to make all the other relatives move in since there was plenty of room. Then he could let the cottage that Cousin Frances occupied on the estate and stop paying the lease on Aunt Judith's house in Bath. Except Cousin Frances would never consent to living in the house, and Bennet wasn't sure he wanted her there. Great-Aunt Flora and Great-Aunt Minerva would fight him —they desired her there even less than Frances wanted to come. Furthermore, Aunt Judith had long ago made it clear that she refused to reside at Aberforth Place with the "afflicted." So while it made economic sense to bring them all under one roof, Bennet couldn't do it. Not only for his own peace of mind but for theirs.

And then there was Aunt Agatha. She couldn't come home either. Bennet had no one to look after her, not in the way that was required.

"You seem to care a great deal for them," she noted softly. "What of your other relatives?"

"My parents are gone, and I have no siblings. I have a cousin who lives on the estate and two aunts who reside in Bath." He wouldn't mention Aunt Agatha or the fact that she lived in a hospital.

"I see." Prudence looked down at her book, and he suspected she'd done the mathematics in her head. He had many relatives and likely cared for them, which was expensive.

She did not, however, confirm this. As with their other conversations, she avoided delving too deeply. In fact, today's questions about his family seemed positively intrusive compared to her usual behavior. It was one reason he saw her as guarded. She strove to keep herself private and gave him the space to do the same.

Normally, he would be relieved and even thrilled by this. He detested revealing anything more than he had, which was to say the bare minimum. Everything else was kept hidden and buried. It was how he'd managed to keep his financial status secret for as long as he had.

But Prudence was different somehow. If she asked more, he wasn't entirely sure he'd avoid answering—at least some things. Perhaps because he wanted to know more about her. "What of your family?" he asked.

"My parents are also dead," she responded quietly. "I also have no siblings. Unlike you, I have no other family either."

"No one?" The question fell from his lips before he could stop himself. He hated thinking of her being alone in the world. "I'm sorry."

"You needn't be. I am quite content."

"You enjoy being a companion?"

"Very much. I hope I may continue." Her eyes narrowed very slightly, as she closed the book over her forefinger to keep her place.

"I promise you will." As if he could control what happened. He'd been utterly unable to manage this situation. What made him think he could guarantee her anything?

"You can't make that promise, but I appreciate you wanting to."

He plucked at a nonexistent thread at his knee. "I'll do whatever necessary to ensure your reputation remains intact. Have you decided what you'd like to do?"

"I haven't yet, so it's just as well that we are stranded here." She stood suddenly. "I should like to find out if the roads are improved. I daresay they aren't." She glanced toward the window. It was still raining.

Bennet got up from his chair and returned it to the table. "I'll go. You stay and read. Please."

Lifting a shoulder in silent response, she sat back down.

"Perhaps the rain will stop soon," he said. "Or at least slow so that the stable master's lad can get to town."

She looked up at him with a benign smile. "We can only hope." Then her attention returned to her book, and he was effectively dismissed.

He'd bloody well trudge to the town himself—the rain be damned.

CHAPTER 4

*P*rudence had spent the afternoon helping Mrs. Logan. Busy assembling the trifle, she startled at the sound of a door clicking shut. She looked up to see Bennet emerging, hair damp from the small bathing chamber off the kitchen. Mrs. Logan rushed to take the clothing he held.

"I'll get this washed and dried out for you right away," she said with a smile.

Wiping her hands on her apron, Prudence stepped around the worktable in the center of the kitchen. "What happened to your clothing?"

"I walked into town to fetch the part for the coach."

She stared at him. While the rain had slowed a few times throughout the day, the past couple of hours had been a steady drenching as the wind had picked up once more. "You must have been soaked to the bone. How did I not see you come in?"

"You weren't in here."

"I must have been in the pantry." She stared at his simply knotted cravat. "You miss your valet, don't you?"

He laughed. "I don't have a valet. Which is unfortunate since I'm rubbish at cravats."

"No, you're not. It looks nice and unfussy, not at all like most gentlemen in London. Do you prefer a more elaborate knot?"

"Honestly, I find them a nuisance. Not having to wear them while boxing is one of the things I like best about the sport." He winked at her, and she hated how her body trembled. No one had ever flirted with her, and she likened her reaction to finding water after days in the desert.

"I still can't believe you walked all the way to town and back. You must have walked very fast."

"I ran partway. It seemed necessary if I was to return before dark." A glance at the window told her he'd barely made it, for it was black as pitch outside now—not that the charcoal rainclouds had permitted the day to ever be bright. "Plus, there was the rain. I was quite eager to get out of it. The last mile was a complete downpour."

"No wonder you needed a bath," she murmured. "Are you warm enough? You had to have been cold to the bone. Why don't you go sit by the fire?"

"Come with me." He went to the door and held it for her.

She looked toward Mrs. Logan, but the woman was already waving her out. Prudence untied her apron and set it on the worktable. "Thank you for letting me help," she said.

"Thank *you*, my lady. The trifle will be especially delicious this evening."

Prudence departed the kitchen, which was situated at the back of the inn, and made her way down a short corridor to the common room. Bennet followed her, and they sat at the table by the fire.

Bennet grinned widely. "I'm pleased to report that the coach is being repaired at this very moment. We'll be able to leave for London tomorrow, provided the weather cooperates."

"That is wonderful about the coach, but forgive me if I don't hold my breath about the weather."

"Are you always this skeptical?"

"Yes. It's best to be prudent when managing one's expectations."

He frowned briefly. "You sound as if you've been disappointed too often."

How did he see straight through her? No, not *through* her, but through her defenses and into her thoughts, into her *feelings*, which she worked so hard to keep buried. It was most disconcerting. She didn't like it one whit. "Did you forget my name is Prudence?" she asked saucily, hoping to distract him. "Who will drive us to London?"

"Ah, well, that is a slight conundrum, but I'm working on it. If necessary, I'll drive us."

She sat straight against the back of her chair and leaned slightly forward. "You can't do that. Is this about money?" She saw his jaw tighten. "Don't bother prevaricating. Haven't I seen you at your worst?"

He laughed, and she was surprised he could find humor about the subject given his clear desperation surrounding his financial state. "It's about a lack of money, yes. Everything seems to be about that." He exhaled in resignation, and she wondered if he'd just decided to surrender. Whatever that entailed.

"I'll pay for the driver." She had some money saved, surely enough for that. "I can compensate him when we get to London."

His blond brows pitched to a V over his eyes. "Absolutely not. You've been through enough. I can drive us."

"Just because you can doesn't mean you should. Let me pay for a driver."

"Just because you can doesn't mean you should." His mouth quirked into a smile, and she would have laughed if he wasn't agitating her with his refusal.

"If you're seen driving your own coach into Mayfair, your reputation will never recover."

He touched his chest. "My darling, I am overcome that you are so concerned."

"I am so glad you're trapped here," Mrs. Logan said from the doorway as she carried in a tray with a bottle and two glasses. "Gives me the chance to enjoy the love you share. It brings such joy to Riverview." She beamed at them as she poured two glasses of light-colored wine. "This is a sack Mr. Logan found this morning. I hope you like it." She left the bottle on the table before bustling back to the kitchen.

Prudence put her hand over her eyes and tipped her head down. They needed to be more cautious. What if Mrs. Logan had overheard them talking about his lack of funds or the fact that he'd abducted her?

She dropped her hand to her lap. "We need to be careful," she whispered.

"Why? So the Logans don't think we're in love?" He smiled as he picked up his wineglass. "I think it's best if they do. Perhaps I should kiss you for good measure."

Heat flushed her neck and probably tinged her cheeks pink. "You most certainly should not." Except the thought of it made her tingle everywhere. She'd had two kisses in her life—one nice and one awful. She wanted to have one that made her body sing. Or at least made her as giddy as Fiona and Cassandra had been. Both had fallen in love while Prudence had been their companion, and both had exuded a joy and excitement that was impossible to ignore. Or not to be jealous of.

She took a deep breath and hoped she wasn't blushing. "We need to be more careful about what we say so they don't

hear the truth. We need to keep pretending we're betrothed."
Perhaps he *should* kiss her. When one of the Logans was
present.

No!

"As I was saying, you can't just drive us into Mayfair." She
kept her voice low and swept her glass up for a substantial
drink to settle herself.

"I meant what I said—I'm delighted you care so much.
Truly." His smile was genuine. "But I'm fairly certain my
reputation is in shreds, as it should be. I deserve to be pillo-
ried, not that anyone knows why. Yet."

"They won't. I'm not going to tell anyone you kidnapped
me or that you'd planned to take Cassandra."

He stared at her in silence for a long moment, his features
registering surprise, then awe and perhaps admiration. "You
aren't?"

She shook her head. She hadn't completely decided until
that moment. Now that she'd said it aloud, it seemed the
obvious choice.

Now he looked at her in gratitude. "For as long as I live, I
will never understand why you aren't leading the charge
against me."

"What good would that do? I'm not in the business of
contributing to anyone's ruin." She spoke rather vehemently
—it was hard not to when discussing this matter—and he
noticed. His gaze centered on her in open curiosity. She
braced herself for his question, but it didn't come.

"You are a singular woman," he said softly. "I am still so
sorry for what you've endured, and continue to endure, but I
must confess I am glad to have come to know you."

She knew he meant it, that he wasn't just flattering her
like some empty-headed buck. "You can stop apologizing.
Really."

"Just because I can doesn't mean I should." He smirked and lifted his glass in a silent toast.

Prudence couldn't halt the giggle that slipped out. She took another drink of the sack. It really was quite delicious. The Logans' wine supply was a marvel.

Sobering—slightly—he asked, "So what are you going to say?"

"I don't know. I woke in the middle of the night and thought about it for some time. I wonder if I should seek help from Lucien. Lord Lucien, I mean."

He blinked. "Do you know him well?"

Calling him Lucien had given her away. Or the fact that she knew he helped people. Ah well, there was no help for it now, she may as well tell him the truth. Or at least part of it. "Well enough to know he helps people, no matter their station. There is no problem too great that he doesn't want to help solve."

"I suppose I've heard that about him, but I didn't realize the scope of his assistance."

"Meaning, you didn't realize he helped people like me?" She tried not to jump to the worst conclusion, but she found herself speaking more freely to him than she did to just about anyone else. She blamed their close quarters and spending so much time together.

"That wasn't really what I meant, but I suppose that's also a valid point. I wouldn't have thought so, no. I meant that I'm surprised he would help with a matter such as this. Anyway, he won't want to help you when he realizes you're protecting me."

Prudence sipped her wine and set it on the table, flattening her palm around the base, with the stem between her thumb and forefinger. "He isn't going to know you're involved."

Bennet stared at her as if she'd sprouted horns. "I didn't

think you could shock me more than you already have, but you intend to ask Lord Lucien Westbrook for help with this catastrophe that *I* created without mentioning me at all?"

"Yes. Keeping you out of it is precisely why we need help." She narrowed her eyes at him. "Please don't question me or my motives. Just be relieved that I wish to keep you out of it."

He gaped at her. "I don't know what to say."

"For once," she muttered with a hint of a smile, teasing him.

His laughter warmed the air around them. "You are incomparable. Can you really be so sure that he'll help you? Just because you're companion to his sister?"

"That's not why. He's helped me before."

"Has he?" His eyes glinted with curiosity, and she knew he was dying to ask. But he'd been careful not to press her on just about everything, endeavoring to keep their conversations light and noninvasive.

She would give him at least a half explanation. The specifics were far too private and would reveal far too much. "He helped me secure my first position as companion—to Miss Fiona Wingate. She was Lord Overton's ward."

"Then she married him. Perhaps over dinner, you'll tell me how that happened under your very nose." Now he was teasing her.

The truth was that Prudence wasn't the most exemplary of companions. She'd aided both of her charges in deviating from propriety. For love. While Prudence endeavored to keep emotion from her own life. It was asinine. Furthermore, if anyone discovered her weakness, she'd never have another position in London Society again.

Grasping her glass, she took another drink, finishing the wine without intending to do so. As soon as she set it back on the table, Bennet refilled it. His curiosity was a living, breathing thing surrounding her. It made her upset.

No, recalling her failures as a companion and that she'd indulged in sentiment made her upset. She really ought to find a position working for an older woman where there would be no chance of being swept into another young woman's love affair. Better still, she should find a position far away from London, from Society where she absolutely didn't belong.

Except she still hoped to find her real mother—the woman who'd given Prudence life before she'd been adopted by the Lancasters. If she left, Prudence would never find her.

Perhaps it was time to let the past go.

"Pru?" Bennet queried gently. "Where did you go?"

Prudence blinked and gave her shoulders a shake. "I was woolgathering in the farthest reaches about nothing of import." She glanced toward the door, wishing Mrs. Logan would come through it.

Then she was there, Prudence's savior toting a tray bearing soup.

"Dinner is here," Prudence said brightly, relieved for the interruption. She didn't want to discuss how Lucien had helped her, and she certainly didn't want to reveal the things she'd been thinking.

She'd distract him with stories about Fiona, nothing terribly personal, of course. So long as Bennet stopped wondering about her, Prudence could manage the rest of the time they were together. Then she would never have to see him again.

Suddenly, he seemed the perfect person to whom she could reveal herself—if she was ever going to tell one person all her secrets. Would he guard them? She suspected he would, and that made him far more dangerous than she'd originally feared.

∾

*B*ennet ought to feel terrible that the weather had worsened the following day, which hardly seemed possible, but instead was glad for the time he had with Prudence. He'd read to her again after breakfast, for a much longer period, and then she'd gone to help Mrs. Logan bake bread while Bennet had checked on the status of the coach.

While the vehicle was repaired and ready for travel, the roads were not. The rain slanted sideways, and the trees shook with every gust of wind.

"Bad luck with this weather, my lord," the stable master said. He was a large, wide-shouldered man with thick, dark hair. "Even if it stops raining tomorrow, you'll be stranded here waiting a few days for the road to dry out. We're too close to the river, and it overflows its banks. The stable's been flooded a time or two."

"How awful."

"Bloody inconvenient, begging your pardon, my lord. But it's late enough in the season that it ought not be that bad."

Ought not.

Bennet would cling to that, for as much as he was enjoying his time with Prudence, he knew she wanted to return to her life. *Needed* to. The longer she was away, the more difficult it became to explain her absence.

He still couldn't quite grasp that she wanted to ask Lord Lucien for help. Bennet didn't know him well and doubted he ever would. The man had personally delivered Bennet's invitation to the Phoenix Club, however, and asked him to come that very night. Bennet now knew it was so he could dance with Cassandra. It was one of the reasons he'd felt confident in her interest in him. She'd gone to the trouble to have her brother invite him to his club. How could Bennet have *not* thought she was open to his courtship?

Anyway, he'd dragged his feet with her. If he hadn't, they

might already have been betrothed before her father had learned of Bennet's financial problems. It would have been too late to back out.

Why had he hesitated? Because as much as he needed to marry, he didn't particularly want to. A wife would have to understand—and accept—certain things, which meant him revealing that which he could not.

It was a bloody tangle, but then everything to do with his father and family was.

"I appreciate you repairing the coach," Bennet said to the stable master.

"My pleasure, my lord. Though, I'd have words with your head groom or whoever oversees your equipage. Your coach was in need of a great deal of maintenance."

Bennet smiled to mask the reality—that Tom, his coachman, was well aware of the state of things and that he did his best to maintain everything given the complete lack of funds to do so. "I'll do that, thank you."

Despite dashing across the yard to the house, he was quite wet when he stepped inside. He removed his hat and shook it off, then did the same with his coat, hanging both on a rack near the door.

He probably shouldn't wander around half-dressed, but he'd done it before—that first morning after they'd arrived. And his coat was wet. Grabbing it from the hook, he took it to their table near the fire and hung it over the back of his chair, then turned it toward the hearth so it could dry more quickly. Bennet rubbed his hands together and soaked in the warmth from the fire.

"I thought I heard someone come in." Prudence walked in from the kitchen, a strand of blonde hair caressing her cheek. Oh, to be that lock...

She stopped short, her gaze moving over his coatless form and provoking a rather indecent response below his waist. He strove to keep his body under control. She didn't need to see how she affected him. Hadn't he already subjected her to enough?

"I was just checking on the coach, and I'm afraid my coat got rather wet when I ran back from the stable." He felt a need to explain why he wasn't wearing it. "The coach will be ready to go whenever we can leave." He sent a perturbed glance toward the window. "Which may not be for some time, unfortunately."

"How much time?" she asked cautiously.

"The stable master said the river has overrun its banks, which has made the road impassable. He said it could be a few days before we can travel. *If* it stops raining tomorrow."

"Perhaps we should build an ark."

Bennet laughed. How he enjoyed her dry wit. "I would if I could afford it." That he was now jesting with her about his financial state indicated just how comfortable he felt with her. Too comfortable, perhaps. He needed to be careful not to expose too much.

"There's plenty of wood around here," she said, standing on the other side of the chair that held his coat. "And if the wind continues as it has, there may be a tree—or ten—felled."

"I hadn't thought of that," Bennet said. "But given our luck thus far, I'm confident one will fall across the road, further delaying our departure."

She smirked. "We may have to walk."

He turned fully toward her. "I'll get you back to London as soon as I can. I'm so sorry."

With a shake of her head, she held up her hand. "I told you to stop doing that. No more apologies, especially for this weather, which isn't your fault."

"I'll try, but I can't promise anything. I'm afraid my remorse is quite towering." He looked toward the fire lest he fixate on that errant lock of hair. He longed to take it between his fingers, to feel its softness before he tucked it behind her ear. Then he'd stroke the delicate shell of that ear and caress her jaw. It would be so easy to lean in and kiss her...

He was an absolute beast.

"I've forgiven you, so please set your remorse aside. I am quite fine, and while your scheme was ill planned and horrid, there was no real harm done."

Unless he'd ruined her for future employment. It wasn't as if he could offer to take care of her the rest of her life. Not only could he not afford to do so, it would imply a rather scandalous connection between them. He wouldn't want her to suffer that, not even for five minutes, let alone forever.

"I won't forget, however," she added, her eyes glinting with promise.

"I won't either," he said softly. "Is it terrible that I'm enjoying this time here with you?" There, he'd said it.

She fidgeted with her hands for a moment, then thrust them down to her sides, as if she'd caught herself doing something wrong. "I can think of worse things. Such as the kidnappers not bringing me to you at all."

He drew in a breath. "Hell, don't even think that." He would have tracked them down and found her, whatever the cost. He said that now, knowing her and liking her as he did. But it would have been Cassandra he would have gone after —or so he'd thought. He would have done the same; however, his reaction was different. Prudence had grasped on to something within him, something that would do anything to keep her safe.

"I try not to think of the worst," she said. "Sometimes, I can't help it."

"Why?"

She fidgeted with her fingers again. "When bad things happen, you begin to wonder if they always will."

"Bad things such as your parents dying?"

Her gaze met his, and he basked in the fleeting vulnerability she allowed him to see. "Among other things." Her eyes shuttered, and she looked toward the window. "Perhaps we'll just be here forever. We could ignore everything else."

He indulged the fantasy, smiling. "Well, that would certainly simplify things."

"But entirely unrealistic. You have responsibilities, people who rely on you."

"Yes."

"I suppose it's nice to think about not having that sometimes. I'm quite free to make my own choices based only on what I want and what is best for me."

A brief flash of jealousy shot through him. He didn't have that luxury. That also meant she didn't have the joy of family, no matter how complicated and exhausting they could be. They could both make an argument for contentment—and discontent.

"Are you lonely?" he asked, knowing he shouldn't but unable to stop himself. Would she answer or deflect and avoid as he expected her to do? "You said you were alone, but are you lonely? That's not the same thing."

A long moment stretched before she responded, and he realized he was holding his breath. "Not usually. Sometimes—"

He would never know what she was about to say because a loud crash sounded as a tree fell against the inn.

CHAPTER 5

*P*rudence followed Bennet to the door. He threw it open and started outside but in his haste hadn't grabbed his coat. She pulled his hat from the hook and stepped out into the howling wind and sideways rain. "Here!" she called.

He turned his head, his brows pitched low over his eyes. "Get back inside!"

"Take the hat!" She thrust it toward him. "And you need your coat."

Grasping the hat, he slammed it on his head. A branch sailed past them, and his face creased with distress. "*Please*, go back inside!"

She turned and stopped short. "Bennet!" Pointing to where the tree leaned against the corner of the house with one hand, she clapped the other over her mouth.

He came to her side and took her arm, guiding her back to the door. "Go inside and stay away from this corner. Tell Mrs. Logan what's happened."

"What's happened?" Mrs. Logan's face appeared in the doorway.

"There's a tree leaning against the house," Prudence said.

Bennet let go of her arm. "There's Logan and Tasker, the stable master. I'll go help them. Remember, stay away from this corner." He looked up and around. "Too many damned trees."

Prudence went inside, but didn't close the door. She craned her neck to see what the men were doing.

"Come in, dear," Mrs. Logan said gently. "I know you're worried, but they'll be fine."

"He doesn't even have his coat," Prudence said, though that was the least of her concerns. What if a branch fell on him? Or worse, another tree?

"Let me get him a greatcoat." Mrs. Logan turned. "I'm sure I can find something that will suffice."

Prudence wrung her hands and allowed herself to fidget —a bad habit she'd worked hard to overcome before assuming her position as a companion. A gust of wind pulled at the open door, and Prudence swung it closed before it blew off.

Mrs. Logan returned with a dark brown coat.

"I'll take it to him," Prudence said.

"You're going to get soaked." Mrs. Logan eyed her doubtfully, but gave her the coat.

"I'll be quick." Prudence dashed outside as lightning flashed overhead. She ran toward where Bennet stood with the others, the mud sucking at her booted feet. They seemed to be assessing the situation with the tree. "Bennet!" she called just before she reached his side.

He turned, his eyes widening. "Pru, you shouldn't be out here."

She thrust the coat toward him. "Put this on before you're drenched to the bone."

"Might be too late for that," he said with a smile, taking the garment and throwing it over his shoulders. "Go back in.

We won't be long. We can't move the tree until the storm is over."

"Be careful," she said, her gaze holding his.

"I will. Go." He smiled at her as she turned. Another bolt of lightning lit the sky followed by a loud crack.

"Prudence!"

Prudence heard her name just before she felt a weight crash against her. She fell forward, turning her head just before she hit the muddy ground.

Her breath had been knocked from her, but she didn't feel hurt. It took her a moment to realize it wasn't a branch that had sent her falling, but a person whose weight now held her down.

Turning her head farther, she tried to see who was on top of her back, but she couldn't. She inhaled deeply through her nose because there was mud on her lip. Then she knew who it was—by scent.

"Bennet, are you all right?" He hadn't moved since they'd fallen.

He let out a groan. "Yes."

"Your lordship!" One of the men called just before the weight was removed from Prudence's back.

She instantly turned over and scrambled to get up. The stable master, Tasker, had pulled Bennet up.

"Bloody hell." Bennet stared toward the stable, provoking Prudence to pivot.

A tree had crushed one side, falling completely through the roof.

"Go," Bennet said to Tasker. "I'll be fine."

Prudence looked to him and saw blood trickling from his temple, mingling with the rain. "You are not fine," she said, rushing to his side.

"I wager I'm better than my coach." He winced as she touched his cheek.

"You're coming inside," she insisted, grabbing his arm and dragging him toward the house.

"All right." He sounded resigned. Defeated almost.

Mrs. Logan met them at the door. "Did that branch hit you?" She gestured toward the very large piece of wood that lay in the mud next to where Bennet had fallen on top of Prudence.

"I think it hit his lordship, yes," Prudence said as they moved inside. She pulled the sodden coat from Bennet and cast it behind her, careless of where it landed. "Come to the settee so I can look at your head."

"Better me than you," he said, touching his head gingerly.

Prudence settled him on the settee in the seating area near the front window. "What do you mean?"

"That bolt of lightning hit the tree. It split, and the branch was diving straight for you." He looked up at her, his blue-green eyes stark with distress. "It might have killed you."

"You saved her life," Mrs. Logan whispered, sounding as if she were awed. "It's a miracle you weren't more seriously injured. Or killed yourself."

"I tried to move us out of the way." Bennet didn't take his eyes from Prudence. "I'm sorry if I hurt you when I tackled you."

"You didn't." She couldn't believe what he'd done, how quickly he'd acted. And with no thought to himself. "You shouldn't have done that."

"Don't say that." His voice was low and raw. "Please don't say that. I'd do it again." He wiped at the blood that was still streaming down his face. "Might I have a towel or something to press on this?"

"Good heavens, look at me standing here doing nothing!" Mrs. Logan dashed toward the kitchen, delivering a commentary as she went, "I hope Mr. Logan and Mr. Tasker come in before too long. It's far too dangerous out there!"

Prudence sank down beside him on his injured side. "Does it hurt?"

"Yes."

"Did you lose consciousness?" she asked. "You didn't move for a moment."

His brow furrowed, then he winced. "I don't think so, but I'm not sure. Everything happened so fast. All I could see was that branch coming straight down toward you. If anything had happened to you..." He closed his eyes and pressed his lips together until they whitened.

"Nothing happened, save my sudden need for a bath."

He laughed and winced again.

"No more laughing," she admonished.

"Then stop being witty and charming." He opened one eye. "If you can, which I daresay you can't."

"Nonsense. I'll be ruthless in my care of you."

His other eye opened, and he regarded her with a heat that shocked and thrilled her. "Promise?"

Before she could summon an appropriate response—and she wasn't at all sure she could—Mrs. Logan returned with warm water and toweling.

"The love you share is so wonderful to see," Mrs. Logan said, handing Prudence a cloth. "I'm so relieved you're both all right."

Prudence wanted to roll her eyes or in some way dismiss Mrs. Logan's observation, but she couldn't. And not just because it would reveal their deception. She didn't want to upset this moment.

Because Bennet was injured. Yes, that was the reason.

She gently put the cloth to his forehead. "Is this all right?"

"Yes, thank you. You can press a little harder."

She applied more pressure, but he winced so she lightened it again. "Just try to relax. Perhaps some brandy, Mrs.

Logan." She glanced toward the woman, who nodded and presumably went to fetch it.

"I'd like to know the state of the coach." He grimaced, and she wasn't sure if it was from pain or the likelihood that they'd lost their only mode of travel. A terrible thought occurred to her—given his financial state, was it *his* only mode of travel? Could a gentleman be a gentleman without a coach?

"We'll ask when they come in. They can't remain in the storm too long." Gusts of wind rattled the inn. Prudence glanced up at the ceiling. "Will it tear the house apart?"

"Only if it sends another tree our way. But I don't think there are any others close enough to damage the house."

"What of the one resting over there?" She inclined her head toward the corner.

"We'll pull it off tomorrow probably. Hopefully. The damage is minimal. The stable, on the other hand…" He frowned, and she knew he was concerned.

"We can hire transportation or ride the mail coach if necessary," Prudence said.

He arched a brow, but only for a second because he winced and relaxed his features. "How are we to pay for that?"

"I've a bit of money hidden in the lining of my case." Her mother had taught her this trick years ago—always have something stashed for emergencies. "Don't tell me you refuse to use it."

"I'm not taking your money," he said firmly. "However, you could use it to return to London on your own, I suppose. Though, I'm loath to let you go alone."

She gritted her teeth. "Are you worried something will happen to me? That perhaps I'll be abducted?"

He laughed and immediately sobered. "Ow. You aren't supposed to be witty."

"Then stop saying stupid things. You don't get to 'let' me do anything."

"Yes, my lady." He sounded as though he'd been reprimanded, but didn't necessarily look it.

Mrs. Logan returned with brandy, setting a bottle and two glasses on a table next to the settee. "Pardon me for taking so long. Mr. Logan came into the kitchen, and I was helping him take off his wet coat. I'm heating water for baths now. I daresay you should both get out of your sodden clothing before you catch cold."

Prudence nodded. She was all too aware of her damp clothing and the mud drying on her face. "Thank you, Mrs. Logan, we'll do that."

Mrs. Logan's features tightened as she briefly clasped her hands. "Mr. Logan said the horses are fine, but I'm afraid your coach is rather damaged, my lord."

"Did he say how badly?" Bennet asked, noting her sudden pallor. "It's all right. You can tell me the truth."

"Irreparably, I'm afraid." She looked at him with sympathy.

"Thank you, Mrs. Logan. For everything."

Mrs. Logan returned to the kitchen, and Prudence fixed her attention on Bennet. She pulled the towel from his wound and was pleased to see the blood was no longer flowing. Although, it hadn't quite stopped either. "Hold this," she instructed as she folded the towel over to a fresh side.

Bennet took over from her, and she poured the brandy, putting a glass in his free hand, then taking the towel duty back from him. She took a long, fortifying drink, glad for the heat working its way down her throat and into her abdomen.

"We'll find a way to get you home—tomorrow," he said. "Not that you can leave tomorrow, but I'll come up with a plan."

Prudence pulled the bloody towel away and set it aside.

Grabbing a fresh one, she wet the cloth in the small basin of warm water Mrs. Logan had set on the same table as the brandy. "Tomorrow is Sunday, in case you've completely lost track of time."

"I had, somewhat."

"I daresay you'll be busy helping with the tree and whatever else." She cleaned the dried blood from his cheek.

"Yes, the yard is a mess, and the storm isn't over yet. I'll still do what I can to make plans for your return to London."

Turning the towel, she wiped at the mud on his face. "When it's possible. This storm has worsened the roads, and they're going to take some drying out."

"As will we," he noted, glancing at her hand. "You're shaking."

She hadn't noticed. "I'll be fine."

"Enough." He pulled his head back and took the towel from her. Plucking up the remaining clean towel, he dipped it into the water and wrung it out before setting to work on her face. His strokes were a bit rough.

"You aren't a very good nursemaid," she murmured.

He gentled his ministrations. "Better?" At her nod, he went on. "I'm afraid the dirt is quite caked onto your skin. It looks as though a beast squashed you into the mud."

"That's precisely what happened." She barely suppressed a smile.

He dropped the cloth into the basin. "That's the best I can do, I'm afraid. Now, upstairs with you. Get out of those clothes and warm up in the bed until the bath is ready."

"What about you?"

"I'll come up in a while and fetch a change."

She stood from the settee. "I'll close my eyes while you dress."

"You don't have to."

Was he flirting with her? It seemed so, though she had no

experience. "Of course I do." Though the invitation was most alluring. The muscular lines of his chest were imprinted on her memory. If she saw more than that, she wasn't sure what she would do.

Straightening her shoulders, she gave him a prim stare. "Don't tempt me, Ben. You owe me that much."

As she walked away, she heard him say, "I owe you far more than that."

~

Somehow, things had changed between Prudence and Bennet. Or at least it seemed that way to her. Was it that he'd prevented her from suffering harm? That he'd openly flirted with her? That they were now stranded here indefinitely?

Prudence didn't know the precise reason, only that things were different. Last night, she'd been far too aware of him sleeping, probably shirtless, mere feet from her bed. Breakfast had been awkward, and while he'd read to her afterward, the interlude had been short. He'd wanted to get outside to help clean up the yard. Thankfully, it had finally stopped raining. The sun had even made an appearance that afternoon.

Not that Prudence had spent any time in the yard. She'd committed herself to tidying the bedchamber and helping Mrs. Logan in the kitchen. After cleaning up from breakfast, she'd helped Mrs. Logan prepare a midday meal for the men working so hard to clear the yard. They'd managed to move the tree from against the house, and someone was busy sawing it into pieces for the fire.

Prudence pulled a loaf of bread from the oven and set it atop the worktable, pleased with the golden crust.

"My goodness, your bread looks wonderful," Mrs. Logan

sang as she strode into the kitchen carrying an empty tray of mugs. She'd taken ale out to those laboring.

"Let me help." Prudence took the tray and went to the sink to clean the mugs.

Mrs. Logan followed her and pumped water into a basin. "You have an ease with cleaning and cooking for a lady of your station, if you don't mind my saying so."

She hadn't asked a question, but Prudence had heard one just the same. "I grew up more humbly. My father inherited when he didn't expect to. Things changed, but I haven't forgotten my earlier years." It was only a half lie. She *had* grown up humbly. But happily. "My mother taught me to make bread."

"That explains why you seem so unassuming, so approachable," Mrs. Logan said. "I've not met a great many Society ladies, but you aren't like any of them."

Because she *wasn't* one of them, even if she mingled in their circles. However, her real mother *was* one of them, as was her real father, whose identity she knew. When Imogen Lancaster had revealed the truth of Prudence's birth, she'd given her a ring that had belonged to her real mother. The ring was a family crest, something only a woman of means and position would have owned. That she'd gifted it to Prudence seemed to indicate she wanted Prudence to find her. In truth, if the woman had wanted her identity known, wouldn't that information have been shared along with Prudence's father's identity? Prudence had since learned her father was dead. It was possible her mother was as well. Perhaps it was time to stop wondering and searching.

"How did you and his lordship meet?" Mrs. Logan's query jolted Prudence back to the present.

Prudence plucked a dishcloth from behind the sink and washed the first mug. "At a ball." It was the first thing that came to her mind—and the most innocuous.

"Did you fall in love immediately?" Mrs. Logan grinned.

"No." Prudence hoped the woman didn't press her for details. She'd have to inform Bennet of what she said so they could keep their stories straight. Anxiety stabbed at her as she wondered whether Bennet had already told her anything.

"Why did you decide to elope?"

"What did his lordship tell you?" Prudence asked, hoping to avoid giving her conflicting information if Bennet had in fact spoken to her already. She handed the mug to Mrs. Logan to dry.

Mrs. Logan's cheeks tinged faintly pink. "I didn't ask him. I shouldn't have asked you either."

Prudence didn't want the woman to feel bad. Mrs. Logan was very nice, and Prudence didn't like that they were lying to her. The woman wouldn't appreciate having them sharing a room under her roof given the truth of their circumstances. It was beyond indecent.

"I'm afraid we were impatient to be wed," Prudence explained. "The banns take too long. Although, if we'd known the weather would keep us here for so many days, we wouldn't have bothered." Prudence finished washing the next mug and gave it over to Mrs. Logan to dry.

"Oh, it is certainly bad luck."

"I wonder if that means we shouldn't wed," Prudence mused.

Mrs. Logan gaped at her. "Of course not! Anyone can see you are meant to be together. You must marry!"

Prudence had picked up the next mug and promptly dropped it into the sink. Thankfully, it didn't break. "I don't know how you see what you do, but I appreciate your support."

"About what?" Bennet's question sounded through the kitchen as he moved inside from the exterior door followed by Mr. Logan, the stable master, and a few other men.

Mrs. Logan moved on to drying another mug Prudence had washed. "I was just telling her ladyship that it's clear you and she are meant to be together, in spite of this bad luck with the weather and your poor coach."

Bennet's gaze found hers as she looked over her shoulder at him while scrubbing the final mug. There was mirth—and heat—in his gaze.

Prudence finished with the mug and handed it to Mrs. Logan. She turned, drying her hands on her apron. "I told her we eloped because we were impatient."

"That is certainly true," Bennet said with a nod. "What else did you tell her?"

"That we met at a ball." Prudence gave him a look in which she tried to convey her concern at having to answer such questions.

"There's soup and fresh bread, baked by our very own Lady Prudence," Mrs. Logan said proudly.

Bennet looked toward the loaf Prudence had taken from the oven. "You baked that?"

"I did."

"Astonishing," he murmured. "It looks delicious."

Mrs. Logan took several bowls down from the shelf. "My lord, why don't you and her ladyship go sit in the common room. I'll bring your food in."

"I can eat in here with everyone else."

"Nonsense," Mr. Logan said. "You've been kind enough to help us, dirtying yourself as you have when the storm has destroyed your coach." He shook his head. "I feel quite terrible about that."

"It isn't your fault," Bennet assured him.

"Still, I'd feel better if you and her ladyship sat down together."

"All right, then." Bennet smiled at him and moved toward the corridor leading to the common room.

Prudence looked to Mrs. Logan. "Shall I slice the bread?"

"Go on now." Mrs. Logan waved her out of the way. "You've more than earned a respite."

"Come, we are being expelled," Bennet murmured as he gently took Prudence's arm and guided her from the kitchen.

His touch was warm and familiar. She liked it more than she ought.

When they reached the common room, Bennet released her and tended the fire. Prudence realized she was still wearing the apron.

"You look exceedingly domestic," he said, straightening from the hearth to hold her chair.

"Is that a good thing?"

"If you were actually my betrothed, yes. My future wife may need to be able to cook and clean." He grinned at her as he slid into his chair.

There was dirt on his cheek, and his clothing was disheveled. He wasn't wearing a cravat. She avoided looking at the small triangle of flesh exposed at the base of his throat. Mostly.

"Then perhaps it's too bad for you that I'm not your betrothed," she said sweetly, provoking him to laugh. She gave him a serious look. "I was worried I might say something to Mrs. Logan that would contradict something you said. About us, I mean."

"I didn't tell her anything specific. Certainly nothing so detailed as us having met at a ball."

"What was I supposed to say?" she asked in a hushed tone. "That you kidnapped me by mistake, and we just fell completely in love?" She rolled her eyes.

He reached across the table and took her hand, surprising her so that she froze. "Thank you for saying what you did. I think I'd like to see you at a ball. Dance with you, even." He let her go and settled back in his chair, his eyes dancing.

Heat flushed through her again. Thankfully, Mrs. Logan came in to provide a welcome distraction. She served their bowls of soup, bread with butter, and two mugs of ale. "I'll bring tea in a while."

"You look rather domestic too," Prudence said. "What sort of things do you do at your estate?"

"Nothing like this," he answered, buttering a thick slice of bread. "Yet. The number of retainers has been whittled down, but there are still people working there." He set down the knife and stared at her. "How do you do that?"

"Do what?"

"Provoke me to say things I would normally never reveal."

Prudence shifted in her chair. He'd done the same thing to her more than once. They were sharing secrets, flirting, behaving domestically, and apparently seemed as if they were madly in love.

She took a long drink of ale. Their departure—and separation—couldn't come soon enough.

CHAPTER 6

ennet hadn't meant to sleep as late as he did, but he'd been fairly exhausted yesterday after cleaning up from the storm. He'd nearly fallen asleep at dinner which had prompted Prudence to offer him the bed, meaning she'd take the pallet. He'd soundly refused. Honestly, he could have slept suspended in midair and wouldn't have noticed. He couldn't remember ever being that tired.

Today, they would work on the damaged stable. The rain had stopped, and the sun was even peeking from behind a cloud. Bennet went to join the others, who'd already been at work for a while, it seemed.

"You should have woken me," Bennet said with a smile to Mr. Logan.

"I considered it," Logan said. "But then Mrs. Logan threatened me if I did. She said you needed to rest. If I can give you one piece of advice about marriage, it's that you should listen to your wife. Especially if she threatens you."

Bennet laughed softly. "What did she say?"

"That she wouldn't make my favorite kidney pie." He

grimaced as if she'd actually threatened bodily harm. "Come, to the back of the stable, where your coach was parked."

Was.

"Well, I suppose it's still parked there," Logan said with another grimace.

Bennet followed him. "I confess I came in to see it yesterday. It's as you said." *Irreparable.*

"I feel as if it's my fault." Logan shook his head. "It was in my stable."

"That's nonsense." Bennet stared at the wreckage where the roof had caved onto the coach, squashing it. "I'm sorry your stable was so badly damaged—none of us escaped the wrath of the storm, it seems."

"What will you do without a coach?" Logan asked.

"Not elope." Bennet smiled then noted the distress in Logan's features. "It's all right. Lady Prudence and I have discussed it. She'll return to London as soon as possible. Ah, her family knows we planned to wed. I will try to get a special license instead." He'd need to tell Prudence about these lies.

"I'm so sorry your plans were ruined. Aren't you going to return to London with her?"

Hell, he should. A young *lady* oughtn't be traveling about on her own. "It depends on the transport we arrange."

Furthermore, Bennet had begun to wonder if he should go to Aberforth Place instead of London. He might do better trying to find an heiress in Bath. London would likely be rife with the gossip of his destitution. But he'd be more likely to find a bride in London. It was a bloody conundrum.

"I'll see what I can do," Logan said with determination. "I promise we'll get her ladyship back to London as soon as possible. I don't know if the road will be better by tomorrow, but certainly Wednesday, provided the rain stays away."

"I appreciate your support," Bennet said. "Now, I've

distracted you long enough from your work. How can I help?"

~

*A*fter a few hours of grueling work, Bennet went inside with the others. As with yesterday, Mrs. Logan insisted he take his meal in the common room with Prudence. He sank into the chair as yesterday's exhaustion coupled with today's efforts weighed him down.

"You look rather spent," Prudence commented as she poured him some tea.

"I'm all right." He picked up the cup, eager for the warmth of the brew. "Thank you."

"Did you make this bread?" he asked as he picked up a slice from the plate in the middle of the table.

"I did. It's good to know I can probably find work as a housekeeper if I'm unable to be a companion anymore."

He flinched. "Don't say that. Of course you'll be able to be a companion."

"I hope so. I plan to go directly to Lord Lucien's when I get to London. I assume I will no longer be needed as Lady Cassandra's companion. Hopefully he can find something else for me."

"What do you plan to tell him?"

"That I eloped and then changed my mind. It's simple and the only thing that makes sense given the note you wrote."

Bennet exhaled, setting his cup down. "Why you are so friendly to me after that idiocy will forever remain a mystery."

"You made a mistake. Haven't we all done that?"

"A mistake is forgetting to thank your hostess or dropping a glass of champagne in the middle of a ballroom. This was a catastrophe." He cocked his head. "Are you thinking of a particular mistake of your own?" Was that why she'd forgiven him? Had she done something for which she'd wanted to be forgiven?

"No." Had she answered too quickly? "I just think our time in this life is too short to worry over things we can't change. Better to make the best of it and get on."

He couldn't argue with that even if he struggled to do it himself. It was hard to make the best of something that hung over your head like an executioner's axe.

They ate their stew, and Bennet was grateful for her quiet company.

"Are you anxious to get back to your life?" she asked. "This is a far cry from what you enjoy as a gentleman—no parties, no boxing, no whatever else you do to fill your time that isn't this."

"I suppose." He said that because he thought he should. "Actually, I don't miss it. Trying to find a wife and meet my obligations is incredibly vexing. These days in the country—with you—have been a welcome respite."

She fixed her attention on her stew and fell silent for a moment. When she looked back to him, there was a determined fire in her gaze. "You must sleep in the bed tonight. I should have insisted last night. You were exhausted, and you're working much harder than you're used to."

"I am not sharing your bed. You were quite clear on that point," he said wryly.

"I've changed my mind. I won't accept your refusal. I'll roll up one of the blankets from your pallet and put it between us."

A barrier was smart, but he wasn't sure he'd be able to sleep knowing she was within arm's reach. He wanted her, damn his eyes. What if he did something untoward while he was sleeping?

"I can see you're concerned, but I trust you."

"I don't know why." He didn't deserve her kindness or trust. He finished his stew and stood abruptly. "I should get back to the stable."

She got up and moved to him. Then she took his hand, and he felt hot and cold at the same time while his heart thundered in his chest. "Stop berating yourself. You're sleeping in the bed. It will be fine."

She held his gaze, her hand warm around his. He wanted so badly to pull her closer, to kiss her forehead, to stroke her cheek.

But then she did the most astounding thing. She kissed him. Soft and fleeting, her lips brushed over his.

Without thinking, he grasped her waist. He bent his head, intending to kiss her again, his pulse thrumming with excitement, his body trembling with want.

He hesitated, searching her face.

"Yes," she whispered, placing her hand on his chest.

How he wanted her.

"No." He pulled away and turned on his heel, escaping to the kitchen where he'd left his hat. He wouldn't sully her more than he already had.

~

*I*nviting Bennet to share the bed had seemed a good idea—the right thing to do given how hard he'd been working. But now, in the dark of night, with him breathing so close beside her, Prudence doubted the wisdom of her actions.

At least there was the blanket between them.

Was she worried that she'd snuggle against him? Ask him for the kiss he'd denied her earlier? Kiss him again?

No, she wouldn't disturb him. He needed his sleep after

the hard work of the past two days. Never mind the scandal of it.

Scandal, really?

Prudence smiled into the darkness. She'd spent five days at an inn with a man who wasn't her husband. He wasn't even her betrothed. And she'd been masquerading as a lady.

Everything that had happened here would, out of necessity, remain secret. She'd never tell anyone, not Cassandra, not Fiona, not even her closest friend, Ada, where she'd been or what she'd been doing. So what did it matter if she kissed him again?

What if this was the only romantic interlude she'd ever know?

A week ago, she wouldn't even have considered such a thing. Romance was for other people, not her. She'd never thought about love or marriage or even sex. Well, maybe not never.

The last couple of days, however, she kept thinking of what it might be like to kiss Bennet, to have him touch her, to lose herself in something that wasn't planned or necessary. So she'd kissed him that afternoon.

His reaction had been difficult to gauge. There'd been a flash of heat in his eyes, and he'd seemed to want more. But then he'd paused and ultimately left her. What if he thought her a wanton?

A kidnapper wouldn't judge you, her mind argued. Or shouldn't, anyway.

What she knew of Bennet said he wouldn't. She had a hard time reconciling the man she'd come to know the past several days with the scoundrel who'd paid brigands to abduct her.

She ought not forget the scoundrel existed, she reminded herself.

Turning her head, she looked over the blanket roll

between their pillows. He lay with his back to her so that she could only see the blond of his hair. Unlike when she'd gone to check on him, he wore a night shirt. Why was he wearing it now?

As if she didn't know the answer to that. He might have scoundrel tendencies, but he'd kept them well reined in since they'd been stranded here together. Pity that.

Did that mean she had scoundrel tendencies? Prudence clapped her hand over her mouth to keep from giggling.

Rolling to her other side to face the wall instead of her tempting bedmate, she told herself to sleep. Tomorrow could very well be their last day at the inn. The rain had stayed away, and the river had receded, leaving the road to dry out. Now, she just needed a mode of transport.

Likely there would be a mail coach or something she could hire in Hersham. And Mr. Logan would certainly take her that far. Tomorrow, she'd settle the details. She was ready to get back to her life, even though she wasn't entirely sure what she was returning to.

She would likely need a new job, unless Cassandra and Wexford had suffered a falling-out in Croydon. Prudence highly doubted that.

Perhaps it would be best if she sought employment away from London. Then she'd never risk seeing Bennet, and she could settle into a long-term position with someone older. No more young ladies falling in love.

Did she think it was catching? What a preposterous thought.

She felt nothing for Bennet beyond a warm affection due to the time they'd spent together. The day after tomorrow, she'd leave this idyllic time—and the scoundrel beside her— in the past. She'd look forward and leave everything behind, including the truth of her birth, the hope of finding her real mother, and all the nagging emotions that accompanied those things. Clearheaded and unencumbered, she'd embrace the future and whatever it brought.

~

*T*heir forced sojourn was about to come to an end.

After six long days, half of which had seen them nearly flooded away, they could finally leave on the morrow. Provided they had a means of departure. Bennet was waiting for Logan to return with good news.

Unsettled, he went out into the yard, where the dusky sky was overcast. Despite the coming of night, it was still warm, quite different from the storms that had ravaged the area just a couple of days before. The tree had been removed from the stable roof, but the repair to the building would take some time. His wrecked coach still sat beneath it.

Of course he was unsettled. He'd lost his only coach, and he didn't have the funds to replace it. He supposed he could sell his horses since they didn't have a coach to pull. That was a very small benefit. Except he liked those horses. Ah well, it wasn't as if he hadn't parted with many things he would rather have kept.

If he were honest, and he wasn't always, as evidenced by what had brought him here, he'd realize there was more to his agitation than the loss of his coach. Or the fact that he'd nearly ruined poor Prudence's life. He'd become rather fond of her. Fond? He bloody well thought about her almost every waking moment. And many of his sleeping moments if his dreams last night were any indication.

Sharing a bed with her had been a poor idea, but they'd come through it unscathed. How many times had he nearly turned toward her and gone through with the kiss he'd intended yesterday?

He stroked his fingertips across his lips where the imprint

of her lips still blazed. Shock hadn't been his first reaction but delight, anticipation, desire. He'd nearly kissed her in return before his sanity had returned.

Yet another moment where he'd lost his control.

Clenching his jaw, he lowered his hand to his side. The sound of a horse drew him to turn.

Logan rode into the yard and dismounted. "Evening, your lordship," he said.

"Good evening."

"Looks as though you'll be able to leave tomorrow, and not just because of the weather. My neighbor is going to London and can take both you and Lady Prudence." He paused before continuing. "You should know he'll be traveling in a cart. I will understand if you'd rather not travel in such a state."

"It's fine," Bennet assured him before thinking if it really was fine for Prudence. She deserved an enclosed coach where she would be protected from the elements.

Except she wouldn't care about that, and he'd promised her he'd return her to London as soon as possible. This was as soon as possible, and he thought he knew her well enough to know she would jump at the chance.

"It's more than fine," Bennet amended. "It's wonderful. Pru will be thrilled to get back to London. Not that she hasn't enjoyed her time here. We both have."

"Is that possible?" Logan chuckled. "You've worked as hard as anyone, and she might be the best help Mrs. Logan has ever had. You've got yourself quite a woman there, if you don't mind my saying so."

"I don't," Bennet said softly. Prudence *was* an incomparable woman. He meant that he didn't mind Logan saying so, but he realized it could also have meant that he didn't have her. Because that was the truth—Prudence wasn't his. In that moment, the thought of parting from her was almost agony.

She'd become so much a part of his daily routine. He could see them together at Aberforth Place. He'd take on repairs and working in the garden. She'd cook and keep things tidy.

And what about his family? He'd somehow keep their true natures hidden? With marriage necessary, Bennet had realized his viscountess would learn of his family's affliction, but he'd honestly never thought about the specifics, the how and when he would tell her. He supposed he'd hoped to keep it from her as much as possible.

How foolish that sounded now. Did he really think Prudence wouldn't notice everyone's moods? Or the way his great-aunts obsessed over things to the point of making themselves ill. She would immerse herself in his household, as a good viscountess would.

Except she wouldn't be there at all. This betrothal was a farce, even if it had begun to feel quite real.

Bennet pivoted toward the house. "I'd best go in. I suspect Mrs. Logan has dinner about ready."

"I think she made something special since you'll be leaving us tomorrow. Don't tell her I told you." Logan winked at him before leading the horse to the stable.

Returning to the inn, Bennet paused just inside the doorway. Prudence was in the common room, standing next to the table near the hearth. She wore one of the two gowns she'd brought, and though it wasn't the most fashionable, nor was she bedecked in jewels or sporting an intricate hairstyle, she was breathtakingly beautiful. There was an ethereal quality to her, as if she'd stepped from a folktale. It was quite at odds with her strong, no-nonsense nature.

He envisioned her with jewels, an expensive costume, and sophisticated coiffure. She would steal every bit of attention at a ball.

"You're staring at me," she said, narrowing her eyes slightly.

"I'm struck silent by your beauty." He went to take her hand and bowed gallantly as if they were in a ballroom. "I would ask you to waltz if we were at a ball."

"I don't know how."

"It's quite simple, really. I can teach you some time."

"There's no reason for me to learn. And no, you can't. Or have you forgotten that this is the last night we'll spend in each other's company? That is, if we actually have a mode of transportation."

"I have not forgotten," he said quietly. He moved to hold her chair, and she sat down. "I have good news regarding our trip to London. Mr. Logan has secured us passage with his neighbor, who is driving there tomorrow." He sat opposite her and poured wine from the bottle Mrs. Logan had set out.

"'Us'?" Her brow creased. "I thought I was returning to London alone. I told you that I didn't require your presence."

"Don't become agitated. Mr. Logan arranged it, and I didn't think it wise to provoke his curiosity. Besides, it's not the sort of transport I would prefer you take, and I'll feel better riding with you." She opened her mouth, and he held up his hand. "Please don't argue with me. We'll be riding in a cart, not a coach. I hope you don't mind that I agreed on your behalf."

She pursed her lips briefly. "I suppose it's what a future husband should do. To do anything else would, as you said, provoke curiosity. Anyway, a cart is fine, so long as it delivers me within a few miles of Mayfair. I can walk the rest of the way if need be."

"You won't. I'll make sure you're delivered to Lord Lucien's."

"To the Phoenix Club, I think, depending on what time we arrive. It will likely be afternoon, and that's where he is most afternoons."

"Very well. I do hope you'll let me know if I can be of further assistance. For anything. At any time."

She inclined her head. "Thank you. However, I daresay Lucien will be able to help me secure a new position, and then everything will be back to normal."

He envied her certainty, her positivity. Normal wasn't something he recognized anymore, and he wasn't sure he ever would again.

Mrs. Logan brought their dinner, a lovely roast with a variety of vegetables and a rich sauce made from red wine. "There's another trifle for dessert. I know how much you enjoyed it." She looked specifically at Bennet, who'd had three helpings of it the other night.

"You are too wonderful, Mrs. Logan," he said, grinning. "Truly."

"It is my pleasure, especially with all the help you and Lady Prudence have given us since the storm. I hope Mr. Logan told you he doesn't plan on charging you for your stay."

Bennet hated how relieved that made him feel. "That is very kind of him."

Mrs. Logan returned to the kitchen, and Bennet lifted his glass in a toast. "To mistakes made and overcome and friendships forged."

Prudence raised her glass. "And to not having to pay after losing your coach." She must have seen his faint grimace because a flash of alarm darted across her features. "I know you must be relieved, and there's no harm or shame in that," she said softly.

"Thank you." He wanted to take her in his arms and thank her properly. It had been a very long time since he'd revealed the truth to anyone. If he wasn't careful, he would tell her every one of his secrets. Only, if she knew them, she'd run far away.

And he wouldn't blame her. On the contrary, he'd be the first one to tell her to go.

They ate for a few minutes, and it seemed the air between them grew thick, with things unsaid, perhaps. Or undone.

"You aren't a villain," she said, picking up her wineglass. "I hope you know that."

"So you tell me. I behaved rather villainously, however. It's going to take me some time to get over that." He tried to smile, to take the darkness out of his words, but failed.

She sipped her wine before setting the glass back on the table. "I suspect it's going to take me plenty of time to get over this entire escapade. And not because it was terrible." Her gaze locked with his, and the tension between them changed. A primal sensation seemed to arc across the table. His body tightened with yearning.

"I could almost think we were actually eloping," he said, not looking away from her. "This has all felt very...comfortable."

"Natural," she said. "Pleasant."

What was she saying? He shouldn't hope... Hadn't he avoided kissing her yesterday? And hadn't he struggled to keep his hands to himself in bed last night?

"I wonder if we might pretend to be a betrothed couple— for real." Now she looked down at her plate.

"Isn't that what we've been doing?" His throat had gone dry, his words sounding as if he'd swallowed glass. He took a swift drink of wine.

"I didn't mean pretend. We *are* pretending. For tonight, let us be betrothed. Let us be...together." She plucked up her wineglass and took a longer drink, her cheeks flushing.

He told himself the color could be from the wine, but he knew better. He knew what she was saying. Still, he had to be sure. "You want to remove the blanket between us?" That's what he asked? Couldn't he be more specific?

She nodded.

"Pru, I want to be very clear about what you're asking. You want me to take you to bed, to—" Crude and vulgar words sprang to his mind along with a host of visions of the things he would do to her and she to him. But she was innocent. He couldn't take that from her. He'd already taken far too much.

"Yes."

The single word from her lips stoked his desire, weakening his resolve. He gripped the edge of the table. "I can't. Then I really would be a villain."

She frowned. "How do you come to that conclusion? I want you to bed me. Very much."

He groaned, then finished his wine and quickly refilled his glass so he could take another drink. "You're innocent, aren't you?"

"I don't know what that has to do with anything. I have no plans to wed. Ever. I've never considered a romantic entanglement, and it's possible I never will again. I want to spend this night, this last night that we have, with you. As your future wife."

"But you are not my future wife," he whispered, disliking the sound of that for some ridiculous reason.

"We've shown a great aptitude for pretend," she said coyly. "One night. And I've no wish for a child."

He recalled that—no husband, no children. She was perfect, and in that moment, he would have sworn he'd fallen in love with her. "I can manage that," he said. Did that mean he'd agreed? His cock hardened, proof that it seemed he had.

"That's a yes, then?" she asked, her gaze sultry and seductive.

"Yes." Sexual tension spun through him. He gripped the table even harder, then abruptly let it go, willing himself to relax. He couldn't throw her across the table and ravage her. How delightful that would be, though.

Hell, they still had the trifle to get through.

Plenty of time to come to his senses and change his mind. Or for her to do so.

Mrs. Logan came in a few minutes later and removed their dishes.

"Dinner was delicious," Prudence said with a warm smile.

"Mr. Logan is quite enamored of your bread," Mrs. Logan replied. "He's going to miss it. He hopes he can persuade you to make it next time you come through—as Lady Glastonbury." She looked from Prudence to Bennet, her expression one of great pleasure, before turning. "I'll be back with the trifle!"

When she was gone, Prudence pinned him with a probing stare. "What will you tell her when I don't accompany you again?"

Bennet exhaled. "That you came to your senses and realized you could do better?"

"Stop that," she said softly. "You're much too hard on yourself."

"Shouldn't I be?" Bennet picked up his wineglass.

"It's too much. I think you should tell them I prefer to stay at Aberforth Place. Then, when you do have a wife along, you'll have to tell them I died."

Having just taken a sip of wine, Bennet choked on it.

Distress creased her features. "Oh dear, I'm sorry."

He held up his hand as he finished coughing and caught his breath. "I am not going to tell them you died."

"Why not? You suggested I kill my faux betrothed."

"Apparently we are both rather morbidly minded." He gave her a wry smile. "I'll think of something and try not to denigrate myself too badly. Is that acceptable to you?"

"Yes, thank you."

Mrs. Logan brought servings of trifle to the table. "I'll be back soon with more." She gave Bennet a pointed look and winked.

Bennet tucked into his trifle, but he was far less enthusiastic about it tonight than the last time they'd eaten it. Because what he craved most was sitting across from him. A forbidden temptation suddenly his for the taking. He ought to have refused her invitation, but he couldn't regret it. He wouldn't.

"I find I'm ready to retire." He set his utensil down.

She paused in spooning a bite toward her lips. "You aren't having more trifle?"

"I'd rather have something else."

She froze, her gaze locked with his. He watched her pulse tick faster in her throat. "Should we go up, then?" She put her spoon back onto her plate, her bite uneaten.

"If you'd still like to, yes."

"Mrs. Logan will wonder where we've gone before you had another serving."

He shook his head. "She won't."

Prudence started to rise, and he rushed to hold her chair. When she stood, he leaned close, whispering next to her ear, "You're certain?"

She turned her head, bringing her lips in close proximity to his. "Never more."

CHAPTER 7

*T*he walk upstairs seemed both interminably long and frightfully short. One thing was certain, however: Prudence was wholly aware of Bennet's presence behind her, of the primal desire that seemed to be arcing between them like some sort of electricity.

At the top of the stairs, she turned right toward the wing where the two guest rooms were located. Theirs was on the left. Before she could reach for the door, Bennet was there, opening it for her and waiting for her to step inside.

She walked to the center of the chamber she'd shared with him for nearly a week now, seeing it in a way she hadn't before. It seemed smaller, more intimate. Inviting.

The fire had been stoked to a cheery blaze, making the room quite warm. Perhaps too warm. No, Prudence suspected that was entirely due to the anticipation—or anxiety—curling through her. Was she making a mistake?

The door clicked shut, and she turned. Bennet stood with his back pressed against the wood, his blue-green eyes fixed on her with a smoldering intensity. Whatever this was, it wasn't a mistake.

She took a step toward him, and he did the same toward her. Another two steps, and they were in each other's arms.

Prudence didn't know what she was doing, only that she had to kiss him. Now. He seemed to want the same, as he enveloped her in his arms, practically lifting her from the floor.

His mouth slanted over hers, spiking a desperate need within her. She wanted more, but didn't know what to do or what that meant. Frustrated at her lack of experience and knowledge, she clutched at his coat and pressed herself against him, hoping she was at least conveying the most important thing: she wanted him.

He pulled away abruptly and drew a deep breath. "Forgive me," he murmured. "I was desperate to hold you, to kiss you. But I shouldn't rush this. Allow me to kiss you properly." His lips twisted into a lopsided smile that was far more genuine than the practiced grin of the viscount who gadded about Society.

"Well, not *properly*. At least some would say it isn't proper. However, they'd be wrong. A lover's kiss is given not just with our lips, but with our tongues, our hands, our whole selves. It's the initial intimate contact." He brought his hand from her back and held it up between them. "Perhaps the mere touching of hands is the initial intimate contact."

Prudence put her hand against his, palm to palm. He laced his fingers with hers, and they clasped one another. Then he pressed his lips to her knuckles. "Yes, this," he murmured, looking into her eyes. "A kiss here and perhaps a kiss there." He turned their hands and kissed her forearm.

A shiver danced along her flesh. "Tell me about the other kissing—with tongues." A longing unfurled inside her. She wanted to know everything. And she wanted him to show her.

He released her hand and cupped her face, his gaze holding hers. "Just follow me."

Prudence let her eyes flutter closed as his lips touched hers. He moved slowly and softly at first. She grasped his coat, holding him tightly, as if he'd leave her. Because everyone left. Sooner or later.

His tongue licked along her lip, and she opened her mouth, somewhat instinctively. Somehow, she knew she should touch her tongue with his. But it was so much more than that. He swept inside, captivating her with lush sensation.

He moved his hand to the back of her head, cradling her, making her feel like the most important person in the world. Or at least in his world.

The feel of him against her and the wicked delight of his kiss teased a host of new anticipation. She knew she wanted him, but this sensation was more visceral. Her body reacted to his with a fervent and immediate need. Stretching her arms up, she encircled them about his neck, holding him as surely as he held her.

He intermittently broke the kiss only to renew it with a delicious intent. With each brush of his lips and lick of his tongue, she felt rewarded for this brazen decision she'd made. She had absolutely no regrets.

Not even when he started to shrug out of his coat. In fact, she helped him, pushing the garment from his shoulders. He let it fall to the floor, and she considered whether she ought to pick it up.

"Leave it," he whispered, seeming to read her mind. "The floor will soon be littered with our cast-off clothing. It will make us smile later." A smile teased his lips now, and his eyes —so bright with desire—flashed with humor.

She was amazed at his ability to find lightness in almost any situation. Perhaps she'd ask him about that sometime.

As if they had more than just tonight.

"Should I undress, then?" she asked tentatively.

"May I do it?"

She couldn't help the blush that rose in her face. "If you want to."

"I do. Very much."

"Should I undress you too?" She felt woefully naïve, but knew she couldn't pretend her way through this.

"If you'd like. I don't want you to do anything you don't wish to. At any moment, you must feel free to stop me or what's happening."

She nodded. "I'm not going to change my mind, if that's what you mean."

"I believe that. However, if you're ever uncomfortable, I hope you'll tell me. I want you to."

"Is ravishment uncomfortable?"

He laughed softly. "It's not supposed to be. There can be discomfort or pain during the first time for a woman. I'll do my best to minimize that, but I don't think it's entirely up to me."

"What can I do?"

"Just relax and enjoy yourself? I think. I'm not a woman, so I can't say. I will promise to ensure you enjoy yourself—to the very best of my ability."

"I enjoyed your kisses." She narrowed her eyes slightly, wishing they'd just get back to that. As much as she appreciated his telling her what to expect, she was eager to get on with things.

"I'm pleased to hear that." He ducked his head and kissed her again. "I fear I won't be able to get enough of you, Pru."

Hearing him call her that between kisses only intensified her desire. She stood on her toes and pressed into him as he stroked his hand down her neck, trailing his fingers to the hollow of her throat.

"My dress comes down in the front," she said.

"How fortunately easy." He kissed her jaw, then moved down her neck, awakening a whole new range of sensations.

She thrust her fingers into his hair, shocked by her boldness. But she wanted him and this, and she meant to take full advantage.

Deftly, he released the clasps holding her dress up. The front of her bodice fell to her waist, and she felt a moment's alarm. Only a moment, because his lips moved toward her breast, thoroughly distracting her.

"Hmmm, why are we standing here? Because I was too eager." He swept her into his arms and carried her to the bed.

"Wait," she said. "My boots." He sat her on the bed, then bent to remove them from her feet.

"Such dainty ankles. But then you are entirely dainty. If I didn't know your personality, I would say you could have been a fairy from the forest."

"What about my personality indicates I can't?"

"I don't know. I suppose I think of a fairy being delicate and sweet. Not that you aren't sweet. I would describe you as forthright and strong."

"I would argue that a fairy can be whatever she wants."

He slid his hands up her calf, his fingertips caressing her through the cotton of her stockings. "That is a very fine argument. I would agree that *you*, my lovely fairy, can definitely be whatever you want."

He found the top of her stocking and untied the ribbon before pulling it from her leg. She nearly moaned with the need for him to put his hands back on her. Thankfully, he only transferred them to the other leg, performing the same arousing ministrations he had on the first one.

Prudence slid from the bed as he stood before her.

"Where are you going?" he asked.

"Taking the dress off." She untied it, loosening the fabric around her middle and pushed it to the floor.

He bent and slid it toward the post at the foot of the bed. "I'll just move it aside. Don't want to step on it."

"How considerate of you." She looked at all the clothes he was wearing compared to her standing before him in her underthings. Reaching for the buttons of his waistcoat, she hesitated.

"You can unfasten this. In fact, you can do whatever you like to me."

She wished she knew what that could be.

"Just follow your instincts," he said, again seeming to be inside her head.

"Are you somehow able to see my thoughts?"

He laughed. "You are typically rather difficult to read, but now, in this, you are not. I'm rather enjoying it, to be honest."

She didn't like that she was so transparent, but it was helpful in this situation. Furthermore, she didn't want to hide from him—or from herself—tonight. "I shall have to work on maintaining an aura of mystery." She unbuttoned his waistcoat.

Bennet slipped the garment off and, as with his coat, let it slide to the floor.

Next, Prudence pulled at his simply knotted cravat. "Thank goodness this isn't some elaborate knot, although it's still rather elegant."

"Thank you. I work hard to achieve just that—simple elegance. I'm afraid my lack of a valet doesn't allow for much else."

"Which is why I nearly always wear gowns that fasten in the front. My lack of a maid doesn't permit anything more complicated. Honestly, I would hate to have to wait for assistance to dress or undress." She slid the silk from his neck.

His eyes briefly closed. "It's astonishing how something so simple can feel so deliriously naughty."

Prudence thought she knew what he meant. When he'd unfastened her gown, something had happened to her—a frisson of awareness that danced across her flesh, that had teased her breasts into a state of arousal. She'd never experienced such a thing. Would he touch them? She longed for him to do so, but wasn't sure she possessed enough courage to ask.

Of course she did. She was a bold fairy, wasn't she?

He continued, "I confess that having someone dress you, particularly for an important event that requires complexity and an excess of style, is rather intoxicating."

"I'll have to take your word for it since it's an extravagance I shall never experience."

"Never say never." He leaned down to kiss her, his hands settling on her shoulders before his fingers slid beneath the straps of her petticoat.

Yes, this undressing business was incredibly enticing. He gently pushed the straps from her shoulders, then worked the garment down her hips as she wriggled to help him.

He groaned, surprising her.

"What's wrong?" she asked.

"Nothing at all. Promise me you'll move just like that shortly." His hands moved to her backside, bringing her flush against him.

Though her chemise and his clothing remained between them, she could feel his shaft pressing into her and was again shocked at her body's response. A wonderful expectation, almost a pressure, throbbed in her sex. She moved her hips again as she'd done when he'd removed her petticoat. A delightful friction sparked where their bodies met. Prudence wanted more.

Bennet groaned again just before he kissed her—differently this time. Instead of cajoling with gentle, eager strokes, he claimed her mouth, his kiss commanding her response. She was most happy to give it. Indeed, she reveled in the wild abandon of this kiss, of the way his fingers dug into her backside, of the press of his sex against hers.

He tugged the laces of her corset free, loosening the front. As with the petticoat, he took it from her body, but with more urgent, rougher strokes.

Still kissing her, he cupped her breasts, pushing them up slightly before he flicked his thumbs across her nipples through the thin lawn of her chemise. The craving she'd felt in that part of her sharpened, making her breasts feel heavy and desperate, which made no sense if she thought about it. So she didn't. She arched into him, eager for his touch, for some kind of relief from this wicked torture.

As if he sensed what she wanted as well as he knew her thoughts, Bennet tugged her chemise over her head and tossed it away, exposing her completely to him. The chill in the spring night air pebbled her skin, making her even more eager to have him close.

"You are incomparably lovely." He lifted her onto the bed and guided her to lie back on the coverlet, her head on the pillow. He stood beside her and simply stared at her body.

What should have embarrassed her only heightened her desire. She wanted to scream for him to touch her. And why shouldn't she?

"Ben, aren't you going to touch me again?"

"In so many ways." He cupped her jaw and kissed her, his lips and tongue stroking hers until she was breathless once more. He moved down her neck, his hand ahead of his mouth. His fingertips closed around her left nipple.

She moaned, her back rising off the bed. She closed her eyes and basked in his attention. There was wetness. Her eyes flew open to see his mouth on her where his fingers had been. He licked across her skin before closing his lips over her and sucking—softly at first, then with more urgency. He caressed one breast while using his mouth on the other, driving her mad with want.

Prudence could not have imagined the pleasure his lips and fingers could bring. She twisted and clutched at him, desperate for more. Each time he flicked her nipples with his tongue or squeezed with his thumb and finger, a flash of ecstasy shot straight to her sex. She wanted him against her there, more of that friction.

Suddenly, his hand was there, between her legs, his fingers stroking her most intimate flesh. His mouth pulled on her breast, sending a torrent of desire to her sex just as he pressed against a most sensitive spot near the apex.

"What is that?" she demanded, her voice climbing along with whatever was building inside her.

"This is your clitoris, my love. Do you like when I touch it?"

"Yes. Very much. Don't stop. Please." She clutched at his head as he blew across her breasts.

"Spread your legs for me," he urged, increasing the pressure he used on her, provoking her to move her hips against his hand. "I know you want to come. Soon."

"What does that mean?"

He drew his teeth across her nipple, drawing a cry from her—not because it hurt but because she wasn't sure how much more she could stand. Her body had begun to quiver.

"What do you feel?" he asked, his fingers sliding through her folds.

Eyes closed, Prudence tried to describe the sensations careening through her. "It's wonderful and frustrating at the same time. I want…something. I don't know. Just don't stop. I feel as though you're pushing me close to whatever it is."

"I hope so." He suckled her breast before pinching the

nipple between his thumb and forefinger, tugging hard enough that she gasped as delicious longing arced through her.

"Don't stop. Please." She just kept repeating those words over and over, mindless to anything except the sensations he was arousing within her.

His finger stroked inside her, giving her a sense of what was to come, of what she didn't know she wanted. Of course —him inside her. Then she would be complete. Then she would...come.

"Pru, I'm going to put my mouth on your sex. I'm afraid I can't resist."

She opened her eyes and lifted her head from the pillow to see his head between her legs. "Ben, you can't." Oh, but she was so glad he did. He sucked that spot—her clitoris—and stroked her sex, his finger sliding in and out.

He was suddenly between her legs on the bed, spreading her thighs and using his mouth in the most sinful way. The tremors in her body multiplied, and she clutched at his head as he drove her inexorably toward that *thing* she sought. Her body seemed to convulse, her muscles tightening as a rapture swept over her. She cried out as everything seemed to explode around her. There was brightness and electricity followed by a swallowing darkness awash with ecstasy.

She'd no idea how much time passed before she came back to herself. Vaguely, she realized Bennet was no longer on the bed. She opened her eyes to see him tossing his clothes off.

"Under the covers," he instructed, tugging at the bedclothes beneath her.

Prudence managed to coax her jellylike limbs to move. He slid into the bed and pulled her into his arms.

"That was hardly fair," she said, pouting. "I barely got to see you naked. You looked your fill of me."

"I beg your pardon." He spoke solemnly, but there was a twinkle in his eyes. Peeling the covers back, he lay back on the mattress. "Better?"

"Mmm," was all she would commit to as she feasted on the full expanse of his chest. It was just as magnificent as the bit she'd seen several nights ago. She sat up to get a better view, then frowned at the sight of a few pale bruises on his torso. Gently, she brushed her fingertips over one on his left side. "What's this?"

"From the fight last week."

Of course. "Does it hurt?"

"Not anymore."

"But it did."

He shrugged against the mattress. "I suppose. I admit I don't sustain a great deal of injury fighting."

She arched a brow at him. "Because you're that good?"

He smirked. "Yes, actually. But not last week." His features sobered. "That was a bad fight. I was angry." He shook his head and sat up, caressing her face and threading his fingers into her hair. "I don't want to talk about that just now. If you don't mind."

She didn't mind at all, not when her body was still recovering from what he'd done. "What just happened? Is that…normal?"

He grinned. "Yes. It's called an orgasm."

"Did I come?"

"If you had an orgasm, you came. You had a release. Those are just some examples of what to call it. You can call it whatever you like."

"Absolute bliss. But shouldn't you have that too?"

"I would like to."

"Does that mean I should put my mouth on you?" She glanced down, where the bedclothes still covered him below the waist. However, she could see the clear evidence of his desire—his shaft stood stiff and tall, making a tent of the coverlet.

He grunted, clasping her to him and kissing her thoroughly. "As much as I would love to feel your mouth around my cock, not tonight. What I just did is one of many things people can do to give and receive pleasure."

"That gave you pleasure?"

"Oh yes. I wanted you before, but after tasting you, after bringing you to release…" His eyes closed briefly, his golden lashes sweeping his cheeks as his lips spread into a lazy, seductive smile. His lids rose, revealing his gleaming blue-green gaze. "Now, I want to possess you completely. My body in yours, your body wrapped around mine."

She shivered. "I want that too. You said it would hurt?"

"It might. I'll be honest—I have no experience with virgins."

"But you have plenty of experience. Or so it seems."

Color tinged his cheeks, surprising her. "Plenty is a subjective word, but I am not a novice. I will go as slowly and gently as possible. You tell me when to move and when to stop."

Nodding, she lay back down and pulled him along with her. He laughed softly. "I will treasure you—and this night—for the rest of my days."

He kissed her, and she was rather shocked to find the same need kindling inside her. Only now she knew what was coming, what would set her free. His mouth found her breast again, and she arched up. "Ben," she murmured, cradling his head against her as he settled between her legs.

He stroked her sex, teasing her clitoris. Then his…cock—she liked that word, she decided—was there. She bent her legs to better angle herself against him. Oh, yes, this was better. Lifting her hips from the mattress, she pressed into him.

"Pru," he groaned, kissing her once more as he ground his hips over hers.

It wasn't enough. She wanted more of him. She wanted him inside her. "Please, Ben. Now."

She felt his hand around his cock.

"Ready?" he asked.

"Yes." She arched up, seeking his entry.

He slid into her slowly, his thumb on her clitoris in insistent, swirling strokes. Pleasure flowed through her only to be abruptly quashed by discomfort. She sucked in a breath and held it.

He paused, freezing above her. "Do you want me to stop?"

She shook her head. "It won't feel like this for long, will it?"

"I don't know."

Hearing the distress in his voice, she pulled his head down and kissed him. "Keep going," she whispered. "I want you. I want this."

He pushed forward, and she stretched. He straightened over her and used his fingers on her clitoris, reminding her of the pleasure that had been there just a moment ago. Her body began to tingle anew with anticipation. Seeming to understand this, as if he knew her body so well already, he lowered his head to her breast and suckled her. With lips and teeth and tongue, he sent her barreling into the frenzied state where she lost pieces of herself only to find others she didn't know she had.

His hips twitched against hers, and she wrapped her legs around him.

"Yes, Pru. I need to move. May I move?"

She thought she understood. "Show me."

Again, he went slowly, but she sensed it was difficult. His body shook, and his muscles were taut as she ran her hands down his shoulders and back. "You can go faster," she said.

"I wasn't sure I dared. Does it hurt?"

"Not really. It's better than it was. When you come back inside, it feels good."

His hips snapped as he drove into her. "Like that?"

Deep inside, there was a flash of pleasure. She tightened her legs around him. "Yes, just like that."

He began to move faster, his body thrusting into hers at a steady pace. The discomfort faded entirely until she doubted she'd even felt it at all. There was just rapture and anticipation, her body clamoring for that sweet release.

His hand worked between them, drawing her closer to the finish. "Come again for me, Pru. Please."

"You come," she demanded, sensing it might not be so easy for her this time. "I already did."

He laughed, and she pulled his head down to kiss him, her fingers digging into his nape. She dug her feet into his backside, and he moaned.

Then he let loose a torrent of nonsensical words before he cried out her name and drove deep into her. Apparently, she could come again, because the world broke apart once more, not quite as spectacularly as the first time, but just as wonderfully. Sharing it with him, being joined with him… she would remember this night always—just as he'd said.

But he was suddenly gone from her. She opened her eyes to see he'd pivoted away. On his knees, he held his cock as liquid spurted from the tip. She watched, entranced. "What are you doing?"

He didn't answer for a long moment. "Finishing," he rasped. Then it was another long moment before he climbed from the bed and went to the washbasin, where he found a cloth and cleaned himself off. He rinsed the cloth and returned to the bed to tidy her.

"Is this part of the act?" She found it hard to believe that most men would be so caring.

"Probably not." He gave her a half smile as he finished and returned the cloth to the basin. "To fully answer your question, I finished outside your body to prevent a child."

"Oh!" She hadn't considered that, but then she'd been woefully unprepared for any of this. Because she'd never expected it. She resolved to read everything she could about the subject when she returned to London. Fiona had a book, if she remembered correctly.

Prudence yawned and brought her hand to her mouth. "Pardon me."

He smiled at her. "Let's sleep." Sliding back into the bed, he gathered her in his arms.

She tucked her head beneath his chin, feeling safer and more content than perhaps ever before. "I don't know what I expected, but it wasn't that."

"I hope that's a good thing." He pressed his lips to her forehead.

"It was wonderful." She tipped her head back and looked up into his eyes. "Thank you."

"It was entirely my pleasure." He kissed her, his mouth lingering against hers.

For the first time in Prudence's memory, she fell asleep smiling.

CHAPTER 8

*W*hen Bennet opened his eyes the next morning, he had two immediate thoughts. First, the woman with whom he was entwined was a singular gift. He'd always counted himself unlucky—there were usually bad surprises, rarely good. But this time, he'd found true good fortune, however fleeting.

Second, the sun was shining quite brilliantly, indicating it was indeed time for them to say goodbye.

She stirred in his arms, nuzzling his chest, then pressing her lips to his neck. That surprised him. She'd been wonderfully curious in her innocence, but not necessarily bold. At least not as bold as she was in other aspects.

"Do we have to get up?" she murmured against his skin, tickling him in the most marvelous way.

"Yes. Though I daresay we can delay it a bit." He rolled to his back, and she pushed herself up to look down at him. Her blond hair fell in waves, caressing her face and his chest.

"And what shall we do with that delay?" She moved her leg over his, bringing her mound flush with his thigh. Her hips moved gently against him.

There was her boldness. Not that he'd doubted its existence.

His cock, already hard, lengthened against her thigh. "You must be sore from last night. We really shouldn't."

"We'll never have the chance again," she said, her voice a low rasp.

Why did she have to remind him? As if they had any sort of future. He needed an heiress. And she didn't even want to wed—he couldn't very well ask her to conduct an endless liaison with him. The truth was he didn't want to wed either. He *had* to in order to keep his family safe and secure. If not for them, he'd let the estate crumble to the ground and the title die with him. He didn't want to subject anyone to his family—more specifically, their affliction—least of all her.

"Pru, you are the most amazing woman I've ever met. I should refuse, just as I should have last night, but I am utterly at your command." He cupped her nape and pulled her down for a kiss.

She kissed him with blood-heating skill, and he bemoaned the fact that they hadn't done this at the start. How they could have spent the last six days…and nights.

Grinding her pelvis against him with slow, enticing movements, she trailed her lips along his jaw and down his neck, demonstrating how much she'd learned. Her hand caressed his shoulder and then his chest, her fingers exploring his flesh.

Bennet closed his eyes and surrendered to her touch. Her hand moved lower over his abdomen, stroking his hip and then grazing his cock.

"Prudence," he croaked as lust streaked through him.

"Mmm?" She kissed his chest and closed her hand around his shaft.

He moaned, his hips arching.

"You like that?" she asked.

"Move your hand—from the base to the tip." He gritted his teeth as she did what he said. The urge to ask her to go faster, to bring him to release was overwhelming. Instead, he flipped her to her back and positioned himself between her legs.

She did not let go of him. In fact, her grip was a bit tight, and he loved it.

Bennet lowered his head to her breast, taking her nipple between his teeth before suckling her. She was so responsive, so unabashedly demonstrative that it took his breath away. He stroked between her legs and found her wet.

"Guide me into you," he said, thumbing her clitoris.

Her breathing sped as her body began to quiver beneath him. She bent her legs and put his cock to her sheath. Unable to resist, Bennet wrapped his hand around hers, and together, they positioned him to slide inside.

He thrust into her, moving his hand to her hip and then her backside.

She gasped, and he paused. "All right?" he asked, thinking she had to be too tender.

"Wonderful," she said on an exhale, her body tightening around him as she wrapped her legs about his hips. "Just move. Please."

"Happily." He kissed her as he withdrew and thrust again, starting a slow but steady pace.

She moved with him, her body rising from the bed while her legs squeezed him. She dug her fingers into his back. "Faster."

He readily complied, his hips snapping as he drove into her, mindless until he remembered that he needed to pull out of her. Not that he would have forgotten. He hadn't in years.

Straightening, he watched her face as she moved toward climax. Eyes closed, lips parted, she was the most beautiful thing he'd ever seen. What he wouldn't have given for a portrait of her looking just like this. No, eyes open with that enigmatic spark she possessed, lips curled in a near smile. He saw her a hundred different ways in his mind's eye and clung to every one of them.

He stroked her clitoris, bringing her swiftly to orgasm. Her muscles clenched around him, and she cried out, her neck extending as she cast her head back.

Just a few more thrusts, and his orgasm came crashing down. He withdrew rather inelegantly, his seed spurting as he fought to turn to the side.

"My apologies," he said. "It's rather untidy."

"But effective and necessary." She touched his thigh. "I appreciate it."

He smiled faintly. "Of course." It was as much for him as for her. Neither of them wanted a child.

Bennet left the bed and went to clean up and dress. Reluctantly. This really was the end of an idyllic time.

"It's hard to believe how this started," she said. "Compared to now."

He glanced toward her. She'd also left the bed and was pulling on her stockings. He swallowed, his fingers itching with the desire to stroke her calves once more.

Wearing a shirt and breeches, he went to stoke the fire. She continued with her toilet, braiding and pinning her hair up.

When he sat to don his boots, she came to stand nearby. "I want to give you something."

He looked up at her. "You've given me far too much."

A blush rose in her cheeks, and she looked toward the fire. She cleared her throat and blinked before returning her attention to him.

He finished with his boots and stood. "You look rather serious now."

"You're going to refuse this, but I want you to have it." She held out her hand. A gold ring sat in her palm.

"What's this?" He picked it up gingerly. It bore a crest—a fox and a dagger with a laurel.

"Just a ring that belonged to my mother."

"It looks like a family crest." Not one he recognized, however.

She shrugged. "It isn't ours—we don't have one. It didn't mean anything to her, nor does it to me. It's the only thing of value she left behind, but I won't ever wear it."

"Why didn't you sell it?" Bennet turned it over, acknowledging that it was very finely made. It also seemed rather old.

"You can sell it." She'd gone back to avoiding his questions. He tamped down his disappointment. "I think it would benefit you far more than me. You're in need of a coach, in case you've forgotten."

He laughed softly. "How could I?" The ring wouldn't pay for a coach, but it would fetch a decent sum, and Bennet could use any amount of funds that came his way. Still, he doubted he could bring himself to part with it, not even for money. "You should keep this."

She blew out an exasperated breath. "Would you please stop telling me what I should and shouldn't do? I've been managing myself and my decisions for twenty-four years."

He grinned. "That's how old you are."

"You may also stop interrupting me. As I was saying, I don't need your instruction or advice. Please take the ring. I don't want it and you need it."

Seeing her agitation, he softened his expression and his tone. "All right. I'll take it. But I'll pay you back someday. I promise."

She smiled then and touched his face. "Let's not make promises we can't keep. I want you to have the ring. Truly.

Now, I suppose we must break our fast so we may be on our way."

"Yes, I suppose it is that time." His feet felt rooted to the floor. "I'm tempted to kidnap you a second time. Only this time, it would be wholly on purpose."

Lights danced in her eyes, and he prayed he'd have occasion to see them again some time.

He held out his arm, and they left the room.

An hour later, he stood in the yard watching as the neighbor's cart left. Prudence sat beside the man wrapped in her— rather Lady Cassandra's—purple cloak.

Bennet had decided not to leave with her. She should arrive in London without him. If even one person saw them together, all their planning would be for naught. Furthermore, Logan had found a coach nearby that could be had for a reasonable price. Perhaps not too much more than the ring in Bennet's pocket.

He pulled it out. The gold glinted in the morning sunlight. He slipped it onto his left pinky where it fit perfectly, as if that was where it belonged.

She looked back over her shoulder, and he lifted his hand in farewell.

∼

While riding in a cart made for a rather sore posterior, Prudence was glad to be back in London. The equipage looked odd in Mayfair, so she made haste with her departure, thanking Mr. Logan's neighbor before toting her bag down the stairs to the employees' entrance of the Phoenix Club. She couldn't very well march into one of the front doors since she wasn't a member. She'd entered this way on many occasions—to meet with Lucien when he'd first offered to help her and to see her dearest friend, Ada Treadway, who managed the club's accounting ledgers.

It was far more than that, really. Ada made sure there was ale, brandy, and port on the men's side of the club and madeira, sherry, and sack on the ladies'. That was just a fraction of what she oversaw along with Evangeline Renshaw, one of the ladies' patronesses who also served as manager of the club.

Going directly to the back stairs, Prudence climbed to the second floor, where Ada's office was located. At this time of day, early afternoon, Ada would almost certainly be at her desk perusing ledgers and drinking tea.

The door was slightly ajar, but Prudence knocked nonetheless.

"Come." Ada didn't look up, her dark head bent over her desk.

"I suppose it's too much to hope I wasn't missed." Prudence stepped inside, set her case down, and closed the door.

Ada's head jerked up, her blue-gray eyes widening in shock. "Pru! Where on earth have you been?" She leapt from the chair and threw her arms around Prudence, squeezing her tightly.

Prudence smiled and hugged her back. "It's quite a tale. Did you miss me?"

"Of course I did." Ada pulled back, her brows pitching into a V as she scowled. "What an absurd question."

"That was ungenerous of me. I knew you would miss me. However, Cassandra would not have."

"It seems not." Ada crossed her arms over her chest. "*Because you left a note that you eloped.*"

"You learned that much? Good." Prudence went to sit in a chair, grateful for its cushion on her backside.

"Evie found out from Lucien." Ada returned to her chair, turning it to face Prudence before she sat.

It made sense that Cassandra's brother would know what happened and that he would share that information with his Evie, his closest friend and partner at the club.

"Well, it wasn't true." Prudence didn't hesitate to tell the truth to Ada—and only to Ada. She was the one person she could wholly trust. They came from similar backgrounds and had suffered similar…setbacks that had forced them to change employment and find a new way forward.

Ada sniffed. "I knew it. I didn't say so, of course. Evie didn't believe it either, but she also kept her mouth shut."

Prudence tried not to smile and failed. "And what did the two of you surmise actually happened?"

"That you knew you were soon to be out of a job since Lady Cassandra is now married—"

"Is she?" Prudence interrupted. "I'm quite happy for her, of course, but I'm sorry I missed it."

"They wed by special license on Saturday."

Prudence grimaced. "You were probably quite upset with me on Saturday." They met every Saturday morning to share breakfast and visit. Sometimes they took a walk. Occasionally, they shopped. Most often, they sat in Ada's small, smart apartment of rooms on the uppermost floor of the club just above them. Even though Prudence would have been at Cassandra's wedding, she would have sent word to Ada to that effect. Instead, Ada hadn't heard a word from her.

"Yes, but also worried. The Prudence I know would never elope with anyone. So you must have had a good reason to lie."

Prudence had thought about what she would say to Ada almost the entire way from Riverview. She'd planned to keep everything from her, to protect Bennet as she'd told him she would do. But now that she faced her closest ally, saw the certainty in Ada's eyes that Prudence *had* lied about eloping, her careful plan disintegrated. And it wasn't as if Ada would tell anyone. She'd hold Prudence's secrets as close as Prudence would herself. "I didn't write the note."

Ada slumped in the chair, her shoulders sagging. "I should have realized. I should have insisted they send Bow Street to find you."

"I'm glad you didn't. There was no harm done, even if the original scheme was very poorly planned and would have ruined Cassandra."

Ada straightened, her curiosity clearly piqued. "I do hope you're going to tell me everything."

Not *everything*. There were some things Prudence wouldn't reveal even to Ada, no matter the fact that Ada would guard them. "You mustn't tell anyone. If you promise, I'll continue."

"Of course I promise!" Ada looked as if she were going to leap across the space between them and shake the words from Prudence's mouth. "I am beside myself with urgency."

Prudence let out a short laugh. "I can see that. The Viscount Glastonbury was quite disappointed upon learning Cassandra was not going to accept his proposal of marriage. He hatched a ridiculous stratagem to take her from Croydon after the boxing match for the purpose of elopement. He felt certain she would be amenable."

Ada stared at her. "He didn't really."

"Which part?"

"All of it! Do you mean he took you instead?"

"His hirelings did. Cassandra and I had swapped cloaks so that she could get away with Wexford. I'm afraid the kidnappers thought I was her. They didn't ask my identity when they snatched me from my bed and trussed me up before tossing me into Glastonbury's coach."

With each revelation, Ada's eyes widened more until

Prudence feared she wouldn't be able to close them again. At last, she blinked. "Where have you been all this time?" she asked in a hushed tone, her face creased with worry.

"I've been fine, truly. I was at an inn near Hersham with Glastonbury. We were stranded because of the weather, and then a tree fell on his coach." Prudence put her hand to her mouth to hide her smile, not that the destruction of his coach was funny. She just couldn't help but think of their time together fondly—even the rough parts. "He has quite terrible luck."

Ada exhaled. "Let me make sure I understand. The viscount had you *kidnapped*, then you were trapped with him for nigh on a week. And you don't want anyone to know?" She sounded incredulous.

"That's right."

"He should be in prison!" Ada's lips pressed into a firm line, her jaw clenched with irritation.

"As I said, there was no harm done. I only wanted to be sure my reputation would be intact, that I'd be able to secure employment. Surely you would agree that if I publicize his activities, it would effectively ruin me in the process."

Grimacing, Ada nodded. "You are, unfortunately, correct. I daresay securing employment won't be a problem. I'm sure Lucien would help you, in any case. Especially if you told him the truth."

"Absolutely not," Prudence said. "You must keep this completely secret—you can't tell a soul, not even Evie."

"I understand. Anyway, the only person I'd want to tell is you." A smile skipped across her mouth.

"Good." Prudence felt a good sense of relief, both at having unburdened herself to her closest friend and securing her silence on the matter. "My reputation and employment aside, I do not wish to cause Glastonbury to suffer any more than he already has."

Ada frowned. "What does that mean?"

"He hasn't two shillings to rub together, and if all of London doesn't know already, they soon will. He faces total ruination."

"Ah yes, I had heard that, actually. From Evie."

Prudence wasn't surprised, but she still felt bad for Bennet. The state of his finances wasn't his fault. He was doing his best to manage in the overwhelming destruction of his father's mistakes. "It isn't just him," she said quietly. "He has a number of relatives who rely on him. His father squandered everything."

Ada's brow furrowed in deep contemplation. "I can see you care about him, and that there's more you aren't saying. But I shan't press you. Not today, anyway. I'm just so bloody happy to see you."

Prudence smiled. "I'm just as glad to see you. Now, I must go visit Lucien, for I am in desperate need of employment. I presume he's in his office?" He was typically there—on the men's side of the club—at this time of day.

"Yes, I'll walk over with you."

Prudence stood. "I was going to tell you one other thing. I've decided to stop looking for my mother."

Ada had risen and now slapped a surprised stare on Prudence. "What happened to you during this abduction?"

"It was far less an abduction than it was a...sojourn." Prudence picked up her case. "I had time to think and came to the conclusion that it was better for me to look forward instead of back." Because to do that meant she would also see Bennet, remember him, miss him. She had to focus on the future, now more than ever.

"This is a shift," Ada murmured. "But I understand. It wasn't as if we'd had much luck in finding her anyway. You couldn't exactly swagger around Mayfair flashing that ring or disclosing the identify of your true father."

"No, I could not." To do so would have thoroughly ruined Prudence and any chance she had at living a comfortable life in her current position.

They walked together to the men's side, and Ada left her to knock on Lucien's door alone. First, they hugged again and promised to return to their ritual this coming Saturday.

Prudence rapped on the door and immediately heard Lucien's response. Taking a deep breath, she walked into his office and set her case down just inside the door.

He blinked at her. "Prudence?"

"Yes, and before you ask, there is no husband. I behaved quite foolishly and am only glad I came to my senses. I would have returned sooner, but the weather kept me from traveling."

Lucien jumped up from his chair. Tall and lithe, he came toward her, his long strides delivering him before her in a trice. "Are you all right?"

"Completely. I am concerned, however, as to whether I am still employable." Her shoulder twitched. "I've already seen Ada, and she said your sister married Lord Wexford."

"She did. Our father even approved of the match. I daresay that's what caused that horrible storm." His dark eyes glinted with amusement. "The heavens simply couldn't countenance such a change in the duke's opinion."

Prudence laughed. Lucien and his father shared a rather tumultuous relationship. The Duke of Evesham was incredibly fond of his eldest child, the Earl of Aldington, and possessed a soft spot for his youngest, Cassandra. His middle child, however, seemed to confound him, though Prudence couldn't understand why. Lucien was brave, having fought in Spain, successful with the Phoenix Club, and above all, kind and generous.

"As it happens, there is a perfect position for you. But we

should move quickly since everyone assumed you would no longer be working as a companion."

Because she'd eloped. Bennet really had caused her a great deal of trouble. He'd also given her wonderful memories she'd cherish her entire life. It seemed a fair trade.

"I will most definitely be working as a companion. What is this position?"

"Companion to Cassandra's new sister-in-law, Miss Kathleen Shaughnessy. It won't be what you're used to—fewer balls and the like—but it's with people you already know and who know you."

People who wouldn't be bothered by her disappearing for six days. This was more than she could have hoped for. "Do I need to rush right over there?"

"Not rush, no. I probably didn't need to say we should act quickly. I only meant that if you were interested in the position, you should let them know as soon as possible because I am certain they'd hire you."

"Thank you." She gave him a warm smile. "You've saved me yet again."

He snorted. "I have no doubt you could have found your own position with references from Lady Overton and my sister. But you have to agree this is simpler."

"Indeed." Besides, she was particularly happy to work with people she knew. She'd been lucky enough to move from Fiona to Cassandra, whom she'd come to know while she'd been companion to Fiona. She'd met Miss Shaughnessy, and Lucien was right that this would be different. Wexford's younger half sister had no interest in marriage or participating in the Season. "I take it Mrs. Shaughnessy agreed to let her daughter remain in London with Lord Wexford?"

"Wex talked her into it, apparently. Mrs. Shaughnessy and the other sister are returning to Gloucestershire, if they haven't left already. Shall I drive you to George Street to see Cass and Wex?"

"I don't wish to impose since they are so newly married."

"They've already been imposed upon—his mother and sisters have been there the entire time. I do think Wex and Cass plan to take a trip to Bath or something. I know Cass will be thrilled to see you. She was rather perplexed by your abrupt elopement." He cocked his head. "We all were, but then I've always found you to be enigmatic. If anyone were to have a secret lover, it would likely be you."

Prudence nearly choked. "He wasn't my lover. Just a mistake." Was that how she thought of Bennet? Of course not. Abducting her had been a mistake, but something good had come from it.

Lucien gave her a sympathetic nod. "I'm glad to hear you were able to avoid it and emerge unscathed, but then you're one of the most resilient people I've ever met."

"And enigmatic," she said with a faint smile.

"Yes!" He laughed. "I'm still not sure what brought you to the Viscount Warfield's house in search of employment, but I am glad I happened to be there the very same day."

"As am I." If not for that chance meeting, Prudence would not be where she was today. "I'm ready to leave whenever you are."

He moved to pick up her case, then paused, pinning her with a serious stare. "I hope you know that I will always help you, no matter the issue. And you know I'll keep it between us. If there's anything you need with regard to this…elopement, I hope you'll ask."

She expected nothing less from him. "I will, thank you. It's more than enough that you're looking out for my welfare. Truly. If only everyone knew what a kind heart you possess."

Laughing, he swept up her case. "What would happen to my roguish reputation?"

"I think you can be kind *and* a rogue." She would categorize Bennet in such a way. Perhaps he was more scoundrel than rogue. Whatever he was, she'd do best to cast him from her mind. She needed to move forward.

Straightening her spine, she walked from Lucien's office, her gaze keenly on the future.

CHAPTER 9

Three weeks later...

$\mathcal{B}$ennet hesitated on the corner of Ryder and Bury Streets outside the Phoenix Club in St. James's. He'd just returned to London yesterday after spending the past fortnight or so at Aberforth Place. The timing of his arrival there had been rather fortuitous as Great-Aunt Flora had been suffering one of her dark episodes. She hadn't left her rooms in over a week. Bennet's presence had roused her from the doldrums, and by the time he'd left, she was cheerful once more.

Logan had helped him secure an older, economical coach near Hersham. He'd stopped to pay for it on his return to town—another painting sold to cover the cost.

Tonight, he'd reenter Society, or at least the edge of it. He had no illusions about his standing or how far he'd fallen. The dearth of invitations compared to before he'd left told him everything.

He wouldn't hide, however. He couldn't, not when he needed an heiress to solve his considerable problems. That was not his mission tonight, though. He only wanted to know how Prudence had fared, and Lucien ought to be able to tell him.

This was the first time Bennet had come to the club on a Tuesday, the night they opened the men's side to the ladies. He had to admit the idea of a private club that allowed ladies and gentlemen to mingle more than intrigued him. He wished Prudence was a member.

Upon entering, a footman greeted him and took his hat and gloves. Bennet had been here once before—for an assembly, which they held every Friday night during the Season. He'd come to court Lady Cassandra. Would she be here tonight? He felt a moment's unease. The last time he'd seen her and her new husband, he'd been in a terrible state of mind.

Heading for the stairs, which would take him to the members' den on the first floor, he studied the huge painting depicting a bacchanalia with Pan. It fit the space perfectly, as if it had been painted exactly for that place on the wall in this establishment. He was surprised that he'd somehow missed it on his first visit.

Luck, as usual, was not on his side, for he ran into Lady Cassandra, rather Lady Wexford now, and Wexford when he reached the top of the stairs. He summoned a brilliant smile and greeted them warmly.

"Good evening, Lord Wexford, Lady Wexford." He bowed. "May I offer my most sincere and heartfelt congratulations on your marriage."

Both regarded him dubiously. Wexford, a tall, dark-haired Irishman, managed to say, "Thank you."

Bennet gestured for them to step aside with him, out of the way of the stairs. He spoke in a low tone. "Please accept my deepest apology for my behavior at the boxing match. I was in a very bad way, and I behaved reprehensibly."

"You seemed quite desperate," Wexford said, pity flashing briefly in his gaze.

A tight knot formed in Bennet's chest, but he worked to ignore it. "I was indeed. But in hindsight, I'm very glad things worked out as they did." He looked to Lady Wexford who, with her sherry-colored eyes and dark hair, was quite beautiful. Bennet also found her courageous, forthright, and more charming than was probably fair. "I hope you and Wexford will be very happy. Truly," he added softly.

"I appreciate that. We are quite giddy, to be honest." She flashed her husband a conspiratorial smile, the kind that spouses in love shared. Not that Bennet had seen a great many of those. Perhaps that was why it stood out. "And really, you and I were merely doing what we thought we should," she said to Bennet.

"Just so."

She frowned slightly, her brow puckering. "Though I suppose it was different for you. You were courting me for a specific purpose."

"For money, you mean," he said frankly. He chuckled at the faint grimace that passed across her features. "It's quite all right. I should have been forthcoming about my situation. I extend my humblest apologies for not being honest with you about that." He recalled Prudence admonishing him. What he wouldn't give for her to take him to task again.

Lady Wexford tipped her head slightly. "To be fair, I was looking for any gentleman who had the nerve to court me despite my father's obnoxiousness. You were the only one brave enough."

"Because I had to be." He laughed again. "It's astonishing what one will risk when one is faced with financial ruin."

"It's really as bad as that?" Wexford asked.

Bennet had thought about how much to disclose when confronted with specific questions, which was bound to happen when he returned to town. He decided there was no reason to prevaricate. Better to just be open about his state—and hope fate might reward him. "I'm afraid so. My father gambled away or sold nearly everything. I've the estate to maintain as well as a pile of relatives." Bennet waved his hand. "But never mind that. I'm sure things will come out right." Or not. He had to admit he felt rather helpless at this point. Perhaps he was now trying to find a way to accept that this was how things would be.

"Have a drink with us," Wexford invited, surprising Bennet. "We were just going to the library."

"I haven't been there," Bennet said, eager to continue their conversation in the hope that he'd find out about Prudence.

They walked toward the front of the club, where apparently the library was located.

Bennet attempted to broach the subject of Prudence. "Lady Wexford, it's a bit strange to see you without your intrepid companion. Miss Lancaster, wasn't it?"

Lady Wexford glanced toward him with a glint of admiration. "You've a good memory, Lord Glastonbury. She's not here tonight, but she still resides with me—with us, rather. She's companion to Ruark's sister now."

Bloody brilliant. Bennet barely kept from grinning. He wanted to shout with gratitude. At least someone had good fortune.

"That's wonderfully convenient," Bennet said.

"For everyone," Wexford agreed as they entered the library. There weren't many places to sit, and Bennet wondered if the club was always this crowded or if this was due to it being Tuesday night with both gentleman and ladies crammed into the men's side. The men weren't ever invited to the ladies' half of the club—only into their side of the ball-room on Friday nights.

The assembly! Would Prudence be there with her new charge on Friday? Bennet hoped so. Now he had something wonderful to look forward to. Just to see her across the room would be enough.

"Irish whiskey?" Wexford asked him.

"That's available?"

"There's also the inferior Scottish variety if you're an imbecile." Wexford twisted his mouth in disgust.

Lady Wexford laughed. "Forgive Ruark. He's awfully snobbish when it comes to whiskey." She lowered her voice and leaned toward Bennet. "He does spend a great deal of time defending his homeland's whiskey."

"Because the lot of them have no taste," Wexford grumbled.

"I'd love some Irish whiskey, thank you," Bennet said.

"Always knew I liked you. Even when you beat me at the boxing club." Wexford grinned before taking himself off, presumably to pour drinks.

Lady Wexford led him to stand near one of the front windows. "Did you just arrive back in town? Your absence was noted."

"Last night, yes. I imagine I've attained quite a bit of noto-riety over the past few weeks."

"Thanks in large part to my father." She gave him sympa-thetic look. "I'm sorry about that."

"It's not your fault. I confess I'm surprised at how welcoming you and Wexford are being."

"What would be the point of holding a grudge for how you behaved at the fight? As you said, everything worked out as it should. Well, except for your reputation taking a fall."

He lifted a shoulder. What else could he do? Wail and complain about the injustice of his father's stupidity? No, not stupidity. That was not what had plagued him. What plagued nearly his entire family. "I do appreciate your generosity," Bennet said as Wexford returned with whiskey for him and a glass of wine for his wife. Then he went back for his own drink.

"Glastonbury?"

Lord Lucien Westbrook strode toward them, his eyes slightly narrowed. He arrived just as Wexford did.

"Sorry, Lu, didn't see you or I would have brought you a drink," Wexford said.

"I have a brandy in my office I'm going to fetch." Lord Lucien looked to Bennet. "Why don't you join me, Glastonbury?"

There was an icy expectation in the man's dark gaze that didn't seem as though he would accept refusal.

"Just allow me to make a toast to the newlyweds." Bennet lifted his glass. "May you live together in happiness and love for all the rest of your days, and on into eternity."

Lady Westbrook's face bloomed into a charmed expression. "That was lovely. Thank you, Glastonbury." She tapped her glass to his and then her husband's before taking a drink.

Bennet sipped his whiskey, appreciating the smooth, bold flavor. He glanced toward Wexford. "Why do you try to persuade anyone to drink this?" Wexford's features immediately darkened, and he looked as if he wanted to challenge Bennet to a third bout, which Bennet supposed would settle things once and for all since they'd each won one. Before Wexford could say anything, Bennet added. "Because I would hoard it for myself."

Wexford relaxed and grinned. "You make an excellent point. I'll stop that immediately."

"It's too late for me, I'm afraid," Bennet said. "This is what I plan on drinking whenever I visit."

Clapping him on the shoulder, Wexford chuckled. "Then we shall share many a toast."

"Shall we?" Lord Lucien prompted.

Bennet inclined his head to the Wexfords, then left the library with Lord Lucien. They walked past the stairs, and Lucien led him to a closed door. Opening it, he gestured for Bennet to precede him.

The office wasn't large, but it was imposing, with a large desk and a wall of bookshelves. The fireplace was encased in marble, and a fantastic Reynolds was displayed on the wall above the mantel. A pair of dark green chairs sat before the hearth.

"Shall we sit for a moment?" Lord Lucien asked.

A moment seemed to indicate he intended them to have a short conversation. "Certainly." Bennet sat in one of the chairs and Lucien took the other.

"You didn't come here for brandy," Bennet said, noting that his host had closed the door behind them when they'd come inside.

"No. I wanted to talk to you about your membership. I wonder if you might not be comfortable here after all."

Bennet's mind worked through that rather quickly. "You want me to resign?"

"It might be best."

Anger pricked at Bennet, but he tamped it down. "You were quite eager to have me join."

Lord Lucien rested his elbows on the arms of the chair and steepled his fingers. "Yes, and I wonder if we weren't premature."

"I believe you were desperate to have me attend an assembly so I could court your sister," Bennet said blandly, again trying to keep a rein on his ire.

"That's true. To be frank, we worked very hard to get you approved because Cassandra asked me to."

"And now you regret it." He tried not to sound irritated, but it was very difficult. "I thought the Phoenix Club welcomed those who were often excluded elsewhere." That certainly fit Bennet.

Lord Lucien frowned, deep furrows lining his brow. "We do."

"I won't resign," Bennet said. "Will you expel me?"

"We haven't ever expelled anyone." Lord Lucien grimaced before adding, "Not permanently."

"I'd like to stay. As it happens, I find I'm rather unpopular at the moment since the news of my financial situation became known."

Again, Lord Lucien grimaced. "That's somewhat my fault. I'm the one who told my father, and he decided to share it with all of White's."

"I suppose I should expect expulsion from there too."

Lord Lucien shook his head. "I'm not expelling you."

Bennet finally relaxed. "Thank you."

"Though I do wonder how you can afford the membership fees."

Thankfully, they were less than other clubs, but Lord Lucien made a good point. Perhaps Bennet should resign from everything, even if it did cast him deeper into the pit of public disdain.

"You're right," Lord Lucien continued. "We do invite those who aren't always welcome everywhere else. It's just that, and let me be perfectly honest, we don't know you very well. It's rather embarrassing to me that we extended you an invitation without realizing your financial state."

"If I decide I can afford the fee, does it matter?" Perhaps Bennet *didn't* want to be a member.

Lord Lucien's eyes hardened. "It does when you misrepresent yourself and try to trick my sister into marriage."

"This is a purely personal issue, then." Bennet understood.

He didn't have siblings, but he would do anything to protect his family. "I have apologized to Lady Wexford. My behavior was quite poor."

"You weren't the first to do that to a young lady, and you won't be the last. It's just that she is my sister."

"I understand. If I had a sister, I believe I would be equally outraged. Would you really like me to leave the club?" Bennet hoped not. The ability to perhaps see Prudence wasn't the only reason he wanted to stay. With his invitations all but dried up, he needed somewhere to go to meet potential brides.

"No, stay. But don't withhold information."

Bennet would never agree to that. There were things he wouldn't reveal to anyone. "I shall do my best." That was all he could say.

Lord Lucien stood and went to the sideboard to pour a drink. Bennet sipped his whiskey, liking it even more now than when he'd first sampled it.

"I am sorry for your troubles," Lord Lucien said, retaking his seat. "Can I ask what you're doing to resolve your situation?"

Bennet let out a hollow laugh. "That's all but impossible. My father gambled away everything. Well, nearly everything. If you came to Aberforth Place, you would find a mostly empty estate." Dozens of rooms were completely unfurnished. Others had a chair or perhaps a table. "I'm doing my best to keep things together, but the fact is that the estate hasn't earned enough to support the way my father lived for years. He dug himself a rather deep hole, and I'm struggling to repay his debts." There. He'd laid it all out. "I haven't expressed the situation quite so plainly to anyone before. May I ask you keep it to yourself?" His lips tried to form a weak smile and failed, so he sipped his whiskey instead.

"Most certainly. Would it help to learn of investment

opportunities, something that might help you make some blunt in the short term?"

"Yes, but I've precious little to invest." He'd have to sell something else, and his resources were dwindling. Prudence's ring was heavy around his finger, but he wouldn't sell it. It gave him solace, as if she were close and sharing her quiet strength. "That's why I need to marry an heiress. Then I will have money to invest as well as the ability to repay my father's debts. Furthermore, the estate needs attention so that it may become profitable."

"It isn't now?" Lucien asked.

"Not for some time." Aberforth Place didn't even have a steward. The last one had left more than two years ago when Bennet's father had stopped paying his salary.

Lord Lucien looked into the fire, his expression contemplative.

"Dare I hope you're considering ways to help me?" Bennet asked. "I understand that's what you do."

"It is." He tipped his head back and forth. "To the best of my ability." He looked back to Bennet. "You really want an heiress?"

"I *need* one." In truth, he didn't want a wife at all.

Lord Lucien nodded. "Let me think on it. I hope you'll continue to let down your guard with me. If I help you, we will be friends. And if we're friends, we trust each other. Do you agree?"

"I do."

"Good. You must call me Lucien. Come to the assembly Friday. I will introduce you to as many heiresses as I can."

Bennet finished his whisky. "I appreciate that very much, thank you. And I look forward to it."

Not because of the heiresses, but in the hope that Prudence would be there.

~

*T*onight was only the second time Prudence had been out in Society since returning to London. Being Kat's companion was far different from when she'd been companion to Fiona and Cassandra. They had participated in the Season. Kat preferred to spend time at museums, walking in the park, or reading.

"I'm not staying past midnight," Kat grumbled from beside Prudence on the rear-facing seat of the coach.

"Oh come, you'll have fun," Cassandra said. "You've been to an assembly at the Phoenix Club before. You must admit it's far more entertaining than any other events."

"I suppose that's true. But I'm still leaving at midnight."

"That's fine," Wexford said placidly, rarely ruffled by his sister's quirks. "I only thought it would be nice for you to get out. And I don't mean to the park or to wander around Covent Garden."

Kat shrugged. "I like to see the city. Can you blame me?"

Wexford exhaled, then smiled at his sister. "No."

Not bothering to hide her smug expression, Kat leaned her head back against the seat. She was dressed simply, but elegantly, her dark hair sporting a single scarlet feather that she'd insisted upon wearing despite Cassandra arguing that it didn't suit her pale pink gown. Kat had responded with "What do I care? It's not as if I'm trying to attract a suitor."

Perhaps not, but she was very pretty and the sister of a wealthy earl. She could probably wear a sack over her head and still attract suitors.

The idea of a sack over her head reminded Prudence of when that had actually happened to her. Instead of feeling a shock of anger or relief at having escaped that situation, she was filled with the desire to do it all over again. Which was asinine. Just because things had turned out well didn't mean she should have wanted it to happen.

Wexford's coach stopped in front of the Phoenix Club. A groom opened the door and a few minutes later, Prudence followed them into the ladies' entrance.

Cassandra hung back a bit and moved next to Prudence. "Are you all right? I know this is an odd time to ask, but I can't help myself."

"Of course, I am." Prudence allowed a bemused smile. "Why can't you help yourself?"

"Because I care about you very much. You've been different since your return. I know you don't wish to speak of your time away, but I'd like to be of help. I consider you my friend."

"I appreciate that—and you," Prudence said. "I am fine, truly. It's an adjustment going from your companion to Kat's."

Cassandra laughed. "Yes, that is definitely true. You're happy, I hope?"

"Quite. I like her a great deal. We discuss books, which I find most diverting."

"I've noticed. Honestly, you seem to talk more to her than you ever did to me. Fiona agrees." Fiona, Lady Overton, had been to visit on several occasions. "Perhaps that's what's different. You're less reserved than before."

"I doubt that's true." Prudence certainly didn't reveal any more of herself to Kat than she had to Fiona or Cassandra. It really was that they discussed books. Prudence liked to read and had more time for it now. They didn't discuss anything personal. At all.

"If you've found a confidante and ally in Kat, I'm glad for you," Cassandra said, and Prudence wondered if she was jealous.

"It's not that," Prudence said softly. "I'm still the same me

—nothing happened while I was away, and I don't like Kat any more than I like you. Or Fiona."

Cassandra grinned. "Am I that transparent? How awful of me."

"Not at all."

"Forgive me. I didn't mean to poke or prod. I know you're a private person, but I truly am your friend and would like to support you as such—as family, really. If that's all right with you."

Prudence was taken aback. She'd never thought to have family again. Before she could respond, her eye caught Ada's just outside the ballroom.

Cassandra saw the direction of Prudence's gaze and pivoted as Ada moved toward them. "Miss Treadway! Do you know my sister-in-law, Miss Shaughnessy?" Introductions were conducted before they entered the ballroom together.

"I'm so glad to see you here tonight," Ada whispered to Prudence. "These are far less dull when you're present."

"We're only staying until midnight. That's all Kat would agree to." Prudence had told her friend all about Kathleen Shaughnessy when they met on Saturday mornings.

"Good evening, Lady Wexford, Lord Wexford."

That voice... Prudence pivoted from Ada and nearly pitched forward.

Standing before her, resplendent in a suit of black superfine, stood the man she'd tried so hard to forget. And failed spectacularly.

"Miss Lancaster, isn't it?" Bennet asked with a bit of a sly edge. At least it seemed that way to Prudence.

"Yes." She curtsied. "It's a pleasure to see you again, my lord."

His lip curled just slightly, and she knew he didn't like hearing her call him that. Not when she'd cried out his name as she writhed beneath him.

Don't think about that!

She prayed her cheeks weren't aflame.

"The pleasure is entirely mine." His gaze held hers, and Prudence feared she might melt into the floor.

"Glastonbury, I can't recall if you've been introduced to my sister, Miss Shaughnessy," Wexford said.

"We met at the park, Ruark," Kat said with a hint of exasperation. "Good evening, Lord Glastonbury."

Bennet gave her a courtly bow, provoking a searing jealousy in Prudence. Then he took her hand, and Prudence actually considered jerking the younger woman's arm away from him.

What on earth was wrong with her?

"I hope you'll save me a dance later, Miss Shaughnessy."

Again, Prudence wanted to demonstrate her irritation, but she only gritted her teeth. Bennet and Kat shared the same position in Society. He would bow to her, take her hand, dance with her. Hell, he could even marry her.

A horrible feeling pitched Prudence's stomach to the floor. Kat might not be the wealthiest young lady in the ballroom that night, but she was in possession of a good-sized dowry. And she was here avoiding a scandal in Gloucestershire in which she'd been seen kissing someone else's betrothed. She'd explained that it was for the sake of science and research, but Society wouldn't care. They'd stamp her as ruined goods. For that reason, Mrs. Shaughnessy had ushered her to London with haste and sought to marry her off as quickly as possible. But Kat had resisted. In the end, Mrs. Shaughnessy had agreed to let her stay with her brother in the hope that the scandal would die down back home— and hopefully never find its way to London. She would make a perfect wife for Bennet.

"I will," Kat said to Bennet without much enthusiasm. She didn't care for dancing.

"There's Fiona," Cassandra said. The group broke up as she headed for her friend.

Bennet moved quickly to Prudence's side. "I need to see you. Where can we meet?"

"The top floor. Two hours." Prudence gave the instructions without thinking. Her heart beat like a downpour.

She turned to find Ada, who was still close by. Hurrying to her, Prudence said, "I need to borrow your room in two hours. Please don't ask why."

Ada's dark brows arched so high they practically disappeared into her hairline. "I won't. Tonight anyway. Tomorrow, I shall ask all the questions and then some."

"Fair enough."

Prudence had no idea what she would tell her. It was one thing to have told her about Bennet kidnapping her and quite another to reveal the depth of their...connection. But she wouldn't think about that now.

Now she would suffer through the most interminable two hours of her life.

CHAPTER 10

*B*ennet paced on the uppermost floor of the Phoenix Club, his body thrumming with anticipation. He'd come up the back stairs, which he supposed was the only way to reach this floor and wondered if he and Prudence were just going to meet in the dimly lit corridor. Presumably, the rooms belonged to people, and they couldn't just barge in.

To do what? Drink tea? Play backgammon? Have sex?

Desire pulsed within him. No, he only wanted to see her, to make sure all was well, that he hadn't thoroughly cocked up her life.

The door from the stairs finally opened. He stopped abruptly and held his breath.

Prudence stepped into the corridor, closing the door behind her. Garbed in an understated but stunning light-blue gown, she looked so very different from when they'd been together at Riverview. Her hair was styled smartly, with a pearl comb nestled in the blonde curls. She looked like the ethereal fairy going to a ball. And he supposed she was.

"Bennet."

The sound of his name on her lips was a balm he didn't know he needed. In two steps, he swept her against him and kissed her.

She twined her arms around his neck and stood on her toes, pressing into him. Her animated and thorough response thrilled him to his very bones. Her tongue slid along his as her hands tugged at his hair.

Groaning, he tore his mouth from hers and kissed along her jaw to her ear, using his teeth to tug her earlobe before licking the flesh.

She gasped, her fingers digging into his scalp. Then she pulled away to grasp his hand.

Bennet shook his head with bewilderment as she led him to one of the doors along the corridor. Opening it, she drew him inside to a small sitting room.

"Should we be in here?" he asked softly.

She closed the door. "It's my friend's room. It's fine." She put her hands on his face and kissed him again, taking complete control and driving him mad with want.

Lost in her embrace, Bennet clutched at her waist. It was as if he hadn't been breathing the past three and a half weeks. And now, he was alive like never before.

Moving her hands to his shoulders, she pulled him back through a doorway into a small bedroom. He ought to stop her, to stop himself. Instead, he deepened their kiss and guided her to the bed.

He did pause then. The bed was low, and her gown would crease beyond acceptability. He pivoted them and pushed her to the wall. Grasping the hem, he tugged the gown up and pinned it between them where their bodies were pressed together.

"What about the bed?" she asked as he kissed her neck, desperate in his need to taste her.

"I don't want to ruin your gown." He looked into her desire-clouded eyes. "Trust me."

She clasped his head and kissed him, her teeth catching his lip as she pulled back. He wasn't sure if she'd meant to do that, but then she smiled. A seductive, cock-hardening smirk that left no doubt as to her intent.

Then she surprised him further when her hand massaged the front of his fall, her hand moving along the ridge of his cock. Even more shockingly, she flicked the buttons open and slipped her hand inside his clothing, her fingers finding his rigid flesh.

"Pru," he moaned, his eyes briefly fluttering shut as he gave himself over to the wonder of her touch.

She skimmed her hand up and down along his length, working him into a frenzy of need. His hips moved, practically of their own volition, seeking more and more of her. Her thumb grazed the tip, smoothing the moisture there over his skin. He groaned, desperate to be inside her.

He claimed her mouth once more, driving his tongue into her as he longed to do with his cock. Gathering what little remained of his sanity, he put his hand on her sex and stroked her folds, finding her wet and ready. She whimpered into his mouth, and it was the most erotic thing he'd ever heard.

He circled his thumb over her clitoris, then speared his finger into her. She cast her head back, breaking their kiss to cry out his name.

He grasped her hip. "Lift your leg and wrap it around my waist."

She did as he said, curling her leg about him with his assistance.

"And the other," he managed to rasp through gritted teeth. He helped her once more. "Now put me inside you."

She positioned him so he felt her heat. Thrusting upward, he buried himself deep. She clutched his shoulders.

Kissing her again, he didn't go slow this time. He couldn't. There was a wildness within him he'd never experienced, a primal need to claim her. To completely possess her.

And to be possessed *by* her.

One of her hands tangled in the back of his hair, pulling hard on him as her legs squeezed around him. He thought he might die from the pleasure of it all.

He let go, driving into her with a relentless pace that brought her quickly to release. Her muscles spasmed, her body tightening against him as her orgasm slammed into her.

His came roaring behind. Christ, he had to pull out. He would have given anything not to.

Somehow, he removed himself—just in time—and managed to set her on the floor before taking himself in his hand and making a terrible mess. A moment later, she gave him a handkerchief, then he bent to clean the floor.

"My apologies," he murmured, feeling like an ass, but not regretting a single moment.

She pulled her glove onto her right hand. Bennet hadn't even realized she'd removed it, but her hand had definitely been bare when she'd touched his cock. God, he thought he could easily go again.

"I should apologize," she said, smoothing her hair, which still looked flawless. "I dragged you in here."

He finished buttoning his fall, then swiftly kissed her, his hand cupping her nape. "Don't ever apologize for this, for wanting me, or anything else."

"Anything else?"

"To do with sex," he clarified, smiling. He took in her slightly amused expression, the familiar tilt of her chin, the lush sweep of her kiss-reddened lips. "I missed you."

"I missed you too," she said softly, her gaze darting away,

as if she were embarrassed to admit it. Or that it made her vulnerable—he understood that. She'd seen him at his absolute worst and somehow managed to like him. Perhaps that was why he was so drawn to her and couldn't stop thinking about her.

She looked back to him. "That was a poor idea, however. We can't repeat it."

"I suppose not. In our defense, I don't think we really thought it through."

She cocked her head. "Then why did you ask to see me?"

He blinked. "You thought... You thought I wanted to have sex?"

"You're right. I didn't think it through. I saw you, and I actually stopped thinking."

A giddiness swirled in his chest. "I confess to feeling rather the same," he murmured, taking her hand and stroking her wrist with his thumb. "I wanted to see you so we could talk privately without drawing attention. I just had to see that you were all right, that I hadn't ruined anything for you." While she seemed fine, he held his breath.

"I'm more than all right. I was fortunate to be hired as Wexford's sister's companion. Speaking of Wexford, you seem on good terms with him now."

"I apologized to him and Lady Wexford the other night— for hiding the reasons behind my interest in her and for my behavior at the boxing match. The night I fell into villainy." He grimaced and let go of her hand.

"Thankfully, it was a brief plunge," she said with a wry smile. "Where have you been these past weeks?"

Had she been looking for him? Or at least paying attention to whether he was in town? "Did you know I wasn't in London?"

"You've been a popular topic of gossip," she said sheepishly.

He laughed. "That was to be expected. I stayed in Hersham another couple of days because Logan managed to find me a coach I could afford. Then I went to Aberforth Place to lick my wounds." He winked at her, then immediately sobered. "Not really. I needed to check on some things —and sell a painting to pay for the coach," he confessed wryly, wondering why he felt so comfortable sharing the depths of his financial woes with her.

Because she cared. She listened to him, comforted him, and gave him hope—something he realized he'd been rather short on.

"I'm glad you have a coach, but sorry you had to sell a painting." She looked at him with such sympathy. He would never understand how she'd been able to forgive him.

And he was grateful it wasn't pity, for there was a difference. Lucien's expression had been tinged with the latter. As had Wexford's and Lady Wexford's.

He leaned toward her and whispered, "It wasn't an attractive piece."

"Ah, well, that's a relief." She paused, seeming hesitant. "I suppose we should return to the assembly. I shouldn't be gone too long. Kat is dancing, but the set is likely almost done."

"Yes, of course." He gestured for her to precede him from the bedchamber.

They left her friend's room, and she closed the door firmly behind them.

"What friend of yours has an apartment at the Phoenix Club?" Bennet asked.

"She's the bookkeeper."

He didn't ask more since she didn't seem keen to offer it. After so many days together, he'd learned to read her quite well.

"I'll let you go downstairs alone," he said, stopping in the corridor.

She nodded. "Thank you. I'm so glad to see you well. You'll recover from this."

He only hoped it would happen in time to save his family from ruin. If he couldn't pay for Aunt Agatha's care at the hospital—

He refused to even think it.

"Good night, Ben." She kissed his cheek, then disappeared through the door to the stairs.

Bennet leaned back against the wall, his shoulders drooping. He ought to feel wonderful after their tryst—and he did —but he also felt unsettled. And sad, because he knew he couldn't see her again. Not like that.

Probably not at all.

❧

*A*s Prudence climbed the back stairs at the Phoenix Club the following morning, her mind filled with thoughts of Bennet, specifically with the memory of last night. She'd caught a few glimpses of him at the assembly afterward before leaving at midnight with Kat. He'd been dancing. And he was so elegant on his feet.

It was almost painful to watch him smile at his dance partners knowing he'd been kissing her—been inside her— just a short while before. But she had no time or space for jealousy. He wasn't hers nor would he ever be.

Shaking him from her thoughts, she rapped on Ada's door.

Ada responded with "Come in!"

Prudence stepped over the threshold. "Good morning."

Ada sat near the window that overlooked Ryder Street below. She folded the newspaper she'd been reading and set it on the small table. "How did Kat enjoy the assembly? I saw that she danced with at least three gentlemen."

Prudence perched on the other chair. "She didn't complain overly much."

"I imagine it will be sometime before she—and you—return for another one, however."

"You are right about that, I think," Prudence said. She realized she was a bit on edge. Because she expected Ada to ask about last night.

Ada didn't disappoint her. "Why did you need my room? You were gone nearly an entire set."

"Were you keeping track?" Prudence asked.

"I was paying attention. You know I always do."

That was certainly true. Ada saw more that happened than anyone realized. Prudence was much the same. One learned a great many valuable things by simply watching.

"I just needed a bit of time to myself." It was a weak answer, and Prudence doubted Ada would accept it.

Ada's eyes narrowed, indicating she wasn't going to settle for that response. "What's going on with Glastonbury? Did you meet him up here?"

Hell. Prudence tried not to reveal her sudden agitation. Her heart was thrumming wildly, and a tremor ran through her. "Why would you ask that?"

"Because you two shared a look and I would swear he whispered something to you. Then you asked if you could borrow my room." Ada pressed her lips together and arched her brows.

For the first time, Prudence found her friend's awareness annoying. Which wasn't fair. Prudence was the one keeping secrets. It was in her nature to do so, she argued to herself. Even if she didn't typically keep things from Ada.

This was different. And not just because she wasn't supposed to have told Ada anything. There was more to this than a tale of two people who'd spent a remarkable period of time together. What was it? The connection they shared. Prudence suddenly realized she had *feelings* about it, and she didn't bloody want to. If she discussed it with Ada, she'd likely see it too. And Prudence definitely didn't want to discuss *that*.

"Can you trust me when I say there is nothing between us?" Prudence would make sure there wasn't. "And can you promise not to press me about this topic?"

"Which topic, Glastonbury or what you were doing in my room?"

Prudence narrowed her eyes in silent response. They were the same topic, of course.

Ada smiled faintly. "I won't press you. Anyway, I have news to share. Lucien has asked me to spend a fortnight with the Viscount Warfield to tidy his ledgers."

The discomfort Prudence had felt magnified. She gaped at Ada, for she was the only person who knew the truth about Warfield, that he was Prudence's half brother, that Prudence had gone to him hoping that their shared paternity meant he would at least give her a job. "Lucien can't ask you to do that."

"Of course he can. Warfield is his friend." They'd been in Spain together.

"I doubt Warfield is capable of friendship," Prudence grumbled. Her half brother was as rude and horrible as a person could be. That Lucien still stood by the man given his demeanor made no sense to Prudence, even if they had fought together in the war.

"I knew this would bother you, which is why I wanted to tell you. I don't have to befriend him, and I won't," Ada said with fierce loyalty. "I'll just fix his books and be on my way."

"I'm sorry you have to suffer being in his presence. He won't like that you're there. He doesn't like anything." The viscount had been quite clear about that when Prudence had gone to ask for a job. She could only imagine what he would have said if she'd told him they were half siblings.

But she hadn't gotten that far. He'd been so disagreeable, so unbelievably cold and unfeeling, that she hadn't told him anything. She'd been flabbergasted and had completely lost her nerve. On her way out, she'd met Lucien, and that had changed her life. She supposed she owed the circumstance of encountering him to the fact that she'd gone to see her half brother in the first place, but she gave Warfield no credit whatsoever. That they were blood related almost made her angry.

"I confess I'm eager to go," Ada said. "Not just because I love to fix things. Perhaps there's a way I can avenge you."

"You can't avenge me," Prudence said. "He doesn't know who I am. He likely doesn't even know that he has a half sister. He certainly won't remember the poor young woman who came looking for a job." She'd hoped to tell him about their kinship, that doing so would make him want to help her. How naïve she'd been.

"Perhaps he does know," Ada suggested quietly.

"I highly doubt that."

"But you don't know it for certain. Perhaps the reason for his misery is *because* he can't find his half sister."

Prudence made a sound that was part laugh and part cough. "Sometimes your optimism is misplaced."

Ada shrugged. "I suppose I shall find out for myself."

"When are you going?" Prudence didn't want to care but found she did.

"I'm not certain. Not immediately, however. I'll let you know as soon as it's set."

"Just so long as you know that he's as scarred inside as he is out—Lucien will tell you that if he hasn't already."

Prudence stood. "Shall we go down to the kitchen for breakfast?"

"Yes." Ada joined her, and they left her apartment.

As she descended the stairs, Prudence tried to focus on the future, on moving forward as she'd planned to do. If only the past didn't keep trying to pull her back.

CHAPTER 11

$\mathcal{B}$ennet walked into the Phoenix Club on Saturday evening, eager to find Lucien. Last night, he'd introduced Bennet to two ladies, one with a considerable dowry and the other a widow with a substantial fortune. The former was the daughter of a baron with ancient holdings and a lineage that was oft entwined with members of the Royal Family. And the latter also brought two children into the bargain, which Bennet saw as beneficial—then he wouldn't feel any guilt at not giving her any of his.

When Bennet had heard the pedigree of the baron's daughter, he'd wondered why he ought to even try. She could certainly snare someone who wasn't currently the subject of ridicule about town.

But then he'd met her and understood. She was homely and quiet, almost frightened of her own shadow. Dancing with her had been like dancing with a newborn foal who hadn't yet learned to balance. Except Bennet suspected the horse would have stepped on his feet less.

He felt rather uncharitable in his thoughts of her, but he compared every single woman he met now to Prudence. And the baron's daughter couldn't hold a candle to his former faux betrothed.

The second woman was the widow of a banker. She now ran the bank, an astonishing feat in itself, and had seemed quite eager to meet Bennet. During their dance, she'd made it clear that her interest had only to do with his title. He ought to have had no quarrel with that, but she seemed a severe woman. There were lines at the corners of her mouth that suggested she frowned more than she smiled.

There had to be other options.

And so here he was to speak with Lucien. Perhaps there was a way Bennet could avoid marriage altogether. If he could only cobble together enough money to make a sound investment, he might be able to keep everyone safe.

After handing his hat and gloves over to the footman, Bennet climbed the stairs to the members' den. He ran into Lucien's older brother, Constantine, the Earl of Aldington.

Aldington was another person Bennet would have described as severe; however, he'd seemed to lighten up of late. Bennet could have sworn he'd seen the man smiling at Westminster a few times.

"Evening, Glastonbury," the earl said with a nod. "I'm just on my way out. Say, I was speaking with one of the men who works at your boxing club. He asked if you were here this evening. He's over in the corner." Aldington inclined his head across the large L-shaped room to one of the two corners Bennet could see.

It was Mortimer Dodd, thank goodness, not the man's older cousin, Fred, who owned the boxing club and who likely planned to toss Bennet out if he hadn't already.

"I'll go and say good evening," Bennet said with a smile. He bid good night to the earl and crossed the room to where Mort sat at a small round table. The man's grizzled features were rather implacable—Bennet wasn't sure if the man was pleased to see him or not.

"Evening, Mort. I understand you were asking about me."

"I was." Mort's voice was deep and rough, a perfect complement to his oak-tree arms and athletic build. Though he was fifty, the man could take down someone half his age—and twice his size. "You haven't been to the club in weeks."

Bennet took one of the chairs at the table opposite Mort. "I was at my estate."

"So I heard. But you've been back now nearly a week."

"You're well informed."

"Not me. Fred." Mort sipped his ale and set it back on the table. "He's been waiting for you to show up so he can throw you out on your arse."

"I expected as much." Still, it stung. Bennet had begun training with Fred as a young man fresh from Oxford. Fred had pushed and encouraged him, instilling the confidence and discipline Bennet had needed to become an accomplished fighter—and a man. In some ways, he'd been the father Bennet had been missing and hadn't realized he'd needed.

"You aren't surprised that Fred would toss you out?" Mort squinted one blue eye at him. "What happened at the match in Croydon? You weren't yourself."

Bennet tensed. "I was not. I'd just learned that my financial realities were about to be exposed. I'd hoped winning the fight would solve some of my problems." He assumed Mort knew all this since his cousin did. "I'm afraid I was so desperate to win that I performed exceedingly poorly."

"It wasn't just that. There was something wrong. You seemed...wild."

Gripping the arm of his chair, Bennet tried not to think of the emotions of that night. He mostly kept them at bay. Indeed, fighting helped him do that. He'd sparred at Aberforth Place—one of the grooms fought with him when he was at the estate—but not since he'd been back in town.

"There's nothing more to it," Bennet said evenly, hoping Mort wouldn't continue to question him. "I suppose I will need to find a new club."

"You will. But for what it's worth, I would've let you stay —because Wexford said we should. However, he resigned his membership the other day. Apparently, he's given up the sport." Mort sounded rather disappointed, which wasn't surprising. He'd worked just as closely with Wexford as Fred had done with Bennet.

Bennet was touched that Wexford would speak on his behalf. Touched and perplexed by the man's kindness and generosity of spirit, just as he was with Prudence.

"But it's not up to you whether I'm allowed to stay," Bennet said. "The club belongs to Fred, and he's likely furious with me for losing." They'd already had a falling out before the fight over the scheme that Bennet had proposed.

Mort gave him an earnest stare. "Fred never cared who won. He didn't agree to your scheme to help you. He's motivated by money and money alone."

"I know that now." Bennet had put his trust in the man he'd known for many years. The man he'd thought cared about him.

"Truth be told, I've had about enough of my cousin," Mort grumbled. "I may go out on my own. If I do, you're welcome to come train with me." He took another drink of ale, then speared Bennet with a weighty glower. "Just know that I don't truck with fixed fights or money-making schemes."

"Nor do I anymore." It had taken a botched kidnapping to make him see what a selfish blackguard he'd been.

"Good. Don't bother going back to Fred's even to resign. Don't give him the satisfaction."

"I'll take that advice, thank you." Bennet caught sight of

Lucien coming into the members' den. "If you'll excuse me, I need to speak with Lord Lucien."

Mort nodded, and Bennet stood to approach Lucien.

"Lucien," he said, upon reaching the man's side. "Might I have a word with you in your office? It won't take long."

Lucien's dark brows arched briefly, then he gestured for Bennet to go ahead and leave the members' den. Bennet went straight into the office and heard the door shut.

"How did things go with Mrs. Merryfield and Miss Conkle?" Lucien asked.

"Well enough, thank you. I appreciate the introductions."

"I'm sensing hesitation," Lucien said slowly.

Bennet frowned. "You provoked me to think about alternatives after we spoke the other night. While I do need money as soon as possible, I'd like to find an investment scheme that will offer some security."

"Do you mean in place of marriage?"

Yes, but he wasn't sure he wanted to commit to that out loud. The last thing he wanted was for a rumor to start that although he was marrying for money, he didn't really want to marry at all. Except it wouldn't be a rumor since it was flatly true.

"I don't know," Bennet said. "But I'd like to try to make an investment. Do you have any you recommend? I can't afford much." He rubbed his left hand along his jaw.

Lucien's gaze arrested on Bennet's hand. "Why don't you sell that ring? That looks rather dear."

Bennet straightened his hand in front of his chest, then quickly dropped it to his side. "I couldn't. Besides, I don't think it's worth much." It would never be worth more in money than it was in sentiment—not to Bennet.

Lucien stepped closer, his gaze fixing on Bennet's hand. "May I see it?"

Reluctantly, Bennet lifted his hand. Lucien stared at it a

moment, then sucked in a breath. "I'll be damned," he breathed. "That crest is from my grandmother's family." He lifted his head to pin Bennet with a fiery stare. "Where did you get it?"

Unease rippled along Bennet's shoulders. "I won it in a card game, but I don't remember where or from whom. I've had it awhile." Telling Lucien the truth wasn't an option.

"It belongs to my family, to my Aunt Christina, I believe, since my grandmother is gone. My grandmother is wearing it in a portrait at my father's house. It's in his study."

Bennet's gut clenched. He couldn't give it up. How had Prudence's mother gotten it?

Lucien frowned. "It's not fair of me to ask you to just give it to me, especially with your current hardship." He focused on Bennet, his eyes glinting with determination. "I propose you give me the ring, and I'll invest a good sum on a solid, secure investment—guaranteed to pay good money and sooner rather than later. That would be more beneficial to you than giving you money outright, but I could do that too if you prefer. Would you agree to either of those scenarios?"

Fuck. Bennet didn't want to give up the ring at all. But how could he refuse? He'd dragged Lucien in here out of desperation and to decline such an offer would raise questions, not the least of which would be whether Bennet was sane.

He definitely didn't want to answer that.

He wanted to say that he couldn't agree, that he'd fibbed and the ring actually belonged to someone else for whom he was holding it for safekeeping. But that would only arouse more questions—and Bennet already had plenty of those. He wanted to ask Prudence how her mother had gotten the ring. Perhaps she didn't know.

"You're quite hesitant," Lucien noted. "And you haven't

yet sold that ring despite your need. Does it mean something to you?"

Bennet recalled Lucien's speech about friendship, how honesty was necessary. And here Bennet was lying to him repeatedly. But he had no choice. He couldn't tell him where he'd really gotten the ring or why he didn't want to part with it. Yet again, he was hiding things, as he'd always done. With everyone, including Prudence, the person who'd seen him at his most vulnerable. "I rarely gamble. In fact, I haven't since I won this ring. It seemed a token of good fortune, so I haven't wanted to give it up." The story fell from his lips with ease, but then he'd spent a lifetime crafting tales to appease various members of his family so that it was now second nature. The truth was that Bennet didn't gamble at all. Not after seeing what it had done to his father.

"Let me think on it," Bennet continued. Prudence *had* told him to sell it. Still, he'd speak to her first, particularly since learning where this ring really came from. He narrowed one eye at Lucien. "You're certain this is your family's ring?"

"Completely. It's a very old coat of arms from my grandmother's family, going back many generations. I remember it quite distinctly."

So curious. Bennet was eager to speak to Prudence about it.

"In the meantime, I'll look for an appropriate investment scheme," Lucien said. "I hope you won't be foolish. Furthermore, that ring belongs with my family. I'm not going to let it go without a fight." His tone didn't carry a threat or any malice at all, just a statement of fact.

Bennet nodded, feeling unsettled about having to lie while also knowing it was necessary. "I understand, and I respect that. I'll let you know soon."

He turned and left the room, his mind churning with

unanswered questions and a swirl of unease in his chest. Did Prudence know the truth about this ring?

He wasn't sure what he hoped to find out.

~

"*T*his is lovely, isn't it?" Cassandra asked with a bright smile as she and Prudence strolled along Bond Street. "Just like before I wed Ruark and before you were companion to Kat."

"When I was companion to you," Prudence said.

"I'm so glad we're still in the same household."

Prudence was too. After being uncertain of things while she'd been with Bennet, she was incredibly relieved not only to have a position, but to have one with people she liked and cared about. And who liked and cared about her.

For now. If her time at Riverview had taught her anything, it was that everything truly was temporary. Only one thing was certain: change.

Perhaps that clear realization was why she felt different since returning to London. Or it could be something else entirely. Or some*one* else.

Bennet.

She shoved him away from her thoughts. There was no point in thinking of him.

Forward, not back.

"Let's go in here," Cassandra said, steering Prudence into a milliner's shop. "Those gloves in the window are the perfect shade of ivory." There was no one in London more adept at shopping than Cassandra. Except, perhaps, Evie Renshaw. Prudence had been shopping with her and Ada on a few occasions, and Evie's eye for fashion was nearly unparalleled.

As soon as they stepped into the shop, Cassandra stopped. Prudence nearly walked into her back.

"Good afternoon, Aunt Christina," Cassandra said with a slight edge to her tone.

So slight that probably only Prudence caught it. The Countess of Peterborough, was Cassandra's father's sister, and she'd been Cassandra's sponsor—though a very poor one. While she'd accompanied Cassandra to Society events, she'd often abandoned her upon arrival. On at least one occasion, she hadn't even come to the duke's house in Grosvenor Square to escort Cassandra. That had annoyed the duke no end.

Nevertheless, he'd allowed his younger sister to play sponsor instead of the more earnest and far more committed Lady Aldington, Cassandra's sister-in-law, who'd briefly held the position before the duke had deemed her too timid.

He failed to see that timid was preferable to absent. Or uncaring.

"Cassandra, my dearest!" Lady Peterborough bussed her niece's cheek. They looked a bit alike, with dark hair, though Lady Peterborough's was streaked with hints of gray. Their eyes were quite similar, tawny and warm. "How lovely you look. Marriage certainly agrees with you."

"Thank you, Aunt. I'm fortunate to have Prudence with me today. I don't know if you heard, but she is now companion to Ruark's sister, Miss Shaughnessy."

Lady Peterborough's gaze passed briefly over Prudence. "I hadn't heard, but how nice for all of you. I know how hard it can be to find good help."

Prudence rolled her eyes internally. She'd always found Lady Peterborough to be self-involved, particularly when it came to her niece. One would expect her to make more of an effort since Cassandra's mother had died when she was young. Prudence knew how deeply the loss had affected

Cassandra. Missing their mothers was something they'd shared.

"What are you shopping for today?" Lady Peterborough asked.

Cassandra glanced toward the front of the shop. "I wanted to look at the gloves in the window."

"The ivory pair?" At Cassandra's nod, the countess smiled in approval. "They are quite cunning. Come, let's have a look, and if you like them, I'll purchase them for you."

That was one thing Lady Peterborough did—she bought things for Cassandra and took her on thrilling shopping excursions to Cheapside. Prudence supposed that was something. She tried to imagine doing that with her mother, but of course, they'd never had money for that. They'd been comfortable enough when her father was alive, but after he'd died, they'd both had to work at the school. There wasn't much left for extravagance. And a fashionable pair of gloves from Bond Street was beyond extravagant for someone like Prudence.

Prudence waited near the corner while Cassandra tried on the gloves. She and her aunt admired them, and the purchase was made.

"Well, that was diverting," Lady Peterborough said with a light laugh. "I'm so pleased I ran into you, my dear." She gave Cassandra a brief hug, then glanced toward Prudence. "Good afternoon, Miss Lancaster."

Prudence inclined her head and watched the countess leave. Cassandra clasped her new package and turned toward the door. "Ready?"

In answer, Prudence followed her from the shop. They strolled for a few minutes before Cassandra said, "I wonder if she'll always buy me gifts out of guilt."

"You think that's what they are?"

Cassandra let out a soft but still unladylike snort. "Don't

you? I've told you enough about my aunt, and you've seen for yourself how she is."

Yes, Prudence had. "Is there any chance she does it because she likes to? Everyone shows affection in different ways." Prudence thought of her own mother, who had demonstrated her love by teaching and helping Prudence become independent. If not for her guidance, Prudence might have ended up in a workhouse. That was love just as Lady Peterborough's purchases could be too.

"I suppose you're right. Though, I daresay she may still feel guilty for being a terrible sponsor." Cassandra looked toward Prudence. "Perhaps I should tell her that she needn't feel that way. We've never discussed it."

"Do you think it would help to do so?"

"I don't want her to feel guilty. I confess I did, but that seems rather immature now."

"I don't think so," Prudence said quietly. "You probably hoped she would be more of a mother to you."

Cassandra looked ahead and blinked. "Yes. But I also understand why she was not—she had two sons of her own and an unhappy marriage. I can't imagine things have been easy for her. And now I feel doubly immature for not recognizing that sooner." She shook her head, returning her attention to Prudence. "You are always so wise, Pru. Mysteriously so. I should love to know your entire background—not just the parts you deign to reveal."

"My background is dreadfully dull," Prudence said without guile. Her life had been dull in comparison to the daughter of a duke.

"I doubt your elopement was, however," Cassandra said wryly. "How I would love to hear what happened, but I know you don't wish to discuss it." There was a wistful quality to her voice that made Prudence almost want to tell her. It should have been enough that she'd told Ada, but she hadn't revealed the entire truth. Perhaps that was what she really wanted to share. But again, that meant allowing her emotions to guide her, and she didn't do that.

"I'm only sorry your plans didn't work out as you'd hoped," Cassandra said. "And I meant what I said the other night at the assembly. If you ever need to unburden yourself, I am here for you. Your secrets will always be safe with me."

"That's very kind of you," Prudence said, thinking her secrets would probably shock Cassandra to her bones.

They rode back home in the coach, a luxurious equipage that made her realize just how old Bennet's had been. Why had no one noticed that he lacked the usual trappings of a London gentleman? Prudence had heard he lived in a very small terrace near Bloomsbury Square.

Perhaps they were too dazzled by his striking good looks, charming laugh, and impeccable style. He did dress the part of affluent viscount, at least. She supposed that was all he could manage. He did have to play a role, after all. How else was he to land an heiress?

The thought of him doing so formed a ball of lead in her belly. She had difficulty swallowing as the coach stopped in front of the Wexfords' house on George Street, on one of the corners nearest Grosvenor Square.

As she departed the coach, Prudence looked down toward Queen Street and froze. Was that…? She blinked, certain she must be seeing things. She'd been thinking of Bennet, and her mind had conjured him. Looking again, she saw that she wasn't imagining his presence. He lingered at the corner, seemed to nod at her, then disappeared.

Prudence went inside, her pulse speeding with anticipation. Did he mean for her to go and meet him? She could take a walk…

Twenty minutes later, that was precisely what she did.

CHAPTER 12

Though she wasn't a young lady who shouldn't go walking without a chaperone, Prudence wondered if she was being foolish. If she were seen with the Viscount Glastonbury, someone would surely say something. Such gossip would be too delicious to ignore. A fallen viscount promenading with a paid companion.

It could be so much worse. What if people knew who she really was?

A fallen lord promenading with a viscount's bastard.

She stopped just before reaching Queen Street and nearly turned around.

But then he was there, his hand clasping hers. "Pru. How lovely you look today."

She wanted to say that he was the lovely one. He was immaculately garbed in a bottle-green coat that made his eyes look more green than blue instead of an even mix of the two.

She withdrew her hand from his. "I shouldn't have come out. It wouldn't be good for us to be seen walking together."

"I've considered that." He glanced about, then ushered her across the street and around the corner into the mews. The smell of horses filled the air.

He tucked them into an alcove between two carriage houses. "May I take your hand now?"

"You shouldn't."

Lifting a shoulder, he gave her a dazzling smile. "When have we ever let that stop us?"

Prudence could barely swallow past the tightening of her throat as emotion swelled in her chest. She couldn't keep doing this. It was becoming too painful to walk away. And to keep her feelings at bay.

"How are you?" he asked, taking her hand. She let him.

"Fine. You?"

"Fine is not a real answer. Are you well? Busy? Utterly bored without me?"

She laughed. "You have a rather high opinion of yourself."

"You know I don't," he quipped. "Especially after what I did to you." There wasn't any melancholy in his tone, just a statement of fact.

She needed to put some distance between them. "Have you found an heiress yet?"

He grimaced and let go of her hand. That had been her intent—to push him away—but it still stung. "I wish I didn't need money. Perhaps I should get a job. Is there such a thing as a gentleman's companion? You could train me up."

Another laugh shook her frame. "I'm afraid I've never heard of such a thing. I do know you're good at cleaning up after storms."

"You're right," he said, stroking his chin. "I could work as a gardener or a groom. I do know a fair amount about horses."

"You could also be a teacher. I assume you went to Oxford

or Cambridge and possess a great deal of knowledge to impart."

"Like your father." His eyes glowed with warmth.

"Not like my father. He did not attend Oxford or Cambridge. He was rather brilliant, however." He'd taught her so much about history and science and words.

"He has to have been to have created a child as smart and wonderful as you."

Except he hadn't created her, not in the most basic sense of the word. She inhaled sharply and coughed to cover it up in case Bennet deduced something. "I should get back. And we ought not meet like this anymore."

"I know." He sounded resigned. "But I had to see you. It's about the ring you gave me."

"You sold it." She'd told him to, and yet remorse burrowed inside her.

"Not yet, but I've had an offer. It's the damnedest thing." He shook his head as he removed his left glove. "I must confess that I've been wearing it since you gave it to me."

The gold glinted in the afternoon brightness. The ring looked quite natural and attractive on his hand. Seeing it there made her inordinately pleased.

"It looks nice," was all she could manage to say. She was still waiting for him to explain the damnedest thing.

Her gaze flicked to his, and she saw the barest hesitation. His demeanor sent a jolt of anxiety through her. "Lucien took note of it the other night. He asked how I came to have it."

Her heart felt as though it might jump from her chest. "What did you tell him?"

"That I won it in a card game. He's quite perplexed, however, because he insists it belongs to his family, that the crest is of his grandmother's family." He glanced down at the ring on his finger. "How would your mother have gotten it?"

Everything around Prudence seemed to stop. There was no sound, no scent of horses, nothing but a sensation of falling. Then sound returned, a loud whooshing noise in her ears. Was she actually falling?

"Pru?" Bennet touched her arm. "Are you all right?"

"Yes," she croaked, coughing and taking a breath. "I'm just surprised to hear this."

If the ring belonged to Lucien's family, how on earth had it come into Prudence's mother's possession? No, how had it come into the possession of the woman who'd given birth to Prudence. Unless that woman was from Lucien's grandmother's family. Which wasn't far-fetched. Prudence's real father was a viscount, and the ring had seemed to be from a family of means. Everything pointed to Prudence's real mother being from Lucien's grandmother's family.

That would mean that Lucien—and Cassandra—were Prudence's family.

Prudence felt like she *could* fall. Her legs wobbled beneath her.

Pull yourself together before Bennet puzzles this out!

"I don't know how my mother got it," she lied.

"And you can't ask her, of course." Bennet stroked her arm, his gaze full of concern. "I wonder if she knew the truth about it."

Prudence chose not to speculate with him. The less she said, the better. "Thank you for not telling him I gave it to you."

"I couldn't without revealing how or why. I wouldn't have, anyway."

"Why?"

His brow creased slightly. "I suppose I feel protective of you, whether that's reasonable or not."

Prudence didn't care if it was reasonable. "I appreciate it.

And you." She kissed his cheek but backed away quickly since she was still quivering from shock.

"There's more, I'm afraid," Bennet said darkly. "Lucien wants the ring. He thinks it must belong to his Aunt Christina since their grandmother is gone."

Lady Peterborough. Could *she* be Prudence's mother? It became difficult for her to breathe. She felt as if she'd run long distance at a very fast speed.

"He's offered me an arrangement." Bennet's words drew her back from a swirling chaos.

"What sort of arrangement?" Prudence asked quietly.

"He'll put up the money for an investment scheme on my behalf in return for the ring." He stared at her a moment before continuing. "I told him I'd think about it."

The chaos returned, pulling at her feet. Bennet needed this. What's more, she'd given him the ring to sell for his benefit. Now he had the chance to do exactly that. Why did Prudence need it? Hadn't she already decided to leave the mystery of her mother in the past?

Only, the mystery was nearly solved. Prudence wasn't sure she could turn away from learning the truth at last.

His features softened. "I can see it will pain you for me to give it to him. I can't do that." He worked the ring from his finger and pressed it into her gloved hand.

She wanted to protest, to insist that he sell it to Lucien. Then the secrets of her past could finally be laid to rest. But she couldn't do it. In the end, she couldn't ignore her feelings about this, her need to know and complete the puzzle of her life.

She felt the weight of the ring in her palm. "What will you tell him?"

"Don't worry about that. Take it, please." He wrapped her fingers around the ring, then stroked his bare fingers along her jaw. "You don't have to answer me, but are you somehow related to Lucien's family?"

She responded with the truth, her voice ragged and low. "I don't know. I suppose it's possible." And then the truth spilled from her as the cacophony of emotions became too much for her to contain. "My parents were not really my parents. I was adopted by them." She looked away from him. "The circumstances of my birth are indecent. *I* am indecent."

He grabbed her shoulders and gently squeezed. "Don't ever say that. You can't choose how you are born. You can only choose how you act. I am the indecent one here, never you."

How she adored him in that moment. But it mattered. They came from different worlds, and while blood was important to his class, the fact that her blood came from aristocrats mattered not. The stain of her birth ensured she could never be equal to him. She wasn't going to debate him about that, however. "You're not angry with me for not telling you before?"

"Of course not. That's an awfully big secret to share." One side of his mouth ticked up. "Knowing you, I wouldn't be surprised if I'm the first person you told."

"The second. Sorry." Why she felt she had to apologize for that, she wasn't sure. "My friend Ada—she knows. As you said, it's a very big secret. Too hard to share, but also difficult to keep entirely to yourself.

"I confess I told her that you kidnapped me—but nothing else. I'm sorry. I didn't meant to, but she's a dear friend, and she knows me well enough to realize I would never elope with someone, let alone a man she didn't even know existed."

"Ah. Sometimes logic prevents us from dishonesty, which is probably not a bad thing." His shoulders twitched, and she sensed he was upset, which he had every right to be since she'd broken his trust.

"I really am sorry." She nearly rolled her eyes. "Now it's my turn to excessively apologize."

"Don't. You need never apologize for honesty." He gazed at her in open admiration, clearly *not* upset with her. "You are an exceptionally brave and wonderful woman." He kissed her swiftly, his lips brushing over hers and sparking a desire deep inside her that unfurled as a flower seeking the sun. "I'd like to hold you, but I worry we've already been bold enough." He let her go and took a small step back. "What will you do?"

"I don't know." She ought to speak with Lady Peterborough, if only to return the ring. But then that would provoke questions if Lucien ever learned that the ring had been returned. What a tangle.

"How can I help? Or am I a bother at this point?"

"You are never a bother." She let out a rattled laugh. Tucking the ring into the pocket of her walking dress, she took a sustaining breath. It didn't relax her as much as she'd hoped. But then, she was likely going to feel unsettled for some time. Just the idea of confronting the countess—Cassandra's *aunt*—made her want to toss up her accounts.

Because her idea to confront her half brother had gone so well, she thought sarcastically.

"But I don't think you can help." She gave him a weak smile—it was the best she could do. "I do worry about what you will tell Lucien."

"Don't. You have enough to be concerned about. This could change things for you. If you wanted them to."

He probably didn't mean to sound ominous, but that was how she took it. "I don't think I'd be comfortable suddenly claiming to be a member of Lucien and Cassandra's family." In fact, she nearly returned the ring to Bennet right then. But she'd need it when she went to see Lady Peterborough. After that, she could give it back to Bennet, and he could sell it Lucien.

"I'd like to think about this for a few days. Then I'll likely return the ring to you. I think that's best."

"Do you?" Bennet didn't look so sure. At her slight nod, he went on. "I'll put Lucien off while you work this out."

She finally began to relax—a little. "Thank you. I'm afraid I can't quite grasp this."

He took her in his arms then, holding her close. "It will be all right. Perhaps nothing has to change—if that's what you want."

Prudence pulled from his embrace. "I need to go. Thank you for coming to me and lying to Lucien, though I feel bad you had to."

"I've done far worse." He gave a self-deprecating laugh. "Let me know what you decide. I'll keep Lucien at bay as long as possible."

Bennet took her arm and guided her from the alcove. "In truth, the investment likely wouldn't help in the short term. I will still probably need to marry an heiress." He sounded most unenthusiastic.

A fleeting thought ran through Prudence's mind. If she were the *legitimate* daughter of the former Viscount Warfield, it would be the answer to Bennet's problems. Except she wasn't, so it didn't bear consideration. Which was why she hadn't told him.

He walked her back to the corner at Queen Street. "Try not to worry too much. And please let me know if you need anything. Just send me a note, all right?"

She nodded.

"Promise me, Pru."

"I promise." Then she left him, hurrying back to the Wexfords' house and praying she could dash upstairs without seeing anyone.

∼

*T*elling Prudence about the ring the day before weighed heavily on Bennet. Not that he regretted doing so or could have avoided it. She'd looked so shocked and then almost...panicked. He hated that she viewed her birth as shameful.

The noise of the Phoenix Club was a blur of sound around him, conversation and laughter, people going about their lives while he sat in a chair overlooking Ryder Street, a glass of Irish whiskey in his hand.

"Drinking the good stuff again, eh, Glastonbury?" Wexford asked before sitting down across from him.

"I meant it when I said you'd quite ruined me with it."

"You deserve it," Wexford said with a chuckle before sipping from his own glass. "Mort said he spoke with you about his plans to start his own club. I thought you should know that I'm the primary investor."

"That's why you withdrew your membership from Fred's?" Bennet asked. "Mort indicated it was because you'd married."

"It's both. I'm done fighting."

Bennet frowned. "Then why invest in a new club?"

"Because Mort's been like a father to me, and I believe he'll make a success of it. I think I told you before that he's the best trainer in England."

"I don't know if you said exactly that." Bennet laughed. They'd had a discussion one day at the club as to whose coach was better—Mort or Fred. Mort certainly had the better disposition. What did it say about Bennet that he'd been content to work with the more volatile of the two, that he'd found an affinity with Fred instead of Mort? Was it because when it came to fatherly figures, Bennet expected and deserved someone who was mercurial? Like his actual father.

"So, will you join Mort's new club?" Wexford asked. "It would help him a great deal to have you there. You're a very well-respected pugilist."

Bennet snorted. "Are you sure about that? You beat me quite soundly in Croydon. Furthermore, my reputation is rather tarnished just now."

Wexford made a face, his handsome features distorting as he rolled his eyes. "No one cares about that in a boxing club."

"I'm shocked you don't care, to be honest," Bennet said quietly.

"Did you expect me to hold a grudge?" Wexford sipped his whisky. "Who has the patience for that? Anyway, I'm deliriously happy, and you don't seem disappointed by how things turned out. In fact, I'd say you seem rather…pleasant, all things considered."

He *had* been disappointed in Croydon. And furious. Which had provoked him to commit a terrible act that had somehow turned out to be far from disappointing. Yes, he was pleasant. He was almost *happy*.

Well, he *had* been for a few days. Now, he was venturing toward true disappointment because he had to save his bloody estate and family. His happiness had nothing to do with his duty.

Bennet finished his whiskey. "If you'll excuse me, I need to go find more of this noxious brew you persuaded me to drink." He stood and took himself off to the library where he could refill his glass. He could have asked a footman, but in truth, he found Wexford's happiness a bit constricting.

"Glastonbury, a word, please." Lucien approached him with a rather determined set to his brow.

Bennet finished pouring his whisky, then followed Lucien

to a quiet corner. He could well imagine what was coming next. "Evening, Lucien."

"I don't wish to press you, but I'm rather keen to show that ring to my aunt." Lucien's gaze darted to Bennet's hand, but of course, he wasn't wearing the ring. "Where is it?"

"I left it at home. I don't always wear it."

"Have you come to a decision?"

"Not yet." Bennet sipped his whiskey, his jaw clenching.

Lucien's brows pitched even lower over his dark eyes. "It's a family heirloom. You must understand how important it is for me to recover it."

"I do understand. And I am empathetic. It's just that I've become rather attached to it, silly as that sounds."

Lucien stared at him. "It rightfully belongs to my family. It has to have been stolen."

"You don't know that." Unless he did. Bennet tensed, his hand gripping the glass tightly. "Did you learn something about it?"

"Not yet, but I plan to speak with my aunt."

Bennet realized he was nearly out of time. Which meant Prudence was nearly out of time. He could see that Lucien wasn't going to be able to sustain his patience. "Give me until tomorrow?"

Lucien's jaw worked, but he ultimately nodded. "Tomorrow."

"I'll bid you good evening." Bennet left the library, but didn't want to return to the members' den. Instead, he went downstairs, took one more drink of whiskey, then gave his glass to a footman. Claiming his hat and gloves, he left the Phoenix Club and made his way to St. James's Square, where he hailed a hack.

During the ride to his small terrace near Bloomsbury Square, he planned the note he would dispatch to Prudence first thing in the morning. He'd send it now, but it was far too late to deliver correspondence to a polite address. Not without provoking curiosity.

She had to make a decision. He hated pushing her, but Lucien wouldn't wait any longer. Perhaps Bennet should just tell him the ring had been stolen, that he'd been accosted by a footpad and hadn't wanted to tell him.

Bennet scrubbed a hand over his face. That "explanation" sounded quite weak.

When he arrived home, Bennet went straight to his small office at the back of the narrow ground floor. He penned the note to Prudence, asking her to meet him in the park tomorrow afternoon, if she was able.

"Evening, my lord." Mrs. Hennings, his housekeeper and only retainer save Tom, the aging coachman, poked her head into the open doorway. In her middle fifties, she was widowed with grown children, and one of the hardest workers Bennet had ever met. She was also fiercely kind. "Do you need anything before I turn in?"

"I don't, thank you. I was going to say you're up late tonight, but I suppose I'm home early."

"You are indeed," she said, her light blue eyes perusing him. "If you don't mind my saying, you've been different since returning to town. I know you're going through a bit of a rough time. I hope it's not too troublesome."

Servants were often more knowledgeable about gossip than their employers. Mrs. Hennings was astute and loyal. He wasn't surprised she would mention it, nor did he worry that she was contributing to the rumors. She'd been with him for four years, and his only regret was that she didn't have help to ease her burden.

"Not *too*." He gave her a wry smile. "What have you heard, Mrs. Hennings? No need to soften the blow. Be honest."

She grimaced, her lips thinning. Straightening, she stepped into the office. "The neighborhood was rather taken with the news of your...problems a few weeks ago. The talk died down a bit, but it's picked up again since you returned to town."

"That's to be expected. I hope you aren't concerned that you won't be paid." He would hate for her to think that, and he would never let things come to that. He would find her a new, better-paying position before he couldn't pay her wages.

"Not at all, your lordship. I'm not looking for another position."

"I didn't think you were." Which was perhaps short-sighted and self-important of him. "But if you ever feel as though you must, I hope you won't feel bad. I appreciate your honesty."

"You're a good lad," she said softly. "I wouldn't want to leave you. Is there anything else troubling you?"

Yes, very astute. "Nothing I'm at liberty to discuss. A friend is also going through a rough time. I'm trying to help." Not that he was much use. All he could do was harass her to make a decision about an object that rightfully belonged to her. Lucien wasn't owed it, but Bennet couldn't explain that to him without exposing Prudence's secret.

"I'll leave you to it, then," Mrs. Hennings said with a smile.

"There is one thing. I've a note here that I'll need delivered to George Street tomorrow morning. Can you get John to do it?" John worked in the Bloomsbury Square mews, and his mother was a friend of Mrs. Hennings. He sometimes helped with short tasks, including delivering the occasional letter for Bennet.

"He'll be pleased to help. Just leave it on your desk, and I'll make sure he takes it straightaway." She turned and paused at the door. "Good night, your lordship."

"Good night, Mrs. Hennings."

Bennet finished the note and wrote down the address

along with Prudence's name. He wished he could deliver it in person, but that was impossible. What he wouldn't give to go back to their simple time at Riverview. He closed his eyes and imagined, as he had so often, her in the kitchen and him in the stables or the yard. Both of them working to maintain their house and land, wherever and whatever it was.

But his life wasn't that simple. Nor would it ever be.

CHAPTER 13

*S*eated in the small sitting room she shared with Kat on the second floor of the Wexfords' house, Prudence folded the letter from Bennet that had been delivered that morning. She was out of time. She wasn't surprised, but that didn't make it easier. How she wished she'd never given that ring to Bennet!

But she *had* given him the ring, and Lucien had seen it. Now she knew the likely truth of her birth, and she couldn't unknow it.

"Good morning, Prudence!" Cassandra sailed into the sitting room with a bright, almost giddy smile. "Where's Kat?"

Prudence tried not to look at her oddly. It was so strange seeing her now, knowing they were probably cousins and certainly related in some way. She didn't see much resemblance, but perhaps there was some slight similarity in the shape of their eyes. And in their smiles. "In the library."

Cassandra sat down at the table with Prudence. "Of course she is. I should have known that already." Clasping her hands in her lap, she looked intently at Prudence, still smiling. "Can you keep a secret?" She laughed. "What a silly question. You are the most secretive person I know. I'm still not sure where you go on Saturday mornings. Not that it's any of my business. I'd thought you were visiting the man with whom you eloped, but since you are still absent on Saturday mornings and the elopement failed, I have to assume that was and is not the case."

Sometimes Cassandra talked a great deal. Often, really. And since Prudence didn't like to talk—at least not in her role as companion—she simply listened, usually with amusement. This morning, she was grateful for the distraction.

"What secret are you impatient to share?" Prudence asked, hoping to divert the conversation from herself. Especially since Cassandra's secret didn't concern her. Or did it? Suddenly, Prudence was petrified that Cassandra knew something about the ring or about her aunt probably being Prudence's mother. Cold sweat dappled her nape.

"I probably shouldn't say, but I can't help myself. I am so happy! And I know you won't tell anyone." She looked toward the doorway, as if to confirm they were alone, which they were, then leaned forward. She lowered her voice to a whisper. "My sister-in-law, Sabrina, has confided in me that she's expecting a child. Isn't it wonderful? After all this time, she and Con will finally be parents. And I will be an aunt!"

Prudence's spine bowed, and she relaxed against the chair. Of course Cassandra didn't know anything about the ring or Lady Peterborough. "That *is* wonderful. I won't say a word."

"She's known for some weeks now apparently. Her courses are very regular, so she knew right away when they failed to appear that she may be carrying. The physician confirmed it, but she and Con have kept it to themselves. I don't blame them. They deserve to bask in their happiness together."

Everything she said nestled into Prudence's mind and grabbed hold. Prudence's courses also came regularly. She suddenly realized she hadn't had them in a long while. Too long. Her mind raced. She thought back... It had been before Riverview. Before...Bennet.

But he'd done what was necessary to prevent a child, so it couldn't be possible. Could it? Since then, Prudence had read what she could find about sex and had seen mention of the method he'd employed.

Still, she was long overdue for her courses.

Panic spiraled through her until she felt she might be sick. Was that because she was upset or because she was also carrying a child?

Calm down, Pru. You don't know if you're carrying.

But it wasn't as if she could see a doctor. There *was* one person she could talk to...

"They certainly deserve to be happy," Prudence murmured. "I've just remembered something I need to tell Kat. Please excuse me." She escaped the room on shaking legs.

As Prudence made her way down to the library, her hand flitted over her abdomen. She curled her fingers into her palm and jerked her arm to her side. She refused to believe it.

Kat was curled on the settee, her feet tucked beneath her while she read a book, turning the page as Prudence approached. "One second," she said without lifting her head.

Prudence was used to this behavior and stood patiently, despite the fact that her insides were screaming.

Turning the page once more—Kat was an incredibly fast reader—she set the book on the settee beside her. Then she looked up at Pru expectantly.

"I've an errand to run this morning. Do you mind if I'm gone for an hour or two?"

Kat blinked at her. "I never mind when you have things to

do. Indeed, I find it silly that you should have to ask me permission to do anything." She made a face, then narrowed her eyes, her mouth slanting into a sly smile. "But then you did elope, so I think you find asking for permission just as irritating."

That wasn't true, but Prudence almost wished it was. "Thank you. I'll be back soon."

A short while later, Prudence walked into the side entrance of the Phoenix Club and ran into Ada in the kitchen. "You're here," she said rather stupidly. Seeing her friend made Prudence feel overwhelmed once more. Her heart began to pound.

"Yes," Ada said, her blue-gray eyes sparking with alarm. "What's wrong? You look pale. And distressed." She tugged Prudence to a chair at the table where the maids took their meals—and where she and Prudence ate on Saturday mornings.

No one was about, thankfully. Still, Prudence found she couldn't speak. Emotion clogged her throat, along with the panic she'd barely managed to keep at bay.

"We have to go upstairs," Prudence whispered. "I can't... Not here." She also couldn't ask Ada to have this conversation here. To do so would expose Ada's secrets, and Prudence would never do that.

Ada nodded, and they went upstairs. By the time they reached the top floor, Prudence felt as if she'd run across London. Sensing Prudence's anxiety, Ada held her arm as they made their way to Ada's apartment.

Once inside, Prudence collapsed in her regular chair.

Ada scooted her chair close and took Prudence's hand. "You've well and truly frightened me, Pru. What's the matter?"

"Everything. I haven't had my courses in weeks, since well before I went to Croydon for that stupid fight." Words tumbled from her mouth faster than she realized what she was saying. "Could I be carrying, Ada? How did it feel? How did you know?"

Some of the color drained from Ada's face, but she stiffened her spine. "I missed my courses. I was also quite sick in the mornings. Are you sick?"

"Right now, yes. But not any other morning." She squeezed Ada's hand. "It started when I realized I haven't had my courses in some time."

"This is silly to ask, but is there reason to think you might be carrying?" Ada asked.

Prudence nodded. Then she spilled the truth about her time with Glastonbury. Ada listened quietly, intently, kindly, her hand never leaving Prudence's.

"Why didn't you tell me about Glastonbury? You must know I would have understood. I'm keenly aware of what it's like to be swept away by emotion."

Swept away by emotion. No, it had been physical attraction. Lust. Prudence had worked hard to banish any emotion. "Honestly, I hadn't planned to tell you about Glastonbury at all—not even about the kidnapping. But when you, correctly, pointed out that I wouldn't have eloped, I couldn't lie to you. Neither could I reveal the full truth. I'm not certain why. Perhaps because I was trying to pretend it hadn't happened. Or at least not think about it."

Ada regarded her sadly. "You regret it, then."

"No!" Prudence answered without thinking. When her brain caught up, she added, "Perhaps." If she was with child, Prudence would certainly regret her actions. But would she? She'd never imagined becoming a mother because she hadn't thought it would be possible. "Is there a chance I'm just late getting my courses? I haven't been sick at all."

A faint grimace flashed across Ada's features. "Some

women aren't. How are your breasts? Are they sore? Do they feel hard or full?"

Prudence had found they were sore recently, but hadn't given it much thought. "They do feel odd."

"Any strange taste in your mouth? Sometimes it was as though I'd sucked on iron." Ada stuck her tongue out and made a sound of disgust.

That also sounded familiar. Prudence clapped her hand over her mouth and started to cry.

"My dearest." Ada leaned forward and put her arms around Prudence, holding her while she let the emotion pour out of her.

When at last her tears began to dry, Prudence sat back, wiping her eyes. Ada leapt up and brought her a handkerchief. She sat down again and looked at her with such love and sympathy that Prudence feared she would start to cry again.

"I never do that." Prudence blew her nose. "Cry, I mean."

"It happens more often when there's a babe. One day, I burst into tears when Rebecca did."

Rebecca was one of the children that Ada had been governess to. Ada had fallen in love with their father and he with her. She'd come away with child.

It seemed Prudence really was increasing. She stared straight ahead, seeing nothing but a gray emptiness. "This can't be happening. I can't bear a child who would be known as a bastard."

Ada gently covered Prudence's hands, which were resting in her lap, with her own. "I know exactly how you feel. When I was with child, I was terribly afraid—not necessarily for me as much as for the baby and the stigma with which he or she would have been born. As horrible as it was to lose it, I was so grateful." She took a ragged breath, turning her head from Prudence. "And don't think that doesn't make me feel awful."

The last words were so soft that Prudence had to strain to hear them. She blinked, then focused on Ada. "I'm so sorry to bother you with this, to bring up the past that you never wanted to remember. I couldn't think of what else to do, whom else to talk to."

"You were right to ask me. Of course I can help. I *will* help. We'll find a way through this." Ada hesitated, her expression guarded. "You don't need to have the baby. There are measures you can take..." Her voice was a low rasp.

Prudence was only vaguely aware of such things. "I'm not even certain there is a baby."

"When you are, there are options. If you want them," Ada said quietly. "Have you considered finding a home for it as your parents—your real parents—did for you? From everything you've told me, it wasn't a bad life."

Prudence could barely consider the possibility of a child, let alone what she would do. Except the idea of a son or a daughter wound its way through her and made her feel something she hadn't in a very long time—connected to someone. Even if the child was illegitimate, it would be *hers*.

"I think I might want to be a mother," Prudence whispered, almost afraid to admit it aloud.

Ada gave Prudence's hands a squeeze before letting her go and settling back in the chair. "I presume you haven't told Glastonbury yet, since you didn't even suspect until today."

"No, I haven't. What is he supposed to do, marry me?" Prudence let out a humorless laugh. "Even if he wasn't in desperate need of an heiress to solve his financial problems, a viscount could never be expected to marry *me*. And since he lacks funds to support his own family, I can't expect him to give me an allowance or support me and his child."

"You can and you should," Ada argued, her cheeks flushing. "This is just as much his problem as it is yours. He knew what he was doing when he took you to bed."

"I asked him to," Prudence said with a shuddering breath. "He took precautions. It's an unplanned happenstance." She recalled what he'd said about being unlucky and could only imagine what his reaction would be.

"You still have to tell him. He deserves the opportunity to care for you and the babe, even if you think he can't or won't. Don't be shortsighted, Prudence."

Prudence looked down at her lap and plucked at her dress. "There's more." She glanced toward Ada. "I've found out who my mother is—probably."

Ada's eyes widened. "How?"

"I gave my ring to Bennet—Glastonbury. I wanted him to sell it since he is so in need of funds. Mostly, I didn't want to look backward anymore. The time I spent with him opened my eyes to the future, to possibilities I hadn't ever imagined."

"Did you fall in love with him?" Ada asked softly.

"I don't know. I certainly didn't encourage such emotion." But she was more emotional since then—which she would attribute to the baby growing inside her. A fresh wave of fear and anxiety washed up her throat. She struggled to swallow.

Ada watched her intently. "I take it he sold it, and somehow it found its way back to your mother?"

"No, he couldn't bring himself to sell it." Prudence ignored the flash of surprise in Ada's eyes. "He wore it. Lucien saw it and recognized it." Ada sucked in a breath, but Prudence pushed on. "He said it belonged to his grand-mother, that it bears an old family crest, and that it should be returned to his aunt—Lady Peterborough."

"You think she's your mother?" Ada breathed, her eyes wide.

"It's possible. If the ring is passed from mother to daughter—from Lucien's grandmother to his aunt, it makes sense that it would go to Lady Peterborough's daughter. Except, she has two sons and no daughter."

"Unless you're her daughter, and that's how the ring came to be in your possession."

Prudence wiped her hand over her brow, feeling warm and uneasy. "That seems possible."

"You have to find out for certain. Don't you?"

"I want to," Prudence whispered. "But I'm afraid. What if she never wanted me to find her?"

"Then she should have kept the ring," Ada said crossly. "I think it's more likely that she hoped you would find her—somehow. And now you have. Probably. Where is the ring now?"

"I have it," Prudence said. "Bennet returned it to me, but Lucien says it belongs with his family. He's offered to purchase the ring from Bennet—he'll make an investment on Bennet's behalf. It would have helped Bennet a great deal."

"Yet he returned the ring to you." A quick smile flitted across Ada's lips. "That says something, don't you think?"

"He says he feels responsible and terrible for my abduction and disappearance for nearly a week. It makes perfect sense to me that he wouldn't want to take my ring in the first place—which he didn't—and would return it when it seemed the right thing to do. I refuse to read anything else into it."

Ada's brows arched briefly. "What are you going to do?"

"I don't know." Prudence clasped her hands together and squeezed them tightly. "The baby—if there even is one—complicates things. I wish I'd never given the ring to Bennet." That wasn't precisely true. "I wish he hadn't worn it."

"I think it's rather sweet that he did," Ada said. "He sounds as though he cares about you a great deal. Even if you refuse to acknowledge it," she added.

"We share a bond...or something." Prudence's voice trailed off. She hadn't thought about it too much—the reasons behind her inability to forget him or her yearning to see him despite deciding she had to move on. It wasn't as if they had a future together. Except now there was probably a child. While she'd never entertained thoughts of motherhood or marriage, she now found herself suddenly contemplating both. And she wasn't opposed to either. Indeed, the thought of having her own family was shockingly appealing.

Ada folded her hands in her lap and squared her shoulders. "You came to me for advice, yes?"

"Yes." Prudence was desperate for help.

"You must tell Glastonbury about the baby, or at least the strong possibility that there is one."

Prudence was still resistant, even if the idea of a family now seemed possible. Bennet's situation hadn't changed just because she was perhaps with child. "He can't marry me."

"He'll find a way, or he's an absolute cad. Is he a cad?"

"No." Prudence didn't want to put him in an impossible situation. "There might be a way, but it depends on things that are out of my control." Would he even want to marry her if his situation changed?

Ada pitched forward, her pale eyes alight with interest. "What's your idea?"

"I can take the ring and confront Lady Peterborough. She's wealthy, or her husband is anyway. I'll ask her for money that I can use as a dowry." Prudence had no idea if it would be enough to satisfy Bennet's needs, but it was the only thing she could think of to at least try to put him in a position where he could wed her—if he wanted to.

"With a dowry, you go to Glastonbury with something to offer beyond yourself, something he needs." Ada cocked her head. "That sounds reasonable and rather businesslike. I daresay that's how the best agreements are made, even marriages." She frowned. "However, there is no emotion to it, no mention of love. Which shouldn't surprise me because you're you, and you find *feelings* unnecessary." Ada rolled her eyes. "Perhaps he'd want to marry you because he loves you."

Prudence gritted her teeth. Ada possessed more romantic notion in her little finger than Prudence did in her entire body. "He doesn't have the luxury of marrying for love. We didn't plan for this baby—we tried to avoid it." Prudence hadn't planned for any of this—for Bennet's hirelings to abduct her, to be trapped with Bennet for days, to end up wanting Bennet like she'd never wanted anyone.

Ada was silent a moment. "If you decide to find a home for the baby, you can ask Lady Peterborough about how she did that for you. If you decide to confront her, that is."

It seemed Prudence must see her. She needed the woman's help, either with money or advice. She thought of the innocent life inside her whose family boasted viscounts and earls and dukes. He or she would be raised without any of those benefits, just as Prudence had been. It would be fine, except if they were orphaned and alone in the world, also as Prudence had been.

There was so much to consider. Prudence could barely think straight. Her mind was still awash in anxiety and trepidation.

"There is an alternative to seeing Lady Peterborough," Ada said, her features tensing. "You could ask your half brother for money."

"Absolutely not." That much Prudence was certain of. "I'll speak with Lady Peterborough. Today, in fact." Before she lost her nerve. She ought to see Bennet too—he'd asked her to meet him in the park that afternoon. But she couldn't tell him about the baby in the park, and she still didn't know what to do about the ring. Hopefully, after she saw Lady Peterborough, she would.

"Do you want me to come with you?" Ada offered.

"No, but thank you. I do appreciate your counsel and support. I don't know what I would do without you."

Ada's smile widened. "We may have had some misfortunes, but we were lucky enough to find each other. I'd say we have more than most."

They did indeed. "I think I'd like some tea before I go. If you don't mind."

"Not at all. Let's go down to the kitchen." Ada stood and, when Prudence got to her feet, embraced her in a tight hug. "We'll get you, and the babe, if there is one, through this. There will be happier days ahead. You'll see."

Prudence hoped so, because right now, she couldn't see past the current disaster.

~

*I*n his eagerness to see Prudence, Bennet arrived at the park before five. She was nowhere to be seen, but he hoped she would come. There was plenty of time. Almost right away, he caught sight of Mrs. Merryfield. Tall, with dark hair covered with a plain chestnut-colored hat, she strode toward him, a younger woman—perhaps her maid—trailing just behind her.

"Good afternoon, Mrs. Merryfield." He took her hand and gave her an elegant bow.

"Good afternoon, Lord Glastonbury. What a lovely day for a promenade."

Bennet had no choice but to offer her his arm. They walked along the path as the park began to fill with Society. "I enjoyed our dance at the Phoenix Club the other evening."

"As did I," Bennet said. "You are a unique and independent woman." Her ownership of the bank set her apart from her sex. Many found her intimidating or didn't think she should own a bank. Bennet suspected that was why she'd been invited to join the Phoenix Club. She was precisely the sort of person the club seemed to welcome, those who were excluded or whom Society denigrated in some way.

People like him whose fathers had gambled away their entire fortune, leaving their family to behave as beggars. Perhaps he exaggerated, but not by much.

"I'm glad to hear you say that," Mrs. Merryfield said with the barest hint of a smile. "There is much we can offer each other. A union between us would be mutually beneficial. I know you need money, and I've plenty of it. If I wasn't clear the other night, I would very much like to be a viscountess."

"I did gather that." Bennet was careful to keep the irony from his tone.

"Furthermore, I've demonstrated my ability to bear strong, healthy children. It should be no trouble to provide you with an heir in due haste."

Bennet nearly tripped. How to tell her he didn't want that? He supposed he could just say so. She was being wonderfully frank.

"There is something I wish to discuss, and I hope you will be amenable. I understand you must spend time at your estate in Somerset; however, I expect to reside primarily in London, save a few weeks a year to visit—Aberforth Place, is it?" She looked at him expectantly.

"Yes." Was she saying what he thought she was saying? She didn't want to spend much time at Aberforth Place? She really was close to perfect. He could avoid telling her anything about his family because she'd rarely see them. Surely he could hide their affliction. Until such time as it overtook him as it had his father—*if* it did so.

"I'm afraid I'm needed in London," she went on. "Because of the bank."

"Of course. I completely understand." He smiled widely, pleased with how bloody wonderfully this was turning out. If only he actually *wanted* to marry her. "May I assume your children will stay in London with you?"

"Certainly," she answered quickly, with almost a slight affront. "My son is at school anyway."

"Just so." Bennet appreciated the fact that he could be a stepfather from afar.

"Now, might I ask about your pugilism habit?" She wrinkled her nose, and Bennet could guess her thoughts on the matter.

"I enjoy the sport very much." He wasn't going to pretend he didn't in order to win a wife. Nor was he going to offer to stop.

"It's rather savage. I can't say I'd support it."

"That's unfortunate as I've no intention of giving it up." On the contrary, he felt as though he needed it more than ever.

Glancing toward her, he saw that her lips were pursed. He felt a surge of relief that she was perhaps reconsidering their suitability, which was incredibly foolish. Mrs. Merryfield could be the solution he was looking for.

Turning the conversation to the weather and the spring flowers, he escorted her along the path until she abruptly announced her departure. "Perhaps I will see you at the Phoenix Club assembly on Friday," she said. "Unless you call on me first." She smiled, but he didn't sense any genuine warmth. The entire promenade had felt like a business transaction—and one that hadn't gone satisfactorily.

Bennet committed to nothing as he bowed and wished her a pleasant afternoon. Her maid joined her, and they walked toward the exit. Apparently, she'd accomplished what she'd come to the park to do. He, however, had not.

There were far more people about now, so it was even more difficult to find Prudence. He walked back the way he'd come, nodding and smiling at those who didn't avoid him. No one gave him the cut direct, but some were bloody close.

At last, he spotted Lady Wexford. She stood just off the

path with her friend, Lady Overton. Bennet made his way toward them, drawing their attention as he approached.

"Lord Glastonbury, how fine to see you here," Lady Wexford greeted him. "Fiona, you know Lord Glastonbury?"

He bowed to both ladies.

"I do. It's a pleasure to see you," Lady Overton said. With shocking red hair and a charming, inquisitive demeanor, she'd arrived from the country and commanded quite a bit of attention. That had been before she'd eloped with her guardian, the Earl of Overton, of which Prudence had reminded Bennet. Their elopement had earned even more attention. Bennet knew him vaguely, but they weren't friends.

Bennet looked to Lady Wexford and tried to sound nonchalant. "Where is your lovely sister-in-law and her companion?"

"Kat—that is, Miss Shaughnessy—rarely comes to the park during the fashionable hour," Lady Wexford said. "She finds all this to be nonsense. I would have asked Prudence to join us, but she wasn't at home."

Bennet tamped down his disappointment. Where was she if not at home? Particularly when he'd asked her to meet him? He wondered if she was doing something with the ring since he'd shared Lucien's impatience. Had she gone to him? Had she gone to Lady Peterborough? Unease swirled through him. How he wished he could be at her side to offer support. This had to be a difficult time.

Hell, he wanted to be at her side even if it wasn't difficult. He missed her.

He was suddenly eager to be on his way so he could be alone with his thoughts. "I just thought I'd stop and say good afternoon." He touched his hat and continued toward the gate.

Why couldn't Prudence have been the heiress he needed? How simple everything would be.

What a lie that was. The truth was that he didn't want to marry. He couldn't. His family's illness wasn't something he would subject a bride to, especially one he cared about as much as Prudence. If he did wed Mrs. Merryfield, he'd do everything possible to ensure she didn't learn about his family's illness. Thankfully, her revelation that she preferred to spend most of her time in London would make that far easier than he'd anticipated. It was a considerable point in her favor.

He rubbed his forehead as he left the park, feeling a headache come on. Why couldn't a pile of money just fall into his lap? Surely he was due for some excellent luck.

What if meeting Prudence was the best luck he'd ever had?

Except they had no future together. He needed an heiress, and anyway, she didn't want to get married either. She was also a paid companion, not someone a viscount ought to marry. He wasn't sure he gave a damn about that, no matter what Society said.

His mind indulged the dream of not having to worry about money, of being able to do whatever he wanted. Would he marry Prudence? Of anyone he'd ever met, she would be the one who might understand his family. She might even accept them. Her heart was that generous and kind—that, he was certain of. She'd even called them fascinating, but then he'd barely skimmed the surface of their true personalities. Both of them could become quite angry, particularly Flora when things didn't go the way she wanted or expected, and dealing with their obsessions could be tedious at best and volatile at worst.

Expecting someone to not only put up with his family but embrace them was asking a great deal. He'd long ago promised himself that he wouldn't request it of anyone. But he'd never anticipated Prudence.

Furthermore, she'd have to agree not to have children. That was absolutely imperative.

Wonderfully, that seemed the easiest hurdle since she'd already indicated that she didn't want children. She'd also said she didn't wish to marry. Why, then, was he torturing himself with these thoughts? Things he couldn't have, no matter how badly he wanted them.

Taking a deep breath, he thrust his shoulders back. He needed to get his priorities in order and do what needed to be done.

Tomorrow, he'd pay a call on Mrs. Merryfield.

CHAPTER 14

*P*rudence regretted declining Ada's offer to accompany her to Lady Peterborough's house in Berkeley Square. The stone façade rose tall and imposing as she approached the door. She hesitated, nearly capitulating to overwhelming trepidation. Ultimately, she managed the courage to knock.

Almost immediately, a footman answered.

"Good afternoon, I'm here to see Lady Peterborough." Prudence handed the footman her card and was grateful that Cassandra had insisted on providing them as soon as Prudence had become her companion. That the card misidentified her as companion to Lady Cassandra West-brook—which wasn't even Cassandra's name anymore—was the least of Prudence's concerns.

The footman perused the card, then invited her inside. "Follow me, Miss Lancaster."

She trailed him to a sitting room decorated in muted yellows and browns. The color scheme reminded her of one of the final days of autumn when once-bright hues were tired and faded.

After the footman left, Prudence fidgeted with her gown, then chided herself for the bad habit.

A few minutes later, the countess glided in wearing her typical expression of bland cheerfulness. It was as if she tried to look happy, but everyone knew it was an act, including her.

"It's just you?" Lady Peterborough asked, stopping a few feet from Prudence and clasping her hands in front of her with a patient if bemused expression. "I am surprised you would call on your own." She seemed genuinely curious and not as though she was trying to insinuate Prudence *shouldn't* call.

"This errand doesn't involve anyone else." Prudence loathed confrontation, but this was important. Her entire future depended on what happened in this interview. She'd felt the same when she'd gone to see her half brother, only for everything to fall apart because she hadn't been able to muster the boldness to say what she ought, that they were siblings and he should help her.

The words she'd prepared to say to the countess disappeared from Prudence's mouth as if swept away on the wind. Panic rose in her throat, and heat flushed up her neck. Instead of speaking, she reached into her pocket and withdrew the ring. She took a step closer to the countess and held out her hand. The gold flashed in her palm.

Lady Peterborough tipped her head down, her brow creasing. "What's that?"

"A ring." Prudence coughed to clear the clouds from her throat. "My mother gave it to me before she died."

Tawny eyes met Prudence's for a moment before the countess plucked the ring from Prudence's hand. She stalked to the window where the late-afternoon sun streamed past the draperies and held up the ring.

Prudence held her breath.

Lady Peterborough spun around to face Prudence. "Your mother gave this to you?"

"The woman who raised me." Prudence breathed before plunging forward, "I understand this ring belongs to your family, that it may even belong to you."

Clutching the ring, the countess hurried to close the door to the sitting room. When she came back toward Prudence, her face was pale and her eyes dark with fear. "Please keep your voice down." She barely spoke above a whisper. "My husband mustn't hear this conversation."

Prudence stared at her as words once again utterly failed her.

The countess stared at her in return. "The ring does belong to me—or it did. I gave it to the wet nurse who accompanied my daughter to her adoptive parents. I'm glad to see she passed it on as I instructed." She studied Prudence. "I never really looked at you closely before. You resemble him. Your father, I mean. Do you know who that is?"

Slowly, Prudence nodded. She felt as if she were in a dream. "When my mother was dying, she told me that I'd been given to them to raise. Whoever had delivered me to them had given her the ring and said it was from my mother —the woman who birthed me. She also revealed my true father's identity. You are my mother?"

"It seems so." Lady Peterborough held up the ring between her thumb and forefinger. She smiled, and Prudence swore it was the most genuine expression she'd ever seen on the woman. "She was supposed to give this to you when you married. That's when the firstborn daughter receives it." Her smile faded. "I'm sorry your mother didn't live to see that. I'm glad she gave it to you personally, though."

Prudence could scarcely believe she was looking at the woman who'd given birth to her. "Why did you give me away?" The question was soft but harsh sounding.

"Since you know who your father was, you also know he wasn't my husband. I'm afraid Lord Peterborough was furious that I'd allowed myself to get with child by another man. Never mind the children he sired on his mistress." She sniffed, and Prudence felt a sudden urge to knock Lord Peterborough to the ground. "It was the only way," Lady Peterborough said. "Pete wouldn't claim you, and Walter's wife didn't want you either. I'm sorry. He gave me no choice regarding you. I had to give you away." She reached for Prudence's cheek but didn't touch her before withdrawing her hand. "It was so difficult, but I knew you would be well cared for, that the couple taking you wanted you very badly. That gave me solace. I'm glad you still have the ring. You'll give it to your daughter on her wedding day."

Prudence's *daughter*. That she could very well be carrying right this instant.

Tears blurred Prudence's vision, and she felt wobbly as she had earlier. "I need to sit." She practically collapsed onto the nearby settee.

Lady Peterborough sat down on the same piece of furniture, her features creased with concern. "Are you all right? You look unwell."

"I'm... Never mind that now." She wanted to hear the countess talk first. The countess. Her mother. "I can't believe you're my mother. You're certain?"

"The more I look at you, yes." She studied Prudence's face and smiled again. "You are clearly Walter's daughter. You have his eyes and his nose, the same shape of his face. It's astonishing, really. If I'd ever looked at you properly, I would have seen it." She laughed then, surprising Prudence. "My goodness, but that would have been a shock—for both of us."

"I think this must be a shock right now." Stupidly—and surprisingly—Prudence wanted this woman to want her, to be happy to see her.

"Yes." The countess's tawny eyes clouded, and she blinked several times. Then she wiped a tear away. "It's a wonderful shock. I never thought to meet you. You're so beautiful, so poised."

Prudence worried she might burst into uncontrollable sobs. How she hated all this untidy emotion! "But I'm only a paid companion."

"You rose from middle class to move in the highest echelons of Society." Lady Peterborough shook her head. "You didn't rise. You are *from* the highest echelons of Society. You should have been raised here, with me. You and Cassandra would have grown up together." Her voice broke, and she looked away, her chin trembling.

Prudence didn't know what to do. Instinctively, she wanted to comfort the woman, perhaps touch her hand or hug her even. But everything was strange and awkward. A lifetime of secrecy stood between them.

"Your Christian name is Prudence?"

"Yes."

"It's lovely, as are you."

Unwanted emotions tumbled through Prudence, but she had to focus on the goal for this errand. "I'm afraid Lucien is aware of this ring."

The color leached from the countess's face once more. "What do you mean?"

"I gave the ring to a gentleman. He wore it, which I never expected him to do. Lucien saw and recognized it. That's how I came to know it belonged to your family."

The countess's hand flew to her mouth as she drew in a sharp breath. "Pete can never know that you are here—so close to me. To him," she added in a bare whisper.

"I understand." Prudence wanted to allay the woman's fears—no, her panic. She was obviously very stricken by the notion that her husband should learn that Prudence was nearly in their lives.

Nearly.

"What did Lucien say?" the countess asked breathlessly.

"I haven't spoken to him directly. He doesn't know the ring was in my possession, nor does he know I have it now. He wants the ring because he says it belongs with his family. However, the gentleman returned the ring to me."

"As he should have. It's yours." Lady Peterborough glanced toward the window, her brow furrowed.

"The gentleman has been able to put Lucien off, but your nephew has been most insistent. I'm afraid we're out of time. I need to give him the ring."

"No." The countess looked back to Prudence, her gaze intense. "That's the one thing I will not allow. I've bowed to everyone's wishes where you are concerned, but I won't in this. I will handle Lucien."

"What will you say?" Prudence didn't want to cause trouble for Bennet.

Lady Peterborough arched one shoulder. "The truth, I think. Lucien is very good at keeping secrets—and at helping people. I will tell him the ring is where it belongs and to mind his own business."

Prudence continued to be surprised by the countess. Her mother. She was behaving as a mother ought. Somewhat, at least. "Thank you."

"Why did you give this mystery gentleman the ring?" Lady Peterborough asked.

"I gave it to him as a favor—that he didn't ask for. I'd hoped he would sell it. In fact, I told him to. He's in need of funds, and I wanted to help."

"He sounds rather important to you."

Now was the moment to spill the other reason she'd come

today. "Things have changed since I gave him the ring. I find myself in the same dire straits as you once did." Prudence hesitated the barest moment before plunging forward, heat rising in her face. "I believe I'm carrying a child. I need a dowry."

Lady Peterborough's eyes widened. "His child? Oh, my poor dear."

Prudence didn't answer the countess's question. "Can you help me?"

"I do understand your plight—of course I do. But I can't give you anything for fear my husband would realize some of my allowance was unaccounted for. I take it this mystery gentleman to whom you gave the ring is the father? If he's in Lucien's circle, he must be rather prominent." Lady Peterborough's eyes narrowed with skepticism. "Has he agreed to marry you if you provide a dowry?"

"He hasn't agreed to anything yet." Prudence stiffened her spine and averted her gaze from the countess. "I haven't told him about the child. I'm not even entirely certain."

"Forgive me, but if this man *is* a gentleman or a peer, I can't imagine he'd marry you. I'm sorry to have to say that."

"He would if I had the money," Prudence snapped, her emotions getting the better of her *again*. Reining them in, she straightened her spine and moderated her tone. "He needs money." He also seemed to want her, but that didn't mean he'd want to wed her. She could certainly understand why he wouldn't. "In any case, I will be forthright with him about everything—he already knows the circumstances of my birth." And he didn't seem to care.

"So you don't intend to trap him into marriage with a dowry?"

"Since you don't know me, I will strive not to allow your opinion of me to be disappointing," Prudence said coolly. "No, I don't intend to trap him. As I said, I will tell him about the child—or at least the possibility of one. He would not be free to marry me without a dowry, and I should like for him to have that choice."

A sad smile curved the countess's lips. "I fear you've given the male sex far more credit than they are due. He likely isn't free to marry you at all—dowry or no. His duty will require that he wed someone of his station."

"I can see you aren't going to help me." Prudence stood. "Are you going to give me the ring back?" It seemed as though the countess wanted her to have it.

"Of course. It's yours." The countess rose from the settee. Taking Prudence's hand, she pressed the ring into her palm.

"What am I to do with this?" Prudence asked. "You want me to have it, and yet I can't wear it or otherwise display it for fear that people will discover who—and what—I am. When I pass it to my daughter, am I to tell her that I am a bastard and her grandmother is a countess as well as the daughter and sister of a duke? None of that matters since we can't tell anyone. It's simply a fairy tale I can put her to bed with every night. No, you keep your ring." Prudence tried to hand it back.

The countess's features had creased more deeply with everything Prudence said until she looked thoroughly pained. "I wish you could wear it with pride. I wish I could declare to the world that you're mine. How I wanted a daughter, and look at you—so beautiful and so accomplished. I wish I could help you," she added quietly. "Do you really think this man will marry you if you have a dowry?"

Probably, if only because he needed money. "I want to give him that choice—for the sake of the baby who is as much a part of him as of me. If he refuses, I will not be any worse off than I am today."

"Your heart might be broken," the countess said softly, her gaze warm with understanding that nearly melted Prudence's resolve to turn her back on the woman. "I know how that feels, and in some ways, you never recover. I really would like you to keep the ring."

"I will likely sell it," Prudence said, though the funds wouldn't come close to solving Bennet's woes.

The countess looked her in the eye. "I can see how important this is to you—the dowry. I can't ask my brother. I've never wanted to trouble him with this. The only person I can think to ask is your half brother."

"*No*," Prudence practically snarled. She refused to ask him.

"Such a vehement response. Do you know him? It sounds as though you're familiar with his…demeanor."

"I am. He's a horrible person."

"He wasn't before the war." Lady Peterborough gave a faint smile, then took a deep breath, lifting her chin. "I would like to help you. It's the very least I can do. However, my options are limited. If Pete found out about you, my life would be over."

Prudence gasped. It couldn't be *that* dire. "What would he do?"

"Send me to a convent, probably. He's threatened as much. Which is why I can't do what I would like."

"What's that?" Prudence asked cautiously.

"Claim you as mine, of course. What I can do is speak to Maximillian—I mean Warfield—and insist he provide a dowry for you. His father would want him to do it, I'm certain."

Prudence stared at her, hating the idea of going to him, but beginning to accept that it might be her only path forward if she wanted her child to be born in wedlock. "I desperately want this baby to be legitimate," she whispered, her voice breaking on the last word.

"I understand." Lady Peterborough took her hands and

gave them a squeeze. "Will you let me take care of this for you?"

Prudence couldn't quite believe this woman wanted to help her, but wasn't that the reason she'd come? "Thank you. Please don't tell Warfield I'm increasing. It's humiliating enough that I had to tell you."

"You mustn't feel ashamed, not with me. I'm your mother, Prudence, and I love you—I have always loved you. This is my grandchild, and I will love her—or him—too."

The family she never imagined was not only possible, it was coming to be, whether Prudence wanted it or not. She wanted it. An immense lump formed in her throat, and tears gathered in her eyes. She shook her head, refusing to cry. Bloody stupid emotions.

How had Prudence gone from an independent woman content with her life to pining after a man who'd kidnapped her and hoping she indeed carried his child? Perhaps pining was extreme, but she did think about him far too much.

Lady Peterborough continued, oblivious to the major shift of thought occurring in Prudence's mind. "We'll tell your brother that you require a dowry, that you could make a very advantageous marriage. His father would want that, and Maximillian should too. He won't claim you as his sibling, however. You do understand that?"

Prudence nodded and managed to push out a few words. "Yes, and I don't want to claim him either."

"Good." The countess's expression turned pensive once more. "I'll let you know as soon as I've settled the matter. I'll move quickly—I understand time is critical for you." She glanced toward Prudence's still-flat abdomen.

As Prudence left, she couldn't help still feeling apprehensive. What if Warfield wouldn't give her a dowry?

She couldn't shake one word: trap. She'd no wish to snare

Bennet in a marriage he didn't want. He would be shocked when she told him about the baby.

She hoped he might also be happy, since she was starting to feel that way too.

~

*B*ennet returned from the park to find two of his relatives had arrived unannounced. Shocked, for they never visited him here, let alone at Aberforth Place, he worried something awful had happened.

He rushed upstairs to where they awaited him in the drawing room.

Aunt Judith, his father's youngest sister, perched on the edge of the settee, and Great-Aunt Esther, his grandmother's sister, sat in a chair near the hearth. She straightened as if surprised when he entered—or as if she'd been asleep.

"What a surprise," Bennet said, not bothering to characterize their visit as something pleasant. He loved all his relatives, but these two in particular tried his patience. Was that because Aunt Judith seemed to have escaped the family affliction while Great-Aunt Esther didn't come from the afflicted line? "Did I miss a letter from you that said you were coming?"

"I didn't bother to write," Aunt Judith said, not mincing words, but then she never did. "As soon as I heard the rumor, I readied myself to travel."

"I insisted on coming along," Great-Aunt Esther said. At seventy-four, she was still quite spry. "It's been an age since I was in London."

Aunt Judith cast her a beleaguered look. "We're not staying long." She returned her attention to Bennet. "I told her not to come, that this was a critical errand, but not one that would allow for socializing or sightseeing."

Great-Aunt Esther smiled at Bennet, her cheeks dimpling as lines fanned out from her blue eyes. "I'm certain Glastonbury will insist on squiring us about town for a few days at least."

"And where would we go?" Aunt Judith asked. "I suspect he has no invitations. If the rumor is true." She looked at him expectantly, as if Bennet should know what she was talking about.

Of course he did.

"Is that why you've come?" he asked, provoking her to be explicit, which shouldn't be difficult for her. He lowered himself into a chair closer to Great-Aunt Esther than to Aunt Judith. Hopefully, the latter wouldn't see it was some sort of preference, but she very well might.

"Yes, that's why I've come," Aunt Judith replied. "As someone whose livelihood depends on you, I was horrified to hear that you are practically destitute. I am just glad that rumors tend to be exaggerated. Still, how bad is it?" She leaned forward slightly, blinking and cocking her head so that she reminded him of a bird.

"Practically destitute isn't far off, actually," he said somewhat cheerfully. What was the point in being gloomy about it? "Father left things in quite a mess, I'm afraid."

Aunt Judith's nostrils flared, and she jerked back. "I can't say I'm surprised. Your father was a mess at everything. I should have expected that he would have died poorly too."

As angry and frustrated as Bennet often felt toward his father, he reminded himself that those emotions were directed at the unfortunate situation. His father could no more help his shortcomings than he could stop them from driving him down a regrettable and disastrous path. The best thing he'd ever done was marry Bennet's mother—or so he always said. Since she'd died giving birth to Bennet, there was no way Bennet could know for himself.

"There is nothing to be done about that now," Bennet said, pressing his lips together before he added anything else that would be unhelpful. "I'm doing my best to rectify matters."

"You're on the hunt for an heiress," Great-Aunt Esther said. "That was the other part of the rumor. Perhaps Judith and I can help you on that front. Though, I daresay, we'll need to visit a modiste."

Judith snapped her head toward her aunt. "Don't be daft! There's no money for that. We are not here to gad about Society."

Great-Aunt Esther sent her niece a sullen look. "We could still help," she muttered.

Bennet didn't want her to feel bad. "If you have advice for me, I will gladly take it, Great-Aunt Esther."

This mollified her, and she smiled again, revealing her dimples once more. "You've always been such a good boy. And now you take care of everyone. What a trial it must be."

"It's his duty," Aunt Judith interrupted. She speared Bennet with a dark stare. "That is why I've come. Assuming the rumor was true—and how I hoped it wasn't—you do need advice, though not about whom to marry. There's a simple solution. You must stop paying those exorbitant fees for that hospital in Lancashire."

Bennet rested his elbow on the arm of the chair and gritted his teeth. It was all he could do to keep from massaging his forehead in agitation. "That is neither simple nor a solution. Aunt Agatha is precisely where she needs to be, and I won't discuss her care with you. I'm well aware of what you think."

Aunt Judith pursed her lips, her eyes narrowing in disdain. "You're being foolish. The poor thing is barely aware of her surroundings. I know you love her—we all do; she's my sister for heaven's sake—but it's not an unkindness to save money so the rest of us don't suffer."

"Do you know what *would* be a simple solution?" Bennet asked. "You both could move to Aberforth Place. There's plenty of room." He couldn't decide which aunt looked more appalled.

Great-Aunt Esther spoke first. "You can't ask that of us. Bless you, my boy, for taking care of them, but you can't ask me to live with the crazy people."

Bennet nearly growled. He detested when she used that word. "They are *eccentric*."

Aunt Judith rolled her eyes. "Cousin Frances sometimes doesn't know what day it is. Is she still making her clothing out of old draperies and bedclothes?"

"Yes, and it's quite economical, I don't mind saying." He smiled blandly and enjoyed their exchanged look of discomfort.

Aunt Judith clasped her hands in her lap. "If you insist on leaving things as they are, then I suppose we must help you find a wealthy wife."

Bennet looked to his aunt. "Since you don't care for moving to Aberforth Place, another solution would be for you to marry a wealthy husband."

"You know why I have never married," Aunt Judith said tightly.

The same reason he hadn't and didn't want to. Neither of them wished to pass the family condition on to another generation. "You are past your childbearing years, I should think."

She blew out a breath and glanced toward Great-Aunt Esther as if she expected support.

Great-Aunt Esther shrugged. "He makes a valid point, although I imagine it would be difficult to find a husband at your age. I never could."

"You couldn't even during your Seasons," Aunt Judith retorted.

Bennet ignored their bickering. "My point is, unless you're willing to contribute to improving the financial situation we find ourselves in, I would kindly ask you to keep your opinions and counsel to yourselves. Unless and until I ask for them." He tried to sound pleasant while chastising them.

The two women exchanged another look, but Bennet couldn't be sure what they were communicating.

"Whom are you courting?" Great-Aunt Esther asked. "Or thinking of courting?"

"No one at the moment," he said truthfully. He didn't want to mention Mrs. Merryfield, probably because if he did, they'd make it their mission to ensure the match happened. While he should want that, he just…didn't. "While I appreciate you wanting to help, it isn't necessary. I'm sorry you came all this way for something that could have been accomplished with a letter."

Great-Aunt Esther flicked a glance at her niece. "Judith was sure she could convince you to cut corners with Agatha. I also wondered if you could send Frances away too, then you'd have another cottage on the estate to let." At his answering glower, she lowered her gaze to her lap.

"And why should Agatha and Frances suffer while the two of you make no economies? I will no more turn out Aunt Agatha from the only home she's known these past thirty years than I will Cousin Frances or either of you, despite the fact that I should in order to settle my father's debts and restore the estate to profitability."

"My father promised I would always be taken care of," Aunt Judith said indignantly.

"As his heir's heir, I will take care of you," Bennet snapped. "But your household in Bath is bloody expensive."

Aunt Judith blanched. "Careful, Bennet," she whispered. "You must control yourself or you'll end up like him."

As if he needed her to remind him. Bennet let go of his anger. "My apologies."

Aunt Judith's features softened, and her gaze turned sympathetic. "I understand you don't wish to wed—and you know I support that. That's why I thought you would be open to sending Agatha somewhere less costly."

"I appreciate your concern. Truly. Believe me, I've been trying to find another way. I've sold nearly everything of value at Aberforth Place. Poor Great-Aunt Flora is running out of places to press her flowers."

This prompted smiles from everyone, and Bennet relaxed. They might be a mess of a family, but they were still a family. And he would go to any lengths to keep them all safe and happy, including kidnap an heiress. Put like that, there was no reason he shouldn't marry Mrs. Merryfield.

He knew what he had to do. "Actually, there is a woman who might suit our needs," he said. "She's aware of my…situation and is content to exchange money for becoming a viscountess. Furthermore, she has children already, so I won't feel bad not giving her any."

"That's quite a sacrifice," Aunt Judith said quietly.

He exhaled as resignation swept over him, bringing a melancholy he didn't want. "It's the only way."

Great-Aunt Esther gave him an encouraging smile. "As I always say, you're such a good boy."

CHAPTER 15

*B*ennet's tread was heavy as he made his way back home following his call on Mrs. Merryfield. She'd been delighted to see him—if "delighted" could describe her closemouthed smile and invitation to have tea. He'd wanted to decline, but supposed it made sense to spend time with the woman who would be his wife.

In a month.

She'd been eager to choose a date, and the banns would be read this coming Sunday. Bennet should feel happy, or at least relieved. Instead, he felt hollow.

Just as he reached his house, he heard his name. Lucien was bearing down on him from the opposite direction.

"Glastonbury, I'm glad I caught you." Lucien looked rather intense, his brow furrowed and his eyes especially dark.

Bennet wasn't in the mood to discuss the ring. "Afternoon, Lucien. I'm afraid I'm just on my way back from an errand, and I've relatives visiting."

"Indeed? How pleasant. I just need a few minutes. Might we go inside?" He inclined his head toward Bennet's house.

Resigned, Bennet nodded. He led Lucien inside directly to his small study at the rear of the house. "You've come about the ring, I take it?" Bennet gestured for Lucien to sit, then removed his hat and gloves before taking his favorite chair near the hearth.

Lucien perched on the edge of a chair. "Somewhat, yes. My aunt came to see me and asked me to forget about the ring. She said it's with the person it belongs to—her daughter."

Bennet worked to cover his surprise. It wasn't a complete shock to learn that Lady Peterborough was Prudence's mother, but he wished he'd heard it from Prudence. He longed to know how she'd taken the news, whether she and Lady Peterborough had formed some sort of bond.

Lucien shook his head. "I can't believe my aunt has an illegitimate daughter, that I have a cousin I didn't know about."

Bennet bristled at the word "illegitimate," but said nothing on that front. "I'm glad that's settled, then." He desperately wanted to speak with Prudence, but since she hadn't met him in the park and hadn't sent word, he had to assume their association was finally finished. As it should be. There was no reason for them to continue as they'd been doing, particularly since he was now betrothed. He suddenly felt as though he'd swallowed a cup of broken glass.

"My aunt had another reason for coming to see me," Lucien continued. "She asked me to solicit a dowry for her daughter from the woman's half brother, the Viscount Warfield. Aunt Christina insists he'll come up with the funds. I'm not so certain, and I say that as one of Warfield's few remaining friends." Frowning, he added, "Indeed, I may be the only one."

Lady Peterborough was trying to get a dowry for Prudence? Why? Bennet hated that his pulse sped, and a thrill shot through him. With a dowry, Prudence would be marriageable. He detested that he had to think of her in terms of financial benefit. She was so much more. His thoughts were still filled with her even as he plotted a future without her. He longed for the time they'd spent at Riverview so he could drink tea and wine with her, read to her, share a bed with her. "How wonderful that your aunt wants to support her daughter in such a way." He sounded stiff and bound, which he was—tied to his duties instead of free to do as he wished.

Lucien narrowed his eyes at Bennet. "Aunt Christina also said the dowry was so her daughter could marry the man she gave the ring to—that would be you."

Bloody fucking hell.

"I didn't realize you were getting married," Lucien went on. "The last I heard, you were desperately seeking an heiress. *This* is your solution? To wed my illegitimate cousin?"

Bennet wanted to yell at him to stop calling Prudence that word. And he wasn't aware of any of these plans! Furthermore, he'd just agreed to marry someone else! Wait, did that mean he'd marry Prudence if she got this dowry from Warfield? While it made her marriageable, it didn't change the fact that he didn't want to marry anyone, especially someone he cared about as much as Prudence. He couldn't ask her to suffer him if he fell under the family illness.

Remember, she doesn't want any children. She might be perfect...

Lucien pinned him with an intense stare, startling Bennet from his rambling thoughts. "My aunt wouldn't tell me her daughter's name. I want you to tell me."

Bennet shook his head. "That isn't my secret to share."

"I'll find out when you marry her," Lucien said with considerable exasperation.

"Then that's when you'll find out." Bennet's head was swimming. He had no idea what was going on. He *was* betrothed, but not to Prudence.

"Is this a happy union?" Lucien asked.

Bennet couldn't answer that since this was the first he was hearing of it. "I'm sure it will be," he said blandly. "Now, if you'll excuse me, I really must be getting on."

"Very well." Lucien exhaled as he stood. "Wish me luck with Warfield. I'm going to visit him now. He's a difficult sort."

"So I hear."

Lucien cocked his head. "What happens if he won't provide the dowry? I know how badly you need the money."

"For now, I'd appreciate it if you could leave this between me and the lady in question."

"It's hard to do that when you apparently require others' assistance," Lucien said drily. His features darkened. "Don't break her heart if the money doesn't come through. I may not know who she is—yet—but she's my blood, and I'll defend her honor."

"I would never want to hurt her," Bennet said softly. But he already had when his hired ruffians had ripped her from her sleep and altered the course of her life. To the point that she was now planning marriage when she'd indicated she wished to avoid it.

Why *was* she doing this? Just to help him as she'd tried to do by giving him the ring?

Something had changed. Bennet needed to know what.

Lucien left, and Bennet rose from the chair to pace as agitation raced through him. He'd suddenly gone from being desperate and uncertain to having two potentially viable options. The question was, which would he choose?

Mrs. Merryfield had the money he needed, and he'd already made a commitment to her. Still, if Prudence had a dowry, wouldn't he prefer to marry her? He certainly preferred to bed her. He'd dreamed of her every night since they'd parted at Riverview. But it was more than that. He couldn't see Mrs. Merryfield with his family, whereas he envisioned Prudence picking flowers with Great-Aunt Flora and visiting Great-Aunt Minerva in her painting room. While it seemed potentially charming, he knew it was a dream. What would Prudence do when Great-Aunt Minerva threw her paint and made an awful mess? Or when Great-Aunt Flora shredded her newspapers in a fit only to sob once she realized what she'd done?

He pushed the thoughts away. All this was moot. Prudence didn't yet have a dowry, and he didn't understand what was going on.

He needed answers and he needed them fast—before the banns were read on Sunday.

~

"I just want to make a sketch of this specimen," Kat said, her gaze focused on the bird in the case at the British Museum. "You don't mind?"

"Of course not." Prudence was used to her drawing all manner of things and had brought a book. "I'll just go find a place to sit and read."

"Excellent." Kat was already moving her pencil across the parchment she held on a small, thin board that provided a portable writing surface.

Prudence retraced their steps back to the entry area where there was seating. She found an empty bench and sat, opening her book on her lap.

She didn't read a word.

Her mind was too full of thoughts of Bennet, the baby, whether she was going to have a dowry, the fact that she now had a mother who apparently loved her. It was incredibly overwhelming.

She couldn't deny the joy she'd felt when Lady Peterborough—perhaps she ought to think of her as something less formal—had agreed to help her and even said she loved her. She also couldn't ignore the burgeoning happiness she felt when she thought of the child she probably carried. And what about Bennet?

"Good afternoon."

The deep, familiar voice sent a shock of pleasure down her spine. She snapped her head up and met the disarming gaze of the person most occupying her thoughts.

"Bennet," she whispered, utterly surprised to see him.

He smiled. "Prudence."

He'd sent a note that morning asking to see her today. She'd responded quickly with her regrets since she had plans to accompany Kat to the museum today. He knew she would be here.

She realized she hadn't seen him since before she'd confronted her mother. "I'm sorry," she blurted.

He appeared perplexed despite the smile hovering about his mouth. "For what?" He sat down beside her.

"For not seeing you. For not telling you that I confronted Lady Peterborough. She is indeed my mother."

The smile overtook him then. "I know. That's part of why I asked to see you today. Lucien told me." He glanced about. "Where is Miss Shaughnessy?"

"She's sketching a bird. It will take her a while—she's quite detailed with her work—so I came here to read." She closed the book in her lap. "I'm afraid I wasn't getting anywhere. Too distracted."

"I can only imagine. What happened with Lady Peterborough? I hope she was pleased to see you."

"She was, surprisingly. She hated giving me up, but her husband insisted. Indeed, she's terrified of him finding out about me. I don't know what kind of relationship we can possibly have, but I'm glad to know that she loved me. That she *loves* me."

He grinned. "I'm so happy for you."

"She also insisted I keep the ring and said she'd handle things with Lucien."

He angled himself toward her slightly, prompting her to do the same to him. "Lucien came to see me yesterday. That's why I sent you the note."

"What did he want?" Prudence suddenly felt uneasy. Well, more uneasy than she'd been feeling, which was a goodly amount of late.

"He came to inform me that he has been dispatched on an errand by his aunt—to obtain a dowry for the woman I'm to marry. Lucien didn't know who that was, only that she is his cousin."

Prudence's breath stalled as she stared at Bennet. Lady Peterborough was sending Lucien to see Warfield? Why hadn't she said so? When she'd indicated she would handle Lucien, Prudence never imagined that would include involving him in her problems. While they might be family, they weren't really. Because of her illegitimacy, their ties had to remain secret. She hadn't even considered acknowledging to him or to Cassandra that they were related, despite the fact that it would eat her up inside. "Lucien doesn't know I'm his cousin?"

Bennet shook his head. "He did ask me for the woman's identity, but I told him it wasn't my secret to tell." He paused, drawing a breath. "Pru, why are you seeking a dowry? We haven't ever discussed marriage." He kept his voice low and glanced around to ensure there was no one nearby. Confusion marred his features, of course, since this had to be rather shocking.

She turned her head so that she wasn't looking at him except from the corner of her eye. "No, we haven't discussed it."

"Are you trying to solve my money problems?" he asked. "While I appreciate that, I can't accept it. I know you don't want to marry. The fact is, I've made an arrangement, just yesterday, to marry a widow, Mrs. Merryfield."

She jerked her head back to face him and only barely kept her jaw from dropping. He was betrothed? She oughtn't be shocked or upset. He'd been clear from the moment he'd kidnapped her that he needed to marry for money as soon as possible. She'd known this was coming. That didn't make it any easier since she wanted him most desperately. Yes, she *wanted* to marry him. If he would have her.

Despite clenching her jaw, she managed to say, "I see. I hope you'll be very happy together."

Was she really not going to tell him there might be baby? *Might* was the word that gave her pause. She was going to all this trouble to get a dowry—or Lucien was—but what if there wasn't really a baby? But if she waited to be absolutely certain, it would be too late.

Furthermore, there *wasn't* a dowry yet. What if Lucien wasn't successful? Would she expect Bennet to marry her if there was no dowry and only the probability of a baby? It was far too much to ask.

"I was just trying to help you," she said, her throat dry. "I'm glad you've found a happy solution."

Bennet frowned, lines creasing his brow. "This isn't about happiness. Mrs. Merryfield has the funds I require, and she likes the idea of being a viscountess."

"Then you are both getting what you want," Prudence said, trying to sound supportive.

"I'm getting what I *need*." His voice was a low rasp. "Not what I want." His eyes fixed on her. The desire burning in their depths was unmistakable.

Perhaps she *could* tell him…

"There you are, Prudence," Kat said, bustling toward them, her drawing paper and board tucked under her arm.

Prudence rose hurriedly. "You're finished already?"

"No, but I'll have to come back another day. I just can't get the drawing to come out right." Kat sounded frustrated. And distracted. She didn't even make eye contact with Bennet, who'd risen from the bench.

"Lord Glastonbury happened to stroll into the museum and was kind enough to visit with me," Prudence explained.

Bennet bowed to Kat. "Good afternoon, Miss Shaughnessy. It's a pleasure to see you again." He turned to Prudence and took her hand. "I'm delighted to have been able to spend time with you, Miss Lancaster."

He sounded so earnest, and his touch reached straight into her soul, effortlessly reminding her of their time at Riverview. How could such a period be so fleeting and yet so wonderfully memorable?

"Likewise, my lord." She gave him a brief curtsey, then withdrew her hand before her entire body tried to sway toward him. That she would never kiss him again—worse, that Mrs. Merryfield would do so for the rest of their days— made her want to rage.

Instead, she pivoted and left the museum with Kat, at a loss for what to do. The dowry was no longer necessary, unless she wanted to trap some unsuspecting man and pretend the child that she was probably carrying was his. But she would never do that, not even to save her child from the stain of illegitimacy. Better to escape to America or the continent and reinvent herself as a widow.

Her back prickled as if Bennet was staring at her. Perhaps

he was. She wouldn't turn to look. She had to keep moving forward.

~

*M*usicales were not something Bennet particularly enjoyed. However, when one's invitations all but dried up, one went to a musicale to which one was invited. Particularly when one's betrothed—how he suddenly disliked that word—sent a note ensuring you would be there.

As he walked upstairs to the drawing room, he indulged the memory of when Prudence was his betrothed. It hadn't been real, but it had felt wonderfully genuine.

"Good evening, Glastonbury," Mrs. Merryfield greeted him. She stood near the top of the stairs as if she'd been waiting for him to arrive. Elegantly dressed, her dark hair swept into a neat chignon, she didn't smile, but her eyes gleamed with approval. Or perhaps importance. Actually, he realized he had a very hard time reading her. That was probably not a good thing between spouses.

"Good evening, Mrs. Merryfield," he said, wondering if he'd ever feel comfortable calling her Margaret or whatever nickname she preferred. He suspected there was no nickname. He couldn't envision her as Peggy or Margie or Meg or anything else but staunchly Margaret.

He offered her his arm and wondered if he'd ever feel anything when she touched him. He also wondered what she would say when he refused to finish inside her when they shared a bed.

Suppressing a twitch of distaste, he quickly ushered that thought from his mind. Perhaps they wouldn't even have to share a bed since they wouldn't be having any children.

"I'm quite looking forward to Sunday." Now she smiled,

briefly, her lips tightly pressed together. Bennet didn't think he'd ever seen her teeth—not completely. Were they horribly crooked? It was hard not to compare her to Prudence, whose smile made him want to grin like a boy who'd just been given chocolate.

Bennet didn't respond as they moved into the drawing room. Tonight's musicale was to be a quartet from Edinburgh. "Do you think the music will be lively?" he asked, diverting the conversation from anything to do with their impending nuptials.

"Do you expect them to play a reel?" She sniggered. "There's no dancing tonight."

Pity, for he enjoyed a good Scottish reel. Did Prudence know how to dance one?

He led Mrs. Merryfield into the room, and she withdrew her hand from his arm. Pivoting, Bennet sucked in a breath. Prudence had just come in with the Wexfords. He hadn't expected to see her. It didn't look as if Miss Shaughnessy was with her. How peculiar that she would come alone. Well, not alone. She was with Lord and Lady Wexford.

"Did you hear me, Glastonbury?"

Blinking, Bennet turned his head toward Mrs. Merryfield. "If you'll excuse me, I need to speak with someone." He gave her his brightest smile, then took himself off toward the new arrivals, who'd moved toward the seating area.

Immediately, he acknowledged that he shouldn't have left the woman he was going to marry to speak with the woman who'd captured every part of his imagination—along with every part of his body. Prudence looked lovely tonight, her blonde hair styled with green ribbon that matched the green of her simple but exquisite gown. The silver trimming brought out a shimmer in her sage eyes. He could have drowned in them quite happily.

"Good evening, Miss Lancaster." He bowed to her and

took her hand before realizing he'd completely cocked that up by not addressing Lady Wexford first. He never forgot that sort of thing. What was wrong with him?

Pivoting to Lady Wexford, who stood between Prudence and Wexford, he bowed more deeply. "Forgive me for not addressing you first, but I'm afraid Miss Lancaster deserved my immediate attention—she looks splendid this evening." He glanced toward Prudence, whose mouth quirked into a small, secretive smile.

"No forgiveness is necessary," Lady Wexford said cheerfully. "I am quite pleased for Prudence to be the center of attention."

"I don't care for that," Prudence said quietly, hastening to add "But this is fine—because I know all of you. I only mean that I wouldn't like to draw attention from others."

Bennet wanted to tell her that he would keep her safe from that, from everything, but he did nothing of the sort. "Is Miss Shaughnessy not here with you this evening?"

Lady Wexford adjusted one of her gloves. "No, she vehemently changed her mind and decided to stay home."

"'Vehemently' is an excellent description," Wexford said with a shake of his head.

"And since Prudence was already dressed, we thought she should come with us." Lady Wexford smiled at her former companion. "It's almost as it was before."

"Except for you being married," Prudence said drily.

Lady Wexford chuckled. "Well, yes, except for that." She glanced about the drawing room, which was rapidly filling with people. "Have you seen Lucien, by chance?"

"I have not," Bennet replied, wondering if he'd returned from his errand to visit the Viscount Warfield. Did that mean he was making progress? Perhaps they were working out the settlement agreement.

Cold sweat broke out along his nape and shoulder blades.

His gaze darted to where his betrothed—he suppressed a shudder—stood speaking with another lady. Then he looked to Prudence, serenely beautiful in her spectacular evening gown. Except in his mind's eye, he saw her in a simple dress with an apron, working in Mrs. Logan's kitchen at Riverview. She was as lovely to him in any setting, in any costume. Or in none at all.

Of course he would marry Prudence instead of Mrs. Merryfield. If he had to marry anyone at all, and he did, he would choose her.

He suddenly needed to touch her, to hold her, to kiss her. Someone came to speak with the Wexfords, and Bennet took the opportunity to move closer to Prudence. He bent his head toward her ear and whispered, "Meet me in the garden when the musicale starts."

He gave her a slight nod, then left the drawing room before she could refuse. Bennet made his way downstairs and out to the garden. A few people stood talking near the doors, but they went inside, leaving him alone.

After waiting what seemed an interminable amount of time, he heard the beginning strains of the quartet. He looked toward the door, expectant. Perhaps she wasn't coming. Just because he hadn't given her a chance to decline didn't mean she would do his bidding.

He should have asked her instead of demanding. But he needed to see her. Did she not need to see him? Apparently not.

Frustrated, his shoulders slumped, and he turned to walk through the garden.

"Bennet?"

Swinging back around, he saw Prudence framed just outside the doorway. He strode toward her, but she met him halfway. Heedless of anything and anyone, he swept her into his arms and kissed her. She threw her arms around his neck and held him tightly as he lifted her against him.

He opened one eye to make sure they were still alone, then pulled her into the shadows at the side of the garden where a tree would obscure them from the house. There, he kissed her again, his tongue tasting hers as he longed for far more than they could share in a garden during a musicale.

She was suddenly gone from him. His body went from full arousal to confusion.

Her face was pale in the light spilling from the house into the garden. "I think I'm carrying a child."

The words tumbled from her mouth and slammed into him like rocks.

He stumbled back, and if not for the tree, he might have collapsed completely. "What did you say?" he whispered, his pulse racing and his insides twisting.

"I know you were careful at Riverview, but it seems I may be with child."

Seems. May be. These were not words of confidence.

He took solace in her uncertainty. "You aren't sure, then?"

"Not entirely, which is why I didn't tell you yesterday. I didn't want you to feel entrapped, especially when you've found what you need." She sounded cold, which was how he felt at the moment. "I feel badly about this. We should never have shared a bed. I shouldn't have asked you to." Her cheeks flushed bright with color, and she looked away from him.

Bennet took her hand. "You didn't ask me to do anything I wasn't eager to. I was careful." But even he knew the method wasn't foolproof, no matter how cautious one was. "Have you seen a physician?"

She stared at him, blanching as quickly as she'd turned red. "Of course not. I'm unwed."

He was an ass for asking such a thing. Now he understood why she was seeking the dowry. It wasn't to help him, but to save her. "This is why you want the dowry."

Nodding, she again looked away from him, but only briefly. When her eyes met his once more, they flamed with determination and self-preservation. "I don't want my child to be illegitimate."

Like her. She didn't say it, but he heard the fear in her voice.

"I understand." He took a breath, trying to slow his speeding heart. "No one knows that about you, however. You are legitimately the child of the Lancasters."

"I know. Trust me, however, when I say it matters. I can't expect you to understand."

"Because my life is so easy and enviable." He realized he sounded sarcastic and that he was inviting criticism, but she knew nothing about his reality. Nor would he tell her.

Except she was to be his wife. Or so he'd decided, even before hearing this distressing news. She wasn't Mrs. Merryfield, who would spend her time in London away from his family. Prudence would be at Aberforth Place, and she would see everything. *Everything.*

Bennet pressed back against the tree as panic swirled inside him. When she saw what they could be like, what *he* could be like or worse, end up like, she'd want to run far away.

"Your life is easy and far more enviable than most," she said quietly. "But I understand you have difficulties. This is why I hesitated to tell you about the child. I know how badly you need money."

"This is about so much more than money," he whispered. "It's complicated—my family is *complicated.* You have no idea the mess my father left me."

"No, I don't, but perhaps you'll tell me. *If* my half brother provides the dowry."

He should tell her. Right now. But the words simply wouldn't come. He'd never told anyone. Not even retainers. When new ones were hired, he left it to Mrs. Marian, the housekeeper, or Eakes, the butler and Mrs. Marian's brother, to explain the situation to them. Not that there'd been many new retainers. Aberforth Place had a small staff, and not just because there was no money. It was easier to keep things quiet when fewer people knew the truth.

Prudence took a stuttered breath. "I understand that without the dowry, you can't wed me. Still, I wanted you to know about the baby. I didn't think it was right to keep it from you."

A baby. The one thing he'd never wanted. What if the child was like his father or his Aunt Agatha? How could he bring him or her into this world knowing that he might damn them to a life of anger, delusion, or misery? He wanted to tell Prudence that he would gladly marry her, that he eagerly awaited the birth of their child, but he was bound up with fear. Their child could be afflicted, and he still wasn't sure how badly the sickness would affect him as he grew older. It seemed to worsen with everyone, some declining more quickly than others.

He also wanted to tell her that he was glad she'd told him, but the shameful truth was that he was terrified. And he couldn't admit it, not without revealing everything.

"Bennet, did you hear what I said?" she asked, breaking into the tumult of his thoughts. "I don't expect you to marry me if there's no dowry. I don't really expect you to marry me at all. I would never want to entrap you."

That was how he could avoid this problem of telling her about his family—if he didn't marry her. Which meant he'd marry Mrs. Merryfield. He'd never felt more cornered or more frantic in his entire life. The dreams he'd had of

Prudence pressing flowers with Aunt Flora were just that—illusions of a life he'd never have.

Memories of Bennet's father filled his mind. Wide-eyed and panting, he'd rifle through his desk for something—usually money or something important he'd misplaced. This was followed by a rage or uncontrollable despair. Or, in rare cases, a giddy euphoria because he'd found what he was looking for. Those were the best memories because in those moments, he'd seemed happy. The reality was that he'd never been happy. And Bennet wasn't going to ruin her chance for happiness by sharing his family's affliction with her. Perhaps she need never know the real and horrible truth. There was a chance, however small, that their child wouldn't be affected.

As emotion coiled inside Bennet and sapped his control, he fretted the worst would come, that he would succumb to fury or tumble into hopelessness. This situation certainly *felt* hopeless.

Bennet reached back and flattened his palm against the bark of the tree, pressing his hand into the rough grooves. He searched for and somehow found a piece of clarity amidst the tumult in his head. "Lucien will ensure you get the dowry. He's not a man who gives up easily."

"You don't know Warfield," she said darkly, her lip curling slightly. "He's as heartless as anyone can be."

Dowry or not, Bennet would marry her. He might not want a child, but it seemed he was going to have one. "We should still get married." He realized that wasn't a proposal any woman wanted to hear. Nor was the one he'd given Mrs. Merryfield when he'd proposed a "mutually beneficial union." Prudence deserved better.

He took his hand from the tree and drew a deep breath. "Marry me, Prudence." He glanced toward her abdomen, wondering if there truly was a babe within her. His babe. He could be a father. How he wanted there to be joy. But there was only fear.

"What if there's no dowry?" She paused, her anguished gaze meeting his. "Or no baby?" Her voice squeaked on the last syllable.

Then he would be poor but relieved. "We will manage. At Riverview, we demonstrated our ability to clean, cook, and work hard. We'll survive."

Her features softened, and he saw in her the relief he couldn't possibly feel. "Yes, I'll marry you. What about your other…arrangement?"

He would call on Mrs. Merryfield tomorrow—after he obtained a special license to wed Prudence. He couldn't imagine Margaret would be happy, but she would have to understand. It wasn't as if anything had been formally announced, and the banns had not yet been read, of course. "Don't worry about that. Just ready yourself to become Lady Glastonbury on Saturday, assuming I can procure the special license tomorrow." He hoped that wouldn't be a problem.

Her eyes widened. "So soon?"

He couldn't decide if she seemed surprised or tense or apprehensive, or all those things. "The sooner, the better, right?"

He wanted to ask how she was feeling, but realized it didn't matter how either of them felt. Neither wanted to marry or have children, yet here they were. They would make the best of it. At least they liked each other a great deal —or so it seemed to him.

"Yes, I suppose that's for the best." She sounded uncertain, but again, he didn't want to ask her how she felt.

He pulled her into his arms and kissed her forehead. "This isn't what we planned or perhaps what we wanted, but I think others marry with far less on their side," he said pragmatically, hoping to convey the positive aspects of this shocking and perhaps unwelcome development. "We enjoyed each other's company at Riverview, didn't we?"

"After a time," she admitted, provoking him to smile.

"And we certainly enjoyed each other in bed. Or did I imagine that?"

"You did not. I enjoyed that very much."

He pulled back and looked down at her. "Then this is a very good start."

His lips found hers, and he managed to keep the despair at bay.

CHAPTER 16

*B*ennet stood in Mrs. Merryfield's elegant drawing room on Bruton Street not far from Berkeley Square. Her house was larger and far better appointed than Bennet's. He felt the financial difference between them quite keenly. This would have bothered him before.

Before what?

Before Prudence. More accurately, before the time they'd spent at Riverview, where he'd glimpsed a simpler and not unwelcome life.

Now he would marry Prudence and they might need to live that simply. He found he was not upset about that. Oh, he still had to find a way to pay for Aunt Agatha's care. He refused to do what Aunt Judith suggested. He wouldn't sacrifice whatever comfort his aunt enjoyed to save money. That was the problem. He didn't want to ask any of his relatives to change the way they lived because of his father's mistakes. They shouldn't have to suffer. Which was why he found himself in the dire position of having to marry an heiress.

Or not, as he was about to disengage himself from Mrs. Merryfield. He was surprisingly calm about that.

Because he knew it was the right thing to do. The thought of marrying her had done nothing but make him agitated, even if it had seemed the easiest choice.

Mrs. Merryfield strode in, her gait confident and her features set into a pleasant expression of welcome. She was a handsome woman, and in other circumstances, perhaps Bennet would have found her more attractive—she possessed strength and intelligence, which he admired. "Glastonbury," she said. "What a charming surprise."

A bead of dread worked its way up his spine. "May we sit for a moment?" He gestured toward a smaller seating area at one side of the large room.

"Certainly." She went to take a chair—not the settee where they might have sat together. Bennet was glad, for he didn't particularly want to sit close to her to deliver this news.

He took a deep breath and got to the heart of things. "I'm afraid I've come to dissolve our arrangement."

She looked as if she'd frozen. She didn't blink or swallow or move in any way. She didn't even seem to breathe. At last, she spoke. "Did I hear you correctly? You no longer wish to marry me?"

"I'm afraid I find myself in another situation that would prevent me from wedding you. It's not your fault, nothing you have done. I am deeply sorry to cause you any distress."

Her eyes narrowed slightly. "We made an agreement. The settlement is being drawn up today."

He knew that and was thankful he hadn't yet signed it. "I came to tell you as soon as possible. I do apologize for the trouble." He didn't flinch from the rising anger in her gaze.

"This is highly infuriating," she said tightly, her hands clasped together in her lap. "We had an agreement," she repeated. "Furthermore, you need my money." Her nostrils flared. "Did you find a more preferable bride? Someone in the peerage, I'm sure."

"It's not like that. I am going to marry someone else, but not because of money." He wanted to be honest with her—she deserved that.

"What, you fell in love?" Her lip curled. "How foolish you are to choose that over security. Perhaps your current situation is more due to your ineptitude than you would like to admit. Blame your father all you like, but if you would choose love over security, you can't be very astute."

Her vitriol surprised him, but then he didn't know her very well. And he didn't like what she said. What if he was making a bad decision, just as his father nearly always did? Mrs. Merryfield was the better choice: she already had children, she would hardly come to Aberforth Place, and her money was assured. But Prudence...and the baby.

Bennet swallowed, hating the discomfort roiling in his chest. "If it makes you feel better to malign me, please do so. This is rather inexcusable of me, but it must be done." Even if it was a poor choice. He didn't think it was—and perhaps this meant he really was like his father, that he couldn't escape the same end. He clenched his hand into a fist and flexed it back flat again.

"Must it?" Her voice rose. "As I said, we made an agreement. Where is your loyalty, your honor? Have you no shame at all?"

His ire stirred, and his body tensed. "I am doing this because of honor." Trying to redirect the conversation and hopefully extract himself as quickly as possible, he said, "At least the betrothal wasn't announced. There will be no ill effect on you."

Her jaw clenched. "I told my friends, my family, my *children*."

Bennet flinched. He'd met her younger child, a daughter,

briefly. Ten years old, she was sober and exceedingly polite. "I am sorry to disappoint you."

"Then don't. Keep your word, and we'll forget this unfortunate conversation occurred."

Anger coiled within him. "While I understand this is difficult, I cannot continue with our arrangement." Honestly, he hadn't thought she would take it this badly—it wasn't as if he was breaking her heart or causing her to lose anything.

"Perhaps I will consult with my solicitor and see what he says."

Was she threatening him? Now he was becoming well and truly angry. "I have tried to be polite, but your continued refusal to accept this change is becoming tiresome. We will not be married, and that is the end of it." He stood, more than ready to depart.

She also got to her feet. "You do disappoint me, Glastonbury. I liked you. I thought we would suit very well. This was a mutually beneficial agreement, and you can tell me you're a man of your word and of honor, but that is simply not true. You're a fraud and a liar, and given what I know of your father, perhaps I've escaped certain disaster."

It was the one thing she could say that would hit him hard and square. Yes, it was entirely likely she'd just avoided the biggest mistake of her life. And perhaps she was right about his honor. He'd demonstrated a clear lack of it when he'd arranged to have a lady kidnapped. Desperation was an ugly thing—he was seeing it now in Mrs. Merryfield.

He felt bad that he'd aroused this in her. He was trying to do the right thing, but she would pay the price. "I truly am sorry. I didn't want to disappoint you—or hurt you—but it's precisely because of my honor that I must wed someone else."

Her eyes widened. "She's with child, isn't she?"

Christ, how had she guessed that? Bennet said nothing.

"You could at least show me the grace of honesty."

He'd tried to. "I'd rather not discuss it." He ought to deny it, but when his and Prudence's baby came so quickly after they wed, he'd be caught in a lie. He didn't want to be what Mrs. Merryfield had called him—a liar or a fraud. But wasn't he? His family was a shameful secret he couldn't bear to share.

"Then I shall take that as confirmation," she said coldly. "You've behaved reprehensibly and now plan to throw me over for some stupid chit. Anyone foolish enough to give herself to a man outside the bonds of marriage deserves whatever happens to her."

Fury erupted in Bennet sharp and fast. He lunged toward her. "Shut your mouth. Don't speak of her. Ever."

She jerked back, her face pale. Fear glazed her eyes, and Bennet felt a surge of self-loathing so strong that he nearly shouted out his rage.

Instead, he spun on his heel and quit the room.

The footman barely got the door open before Bennet strode through it into the gray afternoon. Stalking down Bruton Street, he tried to push the anger from him, the sense that he had no control. The feeling of loss and despair followed quickly, setting him even more on edge. No, he wouldn't let this happen. He wasn't a bad person; he wasn't lost in anger or emotion.

How he missed boxing. He needed to pour himself into physical exertion. Where was a storm with a resulting mess to clean up when one needed it?

After several minutes, he began to relax. At least that was done. It had gone incredibly poorly, but now he could move forward with Prudence. Into a terribly uncertain future.

~

*a*fter a lovely visit with Ada that morning, Prudence felt almost happy. Ada had been thrilled to hear that Prudence and Bennet would be wed and hadn't let the news that Prudence's dowry wasn't a certainty affect her sentiment. Prudence wished she could share that, but until Lucien returned with a confirmed dowry, she wouldn't be able to rid herself of anxiety.

And now she needed to tell Cassandra everything. *Everything.* Her anxiety tripled.

Oh stop, she told herself. Cassandra had stolen away with her husband on several occasions before they were wed. Prudence didn't know for certain what they'd been doing, but she could guess, and Cassandra wouldn't think less of her for what had happened with Bennet.

She supposed she didn't need to tell Cassandra everything, just that she was marrying Bennet. That was the important part, for she'd be leaving their employ as Kat's companion.

The moment of truth arrived as Cassandra glided into the sitting room. "Mrs. Forth said you wished to see me. Is all well?" Cassandra's brow was slightly creased.

Prudence was already seated in a chair and gestured to the settee near her. "Please sit. I've something important to tell you."

Cassandra went to sit, her ginger-colored skirts draping against the settee in an effortlessly elegant fashion. "I can't tell if this is good important or bad important."

"Good important, I think." Prudence managed a small smile. "I'm getting married. For real this time."

"Oh!" Cassandra lunged toward her, but paused, her expression confused. "Are you happy?"

While she hadn't ever thought of getting married, she couldn't deny she was happy to be marrying Bennet. It was difficult to acknowledge that—even to herself—when she very much doubted that he felt the same. "Yes."

"It took you too long to say that." Cassandra frowned and sat back down. "First you eloped, only to return saying it was a mistake, and now you are unenthusiastically announcing your plans to wed. Are you being forced into something? I hope you're going to tell me what's going on. I've been worried about you, Pru. You just haven't been the same since the aborted elopement."

Prudence took a deep breath. "I never planned to elope. I didn't even write that note."

Cassandra's jaw dropped. "Who did?"

This was the moment—tell her everything or not? Prudence decided to do the former. She had to—they were now truly family and though she'd promised Bennet she wouldn't reveal what happened, he'd have to understand that this was necessary. "The Viscount Glastonbury."

Cassandra's jaw dropped even farther. "*What?*"

"He'd planned to, ah, abduct you. The note was intended to be from you, explaining your disappearance. He felt confident you would be happy to elope with him."

Slumping back against the couch, Cassandra blinked once, then stared at Prudence. "I can scarcely credit this tale, but of course it's true." She sat up, straightening. "He abducted you instead?"

Prudence nodded. "It was because we switched cloaks. He instructed the men he hired to take the woman in the purple cloak."

Cassandra put her hand to her forehead. "My God, this is all my fault."

A laugh leapt from Prudence. "Hardly. This was entirely Bennet's fault, and he takes complete responsibility."

"*Bennet?*" Cassandra asked, her brows arching.

"We spent six days together near Hersham," Prudence

explained. "We were stranded because his coach required repair. Then the weather was terrible, and the roads were impassable. The storm was so bad that a tree fell on his coach, destroying it."

Cassandra gaped once more, her expression growing more incredulous with each revelation. Then she giggled, putting her hand to her mouth. "I'm sorry. I have to ask, was the coach repaired before it was ruined?"

Prudence's lips twitched. "I'm afraid so. He says he has the worst luck, and it's true."

Sobering, Cassandra, put her hand on her lap. "What did he do when he realized his men had taken the wrong woman?"

"He was quite disappointed," Prudence said wryly. "And most apologetic. You see, they'd bound me and put a gag in my mouth as well as a bag over my head."

Cassandra's gasp filled the room. "No! I can't believe you endured that and said nothing."

"When you say it like that, it sounds as though I should have said something, but I wasn't hurt. I was far more concerned about what my absence would mean for my reputation and my future chances for employment."

"You should know that I would always protect you—no matter what. We are friends, Pru."

They were more than that, but Prudence wasn't at that part yet. "I appreciate that."

"Why didn't you tell me the truth when you got back?"

"I didn't want anyone to know what Bennet had done. He was incredibly remorseful—almost irritatingly so, truth be told—and I wanted to see if I could return to my life without having to say what happened—for both our sakes."

"There is something you aren't saying," Cassandra said slyly, looking at her intently. "You keep calling Glastonbury, Bennet. He kidnapped you, and you went to great effort to protect him from all manner of trouble. If people knew what he'd done…" Her eyes widened once more. "Ruark can never know."

"Thank you for saying so," Prudence said. "I was hoping you would agree to that. I wanted to tell you the truth, but this isn't something anyone else needs to know."

"Agreed." Cassandra gave her head a shake. "Ruark might try to kill him. Or at least trounce him in a boxing match again. Yes, we'll keep this between us."

"Thank you. I'd also ask you not to let Bennet know that you're aware of what transpired. Trust me when I say you do not want to be on the receiving end of his regret." She rolled her eyes, and Cassandra laughed.

"You sound as if you know each other rather well."

"We do, I think." Prudence recognized there was much she didn't know about the man she was to marry. "In some ways more than others," she added with a meaningful look.

Cassandra stared at her a moment, then her nostrils flared, and she gave a single nod. "Ah. I understand." Once again, her features registered surprise. "Oh! You're marrying *him?*"

"I am."

"But… How?" Cassandra sputtered. "I mean, I thought he was desperate to wed an heiress."

"He was. He is. His financial troubles have not magically improved. In fact, when we parted before I returned to London, I gave him the only thing I had of value so he could sell it."

"What was that?"

"A ring my mother had given me. However, he couldn't bring himself to sell it, apparently, and wore it instead." She took a deep breath before relating the next part—perhaps the most important part of this confession. "Lucien recognized the crest on it and said it belonged to your family."

Cassandra's face scrunched briefly. "I remember my grandmother telling me about that ring. She was sorry there was no such tradition for me and was disappointed that my aunt hadn't birthed any girls to give it to." She focused on Prudence, drawing in a sharp breath. "Your mother gave it to you?"

"It was given to her by the woman who birthed me, and she passed it on to me before she died. Lady Peterborough is my true mother, and the former Viscount Warfield was my father."

Cassandra gaped at her. Then she suddenly smiled. "This means we're cousins."

"It does." Prudence smiled too.

This time when Cassandra lunged toward her, Prudence also rose from her chair. They embraced tightly, and Prudence felt wetness on her cheeks. To have a family was a gift she hadn't dared to imagine.

After several moments, they broke apart, but Prudence joined Cassandra on the settee so they could sit close.

"This is the very best news," Cassandra said, glowing with joy and...pride? "I've always wanted a sister, and I shall count a cousin as the same thing."

"I've always wanted a sibling too. My adoptive parents weren't able to have children—my mother didn't tell me that until she was dying. They adopted me, and she said it was the happiest day of their lives."

"How wonderful. I wish I'd known her," Cassandra said warmly. "Does Aunt Christina know who you are? She certainly never gave the indication that she did."

"She did not. Though, I had to go see her once Lucien recognized the crest. She admitted she'd never looked at me closely and that if she had, she would have realized how much I looked like the former Viscount Warfield."

Cassandra snorted. "Typical Aunt Christina." Then she

grimaced. "My apologies. I don't mean to disparage your mother."

"I can hardly think of her as my mother, especially when we can't have that kind of relationship. She made it clear that Peterborough would be furious if he finds out who I am."

"He's an ass," Cassandra said vehemently. "I forgive Aunt Christina most of her idiosyncrasies because I know she resides in a very unhappy union. I wish they would just live apart."

"Is that a possibility? She made it seem like she was completely under his control."

"That could very well be. Honestly, I don't know my uncle very well. I only saw him a few times a year, and even then it was for short periods—he never liked children. My father can't stand him. More than once, he's said he wished his sister had married someone else."

Prudence vaguely recalled the duke mentioning something like that. "Do you think that's why he was so keen to have her be your sponsor? He wanted to give her something to focus on away from Peterborough?"

"That's possible. It would certainly explain why he forgave her lack of attention as my sponsor."

Whereas Prudence had once found Lady Peterborough frustrating with regard to her blasé treatment of Cassandra, she now felt bad for the woman. Probably because she now knew the countess was her mother, but also because her life seemed quite sad. Suddenly, she wished they *could* have a deeper relationship.

Prudence returned her thoughts to the matter at hand—it was time for the final piece. "You see, the other reason I had to see her was to ask for money—and she wasn't able to help me because she couldn't risk her husband finding out."

"Why do you need money? I can help you, certainly."

"Specifically, I need a dowry—to marry Bennet."

"Oh! Of course. As you said, his financial situation has not changed." She frowned slightly. "Did you find a dowry? That's more than I can afford, unfortunately."

"Not as yet, but Lucien is apparently working on that. Lady Peterborough sent him to see my half brother and demand he settle a dowry on me."

"Oh, do stop calling her Lady Peterborough, please. Call her Christina or your mother—at least with me." She narrowed one eye. "If you're comfortable with that."

"Lady Peterborough is a mouthful," Prudence admitted with a smile. "I confess I was surprised that she offered to help me. I hated asking her for money."

"But it was necessary since you and Glastonbury had fallen in love and wished to marry." She made it sound like a fairy tale when it was anything but.

Prudence fidgeted with her dress. "Ah, that's not... That's not exactly right. Our time together at Riverview resulted in an unplanned situation. I believe I'm carrying his child. Marriage became a necessity. Except he needs money, and I have none to give him."

Again, Cassandra's expression registered shock. Recovering, she took Prudence's hands and squeezed them gently. "Oh, my dear. How wonderful for you, but how terrifying too."

"I was foolish to put myself in this position," Prudence said.

"Don't say that. We've all been swept away by passion or longing or whatever it was that prompted you to be intimate with him. I'm certainly not blameless."

"He took precautions, but nothing is guaranteed, so here we are."

"So you aren't in love?" Cassandra looked crestfallen.

"I don't think so." Prudence hadn't indulged such thoughts because they involved emotion. Particularly emotions she preferred to leave locked away. But that was before, when she'd never imagined a husband or children. Shouldn't she at least consider opening herself up to that now? "I was attracted to him during the time we spent together. I saw an opportunity for a night of…passion, and I took it. I never planned to marry *or* have children. I was content in my life as companion. I adored working for Fiona and for you and now for Kat." She hesitated, her voice lowering. "I admit I was glad to be on the periphery of Society. Ever since I learned that my father was a viscount, I wanted to see what it would have been like to live that life. I didn't want it—I wasn't born to it. But I was curious if it was truly in my blood."

Cassandra's gaze was so warm and sympathetic. "I think I can understand that curiosity or at least that question of belonging. Family—or the lack thereof—makes us feel different things. Growing up without my mother, I was always so obsessed with my friends' mothers, with their relationships."

Prudence was grateful for Cassandra's understanding. "I'm not even sure I can manage being a viscountess. I feel as though I've entrapped Bennet in this. He needs money, yet he's agreed to marry me without knowing if Warfield will provide a dowry."

"Then perhaps he does love you," Cassandra said with a smile.

"Oh, do stop with your romantic notions," Prudence scoffed, thinking Cassandra and Ada would get on quite well together. "He's doing what he must because he's a good man."

"Who kidnaps people," Cassandra muttered.

"Who's *sorry* about kidnapping people," Prudence amended.

They laughed, and Cassandra let go of Prudence's hands.

Prudence quickly sobered. "We haven't heard from

Lucien, so I'm worried it isn't going well with Warfield. Which was to be expected since he's a horrible, selfish person."

"You know him?"

"I met him once when I went to ask him for a job. My mother had told me that when I was given to them, two things were conveyed. One was the ring that belonged to Christina. The second was the identity of my real father and the message that if I ever found myself in dire circumstances, I should ask him for help. Unfortunately, he had died, so I saw his son instead."

"And he turned you out, his own half sister? I knew he was disagreeable, but this makes him an utter blackguard."

"I didn't get the chance to tell him who I was. He threw me out, called me a pathetic beggar. Fortunately, I encountered Lucien on my way out—he'd gone to visit Warfield."

"They are friends. Or were, anyway," Cassandra clarified. "They fought together in Spain, but it seems Warfield was quite damaged. Inside and out."

Prudence recalled the scarred left side of his face, the cruel set of his lips, the coldness in his hazel eyes. His inside had matched his outside, beauty ruined so that he'd become a beast.

"I have to think Lucien will return empty-handed." Prudence fidgeted with her dress again, unable to make herself stop. "If that happens, I don't know how I can go through with marrying Bennet. As I said, I feel like a swindler for trapping him like this."

"You've done no such thing! He was an equal partner in making this baby, and he has a responsibility. I won't let him shirk it." Her sherry-colored eyes narrowed with determination.

The butler coughed, startling them both. Prudence

suffered a moment's panic, wondering how long he'd been there.

"Lord Glastonbury is here to see Miss Lancaster," he said. "He is waiting in the drawing room."

"Thank you, Bart," Cassandra said. As he departed, she stood and looked down at Prudence. "Do you need help getting up?"

"Not yet," Prudence replied drily. "I'm not even completely sure I'm with child, but all signs seem to point in that direction. I will feel terrible if I'm not. Bennet actually had an arrangement with a wealthy widow that he is breaking in order to marry me."

"You must cease thinking you aren't good enough for him. Or for any of us. You're my cousin. I was already willing to defend you and advocate for you on any matter, but now it is imperative. We are family, Pru." She squared her shoulders. "Now, let us go and meet your betrothed."

Prudence stood and followed Cassandra from the sitting room. However, she nearly ran into her as Cassandra suddenly spun about. "We shall need a story to explain your sudden marriage to Glastonbury. We can't tell everyone the truth of it, but my goodness, it makes a riveting tale." Cassandra grinned. "So romantic."

It wasn't either. But she didn't correct Cassandra. "I don't have any brilliant ideas."

"Let me think on it," Cassandra said confidently. "I'll come up with something." She linked her arm with Prudence's, and they walked downstairs to the drawing room on the first floor.

Bennet stood with his back to them, his hands clasped behind him. His wide shoulders perfectly fit his dark blue coat, and his buff breeches hugged the contours of his muscular legs. Prudence couldn't deny the thrill that raced through her when she thought of the nights they would spend together.

Forever.

He turned, and the view was even better. His bright blond hair was styled carefully, an artful curl grazing his forehead, his square jaw twitching slightly as his lips spread into a slow, appreciative smile the moment his blue-green gaze settled on Prudence.

Cassandra strode forward and sent her fist into his belly, doubling him over with a grunt. "That's for kidnapping my cousin, you brute. We'll never speak of it again." She turned to Prudence. "I'm sorry. I couldn't help myself."

Prudence smothered a smile. Bennet's brows arched as he looked to Prudence.

"I told her everything," she said to him. "It seemed necessary. Don't worry, she's not going to tell anyone, especially Wexford. I don't wish to be a widow as soon as I'm wed."

"That's a relief," he said, straightening. He smoothed his hand down his coat. "Has your husband been teaching you boxing, Lady Wexford? That was a well-placed blow. Quite powerful too."

"Not at all. I'm a natural, apparently." Cassandra gave him a smug smile, and Prudence nearly laughed again. She felt an absurd pride that this woman was her cousin. "You may as well call me Cassandra since we are to be related. When is this blissful occasion to happen?"

"In fact, I have just procured the special license and have secured the vicar for tomorrow morning."

Prudence's gut clenched. It was really happening, then.

"You should marry here," Cassandra said, tapping her chin with her forefinger. "I will ensure you have a lavish breakfast. We'll invite Fiona and Overton. Who else?" She looked to Prudence.

"My friend Ada Treadway—she works at the Phoenix Club. She's the person I spend my Saturday mornings with."

Cassandra's eyes lit. "Aha! I assumed you spent those mornings with the man with whom you eloped." She cast a scowl toward Bennet. She might not mention it again, but she wouldn't soon let him forget his transgression. Prudence found it rather sweet, as if they really were like sisters.

"We should also invite Evie Renshaw." Prudence wanted her to be there. "And probably Christina," she added softly.

"Yes, she will want to see you wed—even if the world is only aware that you are my former companion. Do you mind if I invite Con and Sabrina?" Cassandra gave her a sincere look. "Do you plan to tell him you're our cousin?"

"I hadn't considered it." Prudence had so much in her head. It was hard to think of everything. "Lucien doesn't even know yet. He knows Bennet is marrying his cousin, but isn't yet aware of who that is. Bennet refused to tell him. He said it wasn't his secret to share."

Cassandra looked at him with admiration. "Perhaps you aren't a blackguard after all. For that and for marrying Prudence when you don't know yet whether she'll have a dowry or not. I'm so glad you're doing right by my cousin."

His brow furrowed. He looked toward Prudence. "There's still no word, then?"

She shook her head, feeling his anxiety as strongly as she felt her own.

"So we're settled that you'll have the ceremony and breakfast here tomorrow?" Cassandra said.

"Thank you," Prudence said, a surprising but welcome love surging for this woman who was now her family. She was getting married, and her *family* would be there.

"My family will also be coming," Bennet said. "My aunt and great-aunt are visiting from Bath."

Prudence was surprised to hear that. "You didn't mention that."

"There's been a great deal happening at once," he said with a faint smile.

"Indeed," she agreed.

Cassandra beamed at them. "Excellent, we'll have plenty of room. I must get moving on these plans, so please excuse me!" She hastened from the room, closing the door behind her.

"That was thoughtful of her," Bennet murmured. He walked quickly to Prudence and pulled her into his arms.

She went willingly, glad for his touch and his embrace. He kissed her softly, and she thought in that moment that everything would be all right.

Laying her head on his shoulder, she asked, "How did things go with ending your arrangement?"

"It's done, and that's all that matters."

Prudence pulled back and looked up at him. "That doesn't sound as if it went well."

"It doesn't matter." He gave her an encouraging smile, then kissed her again, his hands moving over her back as he held her close.

After several minutes, they parted, panting slightly. "This is strange, but nice. I suppose we can do this whenever we want after tomorrow."

"Yes, this and many other things." He stroked her jaw and gazed into her eyes. "I look forward to reclaiming your body, Pru."

She shivered with anticipation even as her anxiety persisted. She couldn't forget the circumstances of their unwanted union or the uncertainty they faced. "You can still change your mind if there's no dowry. I'll understand."

"Not a chance." He kissed her again, and she surrendered to a moment of joy.

CHAPTER 17

*B*ennet arrived early at the Wexfords' house and sent his secondhand coach back to pick up his aunts. They'd been shocked to hear he was getting married, but delighted. Probably because they assumed that meant he would be getting a settlement upon the marriage. He hadn't told them otherwise.

Hopefully, he wouldn't have to. He hoped Lucien was already here with news that the dowry had been obtained.

His mind returned to his aunts and what Prudence would think of them. He'd instructed both Aunt Judith and Great-Aunt Esther that they weren't to discuss anything regarding their family with his bride. They'd asked if he planned to hide the affliction and how he could possibly do that while taking her to Aberforth Place.

He couldn't, of course, and he was only delaying the inevitable. However, there was so much happening right now, and with the weight of the unknown dowry hanging over them, he thought it best to put off telling her about their family's illness. That he dreaded doing so only made the decision easier.

Then Aunt Judith asked if he planned to tell her about Agatha. Was there really a need?

Before he could think too deeply about that, the butler showed Bennet to Wexford's study, where the Irishman was waiting. "Morning, Glastonbury. Seems like we just had a wedding by special license." He chuckled.

"Yours, you mean," Bennet said. "I wasn't invited." He'd been stranded at Riverview with Prudence anyway. He wouldn't trade that for anything.

"An oversight, I'm sure." Wexford's gaze simmered with humor. Apparently, he truly had forgiven Bennet for his behavior at the fight. He wouldn't do the same if he knew Bennet had tried to kidnap his wife. He was glad he'd only had to suffer an excellent uppercut from Cassandra.

"Anything from Lucien?" Bennet asked, hating that he sounded as tense as he felt—as though he were strung out on a rack.

"Nothing. Cass did invite him to the wedding this morning."

Bennet wondered if her invitation had included the name of the bride or if Lucien would be surprised when he arrived.

"I'm still so surprised that you and Prudence managed to fall in love under our very noses." Wexford grinned. "How wonderful for you both."

That was the story Cassandra had concocted. There was no other way to explain the haste of their marriage, particularly given the lack of dowry, of which this intimate group of people was, of course, aware. They had to say it was a case of true love. There hadn't been time for Bennet to ask Prudence what she thought of that.

Just then, Lucien stepped into the study. Bennet's neck dampened with sweat as anxiety flared through him.

The moment Lucien's mouth pressed into a thin line, his lips almost disappearing, Bennet knew. Lucien looked

Bennet in the eye. "I'm afraid I have nothing to show for my efforts. I'm sorry, Glastonbury."

Bennet managed to nod as his emotions swirled toward the dreaded despair. "You did your best, I'm sure."

"He was immovable." Lucien scowled. "He is not the man I knew. I hate having to tell your bride that he didn't want to help her. His own sister!" His lip curled with disgust.

Bennet appreciated the man's outrage on Prudence's behalf, but then she was also his cousin. "I take it you know whom I'm marrying?"

"Cass included her name in the invitation, along with the fact that she was thrilled to welcome our new cousin into her family. I can't quite believe Prudence is our cousin and that you and she happened to fall in love. What a strange and wonderful life this is."

Bennet didn't find it particularly wonderful at the moment. Now that he knew there would be no money, his mind was scrambling with how to pay for Aunt Agatha, for Aunt Judith and Great-Aunt Esther. Perhaps he should move Cousin Frances into the house at Aberforth Place as Great-Aunt Esther had suggested. But the thought of asking Prudence to deal with that gave him pause. She had no idea what she was getting into.

He should tell her so that she could cry off if she wanted to. Only he knew she wouldn't. Because of the baby. She would protect the child from being illegitimate at any cost, and he didn't blame her.

The circumstances of their marriage were a muddled, complicated, fretful mess. True love indeed.

"What are you going to do?" Wexford asked, looking at Bennet.

"If you're asking whether I still plan to marry Prudence, of course I do."

Wexford seemed puzzled. "That wasn't a question for me,

given that you love her. I mean, what are you going to do about your financial situation?"

"The same thing I've been doing—managing." He wasn't going to discuss this with them. They couldn't understand what it was like.

Prudence would be shocked when she arrived at Aberforth Place to find the skeleton staff and the empty rooms. Would she mind not spending time in London during the Season? He wouldn't be able to afford an appropriate wardrobe for her. That meant they'd be apart since he had responsibilities in the Lords.

God, they just hadn't thought this through. There hadn't been time. The baby had changed—and rushed—everything.

Feeling overwhelmed, he excused himself to go outside. He needed air. And several thousand pounds.

Strolling to the farthest corner away from the house, he crossed his arms over his chest and frowned at the ground. He'd barely allowed himself to think of the baby. What if the poor child was like his or her grandfather? Or worse, like his or her Great-Aunt Agatha—consigned to an asylum by the age of twenty?

He began to sweat again, his breath coming faster as panic and fear seethed within him. His control began to slip. But he couldn't succumb to emotion right now, not when he was minutes away from marrying Prudence.

Her face rose in his mind. He thought of the way she'd scowled at him after she'd first arrived at Riverview, how she'd told him he wasn't sharing her bed. Then, days later, she'd invited him to do so, utterly shocking and seducing him with her passion and sweetness.

They might not be star-crossed lovers, but he wanted her as he'd never wanted anyone else. That was something, wasn't it?

He just hoped it was enough.

≈

The ring on Prudence's finger felt heavy, the gold shining brilliantly in the light streaming through the window. It was a beautiful spring morning, perfect for a wedding.

She could hardly believe she was married, let alone the Viscountess Glastonbury. *A viscountess.*

"I'm sorry there isn't a diamond or an emerald," Bennet said, coming up behind her. The ceremony had ended a short while ago, followed by a champagne toast, and now they were waiting to go into Cassandra's hastily planned but certain to be elegant breakfast. "Someday, I'll replace it with something more befitting your station."

She looked up at him. "Some would argue this fits my station perfectly. And that I have vastly overstepped." She quirked her brow to accompany her sarcasm.

"They would be idiots." He kissed her forehead.

Lucien, Cassandra, and their brother, the Earl of Aldington, approached, along with Christina.

Prudence's mother stood at her side. "Your cousins have something lovely to share. I wish I could claim to be a part of it, but I cannot."

Lucien looked toward his brother before addressing Prudence and Bennet. "Constantine and I would like to offer you a wedding gift of a thousand pounds. It's not a dowry, exactly, but we hope you'll accept it with love." His gaze settled on Prudence.

The floor seemed to tilt beneath Prudence's feet. She looked from Lucien to Bennet and back again. "Is there no dowry?"

A look of surprise quickly followed by regret passed over Lucien's features. "Of course Glastonbury hasn't been able to tell you yet since I just informed him before the ceremony." He looked to Bennet. "My apologies."

"Warfield declined to provide a dowry," Bennet said quietly from beside her.

She turned her head toward his. "You knew this and married me anyway." He'd said he would, but she supposed she hadn't quite believed it. She knew how badly he needed the money.

He clasped her hand and squeezed. In that moment, she knew she loved him. Her mother hadn't been exactly right. Emotions weren't always untidy or unnecessary. The love she felt for Bennet was crisp and clear. It made her feel strong and happy. And it was very, very necessary. She honestly didn't know what she would do without it or what her life had felt like before he was in it.

"I'm moved by your generosity," Bennet said to her cousins.

"Thank you." It was all Prudence could manage to say past the stone in her throat. Today was a dream come true, except these were dreams she'd never nurtured. A family. A husband. A child. Love.

"I want to thank you too," Christina said to her nephews. "I'm so glad my family has embraced my daughter." She looked to Prudence. "I wish it could have come from me."

"I know." Prudence deeply appreciated all of them, but it was going to take time to feel as if she was really part of their world.

"We've discussed telling our father the truth about you," Cassandra said, glancing at her brothers. "Constantine is going to do it with Aunt Christina. Con is his favorite, and his presence makes everything more palatable."

Aldington grunted and rolled his eyes. "It's unfortunately true."

Prudence was nervous about how the duke might react.

He was a very rigid person with high expectations. She recalled what Christina had said about not wanting to tell him about her illegitimate child. "Does he really need to know?" Prudence looked at her mother.

"I think it's time. While we won't tell the world, I want your cousins to be able to include you as a member of the family."

"We want that too," Lucien said.

"Families have such complicated dynamics," Prudence observed, swallowing her anxiety. "I'll have to learn to navigate yours—ours. As well as Bennet's." She glanced up at him, then sought out his aunts across the room where they sat together.

"Will you be going to Aberforth Place?" Cassandra asked.

"Not until after the Season," Bennet said. While they hadn't discussed their plans for anything following the wedding, Prudence was a bit disappointed. She'd been hoping to meet the rest of his family and see his home.

They chatted for a few more minutes before it was time to have breakfast. It was a warm, lovely affair, with an abundance of food, wine, and good cheer. Prudence's face hurt from smiling.

Afterward, she made a point of speaking with Judith and Esther. "I'm so glad you were able to come today," she told them.

"We are too," Esther said with great enthusiasm. "What a lucky happenstance that we came to town when we did, for we never come to London. I only wish we could stay longer. Alas, we must return to Bath tomorrow."

"Can you remind me of whom I'll meet at Aberforth Place?" Prudence asked. "Great-Aunt Minerva and Great-Aunt Flora?"

"Yes, and Cousin Frances," Esther said.

"Oh yes, I think Bennet mentioned her," Prudence said.

Judith's blond brows arched in surprise. "Did he?"

"Yes." Prudence wanted to ask why that was surprising, but his aunt was already speaking.

"You'll find Great-Aunt Minerva and Great-Aunt Flora quite charming." Aunt Judith said quickly.

Esther's white brows gathered together. "I'm not sure charming is the right word. Did you know Minerva has a pet squirrel? Or perhaps there are two."

"Please excuse us, Prudence," Judith said, taking her aunt's arm. "We must thank our hostess before we go." She quickly ushered Esther away, who seemed slightly bemused by her niece's reaction.

Prudence had the distinct sense there were things they wanted to say but didn't. Or couldn't. Had Bennet told them not to talk to her about their other relatives? She was also curious as to why they lived in Bath while the others lived at Aberforth Place, especially since she didn't think Judith or Esther had ever been married. Given Bennet's financial situation, Prudence thought it might be more economical if they lived on his estate.

Ada joined Prudence, her gaze following the aunts. "How are you finding Glastonbury's family?"

"So far, they seem quite pleasant, if a bit secretive." Ada's brows arched in response, and Prudence clarified, "Perhaps not secretive, exactly, but I have the impression there is more to his family than they are telling me."

"Have you any idea what that could be?"

"Not really. There is so much Bennet and I have yet to learn about each other. This happened very quickly."

"Indeed, though you appear happy, and so does he."

Prudence's gaze found Bennet across the room. "You think so?"

"The way he looks at you seems very romantic. There's a

longing, I think." Ada scrutinized her a moment. "And I would say you're happy, wouldn't you?"

"Almost," Prudence said, wishing the dowry had come through, but incredibly grateful for the financial—and emotional—support of her newfound cousins. She also wished she could tell Bennet how she felt, that she loved him. But she didn't dare. He hadn't wanted this marriage, and he believed she didn't either. "Ask me again when you see me next."

"You know I will." Ada grinned. "That's what friends do."

"Thank you." Prudence touched the other woman's arm and smiled warmly. "I may have two new families, but I consider you my dearest sister. You have been a stalwart and wonderful friend."

"I'm glad to hear it because I will need a friend if I do end up going to work at Warfield's estate." Her blue eyes glittered with determination.

"Are you still going after what's happened? I wondered if Lucien might decide you shouldn't go."

"In fact, he mentioned today that he'd changed his mind, but he's angry and frustrated. I expect he'll change his mind back again. Friendship and loyalty always win out for him—as it should."

Yes, Ada was a special kind of friend—a special kind of person. If she did go to help Warfield, Prudence hoped he would realize his good fortune. If he didn't, perhaps Prudence would go and set him straight. He certainly deserved a verbal thrashing. Actually, if Ada went, Prudence wondered if Ada might be the one to deliver it. Ada might be small, but she was mighty, and Prudence had no doubt she would hold her own.

A short while later, Prudence made her way to Bennet's side and asked if they could take a stroll outside in order to have a few minutes alone. Arching a brow, he silently guided her through the doors that led out to the garden.

Prudence tipped her head to look at him as they circuited the small garden. "I confess I wish we were visiting Aberforth Place, even for a short while. But I understand if you can't afford the journey."

"Actually, now that there is money, I should make a trip there. However, you don't need to come with me. I just need to take care of a few things."

"Debts?" she asked, giving him a supportive smile. "You can tell me. I want you to know that you can be honest with me. If I can tell you about my parentage, you must know you can share anything with me."

He clasped her hand. "I do appreciate that."

"Good, because if you're going to Aberforth Place, I want to come with you. We could even stop at Riverview this evening. The Logans would be delighted to see we are finally married."

Bennet laughed. "Finally. Who could have known our faux betrothal would result in a real marriage?"

A real marriage. Prudence didn't think their union qualified as that—at least not yet. "So, we're going?"

He hesitated, lines furrowing his brow. "You really want to leave today? I suppose it would be nice not to spend tonight in the same small house as my aunts."

"Why, Lord Glastonbury, do you have something planned?" She batted her eyelashes, provoking him to waggle his brows at her.

He pulled her into his arms. "Many things, my lady wife. I shall demonstrate them all in good time."

CHAPTER 18

*T*he coach pulled into the yard at Riverview in late afternoon. Unlike their last visit, the sky was clear and the road dry—and they had a coachman. Sixty, with a hitch in his gait, Tom had been sad to hear of the loss of the former coach, but he'd done what he could to make the new one ride as smoothly as possible.

Tom opened the door for them, and Bennet climbed down before helping his wife from the coach.

His wife.

Would that ever sound normal to his ears?

She took his arm, and they went to the door of the inn where Bennet knocked.

The door opened to reveal Mrs. Logan, who gasped.

"Allow me to present the Viscountess Glastonbury," Bennet said with a wide smile.

"My goodness, how wonderful! Come in, come in." Mrs. Logan grinned enthusiastically as she stepped back and gestured them inside.

Bennet closed the door behind them. "Tom is seeing to

the coach—we'll just be here overnight, assuming you have room."

"Certainly. The window still isn't repaired in the second room, but you can have the one you used on your last visit. Let us hope the weather doesn't prevent you from leaving this time. Though, Mr. Logan and I enjoyed having you here for so long." She clapped her hands together. "How wonderful that you are married!"

"Just this morning, in fact," Bennet said.

Mrs. Logan's eyes rounded. "Oh! Then this will require something special for dinner or dessert. My goodness, I will do my very best."

Prudence took the woman's hand. "Anything you prepare will be lovely, truly. Do you require any help in the kitchen?"

"I couldn't ask that," Mrs. Logan replied, looking slightly horrified. "It's just…you're a viscountess now."

Prudence smiled. "I'm the same person who baked bread here with you, so my offer stands."

"Well, you're newly married, and you'll be wanting to spend your time with your husband." She winked at Bennet. "Do you want me to show you to your room?"

"We can find it," Bennet said with a chuckle.

The stable master's lad dashed through the common room bearing their cases. He must have brought them from the coach.

Mrs. Logan pivoted toward the kitchen. "I can't wait to tell Mr. Logan you've come. Dinner will be at half six, but then you already know that." She bustled toward the kitchen, happily mumbling, "So much to do!"

"I hope she doesn't go to too much trouble," Prudence said as they turned toward the stairs.

"Nothing you say can sway her, so just enjoy it."

"True." She preceded Bennet up the stairs and, when they

reached the top, stepped aside so the stable master's lad could descend.

He touched his forehead with a nod. "My lord, my lady."

"Thank you, Davy," Bennet said. He went to open the door to their room for Prudence.

She moved inside, and he followed, closing the door behind him. Leaning against the wood, he watched her walk to the hearth, where it looked like Davy had started a fire.

Untying her bonnet, she removed the hat and set it on the chair he'd slept in that first night they'd spent together here. Her profile was so lovely—the graceful sweep of her lashes, the pert tip of her nose, the provocative pucker of her lips. He'd been waiting all day to devour them. Indeed, he'd planned to ravish her, at least partially, in the coach, but she'd dozed off almost immediately and hadn't awakened until just before they'd arrived.

"Are you still tired?" he asked, pushing away from the door. He stripped off his gloves and hat and set them atop the dresser.

She gave him a sheepish look. "I didn't realize I *was* tired. I've heard that carrying a babe can make one inordinately sleepy, especially in the beginning." Her cheeks flushed, and she returned her attention to the fire.

Bennet came up behind her and wrapped his hands around her middle. "It's not your fault," he whispered. "Neither of us wanted this."

"But here we are," she said quietly, her breath hitching. "Do you feel trapped?"

He thought before speaking. "Yes, but not for the reasons you think. My father trapped me in an impossible situation when he gambled away every last shilling and failed to run the estate so that it would be profitable." He pressed his lips to her neck just below and behind her ear. "You didn't entrap me. As I said, neither of us planned for this to happen."

"No, you said neither of us *wanted* this. That is not the same thing."

"I suppose it's not." Her scent and proximity were making it hard to think. "But that wasn't true either, because I want you rather fiercely."

"Wanting me and wanting to be saddled with me and a baby forever aren't the same thing either."

He moved his hand down her abdomen and pressed his palm flat against her. There was the child they'd created. He didn't doubt its existence. For whatever reason, Bennet *knew* he or she was there. Just as he knew he was terrified for them and their future. But sensing Prudence's trepidation and hesitance, he wouldn't share that with her. Not now.

Her hand crept over his, but she was still wearing gloves, and he wanted to feel her skin against his. "You truly don't mind being married to me? I'm not what you could have wanted. Not just because I have no money. I'm a paid companion. Worse, I'm illegitimate."

Bennet turned her in his embrace so that she faced him. He lifted her chin to catch her gaze, then caressed her cheek. "Not only do I not mind being married to you, I threw over another woman so that I could do so. My only regret remains that I mistakenly kidnapped you in the first place—and only because I put you through a terrible ordeal."

"It wasn't that bad," she breathed.

He took one of her hands and tugged the glove from her fingers. "I recall what you looked like when you arrived. It seemed that bad. You were rather angry, and you had every right to be."

"Fine, it wasn't pleasant, but it could have been much worse."

After dropping the glove onto the chair with her hat, he moved to her other hand, removing the glove and consigning it to the growing pile of her accessories. "Worse than being stranded here with me when you wanted to shoot me?"

"I never wanted to shoot you."

He spun her about again to face the fire and began to unlace her gown. "You should have." He kissed her nape, feeling her shiver as he worked her gown open.

"Why are you removing my clothes?" she asked. "We have to go downstairs for dinner later."

"Aren't you going to change?" he asked innocently before spreading the gown open and pushing it down to her waist.

"I brought one evening gown, and it hardly seems appropriate for dining in the common room downstairs."

He slid his hands to her front and cupped her breasts through her corset and chemise. "I suppose I could help you put this dress back on. Or we could take advantage of your current state."

"That was your plan all along," she said, arching into his touch.

He flicked the laces of her corset, loosening the garment so he could easily slip his hand against her heated flesh. He caressed her, pressing his cock against her backside. "I admit it was." He lowered his mouth to her neck, kissing her with a wild hunger as he pinched her nipple.

She gasped. "You are distracting me horribly. I wanted to talk to you about your family. That was my intent when we got into the coach, but then I fell asleep."

"Ah well, they will have to wait. In fact, can we delay that conversation until we arrive at Aberforth Place? I want to spend our journey there focusing on just us. More specifically, I want to direct all my attention to your spectacular body and the wondrous responses I can arouse."

He teased her breast while he licked and bit at her neck. She tipped her head, giving him free access to a silken expanse of her delectable flesh. He wanted nothing more than to sink into her and let all their stress and worry fade away.

"I think you're trying to put me off. I might even wonder if you're hiding something."

Bennet froze a moment. He was, but he didn't want to talk about this now. He knew he was delaying what he had to reveal, but they were in this together now—for better or worse as the vows said. He just hoped she wouldn't think it was for worse.

He snagged her earlobe with his teeth. "The only thing I'm hiding is my unadulterated lust for you. But I think I'm doing a very poor job of it." He pulled on her nipple.

"Very," she said between raspy sounds of desire.

Bending his knees, he swung her into his arms and carried her to the bed, where he set her on the edge. He knelt, quickly removing her boots, but leaving her stockings in place.

"You're not taking those off?" she asked.

"As you said, we only have an hour. Also, there is something undeniably erotic about a woman who is just partially clothed." He pushed her corset down and tugged the neckline of her chemise over to bare one breast. "Like that," he growled before dropping his head to draw her nipple into his mouth.

She clutched him, her fingers digging into his scalp.

If he'd doubted that she was with child, he wouldn't now. Her breasts were so different—heavier and...firmer. There was no turning back.

Bennet tore his mouth from her and shoved her skirts up to her waist. Putting his hands on her thighs, he spread her legs and bent to taste her sex.

She cried out the moment his tongue touched her folds. "Bennet!"

"Lie back." He slipped his finger into her wet heat and sucked on her clitoris. Her legs shuddered around him, and the muscles of her sex gripped him tight as he thrust in and out of her.

She still clasped his head, pulling on his hair as her hips rose to meet his mouth and hand. He gripped her hip and positioned her leg over his shoulder. She slid her other thigh onto his other shoulder. Now, he was definitely trapped. But there was nowhere he would rather be. Surrendering to her completely, he devoured her flesh, burying his tongue deep inside her.

Tensing around him, she was close to her release. He filled her with two fingers and brought her to the very edge, reveling in her senseless cries of passion. Then she arched up, her body stiffening as she came in a torrent. He held her, kissing and licking her as she rode the wave of ecstasy.

"Bennet," she groaned. "Come with me *now*." She pulled on his head.

He straightened, his hands shaking as he fumbled with the buttons of his fall. He swore, and her fingers joined his. Then her hand was around his cock, guiding him to her sex.

Turning her onto the bed, he crawled over her as she slid him inside her. He drove deep, moaning her name over and over as lust swept him to a place he'd never been. This was a soul-touching desire, a desperate craving that he wasn't sure could be sated.

Her legs curled around him, her heels digging into his backside as she met him thrust for thrust. They moved together in perfect rhythm, the sound of their bodies and their cries of urgency filling the air around them.

He kissed her, his tongue tangling with hers in crazed abandon. His orgasm built, and habit told him to pull away, to finish outside her.

But why? Not only was she his wife, she carried his child.

There was no reason to maintain his sanity. Shouting her name, he let himself go as never before, flooding her with his seed.

There was indeed no turning back now.

~

They arrived late at Aberforth Place, so it wasn't until the following morning that Prudence met anyone except for the butler, Eakes, the housekeeper, Mrs. Marian, and Laura, the housemaid who would be acting as Prudence's maid.

Prudence had protested having a maid, but Bennet had persuaded her to try the situation and see what she thought. As a woman carrying a child, perhaps she would appreciate the help. Prudence had been too exhausted to continue arguing, so perhaps that was her answer.

Entering the breakfast room, Prudence was greeted with a scene of chaos. Newspapers covered half the table, and nuts were scattered about the other half. A loud squeaking filled the air, and it took Prudence a moment to realize it was coming from one of the women—the one in the chair on the newspaper side of the table.

"Just sit still, Flora!" A tall, slender woman of what seemed to be advanced age dashed about the room, bent at the waist. Her rapid movements contradicted how old she appeared to be. "You're scaring him!"

"*I'm* scaring *him*? He's a menace!" This came from the woman who'd been squeaking. Petite with bright white hair, her legs drawn up to her chest, she waved a knife and fork around madly. Presumably, she was Flora. "He tried to take my ham!"

"I'm still training him." The taller woman disappeared

behind the drapery, and the air in the room seemed to still as Prudence held her breath. Reappearing on the other side of the curtain, the tall woman held up a small bundle of fur. "Got him!"

"Thank goodness." Flora lowered her feet to the floor, then turned her head, her gaze landing on Prudence. "It's Glastonbury's bride. Come in, my dear. Sit and eat with us. Oh, the food is over there." She waved her hand toward a long table against the wall with covered dishes lined atop it.

Ignoring the food for now, despite the terrible hunger clawing at her stomach, Prudence moved toward the table. "Good morning, I'm Prudence."

"You're Lady Glastonbury," the tall woman said.

"Yes, but my name is Prudence, so I hope you'll call me that. You must be Bennet's great-aunts."

From the chair, Flora pointed at her chest. "I'm Flora, and this is Minerva." She gestured toward the taller woman, who stood on the other side of the table. "And *that* is her latest creature." Flora wrinkled her nose.

"Some call us Flora and Fauna," Minerva said with a grin that revealed a missing tooth on the upper left side of her mouth. Some of her gray hair had escaped her mobcap. "Because Flora presses a ridiculous number of flowers all over the damn house, and I use my skills for a more helpful avocation. I rescue those in need." She held up the animal in her hand and kissed its head.

"Is that a squirrel?" Prudence asked.

"A menace," Flora muttered.

"This is George." Minerva came around the table, which caused Flora to pull her legs back up onto the chair. Prudence wanted to soothe her and say it was all right, that the squirrel wasn't on the floor any longer, but held her tongue.

"It's nice to meet you, George," Prudence said, unsure if she should try to pet the animal.

"He's quite friendly, but I'm afraid Flora has frightened him with her irrational fear."

"It's not irrational! I was bitten by a squirrel when I was nine."

"You were not. I was there, and it was a badger."

Flora glared at her with dark blue eyes. "It was *not* a badger. I would remember a bloody badger."

"Whatever it was, I'm sure it was traumatic," Prudence said diplomatically. She looked to Minerva. "Does George have breakfast with you every morning?" She wasn't sure how she felt about eating with wildlife.

"Not every morning, but he seemed lonely this morning. He's just a baby, you see. He's motherless, so I took him in a fortnight ago. I'd hoped Temperance could be his mother."

"Temperance?"

"Her other squirrel," Flora responded tersely. She'd lowered her feet to the floor again and was buttering a piece of bread. "She *rescued* her last year."

"I see, and where is Temperance?"

Minerva crossed to the window and held George to the glass. "She wished to dine al fresco this morning. She's just outside there. There's your mama."

Prudence joined her and saw the other squirrel outside. She was busily working her way through a small pile of nuts. "How...charming." Smiling at Minerva, she capitulated to her hunger and went to the sideboard to dish up her breakfast. With a full plate, she went to the table and considered where to sit. Newspaper or nuts? She chose the chair at the end and set her plate on the very edge of the newspaper.

Flora jumped up and snatched the newspaper from beneath Prudence's plate. "You can't put things on my papers."

Reasons that Bennet might have preferred to avoid discussing his relatives became evident. Hadn't he called them eccentric? "My apologies," Prudence said to Flora, who sniffed in response as she set her paper at the other end of the table before retaking her chair.

"What will you do today?" Minerva asked, sitting down next to Prudence and slipping George into a chest pocket on her apron. Then she picked up a nut from the table and gave it to him as if this was the most natural activity in the world.

Having taken a bite of ham, Prudence swallowed before answering. "I imagine I'll acquaint myself with the house." She'd only seen the entry, staircase hall, and their suite of rooms last night.

This morning, she'd passed through a few rooms on her way here. They were mostly empty, with darker spots on the walls where she suspected paintings had once hung. The house looked like it was in the process of being vacated. She knew Bennet had needed to sell furnishings, but she hadn't realized just how much was gone. The burden she felt at having forced him into this union weighed heavily, no matter what he said.

"Here's another!" Flora's head was bent over one of the newspapers. "The Viscount Glastonbury has wed Miss Prudence Lancaster, former companion to the Countess of Overton, the Countess of Wexford, and Miss Kathleen Shaughnessy." She cast a sideways look at Prudence. "You were a companion?"

Prudence ignored the wave of discomfort that swept over her. "Yes."

Flora's eyes narrowed slightly. "I wager that was *fascinating*. I do hope you'll tell us all the good gossip." She snapped her attention back to the paper.

"Pardon Flora. She's a tad obsessed with London gossip, despite the fact she hasn't been there in over fifty years.

You'll see she receives nearly every newspaper that comes from there."

"The papers serve a dual purpose," Flora said with a hint of exasperation. She did not lift her gaze from the paper. "I use them to press my flowers."

"All nine thousand of them." Minerva rolled her eyes. She picked up her fork and moved her food around her plate. "Today you'll see the house, then. Perhaps tomorrow, you'll tour the estate. Just stay away from Frances's cottage if you can." She said the last while sending Prudence a rather intense stare. Then she shuddered.

"Frances is Bennet's cousin?"

"Yes," Flora replied, still not looking up. "Minerva and I are eccentric, but delightfully so." She exchanged a nod and a smile with her sister, and Prudence realized their bickering was good-natured. This made her relax a bit. "Unfortunately, Frances is eccentric in all the wrong ways."

"What ways are those?" Prudence didn't wish to gossip, but her curiosity was getting the best of her. Was Frances what Bennet had been trying to hide?

"There's a reason she lives in a cottage and not here with us," Flora said as if she were imparting a very dear secret.

"She chooses to," Minerva added. "But honestly, if she wanted to live here, we simply couldn't allow it. Though, I suppose we might reconsider if she bathed more regularly."

"It isn't that she doesn't bathe," Flora explained as if to a child. "She simply insists on making her own soap, and it smells atrocious. I think she must make it from whatever she finds on one of her extensive walks."

Prudence couldn't think of a thing to say, so she focused on eating.

"It isn't just that," Flora said. "She has those horrible fits of pique."

Minerva fed another nut to George. "So do you."

Flora scowled at her newspaper. "Fine, the entire family does, but hers are worse."

They all had fits of pique? Did that include Bennet?

"Not the entire family. Judith would be deeply offended to hear you say that." The sarcasm in Minerva's tone was unmistakable.

"I met Judith," Prudence said. "And Esther. They came to the wedding."

Both Flora and Minerva riveted their attention to Prudence. "They were in London?" Flora asked, sounding jealous.

"Yes," Prudence responded. "I'm not sure why. They just happened to be there."

"Right, because the wedding was hastily planned." Flora narrowed her eyes at Prudence's belly. "Are you carrying?"

Prudence nearly choked on the bite of roll she'd just chewed.

"Don't be rude, Flora," Minerva snapped. "What does it matter anyway?" She looked back to Prudence. "Judith and Esther don't like us. That's why they live in Bath. And they refuse to visit."

"Esther is from our sister-in-law's side of the family— she's an outsider," Flora explained with a hint of disdain. "Judith is more like that side instead of ours."

Prudence tried to make sense of Esther's relationship. If Flora and Minerva were Bennet's grandfather's sisters, Esther must be his grandmother's sister? She felt a bit like someone stumbling around in the dark without a candle. "So Judith doesn't have fits of pique?"

Minerva and Flora exchanged looks and burst into laughter. After a moment, Minerva answered. "She has fits of superiority."

"I see." Prudence thought she could imagine that just from the short time she'd spent with Bennet's aunt, but preferred to give the woman the benefit of the doubt. "And which side of the family is Bennet more like?"

"Oh, our side, certainly!" Flora exclaimed.

"Most definitely," Minerva agreed. "He's a St. James to his very bones." She seemed quite proud of that, and now Prudence was more curious than ever.

"Ah, good morning. I see you've met my great-aunts." Bennet stood in the doorway, his expression slightly pained.

"Your bride is delightful," Flora said, rising. She went about collecting her newspapers into a messy pile, then swept them up close to her chest. "I'll be in the library."

Bennet moved into the breakfast room so she could depart.

Minerva stood and plucked up one more nut, feeding it to George in her apron pocket. "I need to take George outside for a runabout. See you later, Prudence!" She wiggled her fingers in a wave and sailed through the doorway.

"I'm sorry I wasn't here to properly introduce you," Bennet said. "I'm afraid I had urgent business to attend to, now that I have some money, thanks to your cousins."

"Do you still have money, or is it all gone?"

He grimaced. "Much of it is spoken for, I'm afraid. But I did reserve a portion for a sound investment. I promise our future will be brighter than our present."

Prudence hated that he was so stressed by the lack of funds. "Was it hard to sell so much of the furnishings?" she asked gently.

Bennet pulled out the chair next to hers at the small rectangular table and turned it toward her before sitting down. "Not as hard as having to tell debtors I can't pay them. Or dealing with people who think this deficit is my fault and will no longer extend me credit. It's frustrating, but it is the reality I must navigate." He sounded completely resigned, but not sad. "How did you find my great-aunts?" Now he sounded a bit apprehensive.

Prudence turned on her seat to face him. "They were lovely, squabbling and all." She decided not to mention Flora's query as to whether she was expecting a child.

"Yes, I'm afraid they are still as sisterly as ever, but then they've lived together their whole lives."

"Did they choose not to wed or—" Prudence shook her head. "Never mind, that's not a question you need to answer." She realized none of the women she'd met from his family had married.

"I don't know that they chose that, but you'd have to ask them for certain," he said. "I hope you didn't mind their eccentricities." His pained expression returned.

"Do you mean George the squirrel or the newspapers everywhere?"

He wiped his hand over his forehead, massaging it slightly. "I hope Flora wasn't obnoxious. She can get carried away with her gossip."

"She asked if I was really a companion."

His mouth twisted. "I'm sorry if she made you uncomfortable." He leaned forward and took her hand.

"What makes me uncomfortable is the feeling that you're hiding something from me. The truth about Cousin Frances, perhaps?"

He stared at her a moment, his features tense. "Did they tell you about her?"

"Only that she makes her own soap that apparently doesn't smell very good. I have the impression they don't care for her very much. Oh, and the fits of pique that you all suffer. Except Judith. Do I have that right? Although, I'm not aware of you having fits of pique."

Some of the color drained from his face, and she grew concerned.

"I wasn't trying to hide her, exactly." He spoke slowly, as if he were choosing his words carefully. Or trying to think of what to say. "I think I mentioned my family was eccentric."

"Tell me about the fits of pique." Again, he seemed uncomfortable. Prudence touched his hand. "If you want to. I don't wish to cause you disquiet."

He seemed to relax. "I love my family, but they are a great deal to handle. I suppose I was afraid you wouldn't like them —and I wouldn't blame you."

"How could I not like them? Aside from the fact that they were actually quite endearing, I would love them simply because they're your family."

His features froze, and he seemed to not breathe for a moment. "Thank you." He rose from his chair and cupped her face before kissing her. It wasn't soft or sweet, but a ravishment that claimed her as his.

When he pulled away at last, she was breathless, her body quivering with desire. "May I escort you up to our chamber?" he asked. "Or should I close the door, toss up your skirts, and bury my face between your thighs right here?"

Slitting her eyes, she cupped his rigid cock through his breeches. "Perhaps you should just sit back down, and I'll get on my knees." She'd taken him in her mouth on two occasions during their journey to Aberforth Place and quite enjoyed the power it gave her. "You don't even have to close the door because the table would hide my presence from anyone who came in."

He groaned. Pulling her up from the chair, he kissed her again—this time hard and fast, his teeth knocking against hers. "Upstairs. Now. I can't remotely behave myself, and I'd hate to shock the servants. We have so few, and if they left in disgust, we would have to resort to doing things ourselves."

She stroked his nape, her fingers tugging on the ends of

his hair. "You know I wouldn't mind. I thought we agreed there would be worse things."

Bennet lifted her into his arms, prompting her to squeal as she twined her arms around his neck. Then he strode from the room.

Yes, there were worse things, but right now, she couldn't think of what those were.

CHAPTER 19

The thousand-pound gift from his new in-laws helped Bennet very much—but not nearly enough. He was able to settle all his father's debts, which meant he wouldn't bleed funds in that direction any longer. However, the estate did not provide enough income to meet his current demands, which included supporting Aunt Judith and Great-Aunt Esther in Bath, Cousin Frances, Great-Aunts Flora and Minerva, and, of course, Aunt Agatha. Never mind paying for a wardrobe that would befit a viscount and his wife or furnishing residences in which they could entertain. He could do without paintings, but an adequate table in the dining room might be nice. However, that was wholly unnecessary since they couldn't afford to feed anyone other than themselves. Why would they need a table to seat twenty or thirty?

Prudence had been so wonderfully understanding and supportive. She hadn't balked at the bare rooms or scoffed at the lack of retainers. As expected, she was ready to put on an apron and help. In fact, she'd done just that after taking charge of the ravishment he'd begun in the breakfast room.

When she was completely satisfied—which had taken several positions, much to Bennet's delight—she'd announced she was going to go clean something.

Thinking of her made him smile. Thinking of how he'd evaded her questions by seducing her made him want to smack himself.

He couldn't avoid telling her the truth about all of them.

Tell me about the fits of pique.

He'd wanted to respond that she didn't really want to know. Instead, he'd taken the coward's way and hidden from the truth. Perhaps he ought to rehearse what to say. Mrs. Marian would probably help him if he asked. Hell, he didn't even have the nerve to do that. What would his housekeeper say when he admitted he hadn't told his new wife anything about the family illness?

Angry with himself, he closed the ledger on his desk and turned to look out the window. His study had a lovely view of parkland. Someone was marching toward the house.

Standing, he went to the window. As the person came closer, he began to recognize her. But no, she was wearing a proper gown, albeit quite old. And a bonnet. That tied beneath her chin. Bennet couldn't remember the last time she'd done so.

He rushed from the room and dashed to the entry hall. The single footman was nowhere to be seen, likely because Eakes had him doing some chore. Bennet opened the door and stepped outside just as she was striding for the entrance.

"Frances?" he asked, shielding his eyes from the sun with his hand against his forehead.

"Benny, you're home."

He loathed that name. Thankfully, she was the only person who called him that. "Yes."

"With a wife, I hear." Her gown was probably three

decades old and rather small for her current frame. "Why wasn't I invited to your wedding?"

"It was in London," he said, surprised that he wasn't recoiling from her scent.

She walked past him into the house and immediately untied her bonnet with a vicious tug. The ribbon came apart from the hat, and she held the satin up with a frown. "What am I supposed to do with this?"

Whipping the accessory from her head, she tossed it across the entry hall. "Bloody nuisance. This is what I get for trying to fit in with you people." She flung the ribbon too, but it landed mere inches from her feet. She swore again and stamped on it with her heavy boot, which didn't at all complement her ancient walking dress.

Prudence walked in from the staircase hall. "I thought I heard voices."

Before Bennet could introduce her to his father's cousin, Frances stalked toward her. "You're very pretty. I'm Cousin Frances."

"I'm pleased to meet you. I'm Prudence."

Frances held out her hand. "Nice to meet you, Prudie."

Prudence took her hand as she looked toward Bennet with a puzzled expression. Probably because of her new nickname. If he could live with "Benny," she would learn to accept "Prudie." He suppressed a smile even as trepidation skipped through him. Frances seemed to be lucid, but once in a while, she had days where she insisted that she had to get ready for a ball or milk a cow, neither of which were things she needed to do.

"I'd planned to visit you tomorrow," Prudence said. "I'm glad you've come today. Will you stay for tea?"

Leaning toward Prudence, Frances inhaled sharply. Then she wrinkled her nose and walked around Prudence, sniffing as she went.

Bennet frowned. Perhaps Frances wasn't as lucid as he thought.

He moved to stand beside Prudence. "What are you doing, Frances?"

Frances stopped when she was once more in front of Prudence. "When is the baby coming?"

Prudence went rigid beside him. He put his hand on her waist.

"How would you know that?" Prudence whispered, her face pale.

"Animals have a certain smell when they're breeding. You have that smell."

"Breeding?" Great-Aunt Flora scurried into the room, her gaze fixed on Prudence. She must have been in the small sitting room just off the entry hall. "You *are* expecting."

"Yes," Prudence didn't look at anyone, and Bennet wanted to whisk her away.

"That would explain the hasty wedding," Great-Aunt Flora added with a nod. "I knew it! I'm surprised there was nothing in the newspaper about it."

Great-Aunt Minerva glided in from the staircase hall, two squirrel heads poking forth from her apron, each in their own pocket. "About what?"

"Prudie is breeding," Cousin Frances said.

"How lovely!" Great-Aunt Minerva beamed at Bennet. "I'm so glad you decided to have children after all. A little St. James running around Aberforth Place is just what we need."

Prudence turned to him. "What does she mean you decided to have children *after all*?"

Bennet's earlier agitation intensified. This was not how he wanted to discuss his preference to avoid children with Prudence. Hell, he'd hoped never to discuss that he'd ever felt that way. They'd deal with the child when they had to, and she never had to know how terrified he was, how desperately he wished she wasn't carrying *his* child.

"He was going to let the line die with him," Great-Aunt Flora said with a tsk. "He wasn't even going to wed."

"Flora!" he bellowed. "Can't you ever remain silent? Can't any of you remain silent?"

Great-Aunt Minerva pet one of the squirrels in her apron. "Of course we can't, and we shouldn't have to. Why wouldn't your wife know that you'd planned to remain childless, that you—"

"Not another word, Minerva," he growled.

"I suppose you haven't told her about Agatha either." This came from Frances, who stood with her hands on her hips. "You can't hide who we are, Benny. Nor can you run from the fact that your offspring will be just like us."

"He or she might be like Judith," Great-Aunt Minerva said unhelpfully. "But that would be a pity."

While they spoke, Bennet watched a range of emotions move across Prudence's features. Shock, dismay, disbelief, anger, and a host of others he couldn't identify.

"Who is Agatha?" Prudence asked calmly, despite the pulse ticking strongly in her neck.

Bennet took her arm and steered her from the entry hall.

"Will you come to my study so I can speak to you without the chorus chiming in?"

She walked toward his study, her back stiff and her shoulders high. Once inside, she stood off to the side, her arms crossed over her chest. She was the visual representation of someone closed up tightly, and he didn't blame her. "I don't understand what's happening. Who is Agatha?"

He moved to stand in front of his desk, emotion raging within him. "Agatha is my father's other sister. He was the oldest, then Agatha, then Judith. She lives in a hospital in Lancashire."

"Why?"

"It's very hard to explain. Which is why I haven't before now." He glanced at the floor, murmuring, "One of many reasons why."

"Try."

"You will already have noticed that everyone is somewhat eccentric, but it's more than that. There are...swings of emotion, including those fits of pique my great-aunts mentioned. There is also delusion—in the case of Agatha and with my father. One of the reasons he lost so heavily at the tables was that he would often think he was actually winning." He struggled to explain everything properly. It was so difficult for others to understand.

"Agatha is in hospital because of this?"

He nodded. "It's an illness of the mind and seems to affect everyone differently. Minerva and Flora can become quite obsessed with their activities. Minerva will paint for days without leaving her painting room. She's typically maudlin during these periods, but if you interrupt her to try to coax her to come out, she can become despondent. Flora is overly protective of her flowers and newspapers. Her moods can range quite heavily from excessive excitement to incredible sadness. She's gone days without sleeping for her love of reading and flowers."

Prudence blinked, but he couldn't remotely tell what she was thinking. "Why is Agatha in hospital and they are not?"

"Agatha's moods are quite severe. Her rages and bouts of despair were so challenging to handle that my grandfather committed her to the asylum when she was nineteen. She's been there ever since."

Prudence stared at him in shock, her eyes round and her mouth open.

He wanted to stop, but knew he had to keep going. "I'm told my father's moods were similar to Agatha's, but he drank a great deal of alcohol, which tended to mellow his emotions. Until it didn't, and he would lose himself to anger and frustration." Bennet recalled so many occasions in which his father went from drowsy intoxication to growling fury, throwing things and driving everyone away from him. "He was also incapable of making good decisions for the most part. He gambled away nearly everything. Many of the things that are gone from the house were sold by him before he died."

"Oh, Bennet, I wish I'd known." She spoke so quietly that he could barely hear her.

"My grandfather wasn't like this, but his sisters were—Flora and, to a lesser extent, Minerva—as was his brother, who died when a horse threw him at the age of twenty-five. Cousin Frances is his daughter, and she is also afflicted. Judith, however, does not seem to have the illness. Nonetheless, she chose not to marry or have children lest she pass it on to them."

Her features seemed to be carved from stone. "You did the same. Or at least, you wanted to."

"I never wanted to marry, but then my father made it so I would have to. I'd hoped to avoid having children. That's one of the reasons I chose to wed Mrs. Merryfield. She already had children. I didn't think she'd mind when I refused to have any."

"You really were content to let the title die with you?"

"More than. The thought of my child ending up like Aunt Agatha…" He pressed his lips together and clenched his jaw.

"You don't know that will happen," she said. "It didn't with Judith, apparently."

"She is in the minority." Bennet didn't want to have to justify his fear or what he knew to be true—the risk was too great. But it was too late now. The baby was coming, its fate already decided. Panic rose in his chest, stoking his fury.

"Furthermore, *I* am afflicted. My emotions get the best of me, as they are doing right now, and I make horrid decisions such as kidnap people." He turned from her and stalked to the window. His fist burned to punch through the glass if he could. He would welcome the pain if it would dissipate his rage and reclaim his control.

The silence in the room was more frightening than if she'd railed at him. He looked back at her over his shoulder and felt a surge of anguish. Her face was unreadable.

"And not telling me about any of this." Her voice was low and dark, and he felt the tremor of it in his chest. "That wasn't a good decision either."

"Perhaps not."

Her nostrils flared. "Now I understand why you didn't want me to come here. I think it's best if I return to London."

~

*O*verwhelmed with hurt and anger, Prudence started to turn.

Bennet turned away from the window and took a step toward her. "Wait."

"For what? I suppose I must ask what else you've kept from me."

"Nothing."

That was good since this was all quite enough. "Just that your family has an affliction that our child may or may not have. You should have told me. You had ample opportunity to."

She'd wanted to discuss his family at Riverview, and he'd pushed her off. They'd traveled for several days before reaching Aberforth Place, and he'd avoided saying anything, even after they'd arrived and she met his great-aunts!

"I couldn't think of how to tell you."

"But I am your *wife*. And I'm carrying your *child*." She recalled what Minerva had said about him not planning to have children, that he'd meant to be the last Viscount Glastonbury. "Were you ever going to tell me about not wanting children? Be honest. Please."

Distress lined his face. "I'd hoped not to. What would be the point?"

"The point is that you're afraid, and you didn't want to share your fear with me." Proof yet again that feelings were useless. Here she was, feeling far too much and she didn't want any of it.

"I was scared. And ashamed."

A tear slid from her eye. She swiped it away furiously, her brows pitching low over her eyes. "You didn't want this. I entrapped you, regardless of what you insist. Furthermore, I didn't want this either." Not originally, but she'd come to want it very much.

Emotion, impossible to hide away or ignore, roiled inside her. She tried to take a deep breath and failed, her chest constricting. She felt like she was drowning, her throat blocked as panic overtook her.

Too much had happened. She'd found out she was carrying a child. She'd discovered her real mother—and that her friends were her cousins. Then she'd gotten married to a man who'd been engaged to someone else and who hadn't even wanted to marry her. She'd entrapped him, and it was no surprise he hadn't told her his deepest secrets. Why would he?

She'd also realized she'd fallen in love with this man, who couldn't possibly return the emotion.

Tuck it away, Prudence.

Her mother's voice sounded in her head, a welcome balm to the chaos tossing inside her. The moment of calmness was fleeting. She needed quiet and serenity. She needed to get away from Bennet.

"Pru, you don't have to go."

"I do, actually. You didn't want me here, and I think that may have been your best decision. I'll leave for London immediately." She pinned him with a cool stare as she shuttered her emotions as best she could. They were still there, boiling beneath the surface, making her feel as though she could burst into tears at any moment. She refused to do that. "You're going to let me go."

Then she turned and left his study, eager to put time and space between them.

~

*T*wo days after Prudence left, Bennet began to rouse from his drunken stupor. That meant it was time for more wine. Or whatever he could find.

He stumbled down to the kitchens and made his way to the wine cupboard only to find it locked. "Bloody hell," he muttered, rattling the door.

"There you are," Great-Aunt Minerva said crossly, surprising him so that he banged his forehead against the wood.

"Ow." He rubbed his hand over his wounded flesh as he turned.

Great-Aunt Minerva was not alone. Hell, she was never alone. Those bloody squirrels were always in her apron. Great-Aunt Flora also stood at her side.

"You look terrible," Great-Aunt Minerva said. "I realize you're upset about Prudence, but this isn't like you."

"I'm more than upset." He felt as though his insides had been torn out and stomped into the ground. There was nothing but an aching despair. He'd been so stupid not to tell her the truth. No, he'd been stupid to think they could have a real marriage after she'd been clear about not wanting one.

He'd been stupid about a great many things.

"We're all stupid sometimes," Great-Aunt Flora said.

Bennet blinked as a headache crept across his skull. "Did I say that out loud?"

Great-Aunt Minerva stroked the head of one of the squirrels. "You need to go after her."

"And we're coming with you." Great-Aunt Flora lifted her chin with an expression that dared him to refuse her. "You never should have let her leave."

"I'm not her jailer," Bennet slurred. "Besides, she saw all of us and doesn't want us. Why would she? We're all tainted. Broken."

"Definitely stupid." Great-Aunt Minerva shook her head. "We're a bit off, but we're not broken. You definitely aren't. As much as we like to claim you as a St. James, you are not like us."

The pain in his head increased. Or perhaps it was always there, and he was merely becoming sober. "What do you mean? I'm drank like my father. Drunk too. And I make very bad decisions. Like kidnapping Prudence. Only it wasn't supposed to be Prudence."

"You kidnapped her and got her with child?" Great-Aunt Flora shrieked.

"Sort of."

Great-Aunt Flora looked at her sister. "I think he *is* like us."

Great-Aunt Minerva waved her away as if she were an annoying insect. "I'm sure you had a good reason for kidnapping her. You do not make bad decisions—at least not like your father did. You've done everything you can to keep this family together and functioning. What would we do without you, Bennet?"

"But I'm so bloody *sad* right now." He was even whining like his father sometimes had when he'd been particularly despondent.

"As you should be. You cocked things up with the woman you love and you're miserable. You've good reason, unlike me when I go into my painting frenzies. I wish I knew what prompted them, but I don't."

"I wish I knew why I become so irritated if my papers or flowers are in disarray," Great-Aunt Flora said. "It really isn't the same as what you're going through right now. You must see that."

He wasn't sure he did.

"When you're sober, you'll understand," Great-Aunt Minerva said with confidence. "Then we'll leave for London. Tomorrow, all right?"

"No. I'm not taking you to London."

"We're not letting you go alone." Great-Aunt Flora sniffed. "Come, Minnie, let's pack our things." They left in unison, marching away as if called to battle.

Bennet blinked after them as another shaft of pain drove through his temple. He winced, cradling his head. Definitely becoming sober.

"Mrs. Marian, where's the key to the wine cupboard?"

The housekeeper materialized as if she'd been a ghost lurking belowstairs. Round figured with a smile as wide as England, she shook her graying head at him. "You'd have to ask Eakes, but he won't give it to you. Your great-aunts are right."

"About what?"

"All of it. You may not want to believe them, but they are aware of their...problems. Just as we are all aware that you don't suffer any of it."

"You don't know everything I've done," he whispered.

"I don't have to. I've known you since you were a small

boy. You have never demonstrated anything that would make me think you share the affliction of your great-aunts or of Frances. Don't forget that my mother worked here in your grandfather's time. She always told me how like him you were. And you know he wasn't like his brother or your father."

Everything she said was true. Could he truly be unafflicted?

He wasn't sure he could believe it. "I don't suppose you have something that would improve my headache?"

"Cook does." Mrs. Marian smiled. "I'll send it up. You should rest before you pack."

"You think I should go to London?"

She laughed. "I don't think your great-aunts are going to give you any choice. But yes, you should go to London. Lady Glastonbury wasn't here long, but I could see how much you love each other. We are all so pleased to see you happy at last. You certainly deserve it." She gave him another smile before taking herself off.

Bennet slumped against the cupboard door. Whether he deserved it or not, he *had* been happy. The fact was that he loved Prudence. When she'd said she loved his aunts because they were family, he knew he loved her too, that he'd loved her for weeks. Since before they'd even left Riverview. She'd seen him at his worst and had grown to care for him in spite of that.

He wasn't entirely convinced he should follow her to London. If they continued as they were, he'd only fall more in love with her and then it would be difficult to pull away— as he *must* after the babe came. He couldn't risk a second child, not when he was already so frantically worried about this one.

When he allowed himself to think about it. For the most part, he avoided thinking of the future. But as Prudence's belly rounded, he would have a harder time doing that. Perhaps being apart was the solution. She'd just reminded him that she hadn't wanted this.

The terrible secret was that deep down, he had. He wanted her. In his bed, as his wife, and as the mother of his child. He didn't care if she was illegitimate or a companion or a charwoman. She was the first thing he thought of when he roused from sleep and the last image he saw in his mind before he fell asleep. She also haunted his dreams and filled his senses. Prudence was everywhere, every*thing*.

He'd burdened her with his family, with their affliction, with his uncertain future. But perhaps he wasn't going to end up like his father. Moreover, he could hope—really hope—that his child wouldn't either. And if he or she did? Bennet wouldn't love them any less. He already loved them quite desperately, just as he did their mother. They would support their child together with his family.

Of course he had to go to London.

CHAPTER 20

*C*assandra, seated in a nearby chair, tapped her foot. "We should go to the park."

Prudence's nerves were still frayed. She had to fight to keep her emotions in check, something that had become a daily, if not an hourly battle. "I've only been here two days. Can't I settle in before you make me pretend to be a viscountess?"

Though it had been nearly a week since she'd learned the truth about Bennet's family and about his desire to never marry or have children because of that family, the emotions of that day were still strong. She wanted to blame the baby, but the fact was that after burying her feelings for so long, every single thing she'd ever felt now rose to the surface at the slightest provocation. She hated how lost she felt, how out of control.

Ada, who sat beside Cassandra on a settee in the Wexfords' drawing room, turned toward Prudence. "You aren't *pretending* to be a viscountess."

Wasn't she? She'd abandoned her husband. She'd been angry with him, but she shouldn't have left. Flora and

Minerva had tried to persuade her to stay, but she'd been overwrought. She hated disappointing them. Already, they felt like her family, even if Bennet didn't want them to be.

"At some point, you're going to have to accept that you aren't a fraud, that you belong here with us," Cassandra said. "We love you, Pru. You're part of our family. And you're a viscountess, whether you like it or not."

Yes, apparently she was. "I love you too. I just don't want to go out. I need to think." About what to do next. She loved Bennet and wanted a real marriage with him. Instead of fleeing in distress, she should have stayed and told him.

The butler entered and announced, "Lady Overton."

Fiona strode into the room looking very determined. And concerned. Her brown-eyed gaze went immediately to Prudence.

Prudence tensed. Every one of her instincts said something bad was about to happen.

"Sit with us, Fi," Cassandra said, gesturing to an open chair next to her. "Why do you look as if you brought a storm cloud in with you?"

"Because I have," she said ominously. "I've just heard the most awful rumor." She snapped her lips closed and glanced toward Cassandra. "Perhaps I should have spoken to you first," she murmured.

"Is this about me?" Prudence asked. "If so, I should like to hear it. No, I wouldn't *like* to hear it, but I must." Stiffening her spine, she clasped her hands in her lap and waited expectantly for the proverbial axe to fall.

"I'm so sorry to be the bearer of this, Pru." Fiona's gaze was warm and compassionate. "You know how much I adore you. I never could have navigated my way here in London without you. That someone could say such things about you makes me so angry!" Her auburn brows pitched low over her furious eyes.

Prudence appreciated Fiona's support and kindness. "I know you wouldn't ever hurt me. Now, get on with it. Please."

Nodding slightly, Fiona took a deep breath. "I was at the modiste earlier, and she was eager to ask me if the rumor was true since I know you. I should add that I won't be using Madame Leclerc again." She wrinkled her nose. "She said she'd heard that Glastonbury only wed you because you were carrying a child and that he was paid to do so by the Earl of Aldington and Lord Lucien Westbrook. They arranged the marriage for their..." Fiona hesitated, and Prudence knew what would come next.

"For their illegitimate cousin," she finished for Fiona.

Fiona's face fell. "Yes, and I wish that was all."

"There can't be more?" Cassandra asked, a look of horror crossing her features.

"I'm afraid so," Fiona said, wincing as if someone had stamped on her foot. "Since Lord Glastonbury did not return to London with you, there is speculation that the child isn't even his."

Anger bubbled within Prudence. Instead of pushing it aside, she welcomed the outrage. She'd felt so many emotions of late, perhaps it was time she embraced them. If she wanted to forge a future with Bennet, she was going to have to find a way to do just that. How could she be a loving wife and mother if she refused to let herself feel? "So I trapped a destitute viscount into marriage with the help of my cousins? I had no idea I was so calculating."

"How can you be glib?" Cassandra asked, her eyes rounding.

"Bravo," Ada murmured as she briefly touched Prudence's arm. "How on earth did anyone learn all this? No one knows about your true parentage, and they certainly wouldn't know that you are carrying a child. Who could be behind this cruelty?"

Prudence thought of all who knew. "The only people who know about my parentage are those who were at the wedding."

"Plus my father," Cassandra said, grimacing slightly. "Con and Aunt Christina told him. He seemed to take it well—in fact, he hardly said a word. But he can be awfully harsh when it comes to expectations."

"You don't think he would spread that information?" Fiona asked. "Not when it would hurt his sister? From everything you and Pru have told me, Lady Peterborough is terrified of her husband finding out that Pru is her daughter."

Cassandra looked from Fiona to Prudence. "That's true, and anyway, I don't think my father is that cruel, particularly because this involves his sister."

Prudence wished she shared the same confidence. As Cassandra's companion, she'd lived with the duke, but she couldn't say she knew him very well.

"Who are our other suspects?" Ada asked. "Could a servant have overheard something and shared the information? A great many rumors are started belowstairs."

"I suppose that's possible," Cassandra said.

Prudence pinned her gaze to Cassandra. "Remember that day I told you everything, and Bart came in to announce that Bennet was here?"

"You can't suspect Bart." Cassandra shook her head. "I realize I've only been in this household a short time, but Ruark values him as more than his butler. He trusts him completely."

"I can't imagine it's him either," Prudence said. While she also hadn't lived here long, Bart possessed a very dry sense of humor and was very personable.

"I suppose it could be any number of people," Ada said, frowning.

It didn't really matter who was behind the rumor. It was true—most of it, anyway—and now everyone would look at Prudence as though she were a conniving interloper. It was already bad enough that she'd been a companion and was now a viscountess. This would be so much worse. There was going to be talk behind her back as well as curious looks and imperious judgment.

The other truth was that Bennet knew all this about her. But what reason would he have to spread this information? Furthermore, he wasn't even in London.

Prudence jolted upright, her spine stiffening. "My mother. Peterborough hears this rumor, things could go very badly for her."

"How badly?" Ada asked, her tone as heavy as the air in the room.

Cassandra jumped to her feet. "I need to go to my father. He'll know what to do." She looked to Prudence. "I'm sorry to leave you just now."

"You must go." Prudence squeezed her hands together so hard that she couldn't feel her fingers. "My mother needs protection. Please. Should I go with you?"

"No, you stay. I can see how distraught you are." Cassandra hurriedly left, but the air in the room remained weighted. Silence reigned for a few moments before Fiona spoke. "What can we do, Pru?"

"I don't know." She tried to summon a smile and failed. "I just feel so…defeated." She wished Bennet were here.

"Don't. The Prudence I know is courageous and resilient and she makes her own fortune. You've survived hardship and kidnapping and come out stronger for it."

"Kidnapping?" Fiona stared at them, her mouth open.

"Oh bollocks," Ada whispered. "I forgot she didn't know."

Prudence actually laughed. "It's all right. I'll tell the story —it will take my mind off this catastrophe." Then she'd make plans to return to Somerset. To her husband.

To where she belonged.

~

"You've no flowers at all?" Great-Aunt Flora asked from the window of Bennet's London study that looked out to his tiny garden. There was a small tree and a few shrubs, and no room for anything else.

"No." Bennet sifted through the correspondence on his desk while Great-Aunt Minerva sat in a chair petting one of her squirrels. George, he thought, thinking it was the smaller of the two.

They'd just arrived a short while ago after a hurried trip from Somerset—no small feat with two older ladies, two squirrels, and far too much luggage.

Great-Aunt Flora turned from the window wearing one of her signature pouts. "Where will I find flowers to press?"

"The park," Great-Aunt Minerva responded. "I need to take Temperance and George for a runabout. They are anxious after the coach ride."

Bennet had tried to convince her not to bring them, but she'd insisted. Eventually, he'd abandoned the argument because he simply wanted to get on the road. He'd been eager to get to London, to see Prudence.

Now that he was here, he was filled with apprehension. There was much to be said. And much to face. The former didn't frighten him. The latter shook him to his core.

"We can't go to the park right now," he told them, not bothering to hide his exasperation. "Great-Aunt Minerva, can you take your pets out to the garden? I don't think they will mind the lack of flowers."

"That is true." Great-Aunt Minerva rose and departed through the door in the corner that led outside.

Great-Aunt Flora huffed a breath. "Do you at least have a newspaper I can peruse? Preferably something with gossip?"

Bennet found a few newspapers in the stack of things on his desk and absentmindedly handed them to his great-aunt.

She thanked him just as Mrs. Hennings stepped into the room.

"None of these have gossip," Great-Aunt Flora complained, setting Bennet's teeth on edge.

Mrs. Hennings held up a finger before dashing from the room. She returned a moment later with another paper and gave it to Great-Aunt Flora. "This should have what you're looking for," she said with a smile.

"Thank you very much." Great-Aunt Flora smiled with anticipation as she settled into a chair to read.

The housekeeper turned to Bennet and inclined her head toward the door, seeming to indicate she wanted to speak with him privately.

Nodding, he followed her into the narrow staircase hall. "Thank you for fetching that for my great-aunt. I wish she didn't like to follow gossip so much."

"I was quite surprised to see you'd brought them with you," Mrs. Hennings observed.

"They insisted on coming, and I thought I could use the support, quite honestly."

Mrs. Hennings's features creased with concern. "Does this have anything to do with Lady Glastonbury? I confess I was curious as to why she returned to London without you. Which brings me to the reason I wished to speak with you." Now she looked positively pained.

Dread stole through him.

"You know my daughter is maid to Lady Basildon," Mrs.

Hennings said. "In her position, she hears an astonishing amount of gossip."

Bennet's breath caught. What now?

"There is a rather unsavory rumor going about that you only married Lady Glastonbury because she is carrying a child, that you were paid to do so by her cousins, to whom she is...scandalously related."

Every curse word Bennet had ever heard raced through his brain, along with an overwhelming need to personally and physically destroy whoever had started this. "Did Lady Basildon start this rumor?"

Mrs. Hennings blinked in surprise. "I don't know. There is more, however."

Fuck! Bennet massaged his forehead. "Do tell."

"There is speculation that the babe isn't even yours since you and Lady Glastonbury seem to be living separate lives." She grimaced, her gaze full of sympathy. "I'm so sorry to have to relay this, but I knew you would want to know."

"I appreciate you telling me," he murmured, his mind working through not only how this could have started, but how this was affecting Prudence. She would be devastated. And rightfully so.

While he was nowhere to be seen. In fact, his absence had made this even worse.

He realized Mrs. Hennings was watching him warily. "Rest assured, Mrs. Hennings, Lady Glastonbury and I are not living separate lives. And though it is no one's business but our own, my wife *is* expecting *my* child."

"Should I ask my daughter to share that information with Lady Basildon?" Her question held a bit of a squeak at the end.

Bennet realized she was nervous, and he didn't blame her. He probably looked furious enough to throttle someone. He certainly felt that angry. "I'd rather not justify their nasty gossipmongering. And by 'their,' I don't mean your daughter. I know she is only trying to be helpful."

"Absolutely, my lord. She was most distressed on your behalf."

He didn't doubt that. Jane Hennings had worked in his father's London household several years ago when there had been more money. Bennet felt terrible that she'd had to leave. "Perhaps when Lady Glastonbury comes to live here, your daughter might want to return to this household as her lady's maid. She could also help you around the house." Not just because it might be necessary—he knew Prudence wouldn't be comfortable having a maid dedicated solely to her.

He was getting ahead of himself. He hadn't even persuaded her to come back. He wasn't sure he could.

Mrs. Hennings's brows lifted gently in surprise. "I'm sure she would be most enthusiastic, my lord."

"Excellent. Don't say anything yet." He didn't regret making the offer, but now he had to determine how to pay for it. Taking a deep breath to halt the rising panic and frustration, he wondered if things would ever be easy.

Mrs. Hennings nodded, then went on her way.

Bennet went to the base of the stairs and gripped the post, bending his head as though he just couldn't support the weight of it any longer. His mind galloped with thoughts and worries and, most of all, a towering rage. He dug his fingertips into the wood, but the surface was, like his current situation, unforgiving.

And his current situation was entirely his fault. Not the rumor, of course, but he'd made it worse by not being at his wife's side.

"I heard what she said," Great-Aunt Flora said.

Bennet jerked his head up to see her just inside the staircase hall. "I would prefer to be alone at the moment, please." He wished he hadn't brought her or her sister.

"I can imagine—what a debacle. However, we can fix it." She sounded quite confident.

"How?" He wasn't sure if he wanted to laugh or cry at the certainty in her gaze.

"We shall reclaim the narrative." She narrowed her eyes at him, and now he saw determination. "Gossips like to hear themselves talk—I should know. We must give them something else to talk about. Something that is better than this."

Every thought in his head vanished. He simply stared at her. "I pray you have an idea, because I do not."

"Not yet, but I will."

The need to see Prudence was overwhelming, but he acknowledged it would be better if he had a plan in place. Not that he was at all confident in whatever plan Great-Aunt Flora might devise. "When can I expect this scheme of brilliance?"

She rolled her eyes at him. "Don't be saucy."

He tamped down his agitation. "I'm quite anxious to see Prudence, and I'd rather do so after we have taken steps to defeat this rumor. Prudence is why we came here, remember?"

"Of course, I remember. It's why Minnie and I insisted on coming. You clearly need our help, now more than ever." She turned and went back into the study, crossing immediately to the desk. "What invitations have you received?"

"Hardly any."

"We need a ball."

Bennet recalled there was one invitation to a ball. He strode to the desk and rifled through the pile until he found the one that he sought. "It's tonight."

"Oh dear. I suppose Minnie and I will just have to make do with what we have."

"I don't mean to be rude, Great-Aunt Flora, but this isn't about you. Why do we need to go to a ball?"

"Because you need to do something to quash those rumors. You need to give them something far more delicious to talk about." She patted his arm. "We'll come up with something."

"That won't be necessary," he whispered, his mind racing. "I need to go."

He spun about, seeing very clearly what needed to happen. He just had to make certain the right people were in attendance.

~

*P*rudence had barely slept last night beneath the weight of her worry for her mother and whether Peterborough was exacting some sort of awful vengeance. Thankfully, that morning she'd received word that the countess had spent the night safely at her brother's house.

That had left Prudence to focus the majority of her worry on the rumors about her as well as her future. What would Bennet say about all this if he were here? Had he heard about it way out in Somerset? If not, he would soon since Flora kept a keen eye on London gossip.

"Well, that was dull." Kat jumped up from her favorite reading chair and went to replace the book on the shelf.

Prudence turned from the window. "You've finished already?"

"I skimmed the last half." Given how quickly she read, Prudence wondered what that looked like. "And now I'm bored. I think I'll go for a walk. I'd invite you, but you'll only refuse again."

Because Prudence had declined to take walks since arriving in London. At first because she'd been wallowing in self-pity. Now, she didn't wish to encounter anyone who would look at her with disgust.

Before she could respond, Bart entered. "Lady Glastonbury, Lady Peterborough is here to see you. She is waiting in the drawing room."

"Thank you, Bart." Prudence glanced toward Kat, who waved her off.

"It's not as if you're my companion any longer," Kat said. "Though I daresay you wish you were. Seems it was more pleasant for you than marriage. I do think this has sealed my decision to remain unwed. I shall be the greatest bluestocking spinster London has ever known." She fairly skipped from the library, and Prudence was grateful for the smile she couldn't hold back.

Hurrying upstairs, Prudence went to the drawing room to meet her mother. The countess stood just inside and gave her a sad smile as Prudence walked in.

"My poor dear," Christina said, holding her arms out.

Prudence hesitated. While she was eager to see that her mother was all right, she wasn't certain she wanted to rush into her arms. Their relationship hadn't progressed quite that far. Had it?

The countess frowned slightly. "I thought you might like to be comforted. Is that not your nature? It seemed as though it was when you came to see me that first time."

"I was rather emotional that day." She was rather emotional every day now. "This also seems...strange. You never behaved this way with Cassandra, and she was in need of mothering."

Christina paused before responding. "I know. I admit I struggled to show her as much affection as she needed. She reminded me of losing you. It was too hard. I wish I'd been a better aunt, but I did my best."

Prudence went to embrace her mother.

The countess wrapped her arms around Prudence and held her tightly. "What a mess this has become."

They broke apart, and Prudence was surprised to realize she felt a bit better. "I'm glad to see you are well. What happened with Peterborough?" Prudence was almost afraid to ask.

"He was livid, but thankfully, my brother arrived just as he was telling me I would be going to live in a convent in Ireland. Evesham whisked me away and took me to his house. I should have told him about you sooner, but even he acknowledges that he likely would have told me to find an adoptive family for you."

Prudence tensed. "Is he upset that I'm here now?"

"No, he's far more upset at Pete's reaction. He understands we must make the best of this situation." Christina flinched, then smiled apologetically. "Not that having you here in our lives is something we need to make the best of. It's just a change."

That the duke seemed to accept Prudence was surprising.

Christina continued, "I'll be staying with my brother while I determine what to do next. In the meantime, Evesham is trying to persuade Pete that anything he does will only compound the scandal. If he shrugs and does nothing, acts as if it's old news that he cares nothing about, the sting will be gone." She took Prudence's arm and guided her to the settee. "People only like gossip if it humiliates someone."

They sat down together, and Prudence found she could breathe easier.

"I'm glad your brother is advocating on your behalf."

"It's a little shocking, I must confess; however, he possesses a softer side than anyone would realize." Christina put her finger to her lips and smiled. "Don't tell."

Prudence mimicked the action.

"More surprising than him helping me is the fact that he wishes to lend his support to you, his niece."

"Me?" Accepting her was one thing, but *helping* her? "How?"

"Publicly. There's a ball tonight, and he will stand at your side."

It had been hard enough to accept that the truth of her parentage had somehow become known, but now she was to believe the mighty—and austere—Duke of Evesham was going to be her champion. She shook her head. "I can't."

"My dear, you must. And not just because you risk offending the duke. The fastest way to kill gossip is to give them something else to talk about."

"The duke standing with me at a ball is going to put an end to the gossip about me?" She laughed without an ounce of humor. This was too absurd.

The countess exhaled. "Perhaps not, but it will help matters. There will be many who will see the duke's approval and won't dare to say anything against you. The gossip will die down abruptly."

"You put an awful lot of faith in the power of your brother."

"Of course I do. He's the Duke of Evesham." She gave Prudence a sly smile. "You should too. Now, what will you wear? It must be your finest gown."

As a companion, Prudence had gowns that she wore to balls. However, they weren't ball gowns, not like those Cassandra or Fiona wore. "I was a companion until very recently, and my wardrobe reflects that. Even if I'd had time to order new gowns, my husband can't afford them."

"Of course, I should have realized. I'm sure we can come up with something. I'll send for my maid. She can work wonders."

It seemed Prudence was going to a ball that night. She would rather have crawled under a rock.

The countess cocked her head to the side. "I only wish

Glastonbury was here. Having him at your side would also quash the rumors. Why *did* you return to London without him?"

Prudence was grateful that his family's illness hadn't been part of the gossip. That would have been too much. She wouldn't even share it with Ada or Cassandra or her mother. "The gossip isn't completely wrong," she said quietly. "We only married for the babe."

"Oh." A deep frown twisted Christina's features. "I had the impression you cared for each other, that you were perhaps in love."

"You did?" Prudence hadn't thought her feelings were obvious. Perhaps she really was rubbish at hiding them. She'd definitely become incapable of tucking them away as her mother—the woman who'd raised and shaped her—had wanted. Her feelings aside, she didn't think Bennet was in love with her.

The countess shrugged. "It seemed you shared at least some affinity for one another. Is there no hope that love will come?"

"I don't think so." Prudence heard her own lack of conviction. If her mother had seen something, was it possible she and Bennet just needed to bare themselves completely?

A prickle of unease settled between her shoulder blades. She'd been angry and frustrated with him for not being honest with her, but she hadn't told him the biggest, most important secret of all—that she loved him. That she wanted this baby—his baby—more than anything and would fight for their happiness. If he would let her.

"You don't sound as if you believe that," Christina said. "What will you do?"

"I'm not certain yet. But tonight, I must go to a ball, apparently."

The countess grinned. "Yes. We will make a magnificent

entrance with Cassandra and Wexford, Aldington and Sabrina, Lucien, and the duke. No one will dare say a word against you. I daresay you will be quite popular."

Prudence doubted that, nor did she care. This was a favor she was doing for her mother. Because if it was up to Prudence, she'd be on her way back to Aberforth Place as quickly as possible.

CHAPTER 21

*B*ennet took the stairs at the Phoenix Club two at a time. He went directly to Lucien's office, but found it empty. Next, he went to the less populated library. He wasn't there either. Frustration growing, Bennet stalked into the more crowded members' den, where he noticed several stares directed toward him.

Still no Lucien. Where the hell was he?

Turning on his heel, he strode back toward the stairs, intent on searching the gaming room on the ground floor. But Lucien was coming up the stairs.

When he reached the top, he advanced on Bennet until they were nearly nose to nose. "I ought to hit you for allowing my cousin to return to London alone, but you'd probably trounce me."

"I won't." Bennet took a step back. "Take your shot. I deserve it."

Scowling, Lucien let out a low growl before turning toward his office. Bennet followed him.

"Who started this officious rumor?" Bennet asked as soon as they were inside.

Lucien closed the door with force. It wasn't quite a slam, but it was in the vicinity. "You mean the true story of my poor cousin? It may be a rumor, but it's not wrong." His dark eyes simmered with anger.

Bennet had been trying very hard to keep his own ire in check. He was reminded of how difficult it was because he suddenly wanted to toss something across the room.

"It isn't correct either," Bennet bit out. "You didn't pay me to marry her."

"Didn't we? Just answer me one question. Is there a babe?"

Fury seethed in Bennet's gut. He clenched his fists at his sides. "That's none of your concern. It's none of anyone's concern."

"That's an answer."

"I'm going to try to forget you even asked me. It shouldn't matter."

"It *does* matter. I believed you'd fallen in love. However, it now seems that you wed because of a child."

While that wasn't wrong, it also wasn't completely right. Bennet *had* fallen in love. But he likely would not have married her if not for the child. Christ, he hated how all this had happened. Why couldn't he have fallen in love with Prudence and simply married her? Because his family was broken, he was destitute, and he'd been scared of what he might become.

He couldn't keep torturing himself with all that had gone wrong or all that might go wrong. All that mattered was that he loved Prudence and he loved their child, whatever the future held. He was still scared to death, but he wasn't alone.

He wasn't alone.

Bennet met Lucien's gaze and spoke clearly so there would be no misunderstanding. "The reasons for our marriage are complicated. And *private*. However, I have a plan that involves a rather public spectacle. I need to ask you for one last favor." Lucien frowned, and Bennet nearly laughed at the absurdity of it all. "I need you to make sure Prudence is at the Tilden ball tonight."

"That's rather late notice. Why?"

"I don't have time to explain. Just promise me you'll get her there."

"I can't promise you anything, but I'll try." He narrowed his eyes at Bennet. "I'm trusting you one last time, Glastonbury. You botch this, and I won't just expel you from the Phoenix Club."

"If I fail, you won't have to." Bennet didn't know how he would recover from it. "Do you have any idea where this information originated? Only a few people knew the truth."

Lucien looked pained. "I've been over it a hundred times with Con, with Wex. It could be someone in Wex's household, but so far, he doesn't have any leads. His butler is on the case."

"If you find out, I want to know who it is." Bennet waited for Lucien to nod his assent before continuing, "I've been worried about Prudence's mother. Is Lady Peterborough all right?"

Surprise flickered in Lucien's gaze. "That's kind of you to ask. My father has intervened. She's staying with him for the time being."

Bennet was glad to hear it. "Good." He turned to go, but Lucien stopped him.

"If you don't make things right with Prudence, Con and I will make sure that you do."

Looking back over his shoulder, Bennet held the other man's stare. "If I don't make things right with my wife, there's nothing that you or Aldington or anyone could do that would be worse than how I'll have to live the rest of my life."

*E*vie Renshaw had come through again. She'd saved the day for so many people in so many ways, and tonight was no different. When the need for a brilliant ball gown that would dazzle the entire ton became dire, Evie had calmly delivered. Tonight, she had proven that she was unparalleled when it came to fashion and connections. It was entirely because of her that Prudence looked as though she not only belonged in Society but that she reigned supreme.

The red gown had been only partially constructed when Evie had gone to see one of her favorite modistes. She'd brought the woman to the Wexfords' where the modiste had measured Prudence then finished the gown with the help of Christina's maid.

Christina and Cassandra had gone shopping for shoes and gloves, and they'd somehow procured a pair of ruby combs for Prudence's hair, which Christina's maid had dressed in the most elegant style Prudence had ever worn. There was also a ruby necklace and matching earrings. The jewelry felt heavy on her, and Prudence found herself longing for an apron and Mrs. Logan's kitchen.

When she walked into the Tildens' house flanked by her mother and her uncle, Prudence held her head high and prayed she looked like a viscountess. Lord and Lady Tilden had greeted them quite pleasantly, but instead of a genuine warmth, there was surprise. Whether it was due to Prudence having the nerve to come or the fact that she was accompanied by the Duke of Evesham would remain a mystery.

In the ballroom, they took up a position somewhat near the dancing. Cassandra moved to Prudence's side and leaned close. "You are absolutely stunning. People are seeing you looking splendid in that gown and those jewels."

Prudence touched the ruby necklace at her throat.

"They're gaping at me wondering why I am here. If they're noticing my attire or accessories, it's to question how I managed to swindle all of you into outfitting me like this." Prudence had never felt more exposed or vulnerable. She was desperate to leave. "How long must we stay?"

They'd kept their conversation very quiet so that only the two of them could hear. That didn't mean Christina hadn't noticed. She moved closer. "Don't look so stricken, Prudence. Hold your head high and behave as if there is nowhere else you should be."

The duke approached her. "We should dance, Lady Glastonbury."

It wasn't an invitation. Not that she would have refused him.

She put her hand on his arm, and he escorted her to the dance floor as the next set was about to begin.

"I don't dance often anymore," he said brusquely. "But this is important for my sister, so I will do my best."

"I have rarely danced, Your Grace." She prayed she wouldn't embarrass him.

"Don't 'Your Grace' me. We are social equals now, so you would call me Duke. However, you are my niece, so you will call me Uncle Evesham."

They took their position in the square, and it was all Prudence could do not to panic. The music started, and she managed to get on well enough, recalling the steps, mostly from watching Fiona's lessons when she'd first come to town and then helping her practice on occasion.

When she and the duke were near each other, he said, "As I said, I don't do this often. Lucien will come and replace me soon, and I will circuit the ballroom extolling your grace and virtue."

Virtue. Prudence nearly tripped.

"Thank you...Uncle Evesham." Her uncle was a bleeding duke.

For whatever reason, this new situation, new *life* began to finally take hold of her. Even if she hadn't been the daughter of a viscount and a countess and the granddaughter of a duke, she was a *viscountess*. She was Lady Glastonbury, and she absolutely belonged here, whether she wanted it or not.

The dance ended, and Lucien came to take his father's place. Before departing the dance floor, the duke leaned close and bussed her cheek. "You are my sister's daughter. You carry our blood. That's all that matters."

He didn't look at her as he turned and strode away. She watched him go with overwhelming gratitude and affection.

Lucien took her hand as the music began. "You look as if you're slightly more cheerful," he observed with a smile.

"Surprisingly so." She never would have imagined it.

"Then I can't wait to see what happens as the evening progresses." He swept her into a turn, and they parted so she couldn't ask what he meant.

The rest of the set passed in a breathless whirl. She made only a few missteps, and Lucien was adept enough to cover them for her so that she didn't make a fool of herself.

She thanked him as they left the dance floor. "Please tell me I don't have to dance anymore. That was utterly exhausting."

As she turned her head to find Cassandra or Christina, she froze, her body stopped as if she'd walked into a stone wall. Standing with her relatives were her other relatives: Flora and Minerva.

Their gowns were dreadfully out of style, but their smiles were wide, and Prudence was so pleased to see them. Shocked, but pleased.

Regaining her composure, she hurried toward them. "Flora, Minerva, how is it that you're here?"

A hush seemed to fall over the ballroom. The buzz of conversation halted, and the air thinned.

"I brought them."

The two women parted to reveal Bennet. Dressed in black superfine with his usual simply knotted cravat, he was everything she'd ever wanted. Before she'd known she wanted it.

A smattering of murmurs broke the quiet. But only briefly before silence—and expectation—reigned once more.

"Bennet," she breathed, scarcely believing that she was really seeing him, that he wasn't a dream.

He took a deep breath and spoke in a loud, clear voice. "Good evening, my lady wife. I'm so pleased to join you this evening as we planned." Since the room had gone still, everyone could hear what he said.

Minerva tipped her head as she stepped toward Prudence. "Yes, thank you for allowing our dear boy to delay his trip to London so that Flora could recover from her cold."

What cold?

"So thoughtful of you to spare him," Flora said. "But now we're all here together, as intended."

They were publicly explaining why Prudence had returned to London without her husband. Her breath caught, and her pulse began to race.

"Yes, as intended," Prudence repeated.

Bennet walked toward her, his gaze fixed on her and only her. He took her hand and pressed his lips to the inside of her wrist. "How I've missed you," he murmured just for them. Then he raised his voice once more. "I feel as if I must declare for everyone to hear that I love you beyond measure. I would marry you over and over again, a thousand times, if I could. You are the woman of my dreams and the lady of my heart. And those are the reasons I married you."

His blue-green eyes were so brilliant. Were there tears fighting to spill? If so, he didn't let them.

She worried she wouldn't have the same control. Emotion welled, her throat tightened, and her face flushed.

"Huzzah!" Lucien called out. "To Lord and Lady Glastonbury!"

Several people nearby answered with "Huzzah." Prudence couldn't take her eyes from Bennet.

He offered her his arm. "Shall we promenade?"

She immediately took it, glad for his stability. "Directly outside, please," she whispered.

"Of course." He led her toward the doors, smiling and inclining his head at people as they walked past.

Prudence focused straight ahead, still not wanting to see anyone or the way they looked at her. When they were outside, she exhaled at last, her body wilting.

Bennet clasped her waist and drew her close as he maneuvered her away from the house. "All right?"

"I will be. That was... I don't know what to say." She turned to face him. "You made an absolute spectacle."

"I did. On purpose. It's our spectacle—we own it. No more secrets. I want everyone to know how I feel about you." He frowned. "Perhaps we shouldn't have fibbed about Great-Aunt Flora having a cold. I should have confessed to everyone that I was a fool for not being honest with you and for not accompanying you back to London."

"I'm glad you did *not* do that. I am struggling with a great deal, primarily my emotions and the overwhelming plethora of them of late. I don't think I could have managed all of Society knowing that much. The rumors are bad enough." She winced.

"I'm so sorry, Pru. I should have told you the truth so long ago. The silly part is that I think I always knew you would understand. You are the first and only woman I've ever met whom I actually envisioned in my life, at Aberforth Place, *with* my family."

His words made her want to fly into the air, carried by unstoppable joy. This was a surplus of emotion she enjoyed. "I shouldn't have left like I did. I just couldn't take one more thing. After so many years of burying my feelings, I was overwrought with them."

"I understand. You needed to get away—from me." He gave her a tentative smile. "If you still need to be apart from me, I'll understand."

She didn't. In fact, if she couldn't be with him now and forever, she didn't know what she would do. "Did you mean what you said? You love me?"

His eyes glowed with emotion. "More than anything."

"That was quite a performance!" The shrill voice broke them apart. Prudence stared at the woman who'd come upon them. She was tall and rather harsh looking. "But if you think that will repair the damage, you're fooling yourselves. When that whelp arrives in due time, everyone will know the truth —that you married her because she's a whore, and she was fortunate enough to have relatives who could buy you."

Bennet took two steps until he was close to the woman. "*You* did this?"

"Did you think I was going to let you break our agreement without suffering any consequences?"

Prudence watched Bennet's hands curl into fists, his neck and face redden, and his jaw clench. She'd seen him look this angry once before—at the fight in Croydon on the night he'd hired men to kidnap her.

This was what he was afraid of. Losing control. She wasn't going to let him.

"How did you find out about my wife?" Bennet growled, moving even closer to the woman, who Prudence had to assume was his briefly betrothed, Mrs. Merryfield.

"You confirmed that she was carrying when I guessed," the woman said haughtily.

"I never answered you!" A vein in his neck stood out, and Prudence knew he was about to step over the line.

The people who were in the garden began to turn and watch what was happening.

Bennet leaned forward, his lip curling. "You bitch."

CHAPTER 22

*B*ennet saw red. Heat and fury pulsed through him as he looked at Mrs. Merryfield as if through a tunnel. He couldn't see anything else, just her arrogant, angry face.

He felt a hand close around his. The scent was familiar… Prudence. She pushed in front of him, the top of her head obscuring his view of his former betrothed.

How had he ever planned to marry this harpy?

"I don't know how you learned about my parents," Prudence said softly, but with an edge of menace Bennet could never have imagined. "However, I will assume it was by nefarious and scandalous measures."

Mrs. Merryfield opened her mouth, but slammed her thin lips closed once more.

"You should be ashamed of yourself. Imagine being so pathetic as to start a rumor about someone out of sheer jealousy. You couldn't have been more wrong." Prudence stepped back and put her arm around Bennet's waist. She leaned into him. "As you can see, we are deeply in love."

"We had an agreement," Mrs. Merryfield growled.

Bennet had just begun to relax, but a new wave of anger rolled through him. "Not that again. If you—"

"Bennet, allow me, please," Prudence said sweetly. "Mrs. Merryfield, think of your children and the example this sets for them. I can't imagine they'd be proud of your behavior, for whatever reason you felt it was justified. It simply was not. Furthermore, there is no damage done here. Bennet and I are married, we are happy, and we will continue to be happy. I hope you can find an opportunity to do the same. Now, do yourself the greatest of favors and leave."

With a final glare, Mrs. Merryfield spun about and stalked toward the house. Bennet saw that his family—and Prudence's—had come outside and were standing near the doors. As Mrs. Merryfield walked near them, it seemed as though his great-aunts and Cassandra might prevent her progress. All three of them looked as if they might commit some act of physical violence. Thankfully, Wexford was there to step in front of them. Nearly in unison, they turned their attention to Prudence and Bennet, their glowers turning to bright smiles of joy.

Then a smattering of applause broke out in the garden, accompanied by a few cheers. Bennet felt Prudence relax, and his anger flowed away. That had never happened so quickly before. It generally took hours for him to truly calm down.

He looked at his wife and felt more peace than he'd ever known.

She was smiling at people who waved and inclined their heads. A gentleman walked near them and called out, "Bravo!"

Now Prudence blushed.

"Should we go speak with our families?" she asked.

"No, I need you to myself for a moment." Bennet put her arm around his and guided her to a darkened corner. Then he pulled her behind a shrubbery and cupped her face. "I love you." He kissed her, softly at first, then more deeply as she twined her arms around his neck.

At last, he pulled back and brushed his lips across her cheek, her forehead, her temple. "I have loved you for so long."

"How long?" she asked breathlessly.

"Since Riverview—the first time," he added. "I like to imagine those days we spent together, except I didn't have you kidnapped, and I wasn't beholden to my family or duty. I was worry-free and able to choose my own path without fear. I would have chosen you then. I would have begged you to marry me." He traced his finger along her hairline from her forehead to her cheek. "Now, I beg your forgiveness. I'm so sorry I wasn't honest with you. I was afraid for my future and for the future of any child I will have. That fear prevented me from wanting to marry, from allowing myself to love."

She laid her palms flat against his upper chest, pushing them out to the sides near his shoulders. "I didn't want to marry either. After my father died, my mother urged me to bury my emotions, assuring me they weren't helpful. I believed that, especially after she died and I felt so alone. If you don't allow yourself to feel, it's much easier to bear loneliness."

Her words twisted his insides so that he could scarcely breathe. "Oh, Pru. You always seem so strong and confident."

"I didn't even realize I was lonely until I met you." She touched his cheek. "But I think I was—am—strong and confident too. I'm confident that I love you. I was not, however, confident that you loved me. I was sure you didn't, especially when I learned you'd kept the truth of your family from me."

Agony and regret washed through him. "If I could go back and tell you everything from the start, I would."

One of her brows arched. "From the start? You would tell me about your family's troubles when I was trussed up like a pheasant? I think that's what you said, isn't it?"

He couldn't help but laugh. "Perhaps not at that precise moment." He grew serious once more. "Don't ever doubt my love for you. I vow to tell you every day, multiple times a day, for the rest of our lives." He kissed her again, a leisurely exploration filled with promise.

She pulled back and looked up at him intently. "What about the baby? Are you still afraid?"

"Yes." He wouldn't lie to her. Not anymore. "But with you, I'm less so. My great-aunts have also pointed out that I am not—probably—afflicted with the family illness. It seems I'm merely, ah, emotional. Or can be, anyway. And that while I have made some rather poor decisions, they don't compare to anything my father did. They don't think I demonstrate any behavior that's out of the ordinary for most people."

"How lovely of them."

"Yes, it was, actually." Bennet was extremely grateful to them.

She laid her hand against his cheek. "You've been alone in your fear and worry for so long, shouldering a terrible burden, even when your father was alive, I suspect. But you're the one who holds them all together. Don't you see how wonderful that is? How much love and strength it takes to be who you already are?"

How he wanted to believe that. "You see a better man than I am, but then that's been true since I kidnapped you."

"You are a far better man than you think, but I suppose I shall just have to remind you every day."

"I will never tire of that," he said fiercely. "To think that I get to spend every day with you is a joy I never imagined."

"I know neither of us wanted this, that if not for a series of misfortunes, we would not be here right now. But I am not sorry."

"You say misfortunes, and I would have agreed. I told you I was unlucky. I don't think that anymore. I look at those misfortunes and see the greatest luck a man could have. All of it led me to you. To us." He put his hand over her belly and thought of the life growing inside her. "Whatever the future brings, we will manage it—together."

She stood on her toes and touched her lips to his. "Together."

EPILOGUE

*P*rudence jumped up from her chair the moment she heard masculine voices. She rushed to the entry hall as the Duke of Evesham came from Bennet's study, Bennet following behind him.

"Your husband made an excellent case," the duke said, stopping near Prudence.

"He's very committed to Aberforth Place—and to his family." Prudence wished she could have been party to their meeting, but knew the duke wouldn't have approved. He saw financial discussions as a purely masculine domain.

"So it seems." The duke turned to Bennet and shook his hand. "I look forward to your first report."

"Thank you, sir." Bennet smiled and cast Prudence a look that was a mix of joy and relief.

Prudence wanted to throw her arms around her uncle. "We'll see you at dinner tonight?" They were gathering at the Wexfords' for a celebration later.

"Briefly," he said with a slight scowl. "I don't like to intrude on you young people, but I'll stop in before I go to my club."

Gathering her courage, Prudence went to buss his cheek. "Thank you, Uncle," she whispered.

He grunted in response before taking his leave.

Prudence turned to her husband. "That went well, I take it?"

"Very well." Bennet swept her into his arms and twirled her about the entry hall.

Laughing, she begged him to put her down. "Don't make me ill again." That morning, Prudence had suffered her first sickness from the babe. There was no denying it now—not that anyone had been doing that.

Bennet set her down and kissed her soundly. "I can't remember the last time I felt like this. Probably never."

She grinned up at him, basking in his elation. "How's that?"

"I'm not sure I can describe it. I actually feel like I can breathe, that I don't have to worry whether I'll be able to keep Aunt Agatha in the only home she remembers or if I'll have to force Aunt Judith and Great-Aunt Esther to move to Aberforth Place. No one wants that," he added drily.

Prudence giggled. "I'm so glad the duke agreed to give you a loan."

"Not only that, but the terms were quite favorable."

"What did he mean about a report?" she asked.

"I'm to send quarterly reports detailing my progress. It's to be expected, and honestly, I'm glad to have his input. My father was woefully inept at running the estate, and I was too young to learn much before my grandfather died."

The door opened suddenly, and in walked Flora and Minerva, trailed by Mrs. Hennings. Minerva's squirrels peered from her apron, and Flora carried a basket of flowers. They both looked delighted. Mrs. Hennings appeared slightly beleaguered.

"I see you found plenty of flowers in Russell Square."

Bennet kept his arm around Prudence as he spoke to his great-aunts.

Flora nodded vigorously. "Oh yes, it was worth the extra walk. It's much larger than Bloomsbury. Now, if you'll excuse me, I must begin preserving these beauties." She ambled to the staircase hall and would continue up to the drawing room, half of which she'd commandeered for her flower pressing.

Minerva patted George. "Mr. George seems to have found a friend today. We will need to return tomorrow so they can see each other."

"Mrs. Hennings can't accompany you about town every day," Bennet said evenly.

Blinking, Minerva looked from him to Prudence and back again. "Then you or Prudence shall have to do it." With a happy smile, she sailed from the hall.

"Thank you, my lord," Mrs. Hennings said. "I should attend to some chores."

Prudence stopped her. "Just a moment, Mrs. Hennings. I wanted to let you know that I met with Jane today. She is handing in her notice to Lady Basildon." The day after the spectacle at the Tilden ball, Bennet had suggested they hire the housekeeper's daughter. Frankly, the household needed another maid, and Jane could also serve as Prudence's lady's maid. While Prudence had resisted at first, she liked Mrs. Hennings so much that she'd agreed to meet with Jane. Now, having met the pleasant and enthusiastic young lady, Prudence was eager to have her here. Furthermore, poor Jane was anxious to be away from her gossipmongering current employer.

Mrs. Henning's eyes lit, and she clapped her hands together. "I'm so pleased—and grateful—your ladyship. Thank you."

"I'm glad you'll be together—and to have more help. You

work too hard." She cast a sideways glance at Bennet. He knew Mrs. Henning was overworked. That had been part of his argument to Prudence regarding the hiring of Jane.

"I do what's necessary," Mrs. Hennings demurred. "It's my pleasure and honor to serve his lordship—and now you. I'd best get on." She walked toward the back of the house, where the back stairs would take her to the kitchen below.

"I really ought to hire a footman too," Bennet mused. "But I confess that I'm reluctant. It still feels as if I can't afford it."

"Then maybe we can't. I don't need a footman. I don't really need any of this," Prudence said. "We can always claim the life we enjoyed at Riverview."

"That we can." Bennet lowered his head to kiss her again. Some moments later, they parted, breathless. "Might I suggest we go upstairs to prepare for dinner at the Wexfords'?"

"That's hours away," Prudence said with a laugh.

"Without a valet or a lady's maid, you must recognize that it takes longer for us to complete our toilets." He gave her an innocent look while steering her toward the staircase hall.

Prudence suppressed a smile. "I'm quite looking forward to tonight."

All their friends and family would be there—except for the Bath relatives and, of course, Aunt Agatha. Bennet had promised to take Prudence to meet her in August when he made his annual visit.

"You just want to try to talk Ada out of going to help your ill-mannered blackguard of a brother."

"*Half brother*," she corrected him, scowling. "You may be right. However, it's too late, since she's leaving tomorrow. He doesn't deserve her assistance. In fact, perhaps I'll tell her to make things worse."

Bennet shook his head, a smile teasing his lips as they

started up the stairs. "You won't do that. Your heart is too kind and forgiving."

Prudence wasn't sure she agreed, especially when it came to her heartless half brother. "Don't be too sure. And if I hear that he bothers, insults, or makes trouble for Ada in any way, he will have me to answer to."

"If he knew that, he'd be quaking in his boots." At the top of the stairs, Bennet swung her into his arms, drawing a gasp from her. "This is taking too long. I'm in quite a hurry."

She clutched his neck as he hastened to their chamber at the back of the house. "But we have hours, remember?"

"Oh, I'm only in a hurry to get there. I plan to make good use of our time." His gaze met hers and held it. "*Very* good use."

Anticipation shivered across her skin, and she wondered if that sensation would ever go away. She hoped not. "What do you have in mind?"

He put his lips next to her ear and whispered a variety of activities, each one eliciting a wave of desire until she was nearly panting with want.

"Why, Lord Glastonbury, you are most indecent."

His eyes gleamed with seductive promise. "I hope so, my love."

Want to spend a fortnight with Ada at the Viscount Warfield's estate and see if he's as disagreeable as everyone says? (Spoiler alert: he is!) Ada's curiosity about her surly and reluctant host gets the better of her, and Max wishes she'd just go away—until she gives him a glimmer of hope, which he hasn't had in years. Don't miss the thrilling next book in the Phoenix Club, IMPOSSIBLE! Preorder today and read April 19, 2022!

Would you like to know when my next book is available and to hear about sales and deals? **Sign up for my VIP newsletter** which is the only place you can get bonus books and material such as the short prequel to the Phoenix Club series, INVITATION, and the exciting prequel to Legendary Rogues, THE LEGEND OF A ROGUE.

Join me on social media!

Facebook: https://facebook.com/DarcyBurkeFans
Twitter at @darcyburke
Instagram at darcyburkeauthor
Pinterest at darcyburkewrite

And follow me on Bookbub to receive updates on pre-orders, new releases, and deals!

Need more Regency romance? Check out my other historical series:

The Untouchables

Swoon over twelve of Society's most eligible and elusive bachelor peers and the bluestockings, wallflowers, and outcasts who bring them to their knees!

The Untouchables: The Spitfire Society

Meet the smart, independent women who've decided they don't need Society's rules, their families' expectations, or, most importantly, a husband. But just because they don't need a man doesn't mean they might not *want* one...

The Untouchables: The Pretenders

Set in the captivating world of The Untouchables, follow the saga of a trio of siblings who excel at being something they're not. Can a dauntless Bow Street Runner, a devastated viscount, and a disillusioned Society miss unravel their secrets?

The Matchmaking Chronicles
The course of true love never runs smooth. Sometimes a little matchmaking is required. When couples meet at a house party, what could go wrong?

Wicked Dukes Club
Six books written by me and my BFF, NYT Bestselling Author Erica Ridley. Meet the unforgettable men of London's most notorious tavern, The Wicked Duke. Seductively handsome, with charm and wit to spare, one night with these rakes and rogues will never be enough...

Love is All Around
Heartwarming Regency-set retellings of classic Christmas stories (written after the Regency!) featuring a cozy village, three siblings, and the best gift of all: love.

Secrets and Scandals
Six epic stories set in London's glittering ballrooms and England's lush countryside.

Legendary Rogues
Five intrepid heroines and adventurous heroes embark on exciting quests across the Georgian Highlands and Regency England and Wales!

If you like contemporary romance, I hope you'll check out my **Ribbon Ridge** series available from Avon Impulse, and the continuation of Ribbon Ridge in **So Hot**.

I hope you'll consider leaving a review at your favorite online vendor or networking site!

I appreciate my readers so much. Thank you, thank you, *thank you.*

ALSO BY DARCY BURKE

Historical Romance

The Phoenix Club

Improper

Impassioned

Intolerable

Indecent

Impossible

Irresistible

Impeccable

Insatiable

The Matchmaking Chronicles

The Rigid Duke

The Bachelor Earl (also prequel to *The Untouchables*)

The Runaway Viscount

The Untouchables

The Bachelor Earl (prequel)

The Forbidden Duke

The Duke of Daring

The Duke of Deception

The Duke of Desire

The Duke of Defiance

The Duke of Danger

The Duke of Ice

The Duke of Ruin

The Duke of Lies

The Duke of Seduction

The Duke of Kisses

The Duke of Distraction

The Untouchables: The Spitfire Society

Never Have I Ever with a Duke

A Duke is Never Enough

A Duke Will Never Do

The Untouchables: The Pretenders

A Secret Surrender

A Scandalous Bargain

A Rogue to Ruin

Love is All Around

(A Regency Holiday Trilogy)

The Red Hot Earl

The Gift of the Marquess

Joy to the Duke

Wicked Dukes Club

One Night for Seduction by Erica Ridley

One Night of Surrender by Darcy Burke

One Night of Passion by Erica Ridley

One Night of Scandal by Darcy Burke

One Night to Remember by Erica Ridley

One Night of Temptation by Darcy Burke

Secrets and Scandals

Her Wicked Ways

His Wicked Heart

To Seduce a Scoundrel

To Love a Thief (a novella)

Never Love a Scoundrel

Scoundrel Ever After

Legendary Rogues

Lady of Desire

Romancing the Earl

Lord of Fortune

Captivating the Scoundrel

Contemporary Romance

Ribbon Ridge

Where the Heart Is (a prequel novella)

Only in My Dreams

Yours to Hold

When Love Happens

The Idea of You

When We Kiss

You're Still the One

Ribbon Ridge: So Hot

So Good

So Right

So Wrong

ABOUT THE AUTHOR

Darcy Burke is the USA Today Bestselling Author of sexy, emotional historical and contemporary romance. Darcy wrote her first book at age 11, a happily ever after about a swan addicted to magic and the female swan who loved him, with exceedingly poor illustrations. Join her Reader Club newsletter for the latest updates from Darcy.

A native Oregonian, Darcy lives on the edge of wine country with her guitar-strumming husband, incredibly talented artist daughter, and imaginative son who will almost certainly out-write her one day (that may be tomorrow). They're a crazy cat family with two Bengal cats, a small, fame-seeking cat named after a fruit, an older rescue Maine Coon with attitude to spare, and a collection of neighbor cats who hang out on the deck and occasionally venture inside. You can find Darcy at a winery, in her comfy writing chair balancing her laptop and a cat or three, folding laundry (which she loves), or binge-watching TV with the family. Her happy places are Disneyland, Labor Day weekend at the Gorge, Denmark, and anywhere in the UK—so long as her family is there too. Visit Darcy online at www. darcyburke.com and follow her on social media.